To A[...]
a book
extra[...]

hugs
autumn Bardot

GODDESSES INC.

AUTUMN BARDOT

Flores Publishing

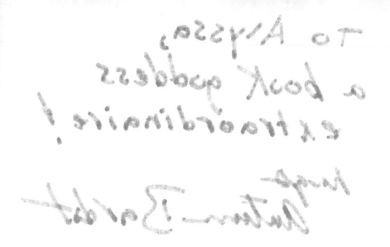

The book is a work of fiction.

Cover art: Sweet & Spicy Designs

Interior formatting: Sweet & Spicy Designs

Paperback ISBN: 978-1-7340897-1-4

E-Book ISBN: 978-1-7340897-2-1

ONE

"Welcome to FEM, the originator of divine, semi-divine, and quasi-divine female empowerment and resources. The records department is located on the second floor. The legal department, the third. Find justice on the fifth floor. War is on the sixth, seventh, eighth, and ninth."

Mnemosyne frowned. Another war floor?

"Love and fertility are on the tenth, eleventh, and twelfth. The grievance department is on the thirteenth. Flora and fauna are on the fourteenth, fifteenth, and sixteenth floors. Artifacts and ancient scripts are located in the basement. Consult the Information Desk for all other departments. Thank you for your contributions to humankind. Have a nice day."

FEM. Female Energy Macrocosm. The all too familiar voice floated like a breeze from above. It was melodious, lyrical, rich, and feminine. Utter perfection. Mnemosyne hated it. Even 'quasi-divine' sounded like an achievement.

Mnemosyne strode across the rosy-hued marble lobby, the four-inch heels of her Louboutin's *clack-clacking* like a woman with places to go. She tossed her head, glossy chestnut hair floating over her shoulders like Aeolis's kiss. The stories about the god of wind were frightfully inadequate!

Mnemosyne stood before a shiny panel next to the gold elevator door, pursed her lips and blew onto the panel. It was breath activated. The entire FEM building. From the security-protected front entrance to the elevator to the water fountain to the lavatories. A breathalyzer for goddesses. It kept them sober. Indulging in a drinking binge with Dionysus the night before wasn't going to open any doors. Garlic breath jammed the system. Raw onions were a no-no. Halitosis! Holy goddess, Shee locked you out of the system for two weeks! Mnemosyne, like all the other goddesses, learned to eat their favorite breath-fouling foods *after* a visit to FEM headquarters.

Mnemosyne—pronounced *nem-o-seen-ee*—glanced about and saw Inna rounding the corner. The Nigerian goddess of the harvest, promises, and justice, looked fabulous as always.

"Mnemosyne." Inna adjusted the ten-strand coral bead necklace that hung like an orange waterfall over her body-hugging striped dress. "Good to see you. It's been a long time."

They cheek kissed. The right cheek only.

"Ages," said Mnemosyne.

"What brings you here?"

Mnemosyne crouched down, her blue-flowered Valentino pencil skirt stretching across her thighs and flicked off a speck of lint from the tip of her Louboutins. "Shee emailed me."

Shee. The CEO of FEM. Nobody messed with Shee. Nobody wanted to either.

"Emailed?" Inna's dark brown eyes widened a mere fraction of an inch.

Mnemosyne straightened up, smoothed her skirt. "I thought it was strange too."

Usually Shee or FEM sent messages the old school way. Via birds. Not carrier pigeons. Shee, or her secretary, spoke through a bird's twitters. Not the social media platform. Real birds. Naturally, no one understood it except goddesses. It's one way to identify a goddess. A woman who suddenly stands motionless during a particularly musical birdsong was probably translating a message from Shee.

Inna stepped close, lowered her voice. "A *real* email?"

Mnemosyne adjusted the cuffs of her blue silk blouse. "That's what I said."

Inna put her hands on her hips. "What did the email say…if you don't mind me asking." The tiniest vertical line appeared between her eyebrows. But only for a third of a second. Maybe less.

Mnemosyne looked past Inna to the lobby beyond. Everyone went about their business. Not one goddess appeared troubled or miserable.

Mnemosyne had always liked Inna, although they *were* miles apart. Not geographically but in terms of status. Mnemosyne considered herself to be ever so much more important. "Your presence is required."

"That's it?" Inna's eyes brightened with curiosity.

Mnemosyne nodded. That was it. Pretty innocuous. It could be about a multitude of reasons. Her free-spirited daughters for one.

"Interesting." Inna's slim hand slipped into her Dolce & Gabbana leopard-print tote and tugged out a pricy bottle of Swiss Mountain water. "Dilution?"

"Thank you, you're a gem." Mnemosyne drank it down. Carefully. So her lipstick did not smear.

Purification by water was not necessary, but Shee always sensed when a goddess's body was not properly hydrated and therefore less fluid in thought and deed. Flow, it was *de rigueur* in the goddess business. Which was pretty ironic since the phrase actually meant unyielding and inflexible. FEM's hypocrisies mirrored that of the world.

Mnemosyne capped the lid, tossed it in the nearby receptacle. "How do I look?"

"Gorgeous and divine." Inna smiled, but it did not reach her eyes. A fake smile.

The elevator door opened.

Mnemosyne stepped inside, turned around, and spoke to the voice-activated ceiling. "Shee."

FEM installed all the latest technology.

Inna wiggled her fingers into a wave. "By the way, you're not the only one who received an email."

Mnemosyne's brows shot up. "Did you—"

The door slid closed with vault-like finality.

Mnemosyne's stomach gurgled with worry. *I'm not the only one? Is this a good or bad thing?*

The email summons meant Shee wanted a digital footprint. Which was odd, because Shee didn't like leaving any kind of footprint. Carbon or otherwise.

Mnemosyne tapped her foot impatiently. The elevator music was anything but comforting. Lyres, aulos, and kitharas melodies designed to infuse her Greek soul with the spirit of her people were neither soothing nor inspiring today. Mnemosyne closed her eyes, let the music wash over her. Nope. Didn't work this time.

Mnemosyne checked her reflection in the mirrored

elevator and preened. Not a day over thirty. Immortality was divine!

The door swished open on the top floor. As usual, her breath caught. Leave it to Shee to hire the world's best architect. A woman, naturally. The optical illusion stole your breath, even a goddess's.

The aerial panorama offered an eagle's eye view. On a smog-free day, a visitor saw from the mountains to the sea. It was a Mount Olympus view.

Mnemosyne stepped out onto the plexiglass corridor. That step alone was proof of faith since the ground was a thousand feet below. The dramatic. Shee embraced it with every atom of her nebulous being. From architecture to miracles to disasters.

Mnemosyne pivoted on her spike heels and headed right. Right. Always *right*. Because Shee was always right, because goddesses were all about rights and doing the right thing. Mnemosyne moved carefully across the clear floor—a sensation like walking on air—and strode toward the only office on the top floor.

Platinum doors glided silently into the walls.

This one is new.

A bald young woman looked up from the pink granite desk. "Shee is waiting for you."

The CEO of FEM appointed the most stunning goddesses in-training as her assistants. Each with a most otherworldly beauty. Were they semi or quasi divine? No one knew or cared much. This one was bare-faced and glowing with health, a caramel-colored knit sweater clinging like a second skin to her curvaceous body. The kind of woman even a heterosexual woman would eagerly get down on her knees for to—

Mnemosyne lifted her haughty chin. "I am—"

Another platinum door to the right (always the right) glided open.

Mnemosyne feared nothing. She was Mnemosyne. A goddess. A very important goddess. So why did the Swiss Mountain water feel like a roiling hot mineral spring in her belly?

Mnemosyne sashayed forward with the fluid, easy stride of purpose and power. Until her heel snagged on the silk Isfahan carpet. It broke her perfect gait for a tenth of a second.

Not. Good.

TWO

Shee's office was the shape of an octagon with five glass walls. Shee, her back to the impressive vista, sat on an ancient ivory chair—more like a throne, really—behind a shiny carved ebony desk.

Mnemosyne dropped to her knees *on the grass*, ready to assume the classic posture of obeisance, forehead to the floor, hands outstretched, palms to the ceiling. The grass was a way of grounding a goddess to the earth. It smelled like heaven, green and fragrant and fresh.

"That's so last millennium." Shee swiveled around and waved Mnemosyne forward. "Take a seat."

Mnemosyne sat in the wingback chair, crossed her ankles, and looked with awe at Shee. The CEO of FEM leaned back in her chair and bestowed a kindly smile. A doting grandmama kind of smile. Her face was every-woman and no woman. Encompassed a spectrum of features, from beautiful to ugly. Young. Middle-aged. Old. Shee was all ages and ageless. Shee was mother and daughter. Lover and enemy. At the same time. Shee was every race. Shee was change and constancy. Shee was All.

Shee clasped her hands together, composed and prayerful. "How have you been, Mnem?"

Very few goddesses called her Mnem. Only her closest friends. Mnem's stomach clenched, the Swiss Mountain water swirled like a turbulent sea in her gut.

"I'm wonderful, thank you." Mnem pushed her lips into a smile.

"Is that so?" Shee tilted her head, compassion flickering across her face.

"Life is wonderful." Mnem sat up straighter. "Beautiful."

"Beautiful?" One of Shee's thumbs tapped with steady slowness atop the other.

Mnem dropped her gaze. It was difficult to look at Shee's face for too long. It was much too…disconcerting. Mnem looked at Shee's clothes instead. Shee always wore a kaftan, this one was tied with a thin braided sash threaded with wooden beads. It was beautiful, the wide stripes of pale blue, bronze, cream, and ginger were timeless hues. The earth's pallet.

"Is this about my daughters?" Mnem prayed to goddess her stomach would not gurgle. "They can be a handful at times. Is it Melpomene? She's such a drama queen."

"Your nine daughters are fine. Quite active in the world." Shee unclasped her hands and set her palms on the gleaming desk. "Which is why I've summoned you here."

Mnem relaxed. Her stomach settled. *This must be about my daughters.*

The nine Muses. What's not to like about them? Creative mortals everywhere called on them regularly. Zeus, their father, however, had little hand in their upbringing. Talk about an absentee father. Well, most of the time. Mnem uncrossed her ankles and leaned forward, eager to hear the good news.

"Your daughters have increased their significance," said Shee. "They are important. Needed. Desired."

Mnem's head bobbed with pride. What mother doesn't love hearing praise about their children?

Shee, her eyes hardening into obsidian, poked a rigid index finger into the air as though tapping an invisible button between her and Mnem. "You are not." Shee settled back in her throne-like chair, her hands draped over the intricately carved armrests.

Mnem blinked. "Pardon me?"

"You are no longer relevant, Mnemosyne. No one knows who you are or what you are the goddess of."

Mnem touched her chest. "I'm Mnemosyne, Greek goddess of memory."

Shee's lips twitched. "I *know* who you are."

"I—"

Shee held out a silencing palm. "Do you have a brand?"

"A what?"

Shee produced a cellphone from the folds of her kaftan and pushed the device across the desk. "A brand. A platform. Do you have followers?"

Mnem glanced at the cellphone. "What kind of followers?"

"Social media followers." Shee tapped the phone with a long oval-shaped nail. "Twitter. InstaPic. Snap chat. Facebook."

"I…" A Charybdis whirlpool churned in Mnem's belly.

"You're a goddess and you don't have a twitter account, let alone a blue checkmark."

"Neither do you," Mnem shot back.

9

Shee laughed, a beautifully ugly sound devoid of mirth. "I don't need one. I am All."

Mnem felt the roiling waters move upwards. "You asked me here to tell me to get a social media account?"

"No." Shee crossed her arms. "FEM and MAS are merging."

MAS, Masculine Alliance Sodality. The cosmic counterpart.

Shee stretched her arm to the vista beyond, to the landscape of skyscrapers, factories, buildings, and domiciles. "The world is always changing. We change with it."

Don't throw up. "What does that mean?"

Shee lowered her arm, the kaftan's fabric fluttering into perfect drapes around her. "It means, Mnemosyne, that we must clean house. Downsize. Free ourselves from goddesses and gods who are no longer relevant."

"I'm relevant." Mnem squeaked, her voice without relevancy.

"No, you're not." Shee's mouth formed into her famous smile-frown. Pitying. Beneficent. Empathetic. And terrifying. "Darling, you haven't been relevant for a thousand years."

"I'll change." Mnem slid her phone from her metallic goatskin Chanel purse. "I'll create a…a brand. I'll start an account. How difficult can it be to get a blue checkmark?"

Shee sighed. "It's too late."

"What do you mean?" Mnem's divine bones chilled to ice. "Are you firing me?"

"I prefer the term dismissed." Shee crossed one leg over the other. "You're one of many. MAS and I are streamlining. Redundancy is neither expedient nor prudent."

All the air whooshed out of Mnem. Her belly

constricted. Her bowels twisted. "What will happen to me?" Mnem's voice cracked. Sounded human. A voice strangled by fear.

Shee graced her with another ghastly pitying smile. "You are now barred from FEM. All your privileges revoked forthwith. Don't look so mortified, Mnem. This is *your* doing after all. You had choices." Shee's finger tapped the air. "You've always had choices. You chose to do nothing."

Mnem squared her shoulders. "I am the mother of the nine muses." *Dear goddess, I sound pathetic.*

"That's not enough anymore." Shee's fingers fluttered in the air. "Look at you. Wearing all the latest designer clothing. You keep current with fashion. Have the newest phone. Enjoy an extremely active social and sexual life."

"People love me."

"No darling, you've become arm candy and a good time for a miles-long string of interesting mortal men."

"I—"

"Your sex life is no concern of mine. What I *do* care about are the goddesses who have an inspirational brand." Shee stood, rounded the desk, and perched on the corner. René Caovilla crystal sandals peeked out between the silk folds.

Mnem swallowed. Shee's proximity was unnerving. "Does that mean I won't be immortal anymore?"

Shee nodded.

Mnem lifted her chin, stared at Shee. "How long do I have left?" *To live.*

"I'm not sure. Immortality is a gift. Maybe you have fifty years, maybe five." Shee shrugged. "Female energy is a collective. A cyclical force of the universe. As an inactive goddess, you have been taking for a long time and not giving back." Shee rose and the air grew oppressive, as though her sheer might pressed down on Mnem's chest and lungs. Like a fat man on top of her.

The office door glided open.

I've been dismissed. Forever.

Mnem would have cried. One thing stopped her. The thought of giving Shee the satisfaction of seeing a fired goddess leak precious water, proteins, lipids, and electrolytes. Besides, tears swayed mortals, not the divine.

Mnem rose from the chair. Her chin lifted despite the tightness in her throat. "Am I permitted to use the archives?"

"The moment you leave the building you will have no access to FEM."

What if I never leave? The thought, silly as it was, dashed across Mnem's mind like an Olympic runner. Other silly thoughts included throwing a tantrum. And groveling. Both were beneath her. Mnem had too much self-respect. Maybe too much. Maybe if she was more reflective, she would have seen this coming. The truth was, immortality was a gravy train Mnem did not realized she was capable of being thrown from.

Mnem's lips twitched into a wide insincere smile. "I understand. Good-bye. Have a nice day." Mnem was thunderstruck. It felt as though Zeus, her baby daddy, aimed his lightning bolt at her head. Mnem walked out, felt the door swoosh shut behind her.

The elevator ride up had seemed interminable. The ride down or, rather, Mnem's fall down, took only a few heartbeats. Mnem found her misty-eyed self staring at the rosy marble lobby all too soon. Goddesses sauntered about without a care in the world.

I'm fired! This can't be happening. Do they all have platforms? Followers? Do they all deserve their immortality?

"Are you getting off, darling?" asked Phra Naret, Thai goddess of water, good fortune, beauty, and blessings. Her voice was calm water, soothing and fluid.

Mnem blinked, snapped out of her astonished stupor. "Yes, I am."

Phra Naret patted her black hair, pulled tight into a shiny tall topknot. A wide gold-threaded ribbon encircled it. A mini tiara. "I hope today showers you with blessings."

More like the curse of mortality. Mnem smiled, realized she hadn't moved. As though she was *afraid* to get off the elevator. Mnem was never *ever* afraid.

Phra Naret smoothed her dress, a modern take on a traditional *chut thai*, and waited patiently.

Mnem roused herself, forced her leaden foot to move forward. "Going up?"

Phra Naret pressed her palms together. "Always, darling. The world is beautiful and divine."

"Do you have followers?" Mnem asked walking out of the elevator.

"Thousands. Perhaps millions." Phra Naret smiled, all white teeth, warmth, and serenity. She blew a kiss as the door *whooshed* closed.

"Millions." Mnem grimaced. For a moment. Grimacing was frowned upon at FEM. Very unbecoming. *I'm not a goddess anymore.* Mnem grimaced harder, her chin wrinkling. It felt good. Freeing. Authentic. Her head hoisted high, Mnem strode through the front door, her needle-thin heels clicking angrily on the shiny marble.

The morning was warm. Fresh. The scent of brewed coffee wafted from the coffeeshop across the street. It was too early for a shot of ice-cold ouzo, so coffee it was. Greek style. A strong brew with one sugar cube in a demitasse cup should do the trick. Mnem needed to think. Think fast and think hard.

The bell over the door jingled as she walked in.

"Mnem!"

Mnem turned to the familiar voice, saw the tear-stained, mascara-smeared face. "You too?"

THREE

M nem swiped her credit card through the machine, picked up her demitasse cup, and joined Inna at the little round table in the corner with a view of FEM. "You knew what was going to happen to me, didn't you?"

"No, not for certain." Inna set down her coffee. Her usual order, a brew spiced with cardamom, cinnamon, and ginger, tasted bitter today.

"You should have warned me," Mnem said, her voice as sharp as the tip of Athena's sword.

Inna's nostrils flared.

"Sorry, I…" Mnem waved her hand, touched her forehead. *Don't cry. Don't cry.*

Inna nodded. She understood and yet she still felt like punching someone in the face. "You're the mother of the nine muses, I couldn't believe Shee would fire *you*. What excuse did Shee give you? No, let me guess. No followers. No platform. You're irrelevant."

"Exactly those words." Mnem fought the urge to break into tears, her chest squeezing with the effort to Not Cry.

Inna leaned forward. "What's going to happen to us?

This has never been done before. How many of us are going to…"

Die. The unspoken word hung in the air like a toxic fog.

"We will wither away like the Celtic goddess Cailleach until we become old crones." Mnem's espresso warmed her throat, took the edge off the Ugly Cry that threatened to erupt.

Inna frowned. "Cailleach regenerates when she finds a new husband." She touched her forearm. "Will we drop dead in the street and turn to dust? Is this my last coffee? My last day?"

Mnem looked out the window, watched as Scáthach, legendary Scottish warrior, entered FEM. "I don't think Shee knows. If Shee did, Shee would have told us."

Inna lifted a skeptical eyebrow. "Shee is All. Shee knows All. It's part of our punishment."

"My head tells me Shee really has no idea how we will age."

"Your head is mortal now." Inna tapped her own. "Fallible."

Evidently, it was already imperfect in immortality or I would have seen this coming.

Inna sat back in her chair. "My heart hurts, Mnem. Hurts bad. I'm lost. I'm the goddess of the harvest, protection, and justice. Now I'm nothing." Her head dropped into her hands.

Mnem reached out, wrapped her coffee-warm fingers around Inna's elbow. "We'll figure something out. There has to be somebody who knows what we can do."

Inna looked up, tears welling. "Can you talk to your daughters?"

"I intend to." Mnem slid her phone from her Chanel purse and sent a group text. **Emergency family meet-**

ing. Tonight. My place. "They're all in town this week for some ridiculous Hollywood awards show where actors give awards to their friends." She studied her petal pink-lacquered fingers as they drummed on the table. Youthful hands. Unlined. Smooth. Free of age spots. *You can tell a woman's age by her hands and her neck. How does Cailleach deal with it? Wrinkles, body aches, saggy breasts, a double chin, a flabby stomach.* Anger roiled in her belly.

"Do you have another source of income?" asked Inna. "Shee said I'm getting the golden handshake."

"What's that?"

"Three months' salary."

"Shee neglected to tell me that." Mnem's drumming fingers quickened. "My olive oil business does well, but I've always given the profits to local charities." The drumming grew louder.

Those charities relied on Mnem's donations. To stop giving, to reduce the amount, felt akin to stealing.

Mnem's phone buzzed, the first of nine responses to her All Daughter message.

"I don't have any secondary income," said Inna. "My country is poor, and there's no Hollywood yam diet."

"Yet." Mnem winked. "Maybe you should start one. I see it now, secret miracle starch found in Nigerian yams melts fat from the body."

Inna managed a smile. She rubbed away the mascara smudged under her brown eyes, looked at the FEM building, and sighed. Then her lips curved into a wicked smile. Her eyes glittering, she turned to Mnem. "We need to take revenge."

"How?"

"Get one of our goddess friends to start a plague. Something with boils and pustules."

Mnem's nose wrinkled. "Plagues are so medieval.

Anyway, mortals make enough lab-created ones. They've far exceeded our talents for creating diseases and pestilence. And remember," she gave her a pointed look, "we're susceptible."

Inna gritted her teeth. "Right, I still don't have a handle on the whole mortality thing yet."

"Besides, involving another goddess is risky. What if Shee finds out?" Mnem shivered. "I do not want to go to *that* place."

Inna swallowed.

That place. Worse than Hell. A Nothingness. Only a few had been sent there. Or so was the rumor.

"I'm okay with risk." Inna rubbed her hands together. "In fact, the more I think about it, the better I like taking revenge. We have nothing to lose. We might even redeem ourselves and earn Shee's respect back. Shee might even reinstate us."

"I doubt it. You know how Shee hates upheaval in the world. People start blaming everyone. The government, each other, Herself and Himself."

"Are you kidding? There's *always* upheaval in the world somewhere."

"I'm talking about the *unusual* kind. The kind that makes Shee uncomfortable."

Inna stared at Mnem over the rim of her coffee cup, sipped, and set it down with a decided thunk. "Fine. Not a plague, but *something*." Her finger stabbed at the table. "I'm going to talk to people. Put out some feelers. I still have contacts. So do you."

Mnem nodded. Or was she now goddess *non-gratis*? "We'll think of something. We're goddesses, after all. I don't care what Shee says, you can't just end our divinity like that." Mnem snapped her fingers.

"Damn right." Inna leaned forward. "Did you check?"

"Check what?"

"That we're really mortal."

"No." The thought didn't occur to Mnem. Why would Shee lie? "Did you?"

"No. I want to, but," Inna picked up her purse, clutched it to her body. "I'm not ready."

"Me neither." *I'll never be ready to see proof that I'm actually mortal.*

Inna reached her hand over the table and set it atop Mnem's. "Thank you."

"For what?"

"For being you. For not joining my sobfest. You know, you have a reputation for being kind of snooty but now I know why. Memory provides the power to reason, to predict outcomes, to *think*. Your reason blew away the revenge fog from my brain. Thank you." Inna rose from the table and kissed Mnem on the cheeks. "Have a nice life."

"You as well." Mnem looked back at FEM. Revenge. The word took on new meaning. Revenge existed because mortals and immortals never forgot a wrong. That wrong forever carved into their brains.

Except there is no forever for me anymore.

FOUR

Mnem's nine daughters were always busy. A twenty-four-hour Walmart kind of busy. Everyone, from an aspiring author to a multi-award-winning director, demanded their services. Creatives were quite the fickle lot. They railed against their muses only to engage in odd rituals to summon them back.

Mnem was proud of her daughters. As long as mortals were permitted to create, her children would be sought out and revered.

Mnem, an iced lemonade and ouzo in her hand, stared out at the sea from the deck of her home. She needed her daughters like never before. Not for inspiration; for comfort. For hugs and love. The phone buzzed. Mnem dropped her gaze to the latest message and sighed. Then she scrolled through all nine.

From Calliope: **Momma, no can do. Have a date with a member of a European royal family. They're speaking to parliament tomorrow about a new law.**

From Clio: **Is this about the same thing as last**

time? History does repeat itself.

From Erato: **Ooooh, is this about that torrid affair you're having with the senator?**

From Euterpe: **Bad time. A Grammy-award winning musician is in a funk.**

From Melpomene: **Oh no! Of course I'll be there. I'm totally getting tragic vibes from this cryptic message. Hugs.**

From Polymnia: **Anything for Momma. I'll circle around after an appointment. Does that square with you?**

From Terpsichore: **I might be late. A choreographer is having a meltdown.**

From Thalia: **What, did they put you at the bottom of the Birken bag wait list?**

From Ourania: **My stars, I'm not surprised. Be there.**

Three definites. Two no's. One late. Three noncommittals.

Mnem's hand tightened around the railing. She didn't blame them. This was last minute. But she needed family. Friends would be nice too, but it appeared word of her fall from immortality already traveled the world over. Every message and call to her goddess friends went unanswered.

Bitches.

Mnem rattled the ice cubes in her drink. What to do? What to do? For the first time in her exceptionally long life she was clueless. Absolutely, positively, horrifyingly clueless. She could not come up with a single memory—which stretched back through the annals of ancient civilization—that might help her solve the problem of mortality.

Her phone buzzed again. The message from *him*. The senator. He was in town this week.

Drinks?

Mnem chuckled. Senator Miguel Flores was *muy caliente*. With a smile like sunshine and the sexual stamina of a demi-god. The political party's fresh new face. Mnem's fresh new lover. They had met at a yacht party in Newport. Mnem was explaining to the bartender how to mix a proper lemonade and ouzo when Miguel interrupted with a request for AsomBroso Del Porto Extra Anejo.

Mnem had glared at him. "Excuse me, wait your turn."

"Over-priced tequila can't wait." Miguel Flores had winked at her.

"Impatience isn't sexy."

"Not in politics, are you?"

Mnem shuddered. *Politics. Such an evil occupation. Mortals trying to rule like gods.* "Goddess, no."

Miguel's dreamy brown eyes—like liquid pools of compassionate honesty—focused on Mnem. "It's not for me." His eyes angled to the lean man in a Newport Harbor Yacht Club t-shirt and Brooks Brothers khaki pants. "Big donor at two o'clock."

"Oh, I see, you're his servant."

Miguel chuckled. "I am the servant of my people." He bowed.

It had been a while since Mnem had anyone, even in jest, bow before her. Warmth flooded her body, made her feel glittery and glowy. "Prove it."

Miguel picked up the shot of expensive tequila. "How?"

Mnem swirled her drink with her finger, stuck it in her mouth and slooowly pulled it out. "Serve me."

Miguel had stared hard. Mnem stared back. Then he turned away and joined the group of loyal party contributors.

Later that night, as the party grew livelier, and

somehow more crowded, a strong hand had taken hers, pulled her down a hall, through a door, and into a cabin. Miguel locked the door, dropped to his knees.

"Your wish is my command." He lifted her skirt.

"Oh my," said Mnem and grabbed hold of his hair.

That was two weeks ago. Five amazing romps in bed ago.

Mnem sighed at the memory.

Riding atop the senator would definitely blow off a bit of pent-up anger.

FIVE

Inna turned her head to gaze out the floor-to-ceiling window. The city stretched before her. It was buildings, freeways, and palm trees as far as the eye could see. However, the view this afternoon was different. It no longer beckoned. Its charms replaced with curses. Uncertainty glared from the buildings. Fears glinted off the glass towers. Worry hovered like smog. The view offered no harvest, no justice, and no protection for her new life as a mortal.

Inna lifted her hand, pinched the top. The skin snapped in place. When would the aging begin? When would the cold hand of mortality grab her by the throat and squeeze the celestial breath from her lungs?

"Are you watching me play today? You'll sit courtside."

Inna turned, her lithe naked body illuminated goddess-like in the window, to regard the gorgeous hunk of handsome sprawled on the custom-made king-size bed.

"You're my lucky fuck."

Inna smiled hard through her wince. She hated that word. It was so…primitive. So base. Goddesses didn't fuck.

They made love, copulated, indulged in hedonist pursuits, engaged in fleshly delights.

Duncan Eze, point guard, playboy, and basketball shoe maven, rolled over and propped himself up on an ebony muscled arm that would make anyone salivate. His whole body looked like a carving of strength and raw masculinity.

Inna stretched her arms to the ceiling, wiggled her body. "Lucky fuck, am I?"

"You're more than that, babe. You've gotten under my skin. You're the first woman I've ever…"

"Ever what?"

"Think about afterwards." His huge hand patted the sheet. "Basketball. Food. You." He grinned. "Damn girl, you wear me out."

Inna pursed her lips and shrugged, a ripple of fear skittering up her spine. Would her luck run out too? How long would she be Duncan's lucky charm?

"What's wrong, babe?" Duncan sat up, swung his long, muscled legs over the bed, and planted size seventeen feet on the Turkish carpet.

"Why do you ask?"

"Usually you beg for round two." He stood, walked across the room in long strides.

"I was fired this morning."

"Fired? I didn't know you had a job." Duncan opened the double-doored closet. Another room, actually. "Thought you were a Nigerian princess or something." He pulled out a custom-made dress shirt.

"Goddess," Inna mumbled under her breath.

"Huh? You say something?" He shrugged on the shirt, buttoned it up.

"I wish I were a princess, then at least I could sell my tiara and jewels to survive."

Duncan stopped dressing, his jaw tightening. "Money. All the bitches want money."

"I don't want your money." Inna stomped toward him. "What did I say about calling women bitches?" She reached out, stroked his face.

"Not to." He flicked her hand away. "You're not my mother."

She caught his hand, kissed the palm. "I was very clear about what I do and do not tolerate when we started dating."

Duncan's face softened. "A woman with relationship rules. That's what I like about you." He smiled. "Here's Duncan's rule. I'm tired of women who are after my money."

"That's not a rule." She ran her hand down his arm, gave his massive bicep a squeeze.

"No money talk."

"A good rule." Inna stood on her tiptoes and kissed him.

Duncan wrapped his arms around her naked body and lost himself in her kiss. "Now look what you've gone and done." He pointed to his crotch as his phone sounded with the jarring noise of a basketball buzzer. "I can't be late again. Coach hates it." He let Inna go, reached for the Seville Row trousers draped over the Restoration Hardware club chair. "You can find another job, babe. You're gorgeous and smart." He worked a Gucci belt through the loops. Duncan Eze liked to look good when he went to work. "What skills do you have?"

Inna shrugged. A goddess didn't need a skill set. She just Was.

"Which tie?" Duncan dangled three from his hand.

"I like the one with the Nigerian print." Inna came

26

forward, slid it from his fingers, and draped it around his neck.

Duncan beamed. "That's one of mine. A prototype. Socks and ties, Nigerian style. I just need to find a few more investors."

Inna adjusted the tie under his collar as Duncan caressed her breasts. "Hold still."

"Mmmm, never." He gave a little squeeze. "You are coming tonight, right?"

Inna adjusted the knot. Smoothed the tie. "I'll be there."

Duncan kissed her deep and hard, then headed out the door, stopped, turned around. "You'll find something, babe, a woman as fine as you. Somebody will hire you for something."

Inna shimmied. "You know it."

"Hey, if you're hungry Maria will fix you something. Got to go, babe. See you at the game and don't forget about the ties." Duncan walked out of the bedroom.

Inna wasn't hungry. Fear filled her belly. Worry stole her appetite. She put on her Altuzarra striped skirt, pulled the clingy Tom Ford top over her head, then surveyed the bedroom. Duncan Eze's decorator had great taste. The headboard was a twenty-foot double door that looked like it came from an ancient Turkish fortress. The rest of the bedroom was minimalistic and modern, creamy sumptuous fabrics softening the gothic-rugged chic style. It was the bedroom of a king. Or rather, a man at the top of his game.

Life as a game. Inna laughed. Except the room, with its vaulted ceilings, made her laughter hollow. As empty as the eternal hope that once nestled without fear in Inna's soul. Life was no longer a game. Life had become cruel in less time than it took Duncan to sink a three-pointer from the free throw line.

A job. Inna rubbed the back of her neck. She did not have any marketable skills. Her goddess talent for inspiring others to keep promises was as defunct as her immortality.

Inna took her purse from atop the chest of drawers. Duncan had left his Nigerian-inspired print ties beside it. She picked one up and smiled. Nigeria. Should she return to her homeland? It might be a good idea. She could lick her spiritual wounds.

Inna took both of Duncan's ties and headed to the front door.

"Miss Inna." Maria bustled from out of the sunlit kitchen. "Are you hungry? I have ogbono soup. Mister Duncan says it's better than his momma's."

"Really? Duncan raves about his momma's cooking."

"I add a bit of Mexican spice." Maria winked. "Don't tell him."

"I wouldn't dare."

Maria giggled. "Let me get you a small container, okay? *Muy pequiñito.* Not enough to add an ounce on your *bonita* body."

Inna's heart skipped a beat. Calories. Weight. Dear goddess, she had mortal concerns now. "A very small container."

"*Muy bueno.*"

Even Maria has a skill, thought Inna as Duncan's housekeeper disappeared back into the kitchen.

"How long have you been cooking?" asked Inna when Maria came out with the sixty-four-ounce container of ogbono soup. Maria's idea of small.

Maria flapped her chapped hand. "Forever, Miss Inna. I helped my father in his restaurant when I was four years old. I washed vegetables. After…" she looked away, her face dark. "After my father lost his life to the cartels, I came to California and found cooking jobs. The last restaurant was where I met Mister Duncan. He loved my chicken mole so much he came into the kitchen and offered me a job." Maria cocked her head. "Made me an offer I could not refuse." She held up a finger. "He had one condition, that I learn to cook his Nigerian food and take good care of his house."

"Duncan is very lucky to have found someone like you."

"Oh," Maria waved her hand again. "Mister Duncan is lucky to have found *you*. Of all the women he brings home, you're my favorite."

"Thank you." Inna, clutching the plastic container, wondered if 'all the women' were pre-Inna or not. That was one of Inna's dating rules, which she made very clear to Duncan at the time. But with her promise-keeping power gone, Inna's hope that the basketball superstar would keep his word was nothing more than a personal foul.

SIX

Light scattered through the Baccarat crystal chandelier, prisms dancing on the walls. Each bright color-infused speck faded before paling into nothingness.

Like my future.

Mnem squeezed shut her eyes. Willed the tears to retreat. Tears did no good anyway. Mnem needed a plan for the rest of her life. She counted on her nine daughters to help her find one. They would come up with a good plan. Probably several. After all, if the muses couldn't, who could?

The *almost* tears receded, and Mnem opened her eyes again. She took a moment to appreciate the beauty of the colorful prisms gracing the hotel suite. An expensive five-star suite. Senator Miguel Flores never settled for second best. It was one reason she liked him. That, and his unflagging energy in the bedroom.

Mnem touched his arm.

Miguel's eyes flew open. "I have a press conference."

"Right this minute?"

Miguel always had somewhere to go. A presser, an interview, a meeting, a fundraiser. The man was busy.

He rolled over, checked his phone. "In an hour."

"What's the topic this time?" Mnem ran a finger along the muscled curve of his bicep.

"Do you really want to know?" Miguel rolled back over and tapped the tip of Mnem's nose.

"Not really." Mnem sighed. Too loudly. It slipped out accidently, her despair leaking out in ways she wasn't prepared for.

Miguel propped up on an elbow. "What? I didn't give you enough orgasms?"

Mnem smiled. "You did a fine job, Senator Flores. No complaints."

Miguel's thick dark brows pinched tight. "Not the response I hoped for."

"If it wasn't great, I wouldn't be here." She tugged on one of his errant dark curls, curls he worked hard to slick back straight and obedient.

"Then why the novella sigh?"

"Do *you* really want to know?"

"Yes, or I wouldn't have asked." Miguel brought her close for a kiss. "Give me the short version." He rolled off the bed. "I can't go to the presser smelling like your pussy." He walked into the bathroom.

"Oh, but I have to walk around the rest of the day with your seed stuck to my thighs?" She followed him in.

"My seed? I like the sound of that." He turned on the hot water. "Tell me what's wrong."

Everything. My life is over. I'm living on borrowed time. I've been dismissed, defunded, defrocked, and disgraced. I've been thrown off the immortality cliff. Tossed in a mortal ocean with no life preserver.

Mnem swallowed the lump of misery that had taken

residence in her throat. The thick ache stuck like glue to her heart. "I'm broke."

Miguel, his dark ringlets glistening with water droplets, poked his head around the marble-tiled corner. "What? How? I thought you were the heiress of an olive oil fortune."

"Who told you that?"

"Remember when we met, and you propositioned me on the yacht?"

"You stared at me and walked away."

"Right. Do you think I'm going to stick this senatorial body part into just any gorgeous woman? I had to find out who you were." Miguel lathered his hair.

"And?" Mnem crossed her arms.

"And Edward told me you were a trust fund baby."

"Oh." It was her standard explanation for not having a job. "Well, it's gone. Along with my accountant."

"That's horrible. I'll get my people on it. Call in a few favors. We'll find the bastard and bring him to justice." Miguel stepped out of the shower.

"Her." Mnem handed him a towel.

"All I need is a name." Miguel shook his head, scattering water.

"She's long gone. And…and I don't want to get you involved."

"Why not?"

"Because." Mnem watched him towel off his body, appreciated the fine mortal specimen before her. She had countless mortal lovers, and they were all fun for a while. But she always moved on. Never became attached. What was the point? They aged and died. And she, goddess of memory, history and knowledge, was eternal. "Because we're not…"

"Not what?" Miguel combed away his curls, slicked them back with gel.

"You're a lot of fun but…"

Miguel strode from the bathroom when his phone buzzed. He picked it up and gave Mnem a give-me-a-minute finger. "I'm not late. What? No, I missed that message. Had an off-the-books appointment. Be there in a minute." He tossed the phone on the bed. "Evidently, there's a pre-presser call-in radio spot." He pulled up his Armani trousers. "We will continue this conversation later. I want to know what I'm *not*. Drinks tonight?" He grabbed his shirt.

"Already booked." *My daughters are visiting. They'll tell me what to do*. Mnem buttoned his shirt.

"I hope you don't consider me a two-week stand." Miguel stood before the mirror to knot his tie.

Mnem tapped her chin. "Haven't decided yet."

Miguel shrugged on his suit jacket. "How do I look?"

"Yummy."

"I was hoping for distinguished and earnest." Miguel opened the door to the hallway. "I'll take a raincheck on your offer. And I want you to seriously consider taking me up on my offer to help you. Justice needs to be mete out."

Mnem blew a kiss and watched as the spring-loaded hotel door closed. Justice had already been meted out. Mnem knew that. She was the one who had leached off the divine domain.

SEVEN

"The royal meeting was postponed," said Calliope by way of a greeting when Mnem opened the front door. "It's good to see you, Momma." She gave Mnem a big hug.

"The traffic!" Melpomene wiped her brow with a theatrical flourish. "Human drivers are ridiculous. Where are they all going in the middle of a weekday afternoon, anyway?"

"Their therapists." Erato kissed Mnem on the cheek. "You don't look too good, Momma."

Terpsichore tilted her head and circled around Mnem with a graceful light step that was more dance than inspection. "Momma looks beautiful."

"Heavenly as usual," said Ourania.

"Perfectly divine." Polymnia gave Mnem a kiss. "Love this top." Her fingers ran down the edge of the sheer, sky blue organza silk blouse. "You always dress like a goddess."

Mnem paled, turned away, and made a beeline for the bar in the living room.

Calliope joined her, made herself a vodka with a twist

of lime. "Why are we having a family meeting?" She dropped ice cubes into the Waterford tumbler.

Mnem removed the ouzo and lemonade from the refrigerator under the bar. "Girls, take a seat."

"Oh dear, Momma, you've made this all sound terribly dramatic." Melpomene gathered her waist-length golden ringlets in her fist, twisted a few times, and tied the curly knot at the top of her head. "I'm all ears."

Erato plopped down on the sofa. "Does this have something to do with Senator Hottie?"

"How do you know about that?" Mnem took a sip of her drink, savored the tang as it cooled her throat.

"Mystery Greek Heiress Seen Dining with Senator Flores." Ourania held up her phone. "This town is gossip central. Probably has more free-lance paparazzi per square mile than anywhere in the world. Want me to read the article?"

"Not really." Mnem splashed more ouzo into the glass.

"Read it. Read it." Erato clapped her hands.

Ourania cleared her throat. "Senator Flores, possibly California's most sought-after bachelor, was spotted leaving a members-only restaurant with a mystery woman sources say is the heiress of a vast olive oil fortune in Kalamata, Greece. One of his aides, who requested to remain anonymous, said, 'it's good to see the senator enjoying his rare free time.' Is the young senator who works hard for his constituents finally going to settle down?"

Mnem flapped her hand. "He's a fling."

Calliope sat in the big club chair, drew up her legs, and draped them over the side. "Okay, Momma, out with it. What's this meeting all about?"

Mnem's heartrate doubled. "I don't know how to tell you this." She looked down at her drink, the words stuck between her mind and tongue. How foolish not to have planned what she was going to say to her daughters. Mnem didn't know where to start. Her own goddess failings? Her summons to FEM. Her new life as a mortal?

"Momma?" Terpsichore sprung cat-like from the sofa, kneeled at Mnem's feet, and set her hand on Mnem's knee. "What is it?"

Mnem's fingers laced through her beautiful daughter's hand and took a deep breath.

"Momma, you're scaring me," whispered Melpomene.

Mnem lifted her chin. "I've been fired."

Five muses looked from one to another, each lovely face pinched with confusion.

Calliope tucked a stray brown lock behind her ear and leaned forward. "From what?"

"From FEM."

If a mouse dared live in the house, it held its breath, the room was that quiet. Only the sound of surf infiltrated the silence.

Terpsichore squeezed her mother's hand. "How is that possible?" Her stunned gaze made an arc from her mother to her sisters.

"Shee summoned me." Mnem set down her drink. "Via email."

"Not birds?" asked Ourania. "How odd."

"Shee told me I was no longer relevant. That I was redundant. That I was a drain on the feminine energy collective."

"I heard they were down-sizing," said Erato.

"Erato," Melpomene scolded. "The goddess of memory, wisdom, and knowledge cannot be down-sized."

"Yes, Momma can," said Calliope. "The world doesn't need her talents anymore. They have the internet."

"Calli," snapped Polymnia. "Whose side are you on?"

"I'm not taking sides," Calliope sniffed. "I'm speaking

the truth. Momma values truth." She settled back in the chair and regarded her momma with a guarded look. "You should have seen this coming."

"You're right." Mnem's fingers wrapped around the drink, its cold condensation identical to the cold sweat at the back of her neck. "The writing was on the wall. I was too busy having fun to read it." She guzzled the drink down, stood, and lifted her arms wide. "Take a good look." She turned slowly around. "Your momma is now mortal."

"What?" Melpomene's hand flew to her breast. "Shee took away your immortality too?"

Calliope rolled her eyes. "What do you think being fired meant?"

"Certainly not that!" Melpomene rushed over and wrapped her arms around Mnem.

Mnem hugged her daughter tight, inhaled the lemon rosemary scent of her hair, basked in the warmth of her skin. Time with her daughters was precious now. Every moment counted.

"How long do you have?" asked Terpsichore.

"Terpsi!" snapped Melpomene. "What an awful question."

"It's okay. It's the first thing I thought of too." Mnem patted Melpomene's hair. "I don't know and neither does Shee."

"I don't believe that," snorted Calliope. "Shee is All."

"Maybe Shee knows and maybe Shee doesn't, but I wasn't going to stomp my foot and demand an answer." Mnem detangled herself from her daughter's arms and headed for the bar.

"Can you become relevant again?" Ourania's voice was icing sweet. "We can help. We will *all* help."

"It's too late. Shee told me I don't have a platform or social media or followers."

"Shee's out of line. The whole world does *not* have a love affair with social media," said Erato. "Millions of humans did not fall sway to its addiction."

"Not according to Shee." Mnem splashed more lemonade into the ouzo.

"Don't take this wrong, Momma." Calliope, always sincere, always just, shifted uneasily in the chair. "No one knows who you are anymore."

"You don't have to dig the mortal blade in." Melpomene threw her sister dagger looks.

"That's right." Polymnia nodded. "Momma needs our help, not our criticism." She tugged her phone from her black patent Birkin bag. "How many Twitter followers do you have?"

"None."

"InstaPic?" asked Ourania.

"Tínota." *Nothing.* "I don't have any of these accounts."

"Surely, you have a LinkedIn?" asked Terpsichore.

"I am—was a goddess. I was linked to all of divine creation." Mnem's voice was too loud, too desperate, too strained.

"Not really," mumbled Calliope.

Terpsichore elbowed her sister.

"You don't need social media to inspire people." Melpomene put her hands on her hips. "Who have you helped recently?"

"Helped?" Mnem peered over the rim of her glass.

"With memory. With wisdom," suggested Terpsichore.

Mnem shook her head. "I don't remember."

Five sets of perfectly groomed eyebrows shot up. Their momma never said, 'I don't remember.' Unlike politicians who forgot campaign promises, Mnem remembered everything.

"You must have helped someone recently." Calliope

paced the room. "A scientist working on Alzheimer's, perhaps?"

"No." Mnem looked out the window to the sea.

"Any neurologists?"

"None." Mnem paled, her inadequacies made perfectly clear by her well-meaning daughters.

The blow to her once-immortal ego was complete. Mnem wasn't just irrelevant, she alone made herself incompetent. Scientific advancements moved as fast as Hermes these days. Mortals barely kept up with the necessary ethics of their progress. Inspiring them to discover more than they were able to handle was counterproductive. Humans neither learned nor applied history's accrued wisdom. They left it to rot in the name of whatever belief was pushed at the time. The more technically advanced mortals became, the shorter their collective memory.

Mnem stared at the horizon. *Mortals are ridiculously shortsighted.*

"Stop badgering her, Calli," said Melpomene. "It's water under the bridge. Momma, what can we do for you?"

"I'm cut off. No more money, no immortality. No divine power."

"That too?" Erato gasped.

Mnem needed only to touch a human. One touch and memory was restored. Like it happened yesterday. Without bias. Recalled through the lens of truth. It was one reason rulers through the ages had a love-hate relationship with her.

"How am I going to live? What am I going to do with the rest of my life?" Mnem's voice was as brittle as a dry twig.

Calliope took a deep breath before delivering the bad news. "You'll have to get a job."

"What kind of job? I have no marketable skills." Mnem wagged a finger at them. "Don't say bartending either. I have no desire to work in bad lighting with drunks."

"Ask your new boyfriend, the senator," said Ourania. "He has lots of contacts. That's how you get jobs these days, Momma. No skills required. You just need to know the right person."

I used to be the right person.

"I don't want his help." Mnem's voice pitched high. "He's nothing, a fling. I don't want to owe him anything."

"You could be a history teacher," offered Polymnia.

"You need a degree for that," reminded Calliope.

Mnem squared her shoulders. "I graduated from the School of Life."

"Don't say that," groaned Terpsichore. "Never say that."

"So overdone, that and the School of Hard Knocks," added Polymnia.

"Well," Mnem gave each one a hard stare. "You're the muses. Get musing! Tell me what kind of job I can get where I can still live like this." She fluttered her hands in the air.

Four muses turned to Calliope, their eyes expressing what they dare not.

Calliope puffed out her exasperation. She was always the lead muse on these things. "You can't, Momma. Not unless you earn a six-figure salary. You have to curb your spending."

Mnem cringed. "For how long?"

"Forever?" whispered Melpomene.

"You mean until I *die*." Mnem banged the empty crystal glass down on the table.

The living room grew hushed, heavy with the thought of their beloved Momma dying. The muses shared furtive glances as Mnem turned their back to them and made her third drink.

"We're going about this the wrong way," said Polymnia. "I think all of us, all nine of us, should pay a visit to Shee and tell Her your new plan to become relevant again. We'll make a list." Polymnia gestured to her sisters.

"Of what?" asked Calliope, ever the pragmatist.

"Of all the things Momma will do. And we will help Momma write a mission statement. Shee will be so impressed Momma's divinity will be returned."

"A mission statement?" Terpsichore rolled her eyes.

"It's worth a try," said Polymnia.

Mnem gulped down her third drink.

Melpomene pointed to Mnem's empty glass. "You're not immortal anymore. Your body reacts differently to alcohol now."

Alcohol was dehydrating. Damaged livers. Made humans act stupid. Addled and aged them.

Mnem set her fingers on both cheeks. "Do I look mortal? Do I look old?"

"Not a day over thirty," said Terpsichore.

"Younger." Ourania nodded.

Mnem looked into the over-sized abalone mirror hanging over the bar, tilted her head from side to side in search of signs that aging already began. Not a wrinkle, not a crease, not an enlarged pore. Yet.

Mnem's attention returned to her daughters. "Well? Get working on the list."

Calliope gave Mnem a troubled smile, all upturned mouth with no confidence behind the eyes. "Okay, we will. But you need to start looking for a job too. You know...in case..." The rest of the sentence withered on her lips.

Mnem closed her eyes and took a deep breath, the

41

effects of the alcohol seeping into her mortal brain. "Group hug." She opened her arms.

Willing herself not to cry, Mnem immersed herself in the warmth and love of her daughters, a whirlpool of emotions dragging her down.

EIGHT

The buzzer blared. A thunderous cheer rose up from the crowd. Duncan's team was crushing their opponents. Inna, sitting courtside at the basketball game, inhaled the heady spice of sweaty players and adoring fans. Of beer and chilidogs. Of over-perfumed women and cigar-smoking men. The fragrance of mortals. A scent Inna had taken for granted since…always.

The arena was deafening, a thousand people talking, laughing, and complaining. Alive with life and mortality.

The sensations sank into Inna's skin. It didn't help. The overwhelming sounds were not enough to drive out the worry that wrapped around her soul like a python suffocating its prey. It squeezed all hope from her.

Never in a thousand years did Inna ever hear of a goddess being fired. It was outrageous! A divine miscarriage of justice of epic proportions! The CEO of FEM threw her—the Nigerian goddess of the harvest, protection, and justice—out like rotten meat. Inna looked down at her lap, found her fingers curled into fists.

Inna's house was paid for. Shee provided that perk at

least. Inna unfurled her fingers, picked up her phone, and checked her bank balance. Not *another* withdrawal. A wine club payment. Another luxury that had to go. Inna scrolled down the page, mentally added the list of monthly expenditures. Even *if* she only paid the necessities like gas and electricity, Inna figured she had maybe, *maybe* five months at most before the FEM well ran dry.

A bump on the shoulder made Inna look up.

"Inna." The center's wife, Alyssa, pointed to Inna's breasts. "You look fabulous! That tie!"

"You like?" Inna touched the tie. It was Duncan's, one of the samples she took earlier. Duncan wanted her to check the quality and fabric. 'I know basketball. You're into all that designer crap,' he had said. After examining the bias cut, interlining, and hand-sewn stitches, Inna deemed it superior and added it to three others on the preferred makers pile. This evening, as she dressed for the game, Inna wore two of those ties on a whim. One encircled her neck, the knot positioned for maximum cleavage-enhancing effect. The other she wound in her hair, part headband, part twisted into her thick braid.

"Your style is seriously swoon-worthy." Alyssa tugged on her tie.

"Ladies, smile," called a photographer.

Inna and Alyssa drew together, their bright smiles photo perfect. A few snaps later, the photographer turned his attention to the ex-supermodel currently dating the shooting guard, a lanky Black-Asian with dreamy eyes and a nightmarish knack for stealing the ball.

Inna stretched out her arm, her phone clasp between her fingers. "Let's take a few more." While they posed and laughed, she snapped away, then posted the best photo.

The basketball game was a blur. Sweaty mortals pounded back and forth across the court. The arena swelled with noise. Duncan might have scored a point, but Inna wasn't sure. Her eyes faced forward, yet her mind was far away. To liquidating her assets and returning to Nigeria. To finding a job. To figuring out what she was going to do with the time she had left in this world. However long *that* was.

The buzzer sounded and the crowded erupted into cheers. Inna checked the scoreboard. A hundred-and-one to a hundred-and-three. Duncan's team won.

Team. The word took on new meaning. Inna was booted from Team Goddess. She was alone. More alone than ever before in her life.

Inna scrolled through InstaPics and glanced briefly at the photo posted earlier. Her brows lifted in surprise. Three hundred likes. Inna didn't have that many followers! She didn't bother reading the comments. Photos of pretty women always received lots of likes. People preferred the young and beautiful. The world had not changed one bit since its inception.

Alyssa leaned into Inna. "Wow, that many already?"

Inna shrugged. It was a photograph. It didn't matter in the greater scheme of life. It was one photo of probably a billion posted every day on InstaPic.

Alyssa shouldered her Chanel bag. "Time to go home and wait for Devon. He's always horny after a winning game. You'd think he would be exhausted but, no, he wants to grind all night."

Inna smiled, was about to slide her phone back into her purse, when it *pinged*. It was a message, or rather a photo— a horrifying photo—from Axtis, Persian goddess of peace, justice, and victory.

Inna's mouth dropped open, her heart thumping in her throat.

The arena was too loud to make a call. A message wasn't enough. She needed to contact Axtis *now*!

Muttering Nigerian expletives under her breath, Inna worked her way through a crowd drunk on victory, the image of Axtis burning in her mind like a brand. The photo left no room for debate. Axtis, goddess of peace, justice, and victory sat cross-legged with an ancient scimitar across her lap.

Inna and Mnem were not the only ones who lost their goddesshood.

Up several flights of steps. Through the corridor. Out the door. Each minute was a countdown.

The parking lot wasn't much better. A few swear words later, Inna decided there was only one option. She forwarded Axtis's photo to Mnem. Mnem would know what to do.

Inna burst through a pack of fans and sprinted for the car. She hoped Mnem arrived there in time.

NINE

Mnem's Mercedes coupe screeched to a stop in Axtis's driveway. She flung open the door, ran up the path as fast as her five-inch heels allowed, and bounded up the steps, almost colliding with Phra Naret.

"Hello, Mnemosyne." Phra Naret, Thai goddess of good fortune, beauty, and blessings, clutched a glass bowl. The single white candle floating inside sloshed in the water. "I just arrived." She bobbed her head at the front door. "Axtis won't answer."

"We'll see about that." Mnem pounded on the door. "Axtis! Let me in!" She pressed her ear to the front door. "Let's go around back."

It wasn't easy. Thick foliage blocked the way. Mnem cursed and fought her way through the tangle of pink-flowering bougainvillea, the thorns scratching her skin and catching on her Valentino silk blouse.

"Will these leave scars now?" Phra Naret dipped under a long thorny branch.

Mnem's head whipped around. "What? You too?"

Phra Naret pushed her lips into a pout. "Axtis too. The

FEM elevator was a one-way ticket to Mortal Land that day."

Mnem lifted a blossoming branch over Phra Naret's head. "How are you doing?"

"I don't think I've processed it yet. It's all so surreal." She lifted the bowl. "Will this work anymore? Will the water and candle help Axtis find comfort? I brought it as habit. Water...flame..." She sighed. "Does it no longer hold the ancient magic?"

"The ancient magic works." Mnem pushed through a thicket at the corner of the house. "Just not for us."

"I should dump this then."

Mnem turned around, set a hand on Phra Naret's arm. "Don't. You never know." She dipped under the branch of an overgrown tree, an unripe avocado hitting her head. "Finally." She broke free of the foliage into the little back-yard and bolted for the sliding glass door. Her two hands splayed wide and her forehead pressed to the glass as she peered into the room. "Axtis?"

The room was dark.

Mnem tried the sliding door. It eased open, moonlight slicing the darkness.

Axtis, Persian ex-goddess of peace, justice, and victory sat cross-legged in the middle of the living room. An ancient but sharp scimitar laid across her lap. One hand rested atop the carved ebony hilt, the other on the blade.

Mnem ran in. "Don't do it."

Phra Naret crossed the room, turned on the lights.

Axtis opened her eyes, swollen and wet with grief. "I'm ready to die."

Mnem crouched down beside her. "They fired me too."

"You?" Dark rings shadowed her eyes and her cheeks were wet and splotchy.

"Four that I know of. Probably more." Mnem sat on the floor.

Axtis gripped the scimitar's hilt, her knuckles white. "What are you going to do?"

"I don't know. We'll figure something out. All of us." Mnem bobbed her head at Phra Naret who took the hint.

"You don't want to do this." Phra Naret took a seat on the opposite side.

Axtis gripped the scimitar tighter. "There's no point. There's no reason to live. I blame myself. Shee is right. I'm irrelevant, a nobody goddess from a worn torn land. I've brought no peace, no victory, no justice." Fresh tears ran down her cheeks.

"It's not your fault," said Mnem.

"I should have tried harder. *Done* something."

"Done what exactly?" Phra Naret's voice was soft.

Axtis choked on a sob. "I don't know. Something. Maybe long ago I should have seduced a ruler or…." She shuddered into another sob.

Mnem rubbed Axtis's back. "We can't berate ourselves for choices made long ago. We thought we'd live forever. Time doesn't—didn't—apply to goddesses. The best thing for us right now is to move forward." *Please don't ask me how. I have no idea.*

The doorbell rang.

"I'll get it," said Phra Naret.

"Move forward." Axtis closed her eyes. "There is no forward for me."

Mnem ran her hands through Axtis's hair. "Yes there is. You, me, all of us, we just have to find our path. Give it some time."

"We don't have the luxury of time anymore." Axtis opened her eyes to stare down at the blade.

"Not eternal time, no. But mortals see time differently,

with hours, days, weeks, and months. We have their time now. Using their time is better than…" Mnem touched the blade. "That."

"Have you looked at the elderly? Really looked? They're ugly. Wrinkled and—"

Mnem's shoulder bumped Axtis's. "Don't let Cailleach hear you say that."

Axtis turned her head. "That's how she regenerates. Cailleach is accustomed to aging."

"Let go of the scimitar." Mnem pried Axtis's fingers from the hilt. "We'll figure something out."

"Damn right we will!" Inna stomped into the room. "Give me the blade. I'm going to stick the pointy end into Shee." Inna wiggled her fingers.

Mnem sighed. "Sure, try to stab Shee. We all need a laugh."

Axtis bit back the beginnings of a smile. "Sounds like a plan."

Phra Naret giggled.

Shee was indestructible. You could no more harm Shee than you could stab a cloud. She was Shee. Immortal divine being. Untouchable. Unflappable. Unkillable. Un-avenge-able.

Inna plopped herself down in front of Axtis. "You can't take your life."

Axis's brows lifted. "Why not?"

"Because you must not give that satisfaction to Shee. Why make Her life easy?"

"What are you talking about?"

"Shee fires a goddess, who then kills herself in despair. Ex-goddess problem solved." Inna snapped her fingers. "No, Axtis, you will not kill yourself. You, me, all of us are going to live in spite of Shee."

"How?" Axtis sniffed.

"I don't know yet. We'll figure something out."

"Mnemosyne already said that. None of you have any answers." Axtis, a reflective and analytical soul, required details. The Why often more important than the How, Who, What, and Where. But not today.

"It's too soon for specifics. It just happened. Do you think mortals who get fired have a job lined up the next day?" said Mnem. "Of course not. But I know this, FEM took our divinity but Shee cannot steal our spirit."

"Or our divine experience." Phra Naret glanced at the unlit candle floating in the glass bowl. Lighting it couldn't hurt. There was power in ritual.

"Nobody puts goddess in the corner." Inna thumped the floor with her fist.

Axtis removed one hand from the blade to wipe away a tear. "It's 'baby,' and that movie is decades old." Her fingers loosened from the scimitar's hilt.

"Who wants a drink?" asked Mnem.

"Champagne," said Inna. "Where's the Dom Perignon?"

Axtis waved her hand toward the kitchen.

After finding the champagne and four crystal flutes, Phra Naret lit the floating candle. Rituals mattered.

"What are we celebrating?" Axtis's fingernails clicked against the blade.

"A new beginning." Mnem held out her arms. "We've never had *that* before. We'll reinvent ourselves."

"That's right," said Inna. "We will join today's hip new crowd. Be the In people."

Axtis winced. "That's all fine but how will we eat?"

"We don't need to figure that out tonight," said Mnem.

"The bubbly is poured." Phra Naret hoisted a glass.

Axtis set the scimitar on the floor, stood, and plodded forward. "Fine." Resignation puffed from her lips.

Mnem pushed the scimitar under the sofa before joining the others. "To us. To a new beginning and a fresh start." She lifted the fluted glass high. "To the next chapter in our lives."

"You mean the last chapter," mumbled Axtis.

"There's always an epilogue," said Inna.

Mnem cleared her throat. "We will rise like the phoenix and live life to the fullest. Who knows what amazing things are ahead for us?"

They clinked glasses, the Lalique crystal *ting* a melodious note of hope.

The ex-goddesses sipped, their eyes wandering from one to the other. They sought hope in each other's faces. Searched for traces of their former goddess courage. Mnem's eyes twinkled with bravado. Inna's glowed with daring. Phra Naret's gleamed with serenity. And Axtis's flashed with skepticism. It was a start.

Axtis felt the champagne fizz for the first mortal time, the effervesce a sensation as fleeting as a mortal life span. "If we're going to join the mortal world, we need new names."

"I like mine." Inna touched her heart.

"Yes, yours is easy to pronounce. What about you, Mnemosyne?" asked Axtis.

"My friends call me Mnem."

"My name is so…" Axtis wrinkled her nose.

"How about Axie?" asked Phra Naret.

"I like it." Axie clinked glasses with Phra Naret. "It sounds fun."

Three heads swiveled to Phra Naret.

"Phra is a title, like Princess." Phra Naret straightened her spine, stood tall, as tall as a tiny woman could.

"What about Fran?" asked Inna.

"My name is *me*." Phra Naret patted her heart. "It's part of who I am."

Mnem nodded. "Naret is perfect. Short and easy to pronounce."

"Okay, now what?" Axie drank half the glass. "Our names don't pay bills or help us find a job."

Mnem splashed more bubbly into everyone's glass. "We drink."

TEN

I nna groaned and forced open heavy eyes. "Ugh." She rubbed her head, squinted at the sunshine pouring through the window.

Mnem was curled on the carpet, her back against the Chesterfield sofa, her head on a pillow, a blanket draped over her body. Naret sprawled on the sofa, one slim arm hanging over the edge. Axie was missing.

Inna sat up and clutched her head, a jackhammer battering her skull. "Mortality sucks." She looked around. "Where's Axie?"

Mnem opened one eye. "In her bedroom sleeping." She moaned and threw off the blanket. "I feel like shit. This must be a hangover. I don't like it."

"It's vile." Inna smacked her lips together and grimaced.

Naret yawned. "I had green tea after the fifth drink." She sat up and stretched her arms. "I'm hungry."

Axie staggered from her bedroom. "I hate you all. I swear this hangover feels worse than death."

"Mortals take two pain relievers." Inna hauled her body out of the chair.

"I don't have any." Axie went into the kitchen. "Never needed them."

"Hydrate." Naret swung her legs over the sofa.

"The goddess associated with water *would* say that," mumbled Mnem.

"Ex-goddess." Axie corrected as she stared at the espresso machine. Coffee good. Obnoxious noise of grinding beans, bad.

Inna staggered into the kitchen, quaffed down a bottle of over-priced water. She wiped her lips, looked at the label. "That was really tasty." She handed a bottle to Naret.

"I think it's the best brand out there." Naret cracked open the lid.

They toasted again, this time with bottled water.

"If it's one thing we all know, it's quality," said Mnem. "One of the perks of being around forever." She clicked the two-espresso shot button and slid a demitasse cup under the spout.

Inna's phone rang. "Where's my phone?" She found it wedged between a cushion. "It's Duncan. He's probably wondering what happened to me. I was supposed to meet him back at his place. Mortals are so needy." The phone *pinged* with a message. "All right, impatient man." Inna read the message and rubbed her temples. "My head feels like it was dropped from heaven. I'm not in the mood for this." She tapped the phone. "Hi Duncan...I'm at a friend's house. A girlfriend...Too drunk to drive...What....Hold on, let me look." Inna scrolled. "I see it...You what...That's wonderful...What? Me? I...okay, I'll do it...I'll come right over...Bye." Inna looked at the others, her eyes wide.

"What is it?" Mnem came forward, a steaming espresso in her hand.

"I have a job," she shouted and punched the air with a fist.

"What kind of job?" Axie stuck a demitasse cup under the espresso machine.

Inna waved them forward and they huddled around her phone. "A paparazzi took a photo of me and the center's wife last night. Look! It has four thousand likes and many of the comments are women asking where they can buy the ties."

"What ties?"

"I wore two of Duncan's sample ties. He has about a dozen."

"I'm confused." Naret wrinkled her nose. "How does wearing a tie give you a job?"

"Duncan has been looking for more investors and today several called him." Inna did a little happy dance. "Which means his new company is a go and he wants *me* to manage the company's new InstaPic account."

"That's a job?" Mnem's brow furrowed.

"Yes!" Inna jumped up and down. "I have a job! I have a job! I won't starve!"

"How much will he pay you?" Mnem sipped on her espresso, felt the caffeine ease the fog of her alcohol-muddled brain.

"I don't know." Inna spun around and snatched her Chanel purse from under the coffee table. "I'll check in with you all later." She hugged everyone and hurried out the door.

"It's the perfect job for her." Axie poured milk froth into her cup. "Inna's an extrovert."

"I'm happy for her." Naret took the tea kettle from the

stovetop. "This is great news for all of us, because if Inna found a job, we can too."

"There's no correlation to Inna's finding a job—which found her by the way—and our job hunt." Axie dropped two sugar cubes into the latte. "I don't have a famous boyfriend and I don't have any marketable skills."

Mnem studied Axie's face, looked for signs of her slipping back into suicidal thoughts again. Axie was a deep thinker, a bottom of the ocean kind of deep. Sometimes, a mortal's problems dulled her divine light. As a goddess she always resurfaced, her sparkling clarity bringing illumination to a mortal's dilemma.

"Think positive," said Mnem. "We all must have some kind of skill." *Goddess, I hope so*. Mnem finished the espresso, considered having another. "I have an idea. Today, we will not wallow or cry or complain or mourn about our situation. We are going to go home and make a list of our skills. Things we know how to do. Things we're good at. We'll meet tomorrow and see what we've come up with. Sound like a plan?"

Naret nodded. Axie shrugged.

"Okay. My house. Tomorrow. Noon." Mnem tapped her gold Rolex. "We have marketable skills. You don't live thousands of years without acquiring skills. Right?"

ELEVEN

Naret sat by the pool, her legs dangling over the edge, her toes skimming the water. A pad of paper rested on her lap, a pen in her hand. The page was blank. Mostly. At the top, in large curvy handwriting, she wrote Job Skills List. The 'o' was a smiley face. But there was no smile on Naret's.

Naret tapped the pen on the pad and stared into cherished memories. The festival of *Loi Krathong*, a full moon bright on the twelfth night sky above and its reflection shimmering in the river lapping at her toes. *Krathong* made from sliced banana tree bark, banana leaves, and spider lilies. The fragrance of incense sticks wafting in the air, the candle's glow, and shiny coins. All offerings to the river spirits. Mortal wishes floating on the water. Mortal desires for forgiveness. Mortals invoking her name. Phra Naret. Phra Naret.

Naret's sigh returned her to the backyard. The ancient rituals no longer held power. They had become a holiday. An excuse to host corporate competitions and beauty contests. A tourist attraction. A photo op to post on social media. The magic was lost.

Naret closed her eyes. Let her mind wander again. Ah, there they were. The orange-robed monks on the riverbank. The countless twinkling boats. Like stars in the river. A breathtakingly beautiful sight. Romantic and inspiring. Otherworldly. But Phra Naret's name no longer fell from their lips. At least, not from enough of them.

Naret blamed herself. She let the magic and purpose and power wilt into nothingness. It was a slow withering. Infinitesimal increments fading away. Too tiny to notice. The world's greatest changes were achieved with barely recognizable alterations. Like a single grain of rice taken from a rice patty. No one noticed until it was too late.

When did the slow erosion begin? Naret did not know. Maybe the erosion began the moment of her inception.

The world was different now. Too different to begin a return to the old ways. People were too busy and cynical to fold banana bark or lily leaves with spiritual hands and prayerful hearts. Few mortals found delight and peace in the simple things. They had become too restless to create beauty. Too distracted to seek peace within their souls.

Naret kicked at the water. The sun filtered through the splash, infused each water drop with a spectrum of hues. She smiled, kicked again, and marveled at the play of water and light. Of the symphony of water in motion. How long would she notice these gifts? Appreciate them? Give thanks for these simple pleasures? Would her new mortality disintegrate like the *krathong* in the water? Would the gift of forgiving transgressions and harmful thoughts wash away in her new mortal current?

There was no doubt. It already began. Phra Naret refused to forgive herself for her carelessness of neglecting her sole purpose in life.

Naret tossed aside the list. Her soul needed an infusion

of hope and serenity. And she knew how. She stood, drew her dress over her head, tossed it aside, and dove in. As her body glided through the water, Naret envisioned her creation.

Several hours later, her wet hair plaited in a tight braid down her back, Naret shouldered her oversized designer tote, her hope wrapped in soft cotton, and headed for the car. The old ways were still best.

TWELVE

"Y̶ou're like a drug. I'm addicted," purred Senator Miguel Flores through the phone.

"How cliché." Mnem lifted her eyes to the ceiling. Mortals! So predictable.

"You don't like my metaphor?" Miguel chuckled. "I'll do better. You, Mnem, are like a field of corn."

"Corn. Mmm…I'm intrigued." Mnem set the phone down on the table, tapped the SPEAKER mode.

"A field of corn is beautiful and bountiful. It is sustenance. It nourishes heart, mind, and soul. I want to walk through the rows of your waving golden stalks. I hunger for your sweet taste."

Mnem cleared her throat to cover her laugh. "Oh my. Stick with politics, Miguel, not poetry." She was too old to fall for flattery, especially the kind wrapped in such a cringe-worthy metaphor. And yet her body warmed.

"I wanted to hear your voice."

"Mm-mm." Mnem tapped her pen on the table and stared at the abysmal list in front of her. She had stared at it all morning. "That's nice."

"You sound distracted."

"Sorry, just working on my résumé."

"Those are always tricky. Experience and education are a good place to start."

Education. Oh dear…

Mnem grit her teeth. Thales of Miletus, Democritus, Anaxagoras of Clazomenae. The early great philosophers. Not to mention the Parthenon of gods and goddesses. The wisdom of the ages. Life schooled her. "I was educated by the world's greatest thinkers." *And I tutored them as well.*

"MIT or Harvard?"

Mnem set down the pen and rubbed her forehead. Three cups of strong coffee, a handful of green olives, and a chunk of feta cheese stopped her throbbing headache but not the pain in her soul. "Neither. I went to a small private college in Greece."

"I have to go—another infernal meeting—but I want to see you tonight."

"Not tonight." Mnem's daughters were arriving shortly.

There was a heartbeat of silence. "Oh." Evidently, no woman ever turned down a date with the hunky senator. "I'm not a gameplayer, Mnemosyne."

"Oh please, you're a politician." *He has no idea how many I've known.* "It's the most game playing profession in the world."

"I'm talking about—be there in a moment—sorry, I'm talking about relationships." Miguel's voice was low, as though he cupped his hand around his mouth.

Mnem bristled. "I'm not playing hard to get, if that's what you mean. I have a life." *A new mortal one that's getting more complicated by the hour.* "I do not appreciate your insinuation that I am toying with you." *Although I did plenty of times in the past.* "Goodbye, Miguel." Mnem tapped END and pushed away the phone.

Another complication she did not need. Especially a high-profile one that came with dating a senator.

Mnem returned to her list. It was too short. A tarantula's knee short. This list was supposed to help spin a resume. Instead it was a venomous reminder of her failings.

Mnem was the ex-goddess of remembrance. She was able to recall with minute detail everything she ever learned. Except there was one huge problem. It was all ancient. Dusty laws and worn philosophies that were no longer relevant. She understood truths, that over time, became twisted and distorted.

Education was simple back then. Reading, thinking, and discourse was the cornerstone of a great mind. Timeless wisdom once reigned supreme. Now entertainment ruled mortal lives. The eternal meanings behind words and ideas were polluted. Fouled in the name of niceness. The world was not nice. It was never nice. The goddesses were not nice. But that did not mean the world was not beautiful and miraculous, and filled with euphoria and wonder.

The doorbell rang and shook Mnem from her memories.

"Momma," Euterpe called from the front door. "Oh, my goddess, Calliope told me everything." She hurried to Mnem, wrapped her arms around her.

Mnem hugged back, then pulled the tiny earphones from her daughter's ears. "That's a lovely melody."

"Isn't it? She's a child prodigy and plays like she is one with the flute."

"Where is my mortal Momma?" Thalia entered the room. "I bought stock in Botox once I heard."

"Not funny." Mnem kissed her cheek.

The front door slammed.

"I need help," called Clio from the foyer. She walked into the room, a stack of books in her arms.

"What's all this?" Euterpe took half the stack.

"Treatises, *vade mecum*, and tomes on the philosophy of death." Clio set the books on the table.

"How awful," Thalia shuddered. "Shall I burn these for you, Momma?"

"What? No." Clio's hands hovered over the books. "Don't you dare. Momma may want to read them."

"Momma doesn't need to be reminded that she's going to...*you know*. Momma needs amusement! Entertainment!" Thalia turned to Mnem. "Let's do something fun tonight."

Her daughters' energy filled Mnemosyne with love. A mortal death was in her future, but at least she would die loved.

Euterpe picked up Mnem's list. "What's this?"

"My skills." Mnem flicked at the corner of the paper. "What do you think?"

"Ancient philosophy expert." Euterpe wrinkled her nose. "Bo-ring. Ancient art expert. Mmmm...master of creativity...I don't know." With a pitying smile, she risked looking at her mother.

Mnem's frustration expelled with a loud sigh. "That bad?"

Clio plucked the paper from Euterpe's fingers. "You need coding skills."

"Like the Caesar Code or the Phaistos Disk?"

"No, computer coding." Clio nodded encouragingly. "Maybe you should go to school and get a degree."

"Goddess, no." Mnem bristled, then stalked to the bar. "That would take too long."

"There's trade school," said Thalia. "You could be a dental assistant."

"Put these," Mnem held up her hand and wiggled her fingers, "once-divine fingers into a mortal's mouth? Never." She flung open the bar refrigerator.

Thalia, Clio, and Euterpe exchanged trouble glances behind their mother's back.

"Momma," said Clio. "You must face reality."

"I *am* facing reality," she snapped, spinning around.

Clio's voice dropped to a whisper. "You have no skills for today's world."

"What kind of muse are you?!" Mnem snatched the list from her hand. "Inspire me, daughters!"

Three muses looked from one to the other. Their faces spoke what their lips dare not. We got nothing.

Euterpe wrung her hands. "You've put us in a tight spot. This never happened before. We need time to process—"

"To ruminate and reflect—" added Clio.

"To ponder, to—" Thalia continued.

"Oh, for goddesses' sake. Spare me." Mnem sipped on the ouzo. "I don't have time for long-term pondering. But then again, what would *you* know about time? I feel time here." She pressed her hand to her gut. "I feel each second, each minute. Gone. *Gone.* Another moment closer to…" The word congealed on her tongue, sour and putrid. "*Death.*"

"Such melodrama, Momma. Let me look at your list again. We *will* think of something." Thalia looked at her sisters. "Right?"

They both nodded with feigned confidence.

"Give us a few days to come up with a better list," said Clio.

"Fine." Mnem grabbed the paper.

The paper's edge sliced razor-like into Mnem's fragile mortal skin. A thin sliver appeared. Red and bright and mortal. Mnem stared. Her daughters gasped. It was one thing to be told your goddess mother was no longer divine and quite another to see the crimson proof.

Clio swallowed the horror in her throat. "Do you have a bandage?"

"No." Mnem watched the blood form a rivulet that traveled down her finger.

Thalia made a beeline for the kitchen, ripped off a sheet of paper towel, then offered it to her mother.

Mnem did not take it. Did not see it. She saw only the blood. Heard only the roar of reality in her ears. "Mortal skin is ridiculously fragile." Her voice sounded hollow, as though she stood at the bottom of a deep well. After what felt like hours, but was only seconds, Mnem felt six warm divine arms encircle her.

THIRTEEN

Axie considered the photo Mnem messaged her. Blood. There it was. The real proof of mortality. Seeing it made it more frightening than she imagined. A few days ago, she contemplated killing herself with an ancient scimitar. Yet she never imagined blood. *Real* blood. Her imagined death was romantic. A stab to the heart. A quick cessation of life. The truth hit hard. Pain, gurgling, gasping, groaning, and lots of blood. Dying was messy.

Axie removed a small paring knife from the kitchen drawer. Killing herself was no longer an option. She refused to give Shee the satisfaction.

Her own blood. She needed to see it.

Axie ran the blade across her palm. The blood emerged, red and fast. Such a precious mortal fluid. Giver of destiny and life. Bringer of tragedy and death.

"Oh my."

Axie must be careful. Avoid sharp things and dangerous places. For thousands of years she walked into battles, into dangerous courts lorded over by bloodthirsty rulers, into villages ravaged by pestilence. She always thought of herself as fearless. Now she saw that courage for what it was. A beautiful lie. There was no bravery if you cannot die. True courage was performing an action that might kill you.

Death and illness had been an abstract concept. One she understood in her head, but never her soul. Broken bones, bruises, sprains, headaches, disease; all these mortal ailments were hers to receive. A fatal gift from Shee.

Axie stuck her finger in the blood and felt strangely reborn. This blood would make her a better person. It would ground her, make her feel empathy in ways she never did before.

"I am one of them," she murmured.

Except she wasn't. Not really. Not by a long—thousands of years long—shot. Once one dined on immortality there was no return. No acceptance of a too-short life. Yet, here she was, having to taste mortality in all of its bitter and sweet sustenance. A meal Axie was force fed by FEM. Made to chew and swallow for the rest of her mortal life.

Axie ran her hand under the running faucet. The blood diluted, dripped over her hand, and ran into the sink. The cut was shallow and stopped bleeding. Axie blotted it with a paper towel, returned to her chair, and stared at the list of her mortal qualifications.

A quick internet search provided the traits most preferred by employers. In small precise script, Axie jotted them down. Motivated, dependable, multitasker, analytical, detail-oriented, independent thinker, quick-learner, organized. She added 'honest' and frowned. These weren't skills that would help her get a job.

Axie pushed the list away, grabbed her Hermès purse, and walked out the front door. Retail therapy. It worked for mortals.

Too bad there was no therapy for ex-goddesses.

FOURTEEN

"That's it?" Inna leaned against the plexiglass wall, her elbows resting on the railing. The cool evening breeze fluttered her Redemption chiffon skirt.

"That's it, babe." Duncan Eze's attention was fixed on the long-legged beauty whose skirt fluttered in the breeze to reveal perfect thighs. "Wear Eze Gear ties." He pulled his phone from his back pocket. "Photos like these build my brand. By the time I launch, people will be hot for my ties."

"No male models?" asked Inna.

"Not yet. You're gorgeous and make style look effort-less." Duncan stepped close, his hand caressing her leg. "I want you."

"I see that." Inna stroked his chin. "I'll earn a salary, right?"

"Mm-mm." Sliding his hand around the curve of Inna's thigh he lowered his head and nuzzled the sensitive spot behind her ear. "You know where I want these gorgeous legs now?"

The man had skills; Inna gave him credit for that. *Major* bedroom skills.

"What's my salary?" Inna pressed her thighs together. Tight. A No Fun Until I Know The Details Of My Employment tight.

"This much." Undaunted, Duncan put his fingers in his waistband and push down a few inches of his joggers.

"I get that for free." She yanked his pants up. "I'm serious, Duncan. I need money. An income."

Duncan stepped back, crossed his arms. "Minimum wage."

Mnem did the math. Three-thousand dollars wasn't enough to live on in this city. Coffee was five dollars alone. An entrée at a decent restaurant over thirty. Designer shoes were over the five-hundred mark.

Inna spread her arms wide and wiggled her hips. "Sugar, does anything about me look minimum?"

Duncan's eyes roved up and down her body. "No, ma'am, it does not."

"That's right. I'm straight up maximum supreme."

"I agree, babe, but it's an easy job. A girl job. Take a few selfies, post them, that's all."

"A girl job?" Inna bristled. "A good photo must be staged and lighted correctly. I'll need to write engaging…" She snapped her fingers. "Copy. It will require researching hashtags, understanding analytics. Planning. Strategizing."

Duncan's eyebrows shot upwards, his lips curling with approval. "Sounds like you already know what you're doing."

"I will not *just* be taking and posting photos. I'll be a social media director for Eze Gear."

Duncan took Inna's hand in his. "Here's my offer. I'll pay you three-thousand dollars this month. That's a hundred dollars a day. After thirty days we'll renegotiate."

He gave her a hard look, then brought her palm to his lips for a kiss. "I work hard for my money, Inna."

"I know you do—"

"I practice more than anyone on the team. Most days, I'm there before anyone else. I stay late. Live clean. Eat clean. Plan for my future." He turned, swept his long arm from right to left. "I'm not frivolous."

Inna cocked an eyebrow.

"Not like the others." Duncan wagged his finger. "Minimum wage until you prove your worth."

Inna folded her arms. "Have you decided who will be manufacturing Eze Gear?"

Duncan's eyebrows lifted. "I see my girl has some business savvy." His eyes widened with newfound respect.

"Don't call me girl."

"Right. I forgot." His eyes tapered for a moment. He was not used to a woman scolding him. He wasn't sure if he liked it or not. "Either China or India. They're the cheapest."

Inna sighed. "Then I will not work for you."

"What? Why?"

"You're selling Nigerian print products. Make them in Nigeria. They once had a thriving textile trade. I will only work for you if your products are ethically sourced and your workers paid a fair living wage."

Duncan spread out his basketball dunking hands. "Girl…um…Inna…"

"A fair wage. Use Nigerian workers." Inna set her hands on her hips, stood tall. "You don't need the money. Many people, the customers you want—that you want to attract—will feel good about themselves. They won't mind paying more for something that's ethically sourced."

"I don't know." His face creased, unconvinced.

"Have a portion of the profits go to scholarships for Nigerian students."

"A scholarship…" Duncan rubbed his chin, the creases blooming into a big grin. "My own scholarship. I like that." He tilted his head. "Since when are you all about justice and good deeds?"

"That's just who I am."

"I like that." He kissed her cheek. "You gave me some great things to think about. My dad would like a Duncan Eze scholarship. And he would definitely want me to manufacture my apparel in Nigeria."

Inna wrapped her arms around Duncan, rested her chin on his hard-muscled chest and peered up. "Then make your dad proud."

Duncan lifted Inna up, cupped her buttocks with both hands, and headed inside. "I'd love to hear more of your business ideas, babe."

"Really?"

"When you're naked I'm bound to agree to anything."

Inna laughed, wrapped her legs and arms around him. For a split second she forgot she was mortal.

FIFTEEN

A thin spray shot high in the air. The watery bloom joined the others, each fountain rising and falling in graceful tempo with the others. The water fountain made a spectacular backdrop to the press conference.

The news crews were out in force, eager to hear Senator Miguel Flores, fresh face of the party, announce his new work program for immigrants.

Naret stared at the forty or so people gathered at the other side of the fountain. Of all days and places to have an announcement. Naret considered her options. Wait for the conference to end. Come back another day. Naret looked into her supersized bag. They wouldn't keep. Besides, everyone was already on their way.

Naret strolled around the wide fountain and toward the group.

"Senator Flores! Senator Flores!" The reporters' shouts started the moment he emerged, smiling and waving, from the black SUV.

Senator Flores strode to the podium, five people taking

their places beside him. Each wore shades of hope, courage, and optimism on their faces.

Senator Flores lifted his hands and the reporters quieted. "Thank you for coming." Confidence, charm, promises, and an uplifting speech about immigrants followed next.

Naret moved closer to listen. She was an immigrant now. A newcomer in this strange land called mortality. It was odd. She always felt at home before. Immortality was its own kind of home. A safe haven from the world's troubles. Troubles Naret watched come and go like a bystander. When one bad leader departed, another replaced him. Often worse. Sometimes better. Humans did not see the big picture. How could they? Their life was short. Only a few generations.

As a goddess, Naret saw it all, many times over. Toil and strife, leaders and governments, war and peace, the new generation's demands for a perfect world. The world was imperfect. It would always be imperfect. Humans were imperfect, and so their world would never be free of poverty, misery, injustice, and suffering. Humans needed those things. Without them there would be no wealth, no joy, no justice, no pleasure. The mortal world required both to function.

Naret was an immigrant. The senator said so. She had the same hopes and dreams as the people who stood beside him. She longed for a job, a purpose, a new life.

The crowd clapped, and Senator Flores held out his arms as though embracing the world with his love and compassion.

A movement caught her eyes.

Mnem hurried towards her with long leggy strides. "I walked for blocks to find a parking spot." Her face strained with annoyance, she flapped her hand at the small crowd.

"This must be the reason why." She hugged Naret. "Why are we meeting here?"

Naret opened her oversized Louis Vuitton tote. "I wanted to share this with you." She pulled a *krathong* from its depths and gave it to Mnem as though it were made of the finest blown glass.

"It's beautiful." Mnem's fingers lingered over the layers of intricately woven banana leaves and artfully arranged blooms. "A Thai ritual?"

The *krathong* was small, it fit into Mnem's palm, the delicate weave and placement of each flower—from a ring of purple to a circlet of palest lavender—was a testament of the perfect union possible between humankind and nature.

"Yes, a rather popular one." Naret pulled another from her tote. "It's a wish boat. You usually set them afloat in a river, but I thought this fountain might be more…" Her arm swept from right to left as though encompassing the whole city. "Fitting."

Mnem inhaled the flowers' fragrance. "Thank you for including me."

"I made one for each of us. We all have new wishes now." Naret shielded her eyes from the sun's glare. "Here comes Axie."

Axie hurried toward them. "What's all this?" She gestured to the opposite side of the fountain.

"Just another pompous politician making promises." Naret drew the third wish boat from the tote.

"I happen to be dating that pompous politician," said Mnem. "His heart's in the right place."

"What about his other body parts?" Axie nudged Mnem.

"Right where they need to be." Mnem winked.

Axie took the *krathong* from Naret and brushed her fingertips across the white petals. "This is beautiful."

Inna, strutting like a runway model, crossed the plaza, her Nigerian-print Eze Gear tie swinging to-and-fro. "Traffic is terrible. You had to pick this fountain? Today?"

"I didn't know." Naret handed her a wish boat. "We'll wait until the press conference is over. Looks like he's leaving now."

Mnem sat on the stone basin encircling the fountain. "I don't want Miguel to see me."

"Why not?" asked Inna.

"He'll think I'm stalking him. I do not stalk. He's a fling." Mnem set down the *krathong*.

"Don't worry about it. He's too busy sucking up to reporters." Inna turned her *krathong* about. "These are all pretty, Naret. Did you make them?"

Naret glowed with pride. "I did, although I made them much faster before...well, you know..." She looked away. "I guess I've made so many my fingers remembered." She lifted hers up and frowned. "They're not p*erfect* anymore."

"Neither are we." Inna gave Naret's shoulder a soft squeeze. "How does this wish boat work?"

"We light the candle and think of our fondest wish. The divinity of water, nature, and light do the rest."

Beyond the watery sprays, the press conference was breaking up. Senator Flores moved through the small crowd, shook hands, and paused for photos. The four ex-goddesses were alone on the other side of the fountain. No one paid attention to them. The handsome senator was the attraction, not four women.

"Close your eyes. Focus on your wish." Naret brought the fragrant *krathong* to her nose. "Inhale the scent of your wish through the flowers. Feel the weight of your wish in your hand."

They did. Ex-goddesses understood the power of ritual. They had a bone-deep knowing that ritual was a sacred way to embrace the universe's power and welcome the divine energy into your soul.

I wish for peace and purpose.
I wish for harmony and direction.
I wish for kindness and hope.
I wish for faith and determination.

Naret opened her eyes and set her *krathong* in the water. It floated, neither listed nor leaned. Thousands of years of making balanced *krathong* perfected. The fountain's current swept it away. It swirled and bobbed, a dancing flower wish.

Mnem went next, lowered her little boat with the reverence of a high priestess into the chlorinated eddy. Inna and Axie followed, their graceful movements careful and solemn. Ritual connected them to the sacred, to mindfulness, to renewal.

The four *krathong* bobbed, rocked, and swayed. They came together, huddled like a football team, separated, taken away by an invisible current, only to come together again with another.

"Is it a sign?" asked Inna.

Axie clasped her hands behind her back. "It's the water pump system, the size of the conduits, and the angle of the jets."

Naret shook her head. "Maybe. Maybe not."

"Inna sees a sign. Axie sees a mechanical function." Mnem watched the four *krathong* spin about, her purple-flowered boat pulled into the center of a cascade, her wish surrounded by sparkling aquatic walls. "I see…" She swallowed her realization. *Mortal life is a prison. A flowing shimmer, a downpour that pummels our dreams to bits.*

Inna nudged her. "What do you see?"

"I see my boat going under." Mnem laughed.

Everyone joined in. They had to. It was that or cry.

They stared at their boats, lost in their thoughts, their dreams for the future as fragile as the petals pummeled by the water.

"Excuse me," a deep male voice interrupted.

They turned to look.

Senator Flores extended his hand. "I'm Senator Miguel Flores. What are those little boats?"

A few tenacious reporters standing behind him lifted up their phones, ready for a photo op.

"*Krathong*. Thai wish boats." Naret smiled. "They're biodegradable. Well, except for the coin in the center."

"Those coins will join the other shiny pennies." Miguel gestured to the multitude of pennies, nickels, and quarters at the bottom of the basin. He flicked his gaze at Mnem but said nothing. Not so much as an eyebrow twitch of recognition. "Are you *all* wishing for something?"

"Everyone has a wish in their heart." Naret reached into her bag and pulled out a fifth wish boat. Goddesses always came prepared. She always made an extra. It was often the poorest—either in spirit or income—that most needed the gift of wishing. "For you."

Senator Flores took the *krathong* with both hands—as it was offered to him, his attention on Naret and not the reporters capturing the moment. He radiated admiration, gratitude, and humility.

He's really really good. Mnem marveled at his respectful manner.

Senator Flores turned the *krathong* this way and that, nodding all the while. He held it out to the reporters. "Let Americans be the granter of wishes."

The reporters and his entourage clapped and cheered.

After Naret lit the candle, Senator Flores glanced

around the crowd, his eyes meeting Mnem's for a fraction of a moment before setting the wish boat in the fountain. The reporters lost interest. No one was interested in a video of a *krathong* swirling in a fountain.

Mnem watched though. As did the other ex-goddesses. The yellow flowered wish boat swirled past the rows of fountains, missing the pulse of the spurts by mere seconds. The *krathong* found its way to the center, still untouched by any watery blasts. And then a jet shot upward, lifted the little boat twenty-feet high into the air. The ex-goddesses looked from one to another. How odd. How *very* odd. The little boat teetered atop the waterspout for a few moments, then it tipped, and went over, as though falling over the edge of a waterfall. Surely the boat would sink.

It did not. It landed upright and swirled around merrily.

"I hope there won't be any problem with the photos taken of us." Senator Flores paid no attention to his sturdy wish boat.

"Problem?" Naret tilted her head.

"Your privacy. Your job."

"Oh." Naret shook her head. "None at all. I'm currently unemployed."

Senator Flores's brow creased with concern. "You don't happen to speak another language, do you?"

"Several."

"More than several," added Inna. "A hundred or so." She nudged Naret. "Right?"

"Almost all of the Asian languages," murmured Naret.

The senator's brows shot up. "Almost all? Did I hear that correctly?"

"Some better than others. There are many dialects."

The senator nodded to the aide, who pulled a card

from his own suit jacket and held it out. "Please call me. I'd like to discuss a job opportunity."

Naret's eyes widened. She plucked the business card from the aide's fingers. "Thank you. I will."

Senator Flores moved away, his entourage and a few lingering reporters surrounding him as he headed for the SUV.

"You have a job!" Inna wrapped her arms around Naret.

"Not yet." Naret hugged her back. "He was cold to *you*." She looked at Mnem.

"Our last phone call didn't go well. I told him I was too busy to see him." Mnem glanced at her gold Cartier watch. "The Plaza is close. Anybody up for some shopping?"

"We have to watch our finances, remember?" said Axie.

Inna drew her phone from her purse. "This fountain is perfect for photos. As the new social media director for Eze Gear, I'm always on the hunt for photo locations."

"Puleeze." Axie rolled her eyes. "A director? You post photos on InstaPics."

Inna took a tie from her bag, unfurled it. "Trust me, it's a job." She put it around her neck, made a Windsor knot, and adjusted it for maximum cleavage enhancement.

"What are you selling? Sex or ties?" asked Mnem.

"It's *always* about sex. You know that. We *all* know that. Sex and power. But at least *I'm* having sex! Here," Inna held out her phone. "Somebody take a photo of me."

Axie crossed her arms. "I'll pass on sex with a playboy basketball player."

"Axie likes them broody." Mnem took Inna's phone.

"I do not." Axie looked sideways, all the men and women in her life lined up in a row in her mind. "Well, maybe a little. I prefer thoughtful mortals. Deep thinkers."

"Broody." Inna grinned before stepping on top of the stone basin. "Should I get in the fountain?"

"Not in your Louboutins," said Naret.

The impromptu photo shoot took fifteen minutes. Out of one hundred shots, Inna pronounced ten of them worthy.

"You're gorgeous in all of them." Mnem scrolled through the photos. "You don't have a bad angle."

"Yes, but only these ten sparkle with energy." Inna tapped the favorite tab.

It was an innocuous statement. From anyone not an ex-goddess.

Mnem swallowed the lump of humiliation in her throat.

Axie looked away.

Naret dropped her eyes, dragged her teeth across her lips.

The goddess glow, the inner light they took for granted for thousands of years, was dimming.

Inna slid on her shoes. "Who's up for some window shopping?"

THE PLAZA WAS one of their favorite shopping destinations. It was a high-dollar mall with designer boutiques for people with millionaire budgets. They knew every store. Salesclerks knew them by name. Thousands of years of eating, drinking, and wearing the finest made goddesses the most discriminating shoppers.

"Gorgeous." Inna slipped a Loro Piana silk and cashmere scarf through her fingers. "It's over my spending limit."

"How much is that?" asked Naret.

"Zero dollars."

Naret circled the display table. "Here's a knock off. It's cheaper by half."

They laid both scarves side by side. There was no contest. The designer scarf was as soft as melted butter, the weave as fine as a summer mist.

"A lot of companies cut costs by exploiting workers in impoverished countries," said Axie.

"It's wrong." Mnem shook her head. "Every year, I scratch off another designer from my list of ethical businesses."

"Profits reign supreme." Inna returned the scarf to the counter. "One of the conditions of my employment with Eze Gear is that Duncan manufacture in Nigeria and pay a living wage. Fortunately, I convinced him to put ethics over profit."

"Wish FEM considered that." Mnem turned away from the counter of designer scarfs to peruse the hats.

"What do you mean?" Axie lifted a hat with a wide floppy brim.

"Shee said I drained the feminine energy collective. Told me I was a taker, not a giver."

Inna frowned. "Me too."

"Same," said Naret.

Axie checked the price tag on a Gucci hat. "Well, it seems FEM has its own kind of divine profit margin."

Four ex-goddesses exhaled, their collective sigh a forsaken breeze.

SIXTEEN

"Impressed?" Inna held up the phone, her eyes alight with pride.

"Two photos. One hundred followers." Duncan shrugged. "Not bad for one day."

"What?" Inna glared at him in disbelief. To a goddess, even an ex-goddess, *not bad* was an insult.

"Babe, stop mad-dogging me. You're new at this. There's a learning curve." He picked up his phone. "I have twenty million on InstaPic."

"Because you're famous." Inna's hands met her defiant hip drop. "You didn't even like my photo."

"I told you I'm waiting to finalize Eze Gear." Duncan flashed his wide killer smile, the one all the women swooned over.

"You're testing me." Nobody tested a goddess!

Duncan's easy grin faded into a let's-not-argue grimace. "I have to." He reached out, his long fingers ensnaring her wrist. "I'm a businessman, babe. It's not personal." He tugged, Inna falling into his lap, and kissed her like a man who wants more than a kiss.

Inna melted into his embrace, let her body enjoy the sensation of lips and tongue and the heat of his arms. She felt Duncan's strong, steady heartbeat. She had felt other heartbeats. Thousands, perhaps. Yet all those previous heartbeats were uncomplicated, a product of mortality. Duncan's heartbeat felt terribly complicated.

Inna pressed closer, her fingers settling on the pulse point under his ear. Every throb was precious. It's rhythm in tune with his emotions. Each emotion moved you forward, day after day until the end of your life.

Inna's heart tightened at sharing this brief moment with Duncan. Her own fleeting life joined with his. Inna wanted...*something*. Not sex. Something else. A meaningful connection. Time swallowed each hour, devoured days like a beast of prey. Inna wanted to chew the minutes slowly. Taste each delicious moment.

Duncan broke the kiss by holding his phone between them. "You didn't use enough hashtags. You need more than five. And you only have likes, no engagement."

The intimate moment soured in her mouth.

Inna leapt from his lap. "It's only the first two pictures." She stood tall. "I haven't even gotten started yet."

Duncan rose from the leather sofa, looked down from his towering height. "What are you waiting for, babe?" He walked past her.

"I need a photographer." Inna trailed him down the wide marble hall.

Duncan entered the large kitchen.

"Mister Duncan." Maria looked up from the bread she was kneading and wiped her hands on a towel. "What can I get for you?"

"Thanks, Maria, but I got this." He opened the indus-trial-sized refrigerator. There was enough food to feed the entire basketball team. He grabbed two bottled waters, handed one to Inna. "You don't need a professional photographer. You have friends, don't you?"

"Of course I do."

Duncan's phone *pinged*. "I have a meeting with possible investors right now. I want to see some serious content tomorrow." He headed for his office.

Inna stood in the hallway, felt Maria's eyes on her from the kitchen. "Are you telling me what to do?"

Duncan looked over his shoulder. "Babe, I'm your boss. That's what bosses do." He walked into his office and shut the door.

Inna bristled. A goddess did not have a boss! Except every goddess did. The mother of all bosses. Shee. Inna's nostrils flared like an angry bull.

Inna looked back at Maria, who slammed the dough on the counter with I'm-not-listening vigor. "Tell Duncan I went home."

Maria looked up, pretended surprise that Inna was still in the doorway. "Yes, Miss Inna." She returned to kneading.

Inna opened her mouth, about to ask Maria if Duncan was a good boss. Then she thought better of it, turned away and grabbed her sunflower yellow Birkin bag from the chair in the foyer.

The drive home was a blur. Ideas for InstaPic content and hashtags and photos rushed by faster than freeway traffic. Inna needed to get InstaPic savvy, and fast.

Three hours and too many how-to videos later, Inna emerged from the internet abyss, a dull thud behind her bleary eyes. This was *work*. And she needed a break.

Inna grabbed the phone. "Any luck finding employment?"

"None." Mnem sounded as aggravated as Inna felt. "How's your new job?"

"Duncan is a taskmaster. He demands content and results. ASAP." Inna rubbed her eyes. "Can you come over and help me take photos?"

"I'd love to. I have nothing else to do."

"Mnem…" Inna's stomach twisted, but she needed to say it. Wanted to speak the truth.

"What?"

"What you said just now, that you have nothing else to do…"

"I'm listening."

"FEM was right," said Inna. "We didn't do anything for thousands of years and lived on the divine coattails of a once relevant life."

"Ouch." Mnem's pain bounced off the cell towers with perfect clarity.

"I'm being honest. We need to be honest with each other and about our future."

Mnem's silence spurred Inna on.

"I just spent hours researching how to build an InstaPic audience and it dawned on me. My new job as social media director requires spending a lot of time and energy to grow Duncan's dream. His dream, not mine."

"That's why it's called work and not play."

"That's not my point," said Inna. "Why didn't I—why didn't we do that when we were goddesses? Why didn't we grow our dream?"

The silence stretched, each second as taut as a drawn back bow string. Honest self-reflection was a pointed arrow. The bullseye their heart.

"I'm thinking." Her voice was stiff. Mnem's throat seized up, crushed by a flood of memories. "I don't remember ever having a goal. I merely…".

"Existed," said Inna.

"Exactly. Why did I need ambition when I lived forever? FEM made us too comfortable. Shee made it too easy for us to live without a goal. There was our mission, our purpose on earth, but that wasn't a goal, was it?"

"You're blaming FEM."

"Yes I am." Mnem's voice tensed with anger. "FEM should have given us fair warning."

"Life isn't fair." Inna spoke these words millions of times to her disciples.

"Yes, but divinity should be."

Did Inna agree? *Fair* was a loaded word. As emotion-ally loaded as words like *justice* and *virtue*. "I'm moving forward, Mnem. I won't dwell on the unfairness of what happened to us. If I do, I'm liable to do a very bad thing."

"Fair enough." Mnem laughed. "I'll be over to help you with photos in a half hour."

"Thank you." Inna ended the call, then swiped to Eze Gear's InstaPic account. As the ex-goddess of the harvest, she knew the diligent farmer produced the best crops. Like growing yams, Inna needed to weed out the bad and stake tall strong poles to secure an abundant yield.

SEVENTEEN

Axie sat tall in the chair, her knees touching, both Fendi-clad feet on the floor. The university office was cheery with light woods and white walls. In her cream-colored Saint John suit, Axie stuck out like a desert rose in a sand dune. Overdressing never made her feel self-conscious before, now she wondered if it would prevent her from getting the job.

Axie patted her purse. Folded neatly inside was the flyer that had been stapled with all the others on the University Jobs Board. Last week she ordered her favorite coffee—sugar, water, cardamom, and fine-ground Iranian coffee beans boiled in a copper ibrik—from the campus coffee shop. The only one in the area who made the aromatic and delectable brew. After drinking it, she read the coffee grinds. The message was clear: share. The how remained unknown. Axie looked up, the University Jobs Board the answer to her question.

Today, a to-go cup of the same brew in her hand, Axie waited patiently in the department anteroom for the interview.

"You can go in now," said a purple-haired woman from behind the reception desk.

Axie went through the open door.

Professor Amir Azam, Doctor of Middle Eastern studies, sat behind a desk stacked with books, folders, and papers. "You must be," he glanced down at a paper. "Axtis Khan."

"I am." Axie set the coffee on his desk. "For you." It was difficult not to gawk at the man. He was swoon-worthy in a dangerous sexy way, with blue eyes that sparkled as though he knew *things*. Sensual delicious things.

Professor Azam rubbed his jaw, which was covered with precisely trimmed five-day scruff. "How do you know I drink coffee?"

Axie pointed to the name plate. "I took a wild guess."

Professor Azam reached out. He didn't look like a stuffy academic. No, he looked more like the roguish Persian prince from an ancient love story. "Please. Take a seat." His eyes traveled up and down, his brow furrowing with confusion for the briefest moment.

Axie sat, eager to begin the interview. She spent days preparing for it, read all about the interview process, what to say, what to expect. She crossed her ankles.

"You have an interesting name. Axtis is the Iranian goddess of peace, justice, and victory." He took his first sip of the coffee.

"Yes." Axie tried to think of something else to say. The most common interview advice was not to give a one-word answer, but Professor Azam did not ask a question. "The name means victorious peace."

"That particular goddess didn't do her job." He took the lid off the coffee, sniffed at it.

Axie's eyes widened. "Pardon?" The remark surprised her, she never heard anyone disparage her before.

"Axtis. The goddess. The middle east is a war-torn land." Professor Azam's fingers ran through his hair, combed back in an effort to tame the waves. Only a few defiant curls rebelled at the ends. "This coffee is made in an ibrik. It's delicious. Never had an interviewee bring me coffee." He smiled. "I need a research assistant who knows her Persian goddesses and—"

"I know them all." Never interrupt the interviewer. Axie recalled reading that rule. This was not going well, at all.

Professor Azam's thick straight brows lifted.

"I am well versed in all Persian history."

The professor's lips pressed into politeness, his disappointment easy to read. Another applicant who did not understand what a *curriculum vitae* was. He tapped the paper. "I'm not familiar with any of these people or institutions listed here."

Because they no longer exist, but Axie could not tell him that.

"I worked for private foundations." Axie was prepared. To lie. Even though falsehoods went against every fiber of her being. There could never be real peace in a world when the opposite sides were dishonest. It was easy when she was immortal. She simply identified a liar. That divine power, unfortunately, disappeared with her immortality. Yet the need to tell the truth still entangled around her soul like a vine. "The people and institutions remain behind the scenes." The half-truth didn't pain her quite as much, but it was still *half* a truth. She pointed to her CV. "This bit of paper does not accurately reflect my knowledge."

"No? It says you speak…" Professor Azam glanced down at the paper. "Farsi, Arabic, Turkish, several dialects, old Persian, classical Persian, and contemporary Persian."

He looked up, skepticism in the creases of his forced smile. "How fluent are you?"

Was this a trick question? "Advanced proficiency. I also am able to translate Classical Sumerian, Middle Egyptian, Old Babylonian, Middle Assyrian, Vedic Sanskrit, Classical Hebrew, Aramaic, Sanskrit, Latin, Syriac, Middle Persian, and Coptic. My Middle Age languages include—"

"That's impressive." Professor Azam held up his hand, his voice was without inflection, flat with suspicion. "Where did you learn all those languages?"

"I had an unusual upbringing and many fine teachers." Axie shifted in her seat, glanced at the walls of books, her fingers itching to open them.

Professor Azam leaned back in the chair. "Why do you want this job? My research grant's budget is small. Not enough to pay what you're worth. Why not work for a private foundation in the US?"

Axie uncrossed and re-crossed her ankles. She didn't prepare for that question. "I don't have a formal degree, which makes it difficult to apply for research jobs in this country. I hoped I could prove my skills to you." She indicated one of the crammed bookcases.

Professor Azam did not look at the bookshelves, instead he gazed at her with renewed interest. "You would be perfect for the job. It's like the goddess Axtis herself walked into my office and offered a chance at an academic victory."

Axie's heart quickened. "Does that mean I have the job?"

"Well…" He tapped a pen on the desk. "I'd like to see your translating skills in action." He stood, his runner's body, lean and fit. "You'll be translating texts of dubious authenticity." He ran his finger over a row of books, stopped at a pile of folders wedged in between. "I'm compiling a list for my new book, the definitive source of Persian myths."

"Sounds wonderful."

Professor Azam turned to her, his expression one of wary suspicion. "I should hope so. You'll translate and categorize. Are you proficient in Excel?"

Axie did not want to lie. "It's not my favorite program."

"Mine either." He pulled a thick stack of folders from the bookcase, slapped them on the desk in front of her, and flipped open the first one. "Read."

"This is a Sabean dialect from the Wādī Hadramawt region." Axie picked up the photograph. "Some call it the Sayhadic dialect. This appears to be an inscription from a building."

Professor Azam's brows shot up. "Go on."

An hour later, Axie walked out of Professor Azam's office. With a job! She skipped down the steps, her heart bursting with accomplishment, and sent **Got the research assistant job** in a group message to Mnem, Inna, and Naret.

The pay was terrible, but the professor was a hottie. The hours were awful, but she would be surrounded by her favorite things, ancient history and mythology. When Axie looked at the photographs of the artifacts, the modern world disappeared. She was home again. To a time and place where she was once revered. When magi and kings consulted her. When consorts and favorites asked for consultations. When her presence alone assured peace between kingdoms. It felt like forever ago.

The research assistant job was a steppingstone to a more lucrative career. The possibilities rippled through her body, nestled in her bones. Looking up into the azure sky, Axie wondered whether Shee was proud or irritated by her mortal success.

EIGHTEEN

"Nothing." Mnem set the five-inch Jimmy Choo spike heel on the display table. She flicked the heel. No wobble. Excellent. It was the wobble trick. If a high-heeled shoe wobbled *off* your foot, it would certainly be wobbly to walk in. A week ago, Mnem would have slapped her credit card on the counter. No price check required.

"Not a single job?" Inna grimaced at the shoe's price.

Mnem tucked the studded yellow suede heels back in the box. "Nothing I want."

Naret and Axie, each with a stack of shoe boxes before them, voiced a collective commiserating sigh.

Inna considered the designer pumps on her feet. Were they a legitimate social media director expense? They ought to be. "Why don't you go back to Greece and take your olive oil business international?"

"Live in a tiny Greek village? Far from all this?" Mnem stacked the shoebox on top of the other four, then turned to Axie. "How's your new job with Professor Sexy?"

Axie slid into a pair of silver Valentino's. "I enjoy the reading and researching but making lists and spreadsheets is mind-numbing. Professor Azam scheduled a meeting with a friend of a friend of a friend in a remote village. I'm looking forward to that."

"Why?" asked Mnem.

"The man is an elder with extensive knowledge of local myths. Or so he claims." She took the shoes for a test stroll. "The professor wants my opinion."

The salesclerk, an older woman with thick legs and granny glasses dangling on a chain around her neck, poked her head around the towering stack of shoeboxes she carried. "You ladies have excellent taste. I brought a few more." She set them down. "Size five, right?" She passed a box to Naret.

"Call me bigfoot." Mnem grabbed the box of size ten Fendi's.

Axie sat down. "What's the point of this?"

"Of what?" asked Inna.

"Of trying on shoes we can no longer afford."

"Because," Mnem glanced at Inna, "I'm not giving up. Because maybe I can't afford them today or this year but I —all of us—haven't lived a millennium without learning how to do *something* worth a decent paycheck."

"That's right." Inna unzipped her Chanel bag. "We're only getting started. We're going places." She pulled out an Eze Gear tie, unrolled it, and draped it over the strappy designer stilettos. "I'm Eze Gear's social media director this year, Neiman Marcus's the next."

Naret giggled.

Axie shook her head. "The odds are it won't happen."

"I don't care about the odds." Inna gave Axie a playful nudge. "You need to feel victorious, goddess of victory."

"I'm trying."

"If nothing else," said Mnem, "it's nice to see each

other every week. You're my support team. It's better than therapy."

"Better than your daughters?" asked Axie.

"Yes." Mnem's smile was half frown. "They don't *get* it. Not really. They don't feel it here." She tapped her heart.

Inna squeezed Mnem's hand. Axie took Inna's. Naret clasped Axie's.

"Awww," said the salesclerk. "A sisterhood moment. Do you want me to bring more shoes?"

NINETEEN

"Well?" asked Mnem while driving home from window shopping with Inna, Naret, and Axie.

"Well what?" Calliope's voice was far away, even though she was across town in the home of a New York Times bestselling author who couldn't finish his novel series.

Mnem called Calliope once a week for a daughter update. Mnem was not a meddlesome mother and mortality didn't change that.

"Did you girls put your nine gorgeous heads together and come up with a plan for my life?"

"We tried, Momma. We really did. But…"

"You've got to be joking. You're the muses! Not *one* of my fabulous goddess daughters has *any* ideas?" Anger and sarcasm made her voice as sharp as a xiphos, a warrior's double-edged sword. Mnem gripped the steering wheel, her knuckles white.

"Not ideas you'd like."

"Try me."

"Do you want to be a history teacher?"

"Heavens, no. Grade papers and read essays? Sounds like Hades."

"What about a research assistant for the ancient history department at a university?"

"Too much researching."

"You're not making this easy." Calliope's voice was as gentle as a summer Aegean breeze. "If it's any consolation, we heard FEM fired others."

Mnem slammed the breaks at the crosswalk to let an old woman pushing a wire utility cart shuffle across the street. *That might be me in a few decades. Haggard. Badly dressed. Wearing comfort shoes with arch support.* She shuddered. "Who? Give me names."

"I don't know. That's the rumor going around. MAS fired gods too. If any goddesses know what's happening, they aren't talking. Everyone's on edge. They're worried about who's next and wondering what the criteria for being fired is."

No longer being relevant. "You girls have nothing to fear."

Mnem's daughters were always in high demand.

"Momma, we decided it's not your fault."

"It's *all* my fault."

"Not really." Calliope's voice shifted, tightened with conviction, like an attorney speaking to a jury. "You were assigned the goddess role. You didn't choose it. Just like we didn't choose ours. FEM made you the goddess of remembrance, knowledge, history, and art."

"I am the daughter of Uranus and Gaia."

"This isn't about them," said Calliope. "Did FEM foresee that your role would wither like a grape on a vine? If Shee did, then why didn't Shee help you? Many companies retrain their employees. FEM chose not to help. Have you looked at social media lately, Momma? Memory, wisdom—mortals don't remember what they posted a day ago. Opinions and positions change faster than Hermes flies around the globe. Our current world conceals all our most sacred values."

Mnem tapped the accelerator. "You're right. I hadn't thought about it like that."

"I believe—all my sisters do—that those values are still there, buried deep under a techno pile of crap."

"Thank you. I feel better. Not inspired though."

Calliope laughed. "Where are you right now?"

Mnem told her the cross streets.

"You're not far from Gallery Hall. How long has it been since you were there?"

"Years." Mnem remembered the art museum's grand opening. A CEO of something or other took her to an event many years ago. It was all premium alcohol, artisan-crafted cuisine, and society gossip. The art was a backdrop. Mnem recalled slipping away to the antiquities wing to admire the larger-than-life Greek statue of Aphrodite—in truth, she's a petite little thing—and to marvel at the cere-monial basin carved with a hippocampos and two wave-riding nereids. The CEO….

His name! His business! Goddess, no, I can't remember!

The back of Mnem's neck beaded with sweat. "That's a good idea. I'll bask in the antiquities room for a few hours before it closes. Thanks, sweetheart." She turned right and headed for Gallery Hall. Ancient art and eternal beauty. Good for soothing her troubled soul.

After Calliope shared news of her sisters' inspirational deeds, their call ended. Fifteen minutes later, Mnem turned into the parking lot of Gallery Hall. Squinting from the reflected glare, Mnem walked to the entrance, a modern concrete structure of white travertine. She preferred museums with ancient architecture. With columns and cornices and arches. With pediments and peristyles. But she was biased, after all.

Mnem paid the admittance fee and entered the bright, airy, and spacious interior. Exhaling with relief, she headed toward the antiquities wing. She remembered right where it was.

The moment Mnem crossed the antiquities threshold, her soul warmed. Neolithic clay figurines. Bronzes from the Hellenistic Age. Roman mosaics. Marble statuettes. Marble vessels from the Cycladic islands. Vases, urns, and mummy portraits. Engraved gems and royal jewels. The pieces hummed with ancient vibrations. Mnem's shoulders relaxed, the weight of her mortality temporarily lifted. She inhaled the rarified aura. It was a nepenthe, suffused her bones and coursed through her veins with the speed of an injected drug.

I am home.

Mnem joined the small group of visitors crowded around a Greek amphora in vivid golds and adorned with figures painted black.

"This amphora was given as a prize for the winner of the four-horse chariot race." The docent, a thin woman with large-rimmed black glasses perched atop her beak nose, pointed to the charioteer side of the amphora.

"A trophy?" asked an old man in a plaid bow tie.

"Yes, they made many of them," said the docent. "The real prize, however, was inside."

"Gold coins?" asked a young woman.

"Precious oil."

"Like olive oil?" The young woman wrinkled her nose, clearly disappointed.

Mnem stepped forward. "Not just any olive oil. It was high quality oil from not yet ripened green olives. You see, oil made from ripened olives doesn't have the same value.

Did you know that olive oil had many uses back then?" Mnem moved into the middle of the group. "It was used for funeral rituals, beauty, as fuel for lamps, and for cooking. But the oil in that particular amphora was sheer luxury. Liquid gold. The winner would sell it and earn about three years of income. Not bad for a single competition."

The small group moved closer to the amphora.

"Four horse chariot races were extremely dangerous, and the charioteers were fearless." Mnem's lips pushed into an impish smile. *Charioteers were wonderful lovers too. Full of energy and strength and stamina.* "If a spoke broke or a wheel came off, the charioteer was thrown from the carriage and pounded to a bloody pulp under the horses' hooves."

"Oh my." A middle-aged woman with chunky jewelry clutched her purse.

"It was a common form of family entertainment." Mnem turned to the docent. "Forgive me for interrupting."

"No problem at all." The docent shrugged. "Sounds like you know your Greek history." She turned to the group. "If you step over here, you'll see *Aurelia,* a mummy portrait from about 100 AD."

"Aurelia? Really? I know her." Mnem hurried over. *It is her! I'd know those earrings and that necklace anywhere!*

"Excuse me?" The docent's brows arched.

The little crowd swiveled their heads towards Mnem.

Mnem laughed. "I know *of* her. The jewelry." She pointed to the gold and pearl earrings. "Very expensive. And the necklaces. Emeralds and pearls. She was one of society's elite." Mnem lowered her voice. "Aurelia, so the story goes, was not a faithful woman. Loved to frolic with the gladiators if you know what I mean. The gold beads on her necklace," she gestured to the mummy painting, "indicate all her dalliances, and the emeralds in between, all the times her husband looked the other way."

"Why did he do that?" asked the young woman.

"Aurelia's father was a wealthy and powerful senator. Her husband dared not divorce her. Rumor has it that Nero's poisoner, Locusta of Gaul, murdered her with a bitter brew."

The little group stared at the mummy painting with newfound curiosity. It wasn't just a painting anymore; it became a real person.

"How interesting." The docent pursed her lips and pushed up her thick glasses. "How do you come to know all this?"

"Oh," Mnem flapped her hand. "I studied art in Greece. I'm Greek. Although the portrait is obviously Romano-Egyptian."

"Yes." The docent looked past Mnem. And paled. "Um…would you like to tell us about this piece?" She led the group to a case with an eight-inch figurine.

Mnem peered into the case. "Etruscan. 500 BC. Bronze. Usil is the solar god." *Where is he now? Haven't seen him for ages.*

"Never heard of that god," said Plaid Bow Tie.

"You might know him as Helios. Or Sol. Look at the intricacy of the artwork. Magnificent."

"His hands are supersized. How come?" asked a man with multiple piercings.

Because he couldn't keep his hands off the ladies. "Art of this time period focused on body language and posture. Most people did not read, therefore the body needed to convey the emotions, strength, and purpose of the subject. Hands were considered to be as expressive as faces."

"Those wings and halo make him look like an angel," said the young woman.

Hardly. "Wings and halos are nothing new," said Mnem. "The earliest art from Mesopotamian has a pantheon of winged creatures and half-man, half-beast chimeras."

"Do you have a story about Usil?" asked Pierced Man.

"I do." Mnem told them how Usil had a terrible relationship with his daughter Catha, and had an ego the size of Nethuns, the Etruscan Poseidon.

The docent looked past Mnem again, her face blanching. "If everyone would like to take a look over here." She shepherded the group toward a statue.

Mnem was about to follow, but a woman stepped in front of her.

"You seem to know a lot about our art." The woman's voice was a millimeter shy of disapproval. She tucked a shiny strand of platinum hair behind her ear. Her Chanel Rouge Coco smile was Hospitality Plus, yet her steely grey eyes bore into Mnem's.

Mnem had never *ever* squirmed under any mortal's gaze. And she wasn't starting now! She did a quick once-over. The woman was in her late thirties or early forties. Hard to tell with all the Botox and collagen injections. The woman had no purse. Dressed to impress in a navy St. John skirt suit and silk camisole. Pearls adorned her neck and ears. Sensible Ferragamo shoes on her feet. Last year's. Footwear meant for walking…around a museum.

Mnem brightened, her eyes meeting the woman's frosty ones. "You must be the Docent Program Supervisor."

"The Museum Educator *and* Docent Program Supervisor." The woman flicked her gaze at the group, like a mother keeping tabs on rambunctious children.

"It's an absolute delight to meet you." Mnem stuck out her hand. "I hope you don't mind my sharing some of my knowledge with your lovely docent."

The woman shook Mnem's hand. "Where is your art degree from?"

Why do mortals value a scrap of paper over experience and wisdom? "I attended a small private college in Greece but have no formal degree." Mnem lifted her palms, brandished a *c'est la vie* but unapologetic grin. "My specialty is ancient art, and I have extensive knowledge about all the pieces here."

The woman's frosty look melted, although her voice was still iced with skepticism. "Really?"

"Oh yes." *More than you know.*

"My name is Phoebe Lawson. You are…"

"Mnemosyne Athanasiou. My friends call me Mnem."

"Mnemosyne? Like the goddess of memory?"

"Yes." Mnem worked hard to keep her face from betraying the conflicting emotions rushing through her body.

Phoebe Lawson pivoted on her sensible Ferragamo flats. "What can you tell me about that piece?" She pointed across the room.

Art spoke to Mnem. Every sculpture, slab, figurine, portrait, bronze, urn, and bit of jewelry. All of it.

Mnem approached the piece. It vibrated with time and place. Quivered with the artist's own energy.

Phoebe Lawson stepped in front of the description card.

Ah, this is a test. Mnem backed away. "This is a marble grave stella from 460 BC. The man is a Greek foot soldier. One can tell this from his shield, spear, helmet, and well-defined musculature." Mnem went on to translate the Megarian script. She pointed out the details, explained what town it came from, and the daily life of a Greek foot soldier. Mnem skipped the part of her quick trysts with a few of them.

"Impressive. What about this one?" Phoebe Lawson's hand touched her cheek with feigned concern. "Oh my, am I keeping you from something? I don't want to take up your time."

"I have all the time in the world. I'm in the middle of job hunting."

"Really? Mmm."

One hour and twenty ancient acquisitions later, Phoebe Lawson, her earlier cool demeanor now warm with respect, turned to Mnem. "I don't usually do this, but it seems you are heaven sent."

More like heaven fired.

"Our antiquities docent quit abruptly for health reasons and I'm in desperate need of another one. As you can see, Ashley, our newest intern, isn't that well versed in antiquities. Would you be interested? The pay isn't very good, but it will open future museum doors."

Interested?! Mnem was ecstatic.

TWENTY

Two weeks? That's all I get paid?

Mnem stared at the rectangular piece of paper in her hand. In first paycheck shock, she read down the list of payroll taxes. Moving to Greece looked better and better. Disheartened by the sad little number on the check, she dropped it in her purse and shut the locker in the employees' room. Time to start her shift. Time to repeat the same stories to museum visitors over and over again.

Mnem once attempted to tell the visitors the real truth, but Phoebe Lawson reprimanded her. Told Mnem never to discuss how sexual violence created new cultures. That museum visitors did not want to hear about warriors raping the women of a newly conquered town, and how those women learned to incorporate their cultures with the victors', blending customs and religions.

People have been conquering others for thousands of years, Mnem explained. It's a good thing. If not, we'd all still be living in closed-off inbreeding communities with no chance for genetic diversity, intellectual growth, and cultural intermingling.

Mnem recalled the conversation with Phoebe Lawson as she headed toward the antiquities department.

Phoebe Lawson, in a gray Armani suit and pewter Marion Parker ballerina flats, stood in the middle of the sunlit corridor. A small two-way radio was clipped to her waistband. She touched the earpiece. "Fifteen ladies from the Pink Bonnet Society arrived for their scheduled tour. Keep it PG."

"I love the Pink Bonnet Society." Mnem smiled. "Women are like olive trees. The older they are, the more beautiful and the more complex their fruit."

Phoebe Lawson looked up from her clipboard. "They'll like that metaphor."

Mnem adjusted her museum ID, which hung from a silver chain around her neck. "You need a goddess exhibit."

Phoebe Lawson blinked. "Pardon me?"

"An exhibit devoted to earth's oldest goddesses."

"Submit your idea to the director."

"A motherhood exhibit would be nice too. A Celebration of Motherhood." Mnem stretched out her arm as though reading the title in the air. She had lots of ideas! Thousands of years' worth of ideas.

"I'm sure the director would like to hear them all. The Pink Bonnet ladies are waiting." She gave Mnem a curt nod and strode away.

Mnem headed to the lobby where fifteen pink-bonneted women flitted about with the chatty energy of teenage girls during a sleepover.

"I'm Mnem, and I'll be your guide."

A woman with a flower-festooned fuchsia hat and matching lipstick gave Mnem the twice over. "We prefer a more experienced docent. You look like you're still in college."

"I'm older than I look." Mnem smiled. She adored feisty, no-nonsense women.

"Don't be rude, Helen." A woman wearing a silk pale pink hat put her hand on Helen's arm. "I'm sure Mnem is perfectly knowledgeable. Besides, what do you care? You're just here for the nudes."

"And lunch in the museum restaurant," Helen said from the side of her mouth. "I really could use a martini."

"Me too," whispered Mnem.

Helen beamed. "Well, honey, what are you waiting for? Show us some nude men."

Mnem escorted the Pink Bonnet ladies to the antiquities wing and past *Greek Mother by the River*, a marble statuette from 101 AD of a woman sitting on a rock, her son in her lap, his hand stretched forward. The one-foot statuette was back on display today after having been in the conservation room for the last few months.

"I remember when I had breasts like that." Helen stopped to admire the sculpture.

"At least you still have breasts." Pale Pink Hat Lady gestured to her chest.

"Why didn't you put in implants after the surgery?" said a woman sporting shiny coral lipstick.

"Didn't want to. I'm a cancer survivor. A warrior. Like those Amazon women who cut off one breast."

Mnem opened her mouth, a correction on her lips. *That's a Greek myth.* She didn't. Instead, she told the ladies about life for the average Greek woman. Somewhere in the first minute of her little speech, her smile slipped. She hoisted it back up again. Like a fisherman hauling in a net.

Something wasn't right. This statuette did not vibrate with ancient energy. Did not emit the sculptor's struggles. No longer hummed with his joy of chiseling it with his own wife and child in mind.

Mnem moved closer.

Aw, hades! Another goddess power gone.

Mnem moved on to the next display.

"Now, that's what I'm talking about." Helen stared up at the life-size bronze of a young man.

"Tsk-tsk. He's a boy." Coral Lipstick rolled her eyes.

"He was old enough to fight in a war," said Mnem.

This statue hummed with angst. It was the artist's first attempt at the copper-inlayed bronze, and he fretted the whole time. Future commissions depended on his excellent execution of this depiction of the emperor's eldest son.

What's happening? Why do I feel this piece but not the other?

The first half of the tour complete, Mnem took the Pink Bonnet Society ladies for a cocktail lunch in the VIP dining area. Once the women were situated, Mnem texted Inna. **Have you felt anything unusual lately?**

The response was immediate. **Yes. We need to talk.**

Two hours later, the Pink Bonnet Society Ladies departed, their heads filled with ancient stories, their bags filled with gift store treasures. Mnem returned to the statuette of *Greek Mother by the River*. Nope, nothing. Not so much as a quiver of ancient inspiration.

"Magnificent, isn't it?" Phoebe Lawson joined Mnem at the statue.

"It's a wonder, isn't it? How the artist breathes life into stone. It's an act of divine creation. It's unfortunate the modern world doesn't compensate artists for their brilliance."

Phoebe's arched brows, bowed higher, dark upside-down V's on her Botoxed forehead. "Are you an artist?"

I am Mnemosyne, goddess of creativity and art. "Not in the traditional sense, but we are all artists in our own way, yes?"

"How so?"

"We all possess some artistry. There is artistry in being good or caring for others. There's even artistry in evil and wrongdoing. Each life, in a sense, is a work of art whether we acknowledge it or not. We are all a canvas—one most of us never complete until our death. And yet for others, they are marble, their destinies carved early in life. Each act, each motion—there is artistry in us all."

Phoebe crossed her arms. "You're a philosopher."

"More like a goddess." Mnem winked.

"Aren't we all." Phoebe laughed and strode away.

MNEM PULLED IN THE DRIVEWAY.

Inna arrived a few minutes later and slammed the car door. "Love."

"What about it?" Mnem unlocked the front door.

"That's what your text was about, right?"

"Do you mean being in-love or the love a goddess feels for mortals?"

"Being in-love." Inna followed Mnem inside, down the hall, and into the living room.

"My message had nothing to do with love." Mnem made a beeline for the bar. "But you obviously have love on the brain." She wagged a bottle of vodka for emphasis.

"Me? Love a mere mortal?" Inna flapped her hand. "Not a chance." Her expression was forced. "What unusual feeling were *you* talking about?"

Mnem poured vodka in a glass, splashed in a bit of cranberry juice, and handed it to Inna. "I was looking at a statuette in the museum and couldn't feel it. Usually I sense the artwork's history."

"Now that you mention it, I haven't been able to tell if someone is going to break a promise." Inna sipped the drink. "We're not goddesses anymore. Our divine gifts are fading or already gone."

"I'm not sure about that. It was only the one piece I couldn't sense. The others were fine."

"FEM is messing with our heads." Inna tapped hers. "Shee wants to keep us on edge and uncertain. It's a way to destroy our confidence. What little is left."

"Shee's a gameplayer for sure." Mnem downed half the glass of her vodka tonic. "It still amazes me that we took all our divine *knowing* for granted."

"If you ask me, our goddess knowing was worthless when it came to knowing we would be fired." Inna got comfy on the sofa.

"So…" Mnem plopped down on the opposite side and kicked off her heels. "You're in love with Duncan."

Inna's head lowered. "Is it that obvious?"

"It was a hunch. How does it feel?"

"Horrible," said Inna. "Like butterflies in your stomach and a hammer to your heart. I don't like not being in control. These feelings are very inconvenient."

"Does Duncan love you too?"

"I don't know." Inna frowned. "Me, the ex-goddess of harvest, protection, and justice. People invoked my name when they made a promise, and now I can't even tell if a superstar basketball player considers me more than a passing fling." She guzzled the rest of the drink, glanced longingly at the bar. "Women throw themselves at him."

"Looks, wealth, and fame are powerful aphrodisiacs."

"Exactly." Inna sprung from the sofa with catlike grace. "Does that mean I'm susceptible too? Like any normal mortal woman?"

"Probably." Mnem finished her drink. "What makes you think he doesn't feel the same way? Was it something he said?"

"Sort of." Inna poured another vodka cranberry. "He's not impressed by my InstaPic skills. He wants more followers, more engagement."

"Argh!" Mnem threw her head back against the sofa. "Social media is ridiculous. You'd think the whole world lives and breathes on someone's posts and photos. Nothing of any real importance in the world can be achieved if mortals insist on dancing for followers."

Drink in hand, Inna crossed the room. The shoe's heel snapped and she stumbled. The glass flew out of her hand and the drink splattered over the carpet. "What the— ?"

Inna yanked off the shoe. "Do you know what these cost me?" She waved the broken shoe in the air. "This designer is awful!" She tugged off the other shoe and tossed them both in the hall.

"What are you going to do?" Mnem headed for the kitchen.

"About the shoes, Duncan, or my horrible InstaPics?"

Mnem handed Inna a roll of paper towels. "The shoes of course. Mortal men are a dime a dozen. There's a learning curve with social media. But shoes…designer shoes should have standards!"

TWENTY-ONE

"Nice view." Senator Miguel Flores stretched out his long legs, a cold beer dangling from his hand.

It was one reason Mnem lived at the beach. The unobstructed ocean view, the few steps away from sand beneath her feet, and the salty sea breeze. It was a reminder of the beautiful Aegean. A daily melody that called to her, come home, come home.

"It's not the Aegean or the Ionian Sea but it'll do." Mnem set down a *chile relleno* plate from Gordito's, Miguel's favorite Mexican restaurant. "Thought you'd be hungry."

Miguel grabbed Mnem's wrist and hauled her close. "There's an ocean view? You're the only thing I see." He kissed her.

"You're so corny." Mnem set down her *ceviche* plate.

Miguel tore open a hot sauce packet. "Your friend Naret is working out well."

Miguel—or rather one of his many assistants—hired Naret to work at RICA, the Refugee and Immigrant Careers Agency Miguel founded and funded. Or rather, fundraised for. Not just jobs, careers! That was their motto.

Both the political left and right and in between had high hopes for the program.

Mnem sipped her margarita. "Naret is intelligent, multi-lingual, and has a really calming manner. I expected nothing less."

"Seriously," he said. "Naret is a godsend. God is good. He sent her at the perfect time."

"He?" Mnem arched her eyebrow.

"He. She. They." Miguel took a bite of his *chile relleno*.

The next half hour flew by. They chatted about their week. Mnem told Miguel about the tour with the ladies from the Pink Bonnet Society. Miguel shared his concerns about passing an upcoming bill.

"You're easy to talk to." Miguel put the Styrofoam container in a bag. "It's a nice change from the other women I've dated."

"I made flan." Mnem rose from the chair.

His eyes bugged. "You *made* flan? For me? Ay *dios mío*, I'm in love." He pressed his hands to his heart.

Mnem kicked at one leg of his chair. "I made flan for *me*. It's not a big deal. It's just milk, eggs, and sugar."

"I love you," Miguel shouted as Mnem walked into the house.

Mnem felt *it* then. There was no mistaking it. Butterflies in her stomach. Thousands. Millions, maybe.

No. No. No. I will not fall for a mortal man. Especially a smooth-talking senator.

Mnem liked Miguel. He was fun in bed. Had moves that made her forget she was no longer a goddess. In fact, he was the best sexual partner she had since…

Mnem couldn't remember.

Which set off a different kind of stomach fluttering. Panic. Her memory was going. Pushing the implications of that down deep—she'd think of that later—Mnem sliced two pieces of flan.

"I like you too," she said handing Miguel a plate.

"How much?"

"A slice of flan much." Mnem sat down. "Is my flan as good as your mother's?"

"Not a chance." He took a bite. "Damn. This is amazing. I can't tell Mom, though."

"I understand."

"I'd like you to meet her."

Mnem's throat tightened. Serious Relationship panic set in. She swallowed, forced a smile. "That's not necessary."

"It is for me." Miguel looked at her. *That* look. The Serious Relationship look. "I really like you."

Mnem pushed the flan around her plate.

"I want to make it public. Make *us* public."

Mnem lifted her head to gaze at the ocean. "That's not a good idea."

"Why not?" His senator's voice—commanding, serious, official—usurped his boyfriend tone.

Mnem pushed away the flan. The conversation soured its sweetness. "You want to be president one day."

"Yes." There was no hesitation. No wavering. His voice matched his intent.

He deserves the truth. Mnem looked him in the eye. "I'm not comfortable having to deal with that."

Miguel cocked his head, a slow smile sliding into a grin. "You don't sound a hundred percent sure. I heard wavering."

Damn. "You don't know anything about me."

"I know you're intelligent and personable." Miguel's voice softened, his senator voice as smooth as expensive bourbon. "You have presence. You walk into a room and command attention." He took Mnem's hand. "You're an old soul. That's what my mom calls people who have wisdom and inner peace."

Inner peace? I'm a mortal rag of wretchedness. "Like I said, you don't know me very well."

"Then let me in. Allow me to get to know you better." His finger tapped Mnem's forehead. "Let me know your mind as well as I do your body."

"My body isn't complicated. I am."

"I like complicated women."

A teasing smile tugging at her lips, Mnem pulled her hand from his grip and folded her arms. "So, this is about you."

"Always." Miguel scooped Mnem into his arms and headed inside. "But tonight, it's going to be all about you."

Much later, Mnem stared at Miguel as he softly snored in bed beside her. His face was serene, his senator-slick hair now curling around his forehead. A slight smile made him appear perfectly content. Serene. Unaffected by politics. A baby's innocent smile.

How many men had she lain with over the years? Thousands? Hundreds of thousands? Mnem never counted. Why count lovers when you live forever. Miguel wasn't the best lover. Wasn't even in the top twenty. Lovers from ancient times were better. They were free from the distraction of a fast-paced life. Free of instant entertainment with a tap of the finger. Hours were spent in love-making. Hours keeping your lover at the edge of almost. Hours frolicking and teasing.

Mnem's finger hooked around one of Miguel's curls. She recalled the first time they met. His masculine take-charge presence. He was more tempting than candy and smoother than aged bourbon. But a politician! Ugh! Politicians hadn't changed in thousands of years. Freedom, liberty, justice. Blah, blah. blah. Those abstract concepts meant different things to different people. One man's justice was another woman's horror. One culture's liberty was another's enslavement. Intangible ideals. Twisted and perverted through the ages. After thousands of years, mortals should have finally understood. Ought to have regarded the history of the ages as a guidebook, not something to be used, abused, ignored, or hidden. The world would never and could never—for countless reasons—be free of oppression and hate and injustice. Not even for a goddess.

On a whim, Mnem had tossed out a dare on the crowded yacht. Miguel took the bait. The sex—oh my— was unexpectedly wonderful. Yet, she never thought it would lead to *this*. To this gorgeous hunk lying beside her. To this ambitious man who wanted more than sex.

With a light touch, Mnem rang her fingers through his hair. What did she really know about this man? Nothing. She didn't believe the internet's version of him anymore than she believed the false engravings on the statues and tombs of kings and emperors.

Who are you?

Sex as a mortal was different. Mnem didn't like it. Feelings were involved. Feelings she could not control. Not that gods and goddesses were unemotional. Far from it. Their anger, jealousy, rage, and passion were the stuff of legends. But those emotions *felt* more pure. More purposeful. More...divine.

Mortal emotions were like those self-storage units that Americans were fond of. Full of useless things. Gaudy, cheap collectibles from grandma. Thrift store treasures. Hand me downs. Heavy boxes and over-stuffed bags of unnecessary possessions. A mishmash of collections with no real purpose.

Dazed and overwhelmed, Mnem was now trapped in the middle of this mortal emotional storage unit. Nothing made any sense. Her emotions were just as useless. Just as ineffective.

What should she do about Miguel? He added a whole new emotional storage unit. Miguel was a big handsome mortal problem. One Mnem must handle pronto.

"Hello, *mi amor*." Miguel opened his eyes and smiled.

Mnem tapped his nose. "You need to go."

He blinked, rubbed sleep-heavy eyes. "Now? Why? It's after two a.m. Do you have a three-a.m. appointment?"

Mnem sat up, threw her legs over the side of the bed, her back to him. "This is happening too fast. I'm not prepared for it."

"What do you mean? We've been f—"

"I hate that word. It's crude." Mnem stood, her hands on her hips. "I need space."

"Space." Miguel's voice was razor-sharp. "You want to have sex with other men? With another woman?"

"Maybe." She turned to glare at him, defiance shining in her eyes.

Miguel grinned. "Damn, Mnem, that's so hot. Look." He threw off the sheet.

Mnem looked. *Impressive.* "It's not the right time for us. For *me*."

Miguel settled himself against the headboard, interlaced his fingers behind his head. "I understand, your accountant ran off with your trust fund and you had to get a job. There are lots of worse things, you know."

Mnem took a deep breath, wished she could tell him the truth. "I'm not..." *Goddess, how do I explain without sounding like a spoiled heiress? Or crazy?*

"Is this about the docent job?"

"No, it's…it's you." Mnem took his pants and shirt from the chair and flung them at him.

"You're kicking me out? Me? A senator?!" He pushed the clothes off his body.

"I don't want to be a senator's girlfriend." Mnem picked up his shoes and tossed them on the floor by the bed.

"Let me see if I have this correctly." Miguel stood, grabbed his pants. "We have amazing sex, get along really great, and you're dumping me because of my career?"

"I thought I already made that obvious."

"I love it." Miguel pulled up his pants. "How long do you intend to keep me dangling?"

"Dangling? I've only ever seen you stand at attention."

Miguel laughed, adjusted his belt. "I don't accept your excuse."

"I don't care if you accept it." Mnem crossed her arms.

"You're making a rash decision based on fear."

"Fear?" Mnem bristled. "I fear nothing!" *Only mortality.*

"Exactly." Miguel tugged on his shirt and strode toward Mnem. He wrapped his arms around her naked body and pulled her to his bare chest. He lifted her chin, stared into her Aegean blue eyes. "Don't give me the brush off just yet."

"You still don't understand. I'm used to being my own person. I never had to worry about making a good impression. Of saying and doing the politically correct thing." *Maybe, if I had, FEM wouldn't have fired me.* "You're asking a lot."

Miguel pressed his lips to her forehead. "Most women would be thrilled to be my girlfriend."

"I'm not most women." She pushed out of his embrace. The skin-to-skin contact wasn't helping. His scent. His voice. His body. The feel of his skin. It was a physical sensation party. And Mnem's decision must be about reason and logic.

"I'll make you a deal." Miguel buttoned up his shirt. "I have a black-tie event on Saturday. Big players but not much press. I would very much like it if you would accompany me. No pressure. I'll introduce you as my friend."

Goddess, I love parties! At least that part about me hasn't changed. "What's the deal?"

"You go with me, and you get a chance to rub elbows with people who may advance your new career. It's all about who you know, not what you know."

"Well," Mnem stuck out her hand, "when you put it like that."

They shook. Miguel was all business. Not even a lusty grin.

"I'll pick you up at five p.m." He scooped up his shoes, shoved his keys and wallet in his trouser pocket and walked out of the bedroom.

"You're leaving?"

"You told me to." A barefoot Miguel headed for the front door.

Mnem threw on her silk robe and followed him down the hall.

At the front door Miguel turned around. "I play in bed. Not in relationships. Don't test me on this." His voice was TV news-special-guest perfect. Friendly, yet serious. "I love my life and I love politics. I understand your hesitation. It's a lot to consider. That my career concerns you is a good thing. Your worry tells me you're a logical person. Emotion is great for swaying voters but it's logic I value most."

"This is about me, not you."

"It's about *me* with *you*."

"True." Mnem was about to kiss him but didn't. It sent the wrong message.

Miguel walked halfway to his car before turning around. "Thank you for a wonderful evening."

"You're welcome." Mnem's heart tugged, she didn't want him to go. "Where is this black-tie event?"

"Gallery Hall."

TWENTY-TWO

"Y ou're going to the Gala at Gallery Hall? Me too."
Inna flung open her closet door.

Actually, it was a room. One room of the house was dedicated to her clothes, shoes, and accessories. The space was lighting and three-way mirror perfection.

"It's the event of the year. Or at least the month. This is the first time Duncan's been invited. His invitation is posted on his subzero fridge like a school kid." She headed for a rack filled with party dresses. Sequined minis. Taffeta gowns. Silk organza frocks. Flowy dresses and skin-tight dresses. Every single item shouted Inna's bold, vibrant style.

"You sound rather excited."

"I am," said Inna. "It's been a while since I looked like the goddess I am."

"Was."

"In my heart I'm still a goddess." Inna gave herself a hug. "Help me choose the right gown."

Mnem's fingers danced over the thick-padded hangers. Valentino. Oscar de la Renta. Marchesa. Naeem Khan.

Zuhair Murad. Dolce & Gabbana. "You have quite a collection."

"Oh please, some of them are almost vintage. Like that Givenchy you're ogling."

Mnem pulled the red and pink gown from the rack. "How's the InstaPic marketing?"

"There's a learning curve but I'm getting the hang of it." Inna studied the Givenchy, one finger tapping her glossy pout. "Duncan wants me to dress more provocatively. Sex sells and all that nonsense."

"Are you?"

"I don't know. I don't like being told what to do." She took the dress from Mnem, hung the gown from a hook, and stared at her shoe collection. "How's your job?"

"Boring. But I like being in a museum. I don't enjoy being told what to do either. 'You're assigned to this group. Take your break now. You took too long for lunch. Go here. Go there.'" Mnem pulled a pair of silver stilettos from the shelf. "Mortals telling me what to do is humiliating." She placed the heels under the dress.

"I don't know." Inna tilted her head.

"About the shoes or the humiliation?"

"The shoes." She took a pink patent strappy pair from the shelf. "We should start our own business."

"Like what?"

"If I knew I would have already started it." Inna sat down on the pink velvet settee in the middle of the room. "Can I be truthful?" She patted the cushion. "Sit with me." She passed Mnem her phone. "I received this private message on InstaPic yesterday."

"This is horrible. Evil and…"

"Racist." Inna pressed her hand to her heart. "It hurt bad. I cried for an hour. I know this mortal woman is lashing out, that I'm the target for her pain and ignorance, but when we were goddesses, I was above it all. My head knows this woman is hurting, but her comments feel like a stab in the heart. I still feel pity for the wretched individual, and yet I wanted to retaliate. Hurt her like she hurt me."

Mnem's brows lifted. "Did you?"

"I sent her blessings and wished her protection from whatever in her life caused her such emotional pain. That's what I do. Or did." Inna tossed the phone aside.

"You sent that in a message?"

"No. That would have only invited more criticism. I closed my eyes and sent her love." Inna sighed. "I don't think that works anymore."

Mnem drew Inna into a hug. "You did the right thing."

"Have you blessed anyone lately?"

"No. I should though. You acted like a goddess. FEM can't take that away from us." Mnem decided that instead of trying to push Miguel away, she should bless him.

Inna leaned back on the settee. "You know what I miss the most?"

"The never empty bank account? The immortality?"

"Well, that too, but I miss feeling good about myself when I helped people. I still want to help people. Don't you?"

Mnem nodded. "That's the one thing I do like about my job at Gallery Hall. For a few hours a day I help people understand a little about ancient history." She lifted her hand, her thumb and forefinger a rice grain-width apart. "What I teach is so tiny. A grain of sand on the beach of millennium."

"At least you have that. I'm not helping anybody by posting InstaPics. I need something to satisfy my soul. Naret helps immigrants find jobs. Axie helps the professor transcribe engravings for his book."

"That only helps his bank account and reputation."

"Yes, but people read books to learn and understand more. What am *I* doing? Helping an already overpaid athlete make even more money."

"Today you are. Tomorrow may be different. Things change. Give it time. This is the beginning of our journey." Mnem took Inna's hand and hauled her from the settee. "Enough sad talk, show me how you're going to sell Duncan's ties in this dress."

Inna laughed. "I *do* have an idea or two."

TWENTY-THREE

A Green Getaway. That was the theme of the Gala at Gallery Hall. The lobby was an atrium of tropical wonders from towering açaí palm trees to a profusion of ferns. A team of party planners transformed the museum into a verdant visit of plants and foliage from around the world.

"We must be in the Amazon," said Miguel Flores, looking as sleek as a jungle panther in his Armani tux. He moved aside a huge frond. "Where are the tree frogs?"

"Anywhere but on me, I hope." Mnem wanted to check her hair, but she dared not risk messing with the profusion of braids in her half updo.

Miguel sidled close. "Don't fear, I will pluck any frog that mistakes your dress for a tree."

"I wonder where Greece is?" Mnem could not see past the wall of bedecked and bejeweled celebrities, politicians, and glitterati. "Do you think they brought in any olive trees?"

"Mnem!"

Mnem turned around.

Inna grabbed Mnem's hand. "Introduce me to the senator."

"Where's Duncan?" Mnem looked past Inna after making the introduction and spotted the six-foot-nine basketball star in the middle of fawning fans.

"Mixing business with pleasure as usual." Inna touched her mock crown, three Eze Gear ties woven together.

"Look," Mnem said after she made the introductions. "Is that Axie?"

"I'll get you a drink." Miguel disappeared into the throng.

As if feeling Mnem's and Inna's stare, Axie turned her head. She lifted her champagne flute in the air when she spotted them, then wove her way through the crowd. "What are you doing here?"

"What are *you* doing here?" asked Mnem.

"No, what are you *all* doing here?" Naret squeezed past two people. "I have an invitation courtesy of Senator Flores." She lowered her voice. "I'm supposed to schmooze people into offering intern jobs for immigrants, but everyone here is only interested in drinking, name dropping, and sex."

Mnem cocked an eyebrow. "Nothing's changed in a thousand years."

"Except us," mumbled Axie. "We're nobodies here. Arm candy. A PR opportunity."

"Who are you here with, Axie?" Inna plucked champagne from a passing server.

"Professor Azam." Axie, looking every inch like a goddess in layers of white gossamer silk, glanced toward where the professor chatted with other PhD highbrows. "Amir knows someone on the museum board because he provides the historical context for a few of their pieces." She shrugged. "I'm here because his wife caught the flu, and he didn't want to waste the ticket. It was very last minute. I found out this afternoon."

"Oh my." After checking out Professor Amir Azam, Inna flapped her hand as though to cool off. "He's positively delicious. All broody and mysterious. Sex oozes from him." Inna quirked an eyebrow. "Is he as good as he looks?"

Axie's lips curled into disappointment. "He's married."

"Don't be such a downer." Inna grabbed a second champagne flute from another server and handed it to Axie. "Loosen up. Enjoy all this. Decadence, luxury, and revelry. Count me in."

Axie held out her hand, each finger stacked with diamonds, emeralds, and corundum set in gold. "Too bad no one here will kiss our hand and beseech us for favor and blessings."

"I always enjoyed a good kowtowing," said Naret.

They laughed. It was forced. Fake. A trying too hard sound that didn't fool any of them.

"Duncan's giving me the Come Here look," said Inna. "He probably wants me to take photos of him in his new Eze Gear bow tie."

"Mnem." The familiar voice was clipped.

Mnem smiled at her boss, Phoebe Lawson. "Good evening."

"This is an invitation only event. It's not for employees." Phoebe, dressed in an elegant but understated Safiyaa gown, stretched her red-lipsticked mouth into a wide phony smile.

Mnem mimicked Phoebe's false grin. "I came with a friend."

Phoebe gave Inna, Axie, and Naret a cursory once-over. Politician, no. Celebrity, no. Glitterati, no. "Is that right?" Disdain dripped from her lips like curdled milk.

"Phoebe." Miguel came forward and gave Phoebe two air-cheek kisses. "You already know Mnem, my good friend." He handed Mnem a vodka with a twist of lime. "So I'll introduce you to Naret," said Miguel. "This amazing polyglot has single-handedly straightened out RICA's Asian division."

Phoebe shook Naret's hand. "It's a pleasure to meet you."

"And this is Inna, Duncan Eze's..." Miguel glanced at Inna. "girlfriend?"

Inna beamed. "Girlfriend and Eze Gear's social media director."

"Duncan Eze's girlfriend? Welcome. Welcome." Phoebe's sour milk tone became milkshake sweet and thick.

Axie stuck out her hand. "I'm Axie Khan. I'm here with Professor Azam. I'm his research assistant."

"Amir's divine, isn't he?" Phoebe purred. "Does he have you translating ancient engravings of some undecipherable language?"

"Quite a few," said Axie.

"Oh dear, how tedious. I know Amir," Phoebe lifted her eyes to the ceiling, "and he's quite the perfectionist. The museum is fortunate to have him."

Axie nodded, hoped Phoebe would go away. She despised patronizing women.

Phoebe turned about. "Mnem, darling, you simply must forgive my earlier comment."

"What comment was that?" Miguel directed his question to Mnem.

"Phoebe thought I crashed the gala with my friends."

"Crashed?" Phoebe tittered. "Oh no, I thought you did not realize it was invitation only."

Miguel, the consummate politician, was gracious. "An

easy mistake. Tell me, Phoebe, how is construction on the new conservation room coming along?"

Phoebe brightened. "We're all very eager for them to finish." She had no trouble speaking for the entire museum board.

Mnem's skin tingled. The conservation room. That might explain why she couldn't sense a few of the art's ancient vibrations. The art was too restored. "Where's the new conservation room?"

Phoebe smiled. A real smile this time. A I Didn't Realize You Dated The Senator smile. "In the basement."

"I'd *love* to see it." Mnem almost cooed.

Phoebe's eyes knit together. "Um…" Her eyes darted around the room.

"I'd love to see it as well," said Miguel.

"Well," she drawled, "I suppose the board would be upset if I denied the senator who assures our funding."

"Don't disregard protocols on my account." A thin sliver of pity sliced Miguel's otherwise understanding tone.

Phoebe heard it. Bristled inwardly. She was not just some lowly museum educator and docent program supervisor. She had friends—good friends—on the board. "This would be a private tour you understand. I'll have to get the keys. Maybe in an hour or so?"

"My lips are sealed," Miguel purred like a content panther.

Phoebe blushed. "Well…um…if you'll excuse me, I must greet the mayor and his wife." She glanced at the four ex-goddesses, her eyes resting on Inna. "I would love to meet Duncan Eze. I'm a huge fan. Perhaps…"

"I'd be happy to introduce you." Inna's serene face revealed nothing but graciousness. Her insides, however, stiffened with disdain. "I don't like that woman," she said when Phoebe was out of earshot. "I want to smack that haughty smirk off her collagen and Botox face."

Miguel swallowed his laughter by clearing his throat. "Mnem, do you mind if I steal you away from your friends for a bit? There's a few people I'd like you to meet."

Mnem gave a quick nod. She *did* need to meet the right people. As long as the right people offered her a better paying job.

Naret watched them merge into the throng of designer gowns and tuxedos. "They make a beautiful couple. Does Mnem have feelings for him?"

Axie wrinkled her nose. "Feelings? Mortal love feelings?"

"She does, but she doesn't know it." Inna loosened her grip on her champagne flute.

"Or refuses to," said Axie.

Inna stepped closer to Axie and Naret. "It's horrible. It makes me feel vulnerable."

"You're in love with Duncan?" Axie's eyes widened.

Inna winced. "You say that like I have a choice. I don't. This mortal love swoops in and takes over your body and brain."

Axie grit her teeth. "Sounds horrible, and being mortal makes me feel vulnerable enough." She sidled close to Inna and Naret, drew them in. "I don't believe Professor Azam's story about his wife being ill. I think—"

"Axtis, my goddess translator, there you are." Professor Amir Azam came forward, his hungry eyes roving up and down Axie's hourglass figure. "Who are these gorgeous women?" Amir's voice was a husky rumble, his clichéd question swoon worthy.

"These are old friends." Axie made the introductions.

"Axie's always so formal and proper." Amir tossed Axie a heart melting grin. "Please, call me Amir."

Naret and Inna shared a glance. They knew that look. The professor was smitten. In love and in lust. He had it bad. They weren't surprised. Goddesses had that effect on mortals. Ex-goddesses apparently still glowed with charisma.

When would that start to fade?

TWENTY-FOUR

After the five-course dinner from world-renowned celebrity chef, Mada Caremyog, the guests headed to the renaissance gallery for dancing. Miguel swept Mnem into his arms and they danced for an hour.

"You're a great dancer for a kid from the wrong side of town," said Mnem.

"Mom made me learn." Miguel winked, spun her around.

"Thirsty?" asked Mnem.

"For you."

Mnem poked his lapel. "You promised. This is business only."

"You're right." His hand on her hip, he pressed a little bit harder. "I'm thirsty for conversation."

Phoebe intercepted them as they serpentined back to their assigned table.

"Are you ready to look at the conservation room?" asked Phoebe.

Mnem's eyes widened. *Did I forget about that? No, the party's distracting me. I did not forget!*

"Thank you, Phoebe." Miguel took two water bottles from a server, handed one to Mnem. "Hydrate."

Hydrate?

FEM insisted her goddesses be properly hydrated. Be fluid in thought and deed. Mnem took the bottle and gave him a questioning look.

"We ought to dilute all the alcohol we drank," he whispered.

"This way." Phoebe strolled from the room, wiggling her fingers in hello to several important people. She walked close to Miguel, as though they were old friends. Wanted everyone to see her with Senator Miguel Flores. "The board was quite adamant about the conservation room not being accessible to guests. They didn't want packs of school children staring into the windows to watch the conservationists work."

"I'm surprised," said Mnem. "Museums like the Rijksmuseum in Amsterdam and Boston's Museum of Fine Arts found that open conservation rooms attract new visitors."

"There's a difference between visitors and donors." Phoebe led them down a wide empty hall. "It's not up to me anyway. The founder's grandchildren aren't interested in that particular change." She looked at Miguel. "Do you happen to know them?"

"I know *of* them. Never met them." It was impossible to tell if Miguel was honest or not.

Phoebe turned right into a small hallway, then made another right into a vestibule with a freight-sized elevator. "Excuse me." She stood in front of the keypad on the wall.

Miguel, standing behind her, looked away. Mnem did not.

Phoebe tapped the numbers. The elevator door slid open. "There's been a lot of change orders. All for the best of course, but it did cause the museum to go over budget."

"What were the problems?" asked Miguel.

"Frayed and old wiring, water damage, mold. All the myriad of things that go with building a first-class conservation room in an old building."

"Are we going to the basement?" asked Mnem as the elevator door closed.

"That's what they call it, but it's really the lower level at the back of the museum where the service entrance and loading dock are located."

The elevator rattled to a stop. The lights flickered above them.

Phoebe stared up. "They're not going to like that."

The door opened into a hallway lit by 1980's fixtures. The lighting was yellow, dim, and depressing.

Phoebe led the way down the hall. "The lower level is a maze. I think it was designed that way on purpose."

They turned left. Left again. Then right.

"This is the old conservation room." Phoebe pointed to the waist high wall, the top half glass. Except for the glow of technology, the room was dark. The other side of the corridor was draped in floor-to-ceiling thick plastic sheeting. The corridor smelled of lumber, like the inside of a newly framed house. "This is the new conservation area." She stopped at a plastic sheet with a small bit of red masking tape tucked to it. The makeshift door. "You understand, this little peek is off the record, Senator Flores."

"We can leave." Miguel stuck his hands in his pocket. "I don't want to get you in trouble with the board."

"I asked, it's fine. It's just off the record." Phoebe nodded, part warning, part self-importance.

"I was never here," said Miguel.

Phoebe pulled back the plastic sheeting.

Miguel flicked on his phone's flashlight, moved the beam of light slowly from side to side. "Looks like they still have a lot to do."

"They told us two months." Phoebe shrugged. "I'll believe it when I see it."

Mnem peeked inside. Sawhorses, plywood, lumber, drills, levelers, half-built counters and electrical outlets with missing faceplates. The usual construction clutter. Minus the dust and trash. Mnem turned away. The other side called to her. She crossed the hall and pressed her nose to the window of the current conservation room. Vibrations of ancient art flowed through the glass. Either that or her wishful thinking was in overdrive.

"They're adding biometric readers too." Phoebe kept up a constant stream of chatter. "Our keypads and cardkey system need updating."

Suddenly, Miguel was beside Mnem, his hand on the small of her back, his shoulder pressed against hers. "Looking for something?"

"Ancient art. The older the better." She recognized what looked like a grave stella from ancient Yemen on one worktable.

"You like all the old stuff?"

"I adore it. It's a link to our collective past. To age-old knowledge and wisdom. A window into another world." *Not by any means a kinder gentler world but one with less distractions and more time for quiet reflection.*

"Mnem is full of interesting stories," said Phoebe. "A few of our regulars ask for her by name."

Mnem, not surprised by Phoebe's announcement, moved away from the window. She wanted to go in the room. Touch the art, feel the artist's happiness and pain. Inhale the fragrance of creativity and artistry. "Who works here?" She wanted to befriend them. Be permitted to enter this bastion of art without the glass and Plexiglas barriers.

Phoebe clasped her hands together. "A few people."

Miguel turned away from the window. "The creative mind fascinates me. Wish I understood it."

"It's pure and diluted," said Mnem. "It's torture and bliss. It's fire and water. Love and hate. It's like a lightning bolt, loud and quick. But it also blooms like a flower, petals unfurling with the sun. It cannot be controlled, and yet it *can* be trained." Mnem's eyes met Miguel's. "Creativity is an enigma."

"And here I thought it was controlled by the nine muses." Phoebe held out her hand. "This way please."

Mnem did not pay attention to Phoebe's namedropping chatter in the elevator. Miguel mouthed the appropriate comments, even his body language appeared engaged. But Mnem recognized when he was in Politician Mode. His eyes creased a certain way in private. His voice was huskier.

"It was an honor to *not* give you a quick peek of our under-construction conservation room," said Phoebe.

"I enjoyed not seeing it," Miguel replied.

When they reached the gallery-turned-ballroom, Miguel paused. "Thank you, Phoebe, now if you'll excuse me, there's someone who's waiting to speak to me." He set his hand on the small of Mnem's back and guided her away. "I've never seen you like that, Mnem."

"Like what?"

"Enthralled by a few random pieces of art you could barely see through the glass. Your eyes sparkled. Your whole demeanor changed. Like someone showed you a cache of gold."

"Art *is* gold. It's too bad no one can touch the art or

feel the alabaster curves and marble engravings. An artist speaks through his hands. Art is humankind's greatest gift."

"I feel that way about politics."

"There's nothing noble or artistic about politics. It's a necessary evil."

"You slay me, Mnem." Miguel slapped his hand over his heart. "For the record, I completely disagree. Politics is its own kind of art. Rhetoric is an art form. The art of using words to persuade and manipulate."

"True enough. It's the foundation of civilization."

Miguel tilted his head, his brows knitted, perplexed and impressed. "Are you sure you weren't a philosophy major?"

I am the first philosopher. "I took a few classes." *Yet despite my understanding the nature of reality, knowledge, and existence, I did not see my own demise.*

TWENTY-FIVE

"Amazing." Professor Amir Azam leaned against the doorway of Axie's tiny office. His eyes were warm and inviting; held the promise of physical pleasures.

Axie looked up, blushed. Blushed! "Excuse me?"

It was wrong to work here. Most of the research assistants worked from home or the library. But Axie liked this small room crammed with three battered metal desks. It made her feel academic and purpose driven. She needed that. Needed somewhere to go and work. To accomplish things. This horrible little windowless room kept her sane. It also kept her perilously close to the sexy married professor.

"I don't know what I'd do without you," said Professor Azam. "Come, look at this."

Axie followed him to his office, where he sat down and pointed to his computer screen. "You've made more connections than I thought possible. Myths. Names. Dialects. I'm astonished."

"Thank you." Axie leaned over. Inhaled his scent. Felt his warmth.

"My project is going to come in well before deadline because of you." Amir angled closer. "You're my translation goddess." He looked into her eyes. "I hope you don't mind me saying this, but you looked like a goddess at the museum gala. Your white gown...simply ethereal."

Axie, her heart thumping with a feeling she did not like at all, straightened her spine. "I enjoyed the event."

They had driven separately. Axie insisted upon it. Today she realized it was the correct decision.

"You took my breath away." Amir's smoky voice permeated her bones, made her think of doing things she ought not.

Axie swallowed. Pretended fascination with his bookshelf.

Amir moved closer. Close enough Axie felt the heat of his desire.

"We share the same interests. The same passions." Amir was smooth. Dangerous smooth.

Axie knew his type. Found his raw sexuality appealing. Men like Amir were skilled lovers.

"How's your wife? Feeling better I hope." She went to the bookshelf, pulled out a random book.

"Much better. Thank you for asking." His tone shifted. The huskiness toned down a notch. "I don't want to talk about my wife. I keep my personal and academic life separate."

Axie flipped through the pages without seeing the words. "That's good."

"I want to talk about your future here."

Axie turned around. "I was under the impression this was a short-term assignment."

"Not anymore. Come to Göbekli Tepe with me. I'll be working with friends from the German Archeological Institute, and I would love your nuanced understanding of the latest findings."

Axie searched her memory. Turkey. A vista of rolling tan hills under an azure sky. The reason for her visit as clear as the celestial sphere over the Mediterranean Sea. The sultan and the three murdered concubines in his quarrelsome harem. Axie had discovered the liar—that was her ability after all. But it was more than finding the murderer, it was restoring peace to the harem. Which she did. It took a month. And to quench the sultan's lust in the meantime, Axie had lain with the sultan every day. A most pleasurable activity.

"It certainly would be a unique opportunity," said Axie.

"Good," Amir drawled. "I'll have more information in the upcoming months." He beckoned, gestured to his laptop. "One more thing."

Axie circled his desk.

He clicked. "Sorry, wrong page." He clicked again, but his stunt was obvious. The 'wrong page' showed a photograph of Amir emerging from the ocean, his swim trunks clinging to his muscled legs, his chest broad and well-defined.

Axie felt the pull of desire. Wanted him. Now. Here. Wanted to lift up her white skirt, sit on his lap, and indulge in a lustful tryst. As a goddess, Axie indulged quite often. But sex with a goddess meant something. It was a way for a man to connect with the divine. To inspire an exalted spark. A spiritual awakening. After sex with a goddess, men lay prostrate at her feet with humility and gratitude.

As a mortal woman, she would only provide physical release.

Axie studied Amir. Wondered what his lips tasted like.

How his beard would feel on her skin, between her legs. She needed only to sit on the edge of his desk…

"Here it is." Amir clicked again and the screen filled with photos of the dig site.

"I don't mind getting dirty," she said.

Amir's eyes lit up. "Me neither." He swiveled the chair toward her.

Axie stepped back. "I look forward to meeting your wife on the trip."

Amir's face darkened. "My wife loathes airplane travel. She's not going."

Axie walked to the doorway, felt much safer.

"Accompanying me on this trip will lead to many opportunities," he said.

"I hope so." She turned to go.

"Axie." Amir's voice was commanding. "Play your cards right and you'll go far."

"I'm not much of a cardplayer, Professor Azam. My specialty is the Game of Ur. I always win."

The ancient board game required skill and luck. Except Axie's luck was no longer divine.

TWENTY-SIX

I nna lay cross a bed, her body strategically covered with Eze Gear ties. The lighting was perfect. The patterns and colors bold and vivid.

"What do you think?" Inna held out her phone to show the ex-goddesses her latest marketing success.

They stood in the middle of the aisle at Neiman Marcus between the shoes and the accessory department.

Mnem's eyes widened. "You have a thousand likes. Holy goddess."

Axie frowned. "It's provocative, Inna. Are you selling ties or sex?"

Inna grunted and slid the phone in her purse. "Sex sells ties." She turned away and stalked to the sunglass display.

"Sex is the greatest sales pitch since the beginning of time." Naret, her voice warm with empathy, handed Inna a pair of supersized Gucci's.

"Exactly, then why am I not comfortable with it?" Inna put the sunglasses on her face, looked into the mirror. "Duncan wants me to do more photos like that. I mean, I'm—was a goddess—"

"All women are goddesses," said the salesclerk with white spiked hair and jumbo silver hoop earrings. She pulled a velvet tray of sunglasses beneath the counter. She knew shopaholics when she saw them. And these four young women were swathed in gorgeous clothing.

"Trust me, we all agree." Inna removed the Gucci's, plucked another pair from the tray. "That photo is the opposite of how I want to portray myself. It felt..." She looked at Naret, Axie, and Mnem.

"Beneath you?" Mnem reached for the sunglasses offered by the eager salesclerk.

"Exactly." Inna swiped off the glasses, reached for a sedate, classic frame style. "Since forever, I've always been about justice, promises, and the harvest." She squared her shoulders. Just saying those words—even though she was no longer their divine champion—made her feel better.

"If you're an agricultural attorney then go with UV protection." The salesclerk offered her a pair of sturdy Ray-Bans.

"You're harvesting potential customers now." Axie picked up a pair of white—her signature color—Versace sunglasses.

Inna set down the aviator-style Ray-Bans, picked up another pair.

Naret didn't bother trying on any. They were all too expensive.

Mnem pushed aside a tortoise-shell pair. "Expensive price tag. Cheaply made. The gold emblem on mine rubbed away and the hinge snapped off."

Naret crossed her arms. "Is quality too much to ask for?"

"What have we decided on, ladies?" The salesclerk swept her hand over the discarded sunglasses.

"Nothing today, thank you." Naret tossed the salesclerk her I'm Sorry face, a shrug with a pained cringe.

The four ex-goddesses turned away and headed for the pavilion outside. Shopping on a budget was as fun as a lactose-intolerant person at an ice cream parlor. What was the point?

"I feel bad," said Axie. "We made a mess in there and didn't buy anything."

"I don't feel too bad," said Inna. "I did manage to do one good deed today."

They all gave her an expectant look.

"Duncan took my suggestion and signed the contract to manufacture Eze Gear in Nigeria."

"Will he pay his employees a living wage?" asked Axie.

"Yes, and he's going to establish a college fund too." Inna didn't smile, her gaze far away.

"That's wonderful," said Mnem.

"It is, but," Inna stopped and closed her eyes. "I need to be honest with you."

They gathered around her.

Inna opened her eyes, took a deep breath. "I hate my life. I feel lost. I have no direction. No reason to get up every morning."

"Me too," said Axie. "I don't understand it. Logically, I do. We once had a divine purpose, even though we didn't do much with it, we still had it. We knew who we were. Why we were put here."

"We have to find ourselves. Damn, that sounds dreadfully cliché." Mnem felt the familiar tightness in her throat. Part rage, part despair.

"I feel dead inside." Naret toyed with the gold bracelets on her wrist. "Don't get me wrong I like working for the senator and helping immigrants. I'm grateful for the job, but it doesn't fill my soul."

They all looked at Mnem. She didn't have answers. Didn't have advice. Was barely keeping it together herself.

"I need caffeine." Mnem plodded to the outdoor coffee kiosk to order a double espresso.

Once their coffee concoctions were in hand, they sat at the tiny bistro table.

"FEM wins. She destroyed our divinity," said Mnem. "But I refuse—*refuse*—to let her destroy what little life I have left."

"You sound miserable." Inna licked froth from her lip.

"My job at the museum is dull. Miguel is pressuring me for a commitment. He wants me to be his official girlfriend. My daughters are busy, and…" Mnem looked solidly at each ex-goddess, "I *am* miserable but not defeated."

Three ex-goddesses peered over their paper cups. They were unconvinced.

"We've been goddesses for thousands of years. We know stuff." Mnem patted her heart. "We have gifts to bestow on humankind. All we need to do is figure out how to use those gifts. How to serve again."

They were quiet as they pondered their lives over trendy coffee concoctions. Mnem drank her espresso as though it were ambrosia, the drink that bestowed immortality to those who imbibed.

Axie's fingers drummed on the table. "Our jobs are all service oriented."

"Yes, but I'm talking about serving humankind," said Mnem.

"Those days are long gone." Axie swirled her coffee with a wooden stirrer.

"Then we've already died." Mnem finished the espresso, lobbed the empty paper cup into the nearby waste receptacle. "We're all still goddesses. Our needs and passions haven't changed. Only our immortality."

Naret stared into her paper cup as though reading her oolong tea leaves.

"We should accept our torture," said Axie.

"Torture's a harsh word," mumbled Naret, her focus on the bottom of the cup.

"We were failures *with* divine powers and immortality," said Axie. "What makes you think we will be better without those celestial gifts?"

"It's true." Naret lifted her head, her eyes clouded with worry. "We didn't keep up with the times."

Axie pointed an accusing finger at Mnem. "What makes you think we can reinvent ourselves now?"

Axie's attitude didn't bother Mnem, it was Naret's dark look that concerned her. "What is it, Naret? What did you read in the tea leaves?"

TWENTY-SEVEN

Naret wrapped her hands around the paper cup. "It's not good."

"Just say it's horrible already," said Inna.

Axie balled up the paper napkin, stuffed it into her empty cup. "Isn't tea leaf reading about the person who drank the tea?"

"I drank this tea for all of us," said Naret.

"Thanks for nothing," grumbled Inna.

Naret threw Inna a frustrated look. "There will be trouble and struggles." She swallowed. "Lost loves and physical danger."

"Sounds like everyday mortal life," said Mnem.

Inna wagged her finger. "Don't try to scare us, Naret."

Naret's eyes widened. "I wasn't—"

"I don't want to talk about this anymore," said Axie. "It's too depressing."

"We *must* talk about this," said Naret. "All of it. A therapist isn't an option for us."

Their heads bobbed in agreement.

Inna rifled through her Chanel bag. "Has anyone heard anything about FEM? Who else was fired?"

"My daughters don't know," said Mnem. "They said it's all very hush hush."

Inna leaned forward, a tube of lipstick in her hand. "I say we get back at FEM."

"How?" Three ex-goddesses voices said in unison.

"I don't know. Blow up the FEM building?" Inna applied her lipstick, a gorgeous apricot shimmer that accentuated her lips.

"How horrible. Don't even think it." Naret scooted away from Inna.

Axie gave Inna a hard look. "Why would you hurt all our goddess sisters?"

Inna's lips twisted into an evil smile. "Shee has an office."

Mnem rubbed her forehead. "We had this discussion already." *I clearly remember that, thank goddess.* "Shee doesn't die. Shee's untouchable."

Inna wadded up her napkin and tossed it at the waste basket. Missed. "I hate not having any power over my life."

"You may not, but I do." Axie plucked the napkin from the ground and dropped it into the receptacle. "For example, the other day my boss hit on me."

"Really?" Inna wiggled her shoulders. "The sexy professor?"

Axie nodded. "He said he could help my career."

Everyone groaned.

"Mortals never change," said Mnem.

"I miss the days where it was a divine honor to enjoy intimacies with us." Naret glanced up at the sky. "Mortality makes everything more complicated. A coworker in the RICA office asked me out for drinks."

"Did you go?" Inna crossed one leg over the other, swung it with pent up energy.

"I made an excuse, but I know he'll ask again. He has that look in his eye. You know the one."

They did. All too well.

"Be careful, Naret," said Axie. "Is he your supervisor or a co-worker? Some workplaces have rules against dating your boss."

"Fuck the rules." Inna smacked her hand on the table.

"Don't use that vile word." Mnem scowled like a mother disciplining a naughty child.

Inna slapped the table again. "I'll say fuck if I want to. You may be the mother of the nine muses, but you're not *my* mother."

"Please stop arguing." Naret pressed her palms together into a plea.

"We need to stop telling each other what to do." Inna looked fierce. Goddess fierce. Defy me and I will smite you fierce. She stood, hands on her hips. "You are all so… so…*argh*!" She turned to Axie. "Make a decision about the sexy professor. Fuck him or don't. Stop making it about your mortality or your morality." Her glare switched to Naret. "Stop being so damn nice. It's annoying and inauthentic."

Naret sucked air between her teeth. "I am not inauthentic."

Axie set her hand on Inna's arm. "I think—"

Inna shook it off. "I don't care what *you* think. I don't care what *any* of you think."

"Inna," warned Mnem.

"Don't Inna me." Inna glared down at them. "The only reason we're all getting together is because we have one thing in common. FEM fired us. But that doesn't make us best friends or anything. Misery brought us together.

Misery is keeping us together. I cannot deal with this anymore." She turned on Mnem. "Stop telling us we have to find a higher purpose. I love you all but count me out of Team Sad Sack ex-goddess." She stamped away from the table.

The others watched Inna cross the pavilion and disappear around the corner of Neiman Marcus.

"She's right, you know." Axie stared down at her lap. "I never spoke but a few dozen words to any of you over the past thousand years. You don't know me, and I don't know you." She got up, looked at Mnem with teary eyes. "We have to handle this in our own way. I know you're trying to be our cheerleader, but I *want* to feel defeated. I *need* to. Mortality will take me time to process."

Mnem rolled her eyes.

Axie jabbed her finger at Mnem. "There it is. That superior attitude. It does not work for me."

Mnem balked. "I just want everyone to be the best they can. I want us to be successful."

Axie fussed with the rolled sleeves of her pristine white blouse. "You expect too much too soon. A change like this —it will take a while for me to adjust." She shoved the chair under the bistro table, the grating sound as unpleasant as the last five minutes. "Bye. Have a nice life." She walked away.

Mnem turned to Naret, who chewed on her lower lip.

"They're right, you know," said Naret.

"We're stronger together than apart."

"Maybe that works for *you*."

"I think you're all too afraid to do what it takes to succeed." Mnem crossed her arms.

Naret stood and gave Mnem a pitying smile. "Not everyone has your drive. For some of us, just *being* is enough. I'm content with the sun on my face, the music of birds, the splish-splash of water, and a breeze rustling through the bushes."

"That attitude got us fired."

Naret's hands clasped together. "You expect too much."

Mnem shook her head. "You're wrong. The problem was I never expected enough. I thought I had all the time in the universe." She glanced at a golden-haired child toddling next to his mother. "How many years do we have left?"

"Don't." Naret whispered.

"We're dying. Right now. We are dying."

"No more. Please."

Mnem lifted her chin. "If I have to die, then I want to have achieved something. Be somebody. I want to have lived a life with purpose. Why don't you? Why are you content to live an unhappy, unfulfilled life?"

"Stop it." Naret's voice was barely above a whisper. "You're lashing out because you're angry at yourself. I don't need that. Goodbye, Mnem. Good luck."

"Luck? We are—*were*—that luck."

Naret shrugged and walked away.

Naret was right. Mnem was angry. At everything and everyone. At the unfairness of the world. Of mortality.

But anger is a more useful emotion than complacency.

TWENTY-EIGHT

Naret, in a blue silk-embroidered dress with a mandarin collar, slid the folder across a desk. "It's our great pleasure to help you. Be sure to fill out the questionnaire and register for the free English classes." Her Cantonese was perfect. She tapped a small flyer stapled to the manila folder. "This place has the best dim sum around." It was one of Naret's favorite immigrant-owned restaurants.

The young woman bowed her head and thanked her profusely.

After the woman left, Daanish Das, RICA's team coordinator, ambled toward Naret. He set his hands on her desk and leaned forward. "You're a natural at this."

"Thank you." Naret straightened the ten-inch high stack of folders at the corner of her desk. Her caseload. Mortal work was a never-ending series of menial tasks that reduced time spent on the real job. Helping people. "It's gratifying to find immigrants jobs."

"Really?" A black swath of hair hung over Daanish's eye. "I find other things much more gratifying."

"Like what?" Naret dropped the binder clip into the top drawer of her desk.

Daanish flicked back his hair and ventured a shy grin. "A great meal and a good movie." He kicked at the aluminum desk with his shoe. "Have you reconsidered having dinner with me?"

Naret clasped her hands together. "I'm not ready to date."

Daanish removed his hands from her desk, rocked back on his heels. "Did you just get out of a relationship?"

Naret hated to lie. Found it almost impossible to do so. "Yes." It was true enough. The thousands' year-old relationship was FEM. Goddesses didn't have relationships anyway, more like dalliances with mortals.

Daanish pointed to the wall clock. "It's lunchtime. I know a great little hole-in-the-wall nearby. Do you like Indian food?"

"Never met a curry I didn't like."

"May I escort you there?"

Naret took her purse from the bottom drawer. "As long as it's not a date."

PUNJABI GRILL WAS ONLY a few feet bigger than an actual hole in the wall. Wedged between a drycleaner and a smoke shop, the take-out place had four tiny tables pushed against the wall. Customers lined up at the pick-up counter, but the tables were empty. The service was lightning fast. In five minutes, Naret picked up her tray and sat across from Daanish.

Naret looked down at her steaming food and laughed. Spicy food was a gift. One that goddesses were not often allowed to indulge in. Nothing worse than a goddess with foul breath, Shee always said. Naret dug into the fiery lamb curry with gusto.

"Do you like working for RICA?" Daanish bit into the samosa.

Naret nodded, heard the odd tone in the question. A leading tone.

"Do you have any plans to do something else? Something bigger?"

"I haven't really thought about it." Naret poked at the chili paneer with the plastic fork.

"The pay isn't all that great." He opened the lid of the tandoori chicken. "I live with my parents. Can't afford my own place. What about you?"

Naret sighed. Questions. Always with the questions. Mortals were relentlessly nosey. "I have a place."

"Where?"

"In the hills." She waved her hand in the general direction.

"You *own* a house?"

Naret nodded, took a bit of the chili paneer, the ginger blooming in her mouth like a fiery flower. "I inherited it." From FEM. Not technically a lie.

"You're lucky." Daanish's eyes widened, impressed. "Well…" He moved his plastic cutlery around, fidgeting. "I've made a lot of contacts over the past few years. I'm thinking of going on my own."

"What does that mean? RICA is a government service."

"RICA is non-profit, but there are businesses who do the same thing. All RICA does is offer dead-end jobs."

"That's not true." Naret's face was creaseless, devoid of the suspicion balling in her belly. Or maybe it was the hot peppers.

"The immigrants at RICA don't care about careers.

They just want all the free stuff—education, EBT card, housing, and an immigration attorney. My business is going to help the immigrants with serious money get set up in this country. And they pay a pretty penny for their immigration to be expedited."

Naret's eyes widened. "You can do that? Is that legal?"

"Of course, it's done all the time." Daanish's chin dropped, his dark hair falling over one eye. "Do you want in?"

"You mean, work for you?"

"Yes. The pay would be much better. I'm thinking of charging a percent of the fee to successfully expedite the immigration process."

Naret's food didn't taste good anymore. Maybe it was the heat. Or the topic of conversation. Goddess ideals and business were like oil and water. They didn't mix. "I don't know."

"Why not? Are you independently wealthy?"

Naret sipped on her sweet lassi, which cooled the fire in her mouth. "Why me?"

"Are you joking? You speak every Asian language there is. Everyone loves you. You have this way about you, you know? Comforting, calm. People trust you."

"I don't know." Naret swirled the straw in the cup.

"You will still be helping people. Rich immigrants need help too and they will provide jobs to the others. A definite plus. It's all perfectly legitimate." He dipped the naan bread into the green sauce. "But I guess if you're not interested in a having a well-paying career…" he shrugged.

A career. Not a job. Naret needed that. Wanted to call Mnem for advice. Mnem always knew the right questions to ask. But Naret didn't dare. Not after what she said to Mnem.

Mnem was right. They needed each other. They

needed to move on. And quickly. Time moved forward. With or without them.

Daanish pushed his hair out of his eyes. "We'd make a great team. I'll show you my business model. I plan on transitioning slowly. We'll both work at RICA until we get enough clients, that way there's no risk. What do you say?"

Naret looked at Daanish. As a goddess, her power was inspiring people to recognize their path to wealth. To feel good about their uniqueness. How ironic that she could not inspire her own. "How much money are we talking about?"

TWENTY-NINE

Axie lifted her head from the microfiche of an ancient Sumerian engraving. She blinked a few times, rubbed her neck. Reading the real engraving was best, but impossible.

Axie typed up her notes. It would be much easier if she could tell Professor Azam which myths were linked. Exactly why. And precisely how. That a ruling clan forced their beliefs on the conquered was obvious. Why the dominant or subjugated clan adapted the beliefs and myths of the other, more subtle. A leader or an insurgent's charisma. The economic, religious, or moral implications. Sometimes weather was the reason. A flood or draught had mortals blaming their gods. A plague. A comet. An eclipse. A blight on crops. Many factors came into play. Ones long buried in the sands of time. Reasons neither quantified or qualified.

Professor Azam wanted real evidence. To Axie, it felt like figuring out the exact ingredients for an unwritten family recipe passed from generation to generation. How much was a handful of flour? How big was grandma's hand?

Axie's knowledge did not come from the engravings. Her understanding came from being there in the thick of it. From witnessing myths stretch and shrink through the generations.

"There's nothing more enchanting than watching an intelligent woman at work."

The professor's voice jolted Axie from her thoughts.

Professor Amir Azam leaned against a wall. His arms were crossed, his biceps straining against his shirt. "I wish I could see into your amazing mind."

Axie shifted in her seat. He made her heart gallop. Made her think things she ought not. About his lips, his muscled body, his eyes that stared into her naughty desires. Axie cleared her throat. "Mind reading is a curse."

Amir laughed. "Why? You know some mind readers?"

She did. Except they were called oracles and prophets.

Heat bloomed across Axie's cheeks. "I find research fascinating." Especially how facts have been distorted, misused, and misunderstood over the millennia.

Amir pushed himself off the doorframe and entered the room. "The nuances you're able to tease out from the writings are outstanding."

"I'm good with ancient languages."

"You're truly astounding."

Axie warmed at his compliments. How long was it since someone used words like amazing, outstanding, and astounding to describe her? Too long. The once-familiar heat of pride flushed Axie's cheeks. Praise felt more than just good. It felt wonderful.

Axie regarded Professor Amir Azam with fresh eyes. Mortal eyes, those unfettered by divine morals and celestial ethics. He wanted her. She wanted him. He needed to flirt. She needed to be adored. Her gaze dropped—she was a master at the dance of seduction—let a tiny smile skip across her lips. "Really?"

Amir moved closer, crouched down across the desk and studied her face like a connoisseur eager to uncork a fine bottle of wine. "Your analytical mind and attention to detail is a professor's dream come true. At least *this* professor's dream."

The praise was like cool spring water in the middle of a desert. It renewed and refreshed.

"Thank you." She gazed into his sexy brown eyes. She craved his devotion, even if it came in the form of sexual release. So be it. She provided inspiration for innumerable mortals over the millennia. It was time she used mortals like they once used her. For comfort, inspiration, and a connection to the spiritual divine. Would a romp with Amir provide those things?

Amir stood, yet Axie never took her eyes off his face.

"I enjoyed the museum gala event," he said. "You impressed quite a few people. Phoebe Lawson for one, and she's not easily impressed."

Axie didn't need her lie-detecting power to know that was a lie. Phoebe Lawson barely acknowledged her. Spent exactly two minutes making light conversation with Amir before directing her attention to more important people.

"Do you know her well?" Axie's tone was professional but her eyes wandered boldly over Amir's body.

Amir puffed out his chest. "I do some work for her from time to time."

Axie met his eyes again. "What kind?"

"Translating engravings and texts. Pro bono. Good for my image." He winked.

"Sounds interesting."

Amir's forefinger drew little circles on the desk corner.

"There's a piece or two from a private collector coming on loan to the museum. Interested?"

Axie's eyes lit up. "I can touch a real artifact?"

"With gloves."

"Obviously." Axie pressed her hands together in prayer. It would be almost like going home. She had questions. What? Where? When? Instead Axie beamed at Amir, a mortal man who offered sex and a chance to touch her ancient past.

Amir smacked his hands together. "Excellent. We'll discuss more about the protocols and procedures over dinner."

"I wouldn't dream of stealing time from your wife." Axie's smile was all innocence.

"She's a homebody."

"As long as she doesn't mind and knows it's…business." Axie pronounced 'business' but the tone was all 'foreplay.'

"Good. I'll set it up when the museum sends me more information." Amir swallowed. He was smitten. Enraptured. Below, he stirred like a lovestruck teenager.

Axie dropped her eyes again. Flirting was a lot of fun. She forgot how much. "I was hoping to finish this today." She turned the monitor around to show him a zoomed in photograph. "It's badly eroded here," she tapped the screen, "and here, but I'm determined to figure it out."

"When they find the lost tablets of *The Epic of Gilgamesh,* I hope you transcribe them."

Actually, Axie *did* know where they were. And why they were hidden. She wondered where Gilgamesh was now. What new name he used. He was, after all, two-thirds god.

Amir's phone trilled. He read the message, his brows lifting, a corner of his mouth curling with satisfaction.

"Good news?" asked Axie.

"Very. If you'll excuse me." He turned at the doorway,

gave Axie a look that made her feel every inch a desired woman. "Axie, you have breathed new life into my work. Thank you."

Axie's breath stuck in her throat. For a split second she was swathed in white garments and glittering jewels and standing in a Persian palace. A ruler, a mage, a witch, an oracle, a high priest...her followers and devotees. They humbled themselves at her feet. Paid her homage. Axie wanted Amir like she had never wanted a mortal man before. He made her feel whole again.

Wife be damned.

THIRTY

"I'm impressed." Duncan Eze, flat on his back, held up his phone with a long-muscled arm.

"Really?" Inna didn't pay attention to the phone. Duncan's sculpted arm was more impressive. She adored making love to him, running her hands over his chiseled perfect body. He was a mortal with a god's physique. "Does this mean I get a raise?"

"You just got a raise." He was naked, a thin sheen of sweat over his chest.

"A real raise. The kind that puts food on the table." Inna tweaked his dark brown nipple.

"Ouch." Duncan set the phone on the nightstand. "I need to see more impressions and interactions on the posts. "Do it again." He pointed to his chest.

Inna rolled onto her side and bit his nipple. Hard. Clenched it between her teeth and tugged.

"Damn, babe, don't take it out on my nip." It stung but Duncan felt himself harden with desire for Inna again. The third time in eight hours. He never met anyone like her before. It made him feel vulnerable. Duncan Eze *did not* like feeling vulnerable. He was too rich and too famous to lose his head over a woman. Most women will take your money, have your illegitimate babies, and make you miserable—that's what his father told him.

"Take what out?"

"Your anger at not getting enough followers." Duncan pressed the intercom on the nightstand. "Maria, bring me a sandwich and lemonade. Inna wants the usual."

"Yes, Mister. Duncan."

Inna had an idea. "What do you pay Maria?"

Duncan's Guatemalan housekeeper looked like she was around fifty years old. She was actually ten years younger. Poverty aged mortals. At eighteen, Maria fled her village in terror and came to the United States. She worked hard for many years. It finally paid off when she met Duncan Eze.

"I pay her a fair wage." Duncan narrowed his eyes.

"Which is what?"

Duncan told her.

Inna's eyes bulged. "She makes more than I do."

"She has skills, babe. She cooks, cleans, and handles guns like a drug runner."

Duncan's insinuation was clear. You have no marketable skills.

Inna rose from the bed and donned her silk designer robe. She tied the sash, yanked it tight. The sash snapped; the seam shredded. "Quality is a forgotten necessity." She stared at the torn sash. "In ancient times, stuff lasted," she mumbled in Nigerian.

Duncan sat up in bed. "Huh? What did you say?"

"In the future, I'm going to check a product's quality before slapping down my credit card."

"Everything's made to fall apart. That way you have to buy more." Duncan smiled, his eyes wandering up and down her body. "I like the robe open like that."

Inna threw the sash pieces at him. "What about your ties? Who's checking the fabric quality? The sewing quality? Your fabric is timeless, it should last forever. In fact, you ought to include that in your marketing copy. Timeless ties make forever memories."

Duncan's eyes widened. "I *like* it. You have some mad marketing skills, babe."

Inna shrugged off the silk robe.

"That's what I'm talking about." Duncan leered.

Inna laughed and headed for the bathroom, closing the door to the sound of Maria's knocks. She stepped into the white marble shower and let the jets soak her skin. Her hot tears mixed with the water. A spiritual cleaning, an emotional purge. She was in great need of one. Mnem was right. Her life lacked direction and purpose. *Real* purpose. When she was immortal, she never thought about making every moment count. Now she did. Doing something meaningful with her life never mattered before. Now it was critical.

Emotionally and spiritually drained, Inna shut off the faucet. Her life, her hopes—it all went down the drain with the water. She stepped from the shower and stared at the fogged mirror. She had become one of Them. A faceless creature obscured by the haze of mortality. Inna rubbed the mirror with her palm, her face emerging from the condensation. The sight didn't cheer her. Made her feel disembodied.

Inna flicked on the fan and in moments the mirror cleared. There she was. And yet the reflected figure was not her. Not who she remembered herself to be. Mirrors were vile. No wonder mortals hated them.

Wait...

Inna moved closer, her nose a hair's breadth from her reflection. Was it a trick of the light? She angled her head from side to side. No, it was real. Inna's horror coiled like a serpent in her belly. This changed everything. And nothing at all. Her fingers gripped the edge of the marble counter, knuckles white, fingers trembling.

A wrinkle. The thinnest crease at the edge of her eye. She was aging. Right this very minute.

"Babe, your lunch is here." Duncan's voice boomed from the bedroom.

"In a minute." Inna opened a drawer. Razors, toothpaste, toothbrush, deodorant, skin care products. She rifled through them. Did a star basketball player buy wrinkle cream? She needed some. Now! No, three weeks ago.

The second, third, and fourth drawers didn't have any either. One medicine cabinet was filled with vitamins. The other with cologne.

Inna leaned over the counter again, flattened the miniscule indentation with two fingers. Yesterday, she nicked herself while shaving her legs. That was traumatic enough. But this? Aging? Already?

Inna wanted to message the others, ask them if they noticed any signs of their body succumbing to mortal life. Cry on their shoulders. Feel their comforting arms and words.

"Inna!"

Inna looked up at the ceiling as though beseeching Shee. But Shee abandoned them. Left them to rot.

Inna sat on the toilet seat and stared at her hands. Hands that once bestowed wishes, clutched soil, blessed crops, offered nourishment, held yams, inspired promise keeping, and meted out justice.

Now they gripped designer purses and held technology. Nothing that really mattered. Nothing that changed lives.

I'm wasting my life selling ties for a basketball superstar.

"Babe!"

Inna curled her fingers into a tight fist. She needed Mnem to talk through the sorrow and anger, those emotions seeming to attack from the tall grass like a lion. One minute she was fine, handled it all with grace and dignity; the next, her spirit devoured by overwhelming emotions.

Inna burned the Mnem bridge. Accused Mnem of pushing them too hard to find a new purpose in life. Hell, Mnem didn't push them hard enough! Sure, their friendship began with their mutual misery, but it grew into something more.

I behaved like a stupid spoiled mortal.

Inna wiped away a stray tear from her cheek, shrugged on a thick cotton robe, and opened the bathroom door.

"Here's that traditional yam meal you like." Duncan bit into his roast beef sandwich. "What's wrong?"

Inna perched on the side of the bed. "I've been thinking—"

"I hate when women do that." He nudged her side.

Inna lightly cuffed his head. "I want to do something with my life. Something meaningful."

"You are. Working my Eze Gear's social media account is meaningful. You know how many people would kill for your job?"

"It's meaningful to you. It benefits you. I need something meaningful to me."

"Like what?"

"I have no idea."

THIRTY-ONE

Mnem stared at the first century BC alabaster statue from the ancient kingdom of Awsān. The once former Awsāni king stood two-feet tall, his shoulders broad, his face kindly yet concerned. The statue, permanently on loan from an anonymous donor, stood behind glass for thousands of visitors to admire. Mnem was unable to transcribe the inscription at the base. But Axie could. She might have known the king as well. Strolled his palace halls. Touched the statue itself. Perhaps even knew the artist.

Mnem missed Axie. She missed them all. Her heart tightened whenever she thought of them. Which was every day.

They abandoned their friendship two weeks ago. It seemed like a lifetime. Mnem needed them. There was no one else to discuss the horrors of mortality like bleeding from a hangnail, stomachaches, and the sorrow that came every evening when the sun went down. Another day gone. *Poof.* Just like that! Each sunset was a countdown. Mnem detested them.

Mnem blinked, focused on the statue again. The Awsāni king statue, like *Mother by the River*, did not emit its ancient past. Mnem did not sense the artist's perseverance or its age-old energy. It was spiritless and sterile.

My divine gifts are receding. Before long, I won't feel any of the art.

"What do you think of that one?" Ashley, the intern turned docent she had first met, stopped at Mnem's side.

"It's remarkable."

"It looks like a square-bodied dude with long hair and wearing flip flops." Asley giggled. "This piece ought to be renamed Ancient Surfer Dude."

Mnem tilted her head. "Imagine being this man—the king surfer dude—and commissioning this statue with the expectation it would stand forever. That future peoples would know your name."

"Guess it's a kind of immortality." Ashley pointed to his hands. "Was he holding something? Like a Beach or Bust sign?"

Mnem smiled. "Probably an obelisk or some other object symbolic of his reign."

"I like modern art better. It speaks to me."

Mnem's head whipped around. "It does?"

"Sure, modern art is in touch with today's problems and global issues."

"Oh." For the briefest second Mnem thought...but Ashley spoke of feelings not the art's vibrations. "There's no such thing as a modern problem or global issue. All of humankind's problems and issues are eternal."

Ashley wrinkled her nose. "What about global warming and genetically modified food and rights for the trans community?"

"The words may have changed, but the fear of losing one's home and lifestyle, fear for one's health, and fear of those who are different are eternal." Mnem gestured to the statue of *Mother by the River*. "This woman had the same concerns we do. Would thieves steal her possessions? Would invaders or a new ruler decree new taxes and burdens, or send her children to war? Would there be enough rain for a successful harvest? Would a flood destroy the crops? Would she be able to eat? Would her goats die of a disease? Would her husband die and leave her in poverty with many hungry children to feed?"

"Never thought of it that way." Ashley rubbed her chin. "But we have corrupt politicians."

"So did they, except they went by the name ruler, king, sultan, and priest. Same power, different name."

"Do you think surfer dude king was an evil dictator?"

"Yes." Mnem crossed her arms.

"Humankind hasn't learned much, have they?"

You have no idea.

Ashley tapped her watch. "I'm off duty now. See you around."

Mnem watched her stride across the gallery, the confident steps of a modern woman who believed she understood life yet had a child's simplistic comprehension.

I missed a golden opportunity to elevate humankind. I could have written a book on wisdom and art, or on the importance of history. Not just the winner's history, the loser's account.

Mnem drifted from statue to statue in the antiquity's gallery.

I ought to write about you…and you. Before I lose all my memory. Before I no longer feel your story in my bones.

Mnem paused in front of two statues without vibrations. It made no sense. There was a total of five in this collection devoid of the ancient energy that should have hummed in Mnem's heart like an eternal melody. Her divine gift did not wilt like a plucked rose in a vase. Instead it was as spotty as a Wi-Fi connection in the Mohave desert.

Mnem checked her watch. Her shift ended a half hour ago and she had a date with Miguel later. As she headed for the employee room, a thought struck her. A struck by Zeus's lightning bolt kind of thought.

"See you tomorrow, Mnem." A sixty-something retired art professor with a gray Van Dyke beard exited the employee's room. "Love listening in on your stories."

"Thank you. Did Phoebe leave?"

"Hours ago."

The visitors were gone. The docents, on their way out. It was the perfect time.

Mnem strode past the employee's room. Turned right into a small hallway, made the second right into the vestibule, and walked to the keypad next to the elevator.

Her memory was another superpower. Correction: *had been* a superpower.

Mnem exhaled, let her body relax and waited for the stress to leave her muscles. She recalled Phoebe's fingers dancing over the numbers. Mnem's mind was a tape she could usually rewind, slow down, speed up…Phoebe's fingers…her red lacquered nails…the tiniest chip on the pinky…her gold amethyst cocktail ring… fingers dancing…skipping over the numbers…

Mnem slowed her mind. Recalled Phoebe's shiny blonde bob—never a hair out of place—and let her mind wander. There it was. Seven digits.

Right center right down up down left.

Phoebe's password. Quite ingenious. Not likely to be known. The numbers corresponded to the letters FAMU-LUS, the artist who painted the fresco for Emperor Nero's infamous Domus Aurea in Rome.

What a lover! Mnem recalled the tickle of the paintbrush hairs as he stroked her back during one particular afternoon tryst in his studio. How he had—

Mnem shook away the fond memory and tapped the keypad. The elevator door whooshed open. Mnem stepped inside. She wasn't nervous. Did not feel like she was doing something she wasn't supposed to. She had lived too long to feel encumbered by mortals' arbitrary rules and procedures.

A minute later, the door swished open into the dimly lit hall. Mnem's black Jimmy Choo's *click-clicked* as she headed for the conservation room. It called to her like a Siren's song since the gala.

The old conservation room was dark. Mnem tried the door. It was unlocked. Mnem flipped the light switch and row after row of overhead fixtures flickered on.

It was a huge space—definitely in need of upgrading—with big worktables, rolling chairs and supply cabinets, and task lighting clamped to smaller workspaces.

A Renaissance portrait and a modern mixed media piece were mounted on vertical stands. An ancient alabaster funerary stela stood on one table; the stone slab burial marker carved to commemorate a celebrated some-one. A six-inch tall skyphos of azure blue glass with a white overlay of a frolicking Bacchus stood on another worktable.

Mnem went to the glass, recalled drinking from others like them. This one portrayed Bacchus lounging on a sofa, three bare-breasted women at his feet while he drank from a goblet. It was an accurate but rather tepid portrayal of the god. New initiates to his cult were required to do much more than just gaze at him adoringly.

The glass should have spoken to her. Thousands of drunken parties should have crashed over her as loud as an ocean wave. This glass had *been* places. Seen and heard the most decadent things. Orgies and treachery. Oaths and betrayals. Yet there was not so much as an echo.

The artists, the glassmaker and lapidary, were mute as well.

The glass skyphos was voiceless.

Mnem reached out to touch it. Perhaps touching the glass might activate her powers. Her finger hovered over it as she eyed the box of gloves on a nearby table.

I might have drunk from this very cup.

Mnem set two fingers on the rim. Closed her eyes and waited for the vibrations of an ancient life to wash over her.

Nothing.

She leaned over the cup and inhaled. She should have been able to smell the vestigial trace of a thousand vintages.

Again nothing.

Mnem straightened her spine, put her hands on her hips. Her eyes swept the room, alighted on the Renaissance painting. She started for it.

The oil and canvas reached out to her like a mist, enveloped Mnem's body in sensations. The naked cherubim were the artist's twin boys. The angel, a boy prostitute he met in a brothel. The young virgin, a woman he loved but never had. Mnem felt the artist's troubled sexuality, his lust for both men and women, his tortured joy at painting the love of his life that was denied by his over-bearing father. Mnem felt this all in an instant. Smelled the artist's studio, the scent of orange blossoms outside his window. Heard children laughing and the shrill voice of his wife's scolding.

Standing in front of the canvas, Mnem appreciated why the artist used such a subdued color pallet to convey his sensually gleeful depiction of heavenly joy.

Mnem glanced back at the Greek skyphos again. It didn't make any sense. Unless…

Another statue caught Mnem's attention, that of an ancient alabaster funerary stela. The cameleer, a sword in hand, sat astride a camel, a waterskin slung on the rear flank. The piece ought to radiate with ancientness. With Arabian sandstorms and the raiding adventures of the man's life who held the high-ranking position in society.

Why am I unable to sense this one? Is it my diminishing powers or the artifacts?

Mnem snapped a photo of it.

Axie translates ancient texts. It will be an olive branch of sorts.

Mnem pressed her fingers to her forehead. Didn't know whether to send the photo or not.

THIRTY-TWO

Gentle waves lapped against the beach. Mnem heard the surf's calming melody through her open bedroom window.

Last night's date with Miguel had been perfect. Delicious food. Interesting conversation. Great sex. And no mention of a relationship. Only one little thing marred an otherwise flawless evening. The disappointment in his eyes when Mnem declined his offer to stay the night.

From downstairs, Mnem's phone chirped nine times. Nine messages. Her daughters.

She shrugged on a blue silk robe and went downstairs.

All the messages were the same. **Did you do it?**

Do what? Mnem messaged back.

Watch the news!

Mnem grabbed the TV remote and headed into the kitchen to make coffee.

"The bomb blew out the first-floor window of this office building," came a chirpy voice. "The front door's sophisticated security required firefighters to enter through the windows."

Mnem turned on the espresso machine and hurried back to the living room.

"Miraculously, no one suffered injuries inside the lobby." The reporter, a pale young woman with poker-straight platinum hair, spoke with an iced caramel-latte emphasis, all sugar and sticky with intensity. "Police are asking for any information regarding this terrorist act to call the hotline on the screen." She stood in front of a modern building with a gaping hole on the ground floor. Glass and debris were scattered everywhere.

Mnem's mouth dropped open.

The FEM building.

While the espresso machine grinded and rumbled Mnem's special Greek blend, her eyes stayed glued to the big screen TV.

Did Inna blow up FEM headquarters?

"Do you know who did this?" The reporter thrust the microphone at a stunning, tall woman with purple spiked hair. The news ticker at the bottom of the screen identified the woman as Tao, the building owner's spokesperson.

Mnem stared at the TV, that woman…

It was Shee's secretary in a wig. Tao. Mnem didn't realize that was her name. Hadn't cared at the time either. She was just another quasi or semi goddess in training.

Mnem tapped her response to her daughters. **Not my doing.**

"We feel very blessed that no one in the lobby was hurt." The secretary pressed her hand to her heart. "We're relieved and happy none of our personnel were injured."

"It's a miracle," said the reporter. "What sort of business is it?"

"We are a non-profit organization dedicated to anonymous worldwide altruism." With eyes warm with global compassion, the secretary looked straight into the camera.

"Worldwide altruism?" Mnem rubbed her forehead.

The sugarfied reporter smiled bright, her too-white locks shining in the sun. "How wonderful, what—"

"We want to convey are deepest gratitude to the fire-fighters and police for their prompt response." The secretary put her hands together in namaste and bowed her head, then she turned away and walked off camera.

"If you would answer a few more questions." The reporter went after her, waved to her cameraman to follow. "Was this an attack on your charity?"

The door of a black stretch limousine opened, and the secretary disappeared inside.

Nice exit.

The reporter hurried across the street and stuck the microphone in a firefighter's face. "You just came from the site of the bombing. How is it possible no one was injured?"

The firefighter shook his head in disbelief. "It's a miracle. There were at least twenty women in the lobby at the time and not one was injured."

"I suppose they were at the right place at the right time." The reporter tilted her head, looked beyond his broad-shouldered dusty bunker gear. "Where are the women now?"

"They…." The firefighter looked over his shoulder. "I don't know…They left."

"Left? Don't you need to talk to them? See if anyone saw the bomber?"

"Ah—"

"What kind of bomb was it?"

"That's under investigation." The firefighter's two-way radio crackled. "Excuse me." He headed toward a fire truck.

The reporter touched her earbud, a faceless voice in a

studio telling her what to do next. She flashed a movie star smile, turned to the side—a nice booty shot—and pointed. "A spokeswoman for the building's owner said they were blessed. The firefighter claims it was a miracle. A blast like that and no one is hurt? What about the owner of that shoe?" The cameraman zoomed in on the single Louboutin shoe, a black patent leather five-inch heel, the iconic red-bottoms skyward. "There are still a lot of questions that need to be answered. This is Candy Dixon for ARC news."

Mnem flicked to the next channel. Same story, different reporter. Mnem retrieved her latte from the kitchen, took a thoughtful slip, and looked down at the phone in her hand. A knot coiled in her stomach. She had to do it.

She tapped out the message. **Turn on the news.**

Inna's response was immediate. **OMGoddess! I can't believe it**.

Mnem tapped a question. Deleted it. Tapped out another. There was no good way to ask Inna if she bombed the FEM building.

Inna sent another message. **Wasn't me. I promise**!

Mnem's fear evaporated like dew on the grass of a hot summer morning. Inna's promises were gold. Better than gold. She was the ex-goddess of promises after all.

Who then? asked Mnem.

She sipped her latte and waited. And waited.

After too many minutes, Inna replied. **Not. Me.**

"Arrgh." Mnem called her.

Inna picked up on the first ring. "I didn't do it."

"I wasn't accusing you."

"Oh." An awkward silence stretched for several moments. "Mnem... I've been thinking about what you said and... you're right. I hate to admit that."

"You were right too," said Mnem. "We were all right. We spoke what we felt. That's never wrong."

"In the moment, yes, but feelings pass, and I had time to think. I miss you. I miss us. All of us. I miss having a purpose too—even though I did a crappy job being a goddess."

Mnem exhaled, relieved. "Me too."

"FEM did more than take away our immortality. She took away our reason to live."

"Don't say that." *Don't think it. It's too dangerous. Too soul killing.*

"How do mortals do it, Mnem? How do they get up every day without knowing why they were put on this earth?"

"Why do you think they're messed up, depressed, and do reckless things? It's who they are. It's all they know." Mnem swallowed the last drop of her latte.

"Will that happen to us?" asked Inna. "It feels like it's already happening. We're lost. Just like them."

"We're different. We've lived too long. We will never be one of them, even on our death bed." Mnem grimaced the moment she said the word.

Death. It was coming for them sooner or later.

"Yet another way Shee cursed us," said Inna.

Mnem's doorbell rang.

"We need to get together again." Mnem headed for the front door. "We're all we've got."

"I agree."

"You don't think Axie and Naret are responsible for blowing up the lobby of FEM, do you?" *Please say no.*

"Naret's too calm and Axie hates violence of any kind. But I know for sure another ex-goddess did. I'm beginning to think it was a mass layoff."

"That could be thousands and thousands." Mnem put

her eye to the front door's peep hole. *This is unexpected.* "I'll call you later. It's good to hear your voice." She disconnected and opened the door.

Miguel held out a bouquet. "Greek blooms for my Greek beauty."

"Larkspur, iris, lily, rose, crocus, and violet. Do you know the significance of every flower?" Mnem took the bouquet and let Miguel inside.

"No, but maybe you'll tell me one day."

"Why are you here this morning?" She filled a vase with water.

"I'm taking you out for breakfast." Miguel kissed her cheek.

"You don't have to make a public statement about the bombing?" Mnem arranged the blooms.

"That's the mayor's job."

"Have you heard anything?" Mnem gathered her hair into a bun at the top of her head and secured it with an elastic. "I need to change clothes." She set the vase in the living room. "Watch the news while I get dressed."

"I'd rather watch you put on your clothes."

Mnem tossed Miguel the remote. "Stay informed, Senator Flores."

Ten minutes later, Miguel was opening the passenger side door to his vintage 1959 black and white corvette.

Mnem slid into the white leather seat. "Any more news about the bombing?"

"The police are not sharing the details with the media." He turned on the ignition and the car roared to life.

Mnem patted the dash. "Pretty fancy car. Did you restore this one too?"

"Sure did, and I'm not going to give this one up." It was one of the things the news media loved about the senator. He restored old cars. Stress relief, he claimed. Found them in junkyards and had them hauled back to California. He donated most of them to his favorite charities to be auctioned off. The media loved it. The regular folks embraced him as one of their own. The Movers and Shakers admired his work-across-the-aisle strategies and policies.

"What do you know that the media doesn't?" asked Mnem.

"Only women were in the building." Miguel turned into the street. "And the utter impossibility of the blast debris not injuring anyone inside *or* bystanders outside."

"Miracles happen." *Especially if you're immortal.*

"The firefighters said every woman was gorgeous."

"Is that a problem?"

"No. Maybe. Sort of. It's just strange."

Mnem shifted in her seat. "Was that the only strange thing?"

Miguel glanced at her. "No. The owner of the mysterious corporation seemed unconcerned. As though they expected it."

"Retaliation?" Mnem put on her pink Dior sunglasses, made her voice as neutral as possible.

"Possibly, but for what reason? They're a philanthropic organization. Or so they claim. The FBI opened an investigation on them."

Mnem stifled a chuckle. *As if the FBI, CIA, or any organization could do anything to FEM. Impossible. FEM will exist forever.*

"You know something you're not telling me? You seem unusually interested in the bombing."

"Me? What could I possibly know?"

Miguel's phone chirped and he stuck in his earphones. "What's up?"

Mnem turned away. She liked this convertible. Imagined driving it through the curving roads along the Aegean Sea. Sunshine. Mountains. Olive Trees. A nymph or two hidden in the tall grass.

"Mnem, I'm sorry, they scheduled me to make a brief statement at the breakfast place."

"Duty calls."

"Thank you for understanding," said Miguel. "Not too many people understand the concept of duty anymore."

"I understand what it is to have a purpose." *Try having a purpose for thousands of years. I can teach you a thing or two.*

Miguel stopped at a red light and gave her an inscrutable look, his brow furrowed. "You think my purpose is press conferences?" His tone was odd, a sharp crease in his usual smooth manner.

"Not at all." Mnem's hand alighted on his thigh. "It's only part of it. Your purpose is to be an excellent steward of our state, to fight for the underdog, and find innovative solutions to our problems. To move we, the people, forward."

Miguel kissed Mnem's cheek. "I may have to hire you as my press secretary."

Mnem forced a smile. That wasn't her new destiny. Was it?

THIRTY-THREE

The phone was like a glass of water. Axie was parched. Thirsty for the voices of the other ex-goddesses. Thirsty to know if one of them set off the explosion at FEM. Axie didn't put it past either Mnem or Inna to do it. Or maybe they both did it, ex-goddess partners in crime. Or maybe it was Naret. Watch out for the quiet ones. They tended to implode.

Axie reached for the phone from the table. Talking to Mnem was like drinking sugared water. Sweet and satisfying but not quenching Axie's real thirst.

Her hand hovered over the phone. To call or not to call?

She picked up the remote instead and flipped through the channels. They all reported the same thing. One stopped her channel surfing.

"Investigators are at the scene and local authorities will update you with any news. I wish I had more to say, but I know as much as you at this point," said the calm voice of Senator Miguel Flores, looking very Saturday morning-ish in khaki pants and a linen shirt with rolled up sleeves. "If you saw anything or have information, please call the tip hotline."

A reporter asked about domestic terrorism, but the senator sidestepped the question with political double speak. The camera panned back. Just enough to show Mnem standing among the senator's staff.

The brief shot of Mnem's face was enough to convince Axie. It wasn't Mnem. Axie knew when someone lied. It was her goddess power. Or had been. She hadn't tested it lately. Was afraid to.

Axie scooped up the phone and sent a message. **Did you see the news?**

Naret's response was immediate. **I can't believe it. I'm stunned. Did Inna or Mnem do this?**

I don't know. Axie waited for the reply. Drummed her fingers impatiently. Tapped out another message. **I miss everyone.**

I need to move on with my life.

There it was. Axie extended an olive branch—wouldn't Mnem love *that* metaphor—and Naret didn't take it. An ex-goddess—because who else could it be—bombed FEM and that still wasn't enough to forgive and forget their argument. Naret, it seemed, didn't need them anymore. Adapted to mortal living. Or maybe Naret didn't want the drama.

Axie dropped the phone, hot tears brimming, and paced the room. The ex-goddess of peace, justice, and victory needed peace in her life. Victory would be their reuniting again. As for justice? That ship sank the day FEM fired them.

Girlfriends. Axie wasn't good at making them. Never had been. Thousands of years of goddesshood and she considered only seven women her friends. Four had been princesses in need of serious counseling. Navigating the treacherous world of court intrigue and royal backstabbing left those innocent virgins in tears. The others were terrified wives of abusive rulers. Axie had done more than console those women, she taught them how to negotiate with and appease a tyrant. More importantly, how to maintain their self-worth and dignity.

The truth was, goddesses didn't have friends. They have sycophants, minions, adorers. Not friends. Was it even possible to make a mortal friend? Axie didn't know. Mortals were clueless. She didn't fault them. Immortality granted a wisdom and perspective that made it difficult to be compatible with a mere mortal.

Axie paused before the full-length mirror. She looked the same. No, that was a lie. She looked different. There was a world-weariness behind her eyes. Her mouth tight with petty annoyances and daily aggravations. The white silk kaftan that once made her look regal, now hung from her shoulders like a large blanket. It wore her, she no longer wore it.

Axie lifted both arms—a gesture she had done countless times in the past. This time the majestic gesture appeared feeble, like a beggar beseeching help.

She pulled the kaftan over her head and dropped it on the floor. A slim, sad-eyed woman stared back. "You had a good run, Axtis Khan. You're not at fault for the Middle East's problems. You did your best."

Axie left her homeland a hundred years ago. Was it a diplomatic reason? Had she come to the United States to help a refugee? She didn't remember. Didn't recall why she stayed either.

"It must have been for a good reason," Axie said to her reflection. "I don't do anything without analyzing every aspect of a decision."

Yet many decisions in life—even immortal life—were

without a better or best option. Often any choice was an awful one.

Axie bent down, scooped up her kaftan and put it back on. She squared her shoulders and lifted her chin. "That's better."

She returned to the living room and channel surfed. One network showed a close-up of the blast at FEM. Axie lowered the volume, Candy Dixon's 'scoop' a repetition of the same facts.

New FEM footage appeared. The glass shards glinted in the sun. The blown-out wall looked more artistic than random. It was definitely a building infused with goddess power. Did mortals not see that?

"I didn't do it," Axie said out loud. "Do you hear me, Shee? This goddess did not blow up FEM. I don't think Inna, Naret, or Mnem did either. Don't blame us. I accepted my fate. I would never terrify my goddess sisters like that."

A loud chirping on the porch made Axie look up. A blue-winged scrub jay perched on the railing, its head cocked and staring at her. A chill ran up Axie's spine. Was it one of FEM's messenger birds?

"I didn't do it." Axie spoke through the screen door. "Tell Shee that."

The bird pecked at its white-plumed underside.

"Go on, tell Shee I didn't blow up the FEM lobby."

The bird ruffled its feathers, splatted bird poop on her porch, and flew away.

Axie pinched the bridge of her nose. "I'm losing it."

THIRTY-FOUR

M nem stood in front of the Awsāni king statue. No
photographs; that was the museum rule. Cameras
were mounted in every corner. Phoebe might fire her for
taking a photo. But how could Mnem ask Axie to read the
inscription if she couldn't photograph it?

Mnem's lips curled with a sudden idea.

During lunch break, she paid a visit to the museum gift
shop and plucked the *Gallery Hall's Antiquities Collection* from
the top of the bookshelf. It took only a minute to find the
photo. Her back to the cashier, Mnem snapped a quick
picture of the photograph, then went outside to the sculpture garden.

Mnem needed Axie's friendship. Her expertise too.
With a sinking feeling in her gut, she tapped out the
message, sent the picture, and waited.

Axie didn't respond during Mnem's lunch break.

Two hours later, while Mnem was in the middle of a
tour, Axie answered.

**I need to see it up close. Engravings are tricky.
Erosion and such.**

"Art-related message, excuse me," explained Mnem to the group as she took a moment to message back. **Do you have time to stop by Gallery Hall? I need a goddess's opinion. It's important.**

It took Axie a half hour to respond but when she did Mnem pumped her fist in victory.

Axie, dressed in white wide-leg trousers and a form-fitting silk blouse, arrived a half hour before the museum closed.

Mnem wrapped her arms around her. "Thank you for coming."

Axie relaxed into the embrace, squeezed back.

"I really appreciate this." Mnem led her from the lobby.

"Why do you want me to read the inscription? What's important about it?"

Mnem paused under the entry arch of Antiquities Hall. "Did you know that I feel a work of art's vibration? That I see the artist's life, emotions, and the location and milieu of the time."

Axie's brows shot up. "You can still do that?"

"Well, that's the thing. I sense the artist in about ninety-nine percent of the art here." Mnem's gaze swept across the room.

"What about the other one percent?"

"Nothing." Mnem shook her head with a sigh. "Nothing at all. Is my ability fading away? Sporadic? Or a hundred percent unreliable?"

"How is my translating an ancient engraving going to help?"

"I'm hoping it will spur the ability."

"But isn't the translation on the display card?" Axie crossed her arms.

"It is but…I have this feeling…I can't explain it."

"Okay, fine." Axie figured this was an excuse to see her. "Lead the way."

"Thank you." Mnem entered Antiquities Hall. "How's work? Do you still like it?"

"Translating texts is like a trip down a very long memory lane. And Professor Azam is problematic."

"Why?" Mnem's pace slowed, gave Axie time to explain.

"Amir makes me feel wonderful. He showers me with compliments. Even calls me his goddess."

"Sounds good to me." Mnem walked even slower, old-woman-with-arthritic-knees slow.

Axie wrapped her arms around herself. "I crave his attention like a drug."

"What's the problem?" Mnem stopped between two Grecian urns.

"Sex." Axie's voice was low.

"When is that ever a problem?"

"It never was before. Then Shee made us mortal." Axie moved close. Best friend close. "Amir wants sex with a human. Not a goddess. It won't be special for him." Axie's quick laugh was strained. "I know it sounds cliché."

"Not to me."

"When I was a goddess, sex brought my lovers closer to the divine. They touched the sacred."

"In more ways than one." Mnem nudged her.

"Even if they didn't know I was a goddess, they felt empowered. Enlightened. Transformed in some way. Now," Axie rubbed the back of her neck. "It's just sex. And Amir is married, which makes it worse."

"Do you want him?"

Axie closed her eyes and dipped her head. "In the worst way. I have sex dreams and daydreams and ..." Her fingers wrapped around Mnem's arm. "He's intelligent and charming and his smile—but I can't shake the feeling that I'm simply another conquest."

"You think too much. Just enjoy yourself. Let loose. Does it matter if you're one of many? You're in it for the pleasure." Mnem continued on. "The statue is right over here."

Axie followed Mnem to the Awsāni king statue. Instead of reading the display card, Axie translated the inscription.

"Does it match?"

Axie leaned closer. "Almost. See that letter? The one that looks like a lower-case *h* with a right slant. That's a *k*. Now look at this letter, it looks like a table with a line in the middle. That's an *s*."

"Did the engraver misspell the word?"

"If he did, the king—who claims to be a direct descendent of the god Wadd—would have killed him and destroyed the statue. One wrong letter changes the meaning."

"What about this one?" Mnem went to another artifact, a narrow pedestal bowl with an inscribed ledge rim.

Axie translated the engraving aloud.

"It's the same as the display card." Mnem tapped her chin. "This one oozes with vibrations. I feel the magi's struggle to retain his power and the craftsman's fear after being commissioned to make this ritual bowl."

"Are you sure you're not just projecting? Feeling what you want to feel?"

"I don't know what I'm feeling." Mnem's eyes darted from camera to camera. Four of them. One in each corner of the room. "Come with me." She led her to an alcove outside of Antiquities Hall, turned her back at the camera across the corridor. "I feel all their histories, except for a few."

"You're being cryptic. What's your point?"

"I think they're fakes," Mnem whispered. "Both this Awsāni king statue and *Mother by the River*. There's two more in the conservation room, a Greek goblet and a funerary stela. I think someone is swapping out the real for the fake and it's happening in the conservation room."

"Oh-oh." Axie grit her teeth. "What are you going to do?"

"There's a huge black market for art. Those people are unscrupulous. If I were mortal, I'd report it, but I bleed now."

"You're not going to tell anyone? Not even your supervisor?"

"Phoebe?" Mnem shook her head. "I don't know."

"You ought to. It's your moral duty. Ask in a round-about way if they have replicas of any artwork."

"I suppose that wouldn't be too suspicious." Mnem didn't look convinced.

"It's an innocent question."

Mnem stepped close. "Come to the conservation room with me."

"It's open to the public?"

Mnem shook her head.

"What if someone sees us?"

"We'll tell them the truth. I'm an art aficionado who's showing my good friend the conservation room."

Axie sighed. "Fine. A quick look."

"Thank you." Mnem said with an intensity that left Axie unsettled. "This way."

"Do you know who bombed FEM?" Axie's voice was light, no accusation implied. Goddesses were experts at saying one thing and thinking another.

Mnem gave her a sharp look. "I didn't do it and neither did Inna."

"Shee deserved it."

Mnem curved her head. "I didn't expect to hear that from *you*."

"Why not? Shee did a horrible thing. Shee could have warned us, put us on probation or something."

"The divine world is crueler than the mortal world."

"Only we know that."

Mnem tapped FABULUS on the keypad. "I miss everyone."

The elevator door slid open.

"Me too. We need each other," said Axie as they descended to the ground floor. "What should I do about the professor?"

"I'll give you the same advice I give my daughters," said Mnem as they walked down the corridor. "If having sex with him makes you feel bad about yourself then don't. Our egos are more fragile now than ever." Mnem tried the door. "It's locked."

Axie looked through the glass into the dark cavernous space. Locked doors never stopped her. But this was different. Best not to get involved. Besides, she didn't have it with her. "Take photos next time you sneak in."

"As a matter of fact," Mnem tapped her phone, brought up the photo she never sent Axie.

Axie squinted, zoomed in. "Take *better* photos. This is too blurry."

They burst into laughter, friendship warming their hearts. Although born in different cultures and for different purposes, they were sisters in goddesshood. No argument had the power to sever that link. No disagreement would ever divide their divine connection.

THIRTY-FIVE

Naret sipped her tea. It was too hot. The server scalded the oolong leaves. Only a few restaurants in the city knew how to prepare tea. This chain coffee and tea shop was not one of them. Over the rim of the paper-sleeved cup, Naret studied the man sitting opposite. Her goddess ability had been helping mortals understand the path to achieve good fortune and make their own wealth. Daanish Das already knew how to do that. In fact, the tables were turned. *He* was helping Naret understand how to earn a decent income. Money enough for one pair of designer shoes a month.

Daanish poured another sugar packet into his coffee. "It's simple. We make sure they fill out the proper forms and comply with the immigration requirements."

"Let me get this right, this is a loophole for extremely wealthy immigrants." Naret's stomach was hollow. The former goddess of abundance, wealth, and prosperity bestowed her gifts on all mortals not just the privileged few.

"No." Daanish's head twitched back as though

insulted. "It's a fast track, an immigration highway instead of a years-long slow road."

"That fast track requires millions of dollars."

Daanish rubbed his three-day scruff. "They're investing in the U.S. They create jobs and usually hire their own people, you know, the poor immigrants you're so concerned with. It's a win-win." He lifted his forefinger. "For them." He lifted another. "For the unemployed." He uncurled the third. "And for us."

Naret sipped the burnt oolong. "Are you certain both the rich and the poor benefit?" As the former goddess, her task was inspiring the poor, plain, and cursed to realize their personal power to attain wealth, beauty, and blessings. To become wealthy. Which meant she loved those in all stations of life.

"The United States is a country of immigrants. You. Me. And millions of others. Those who jump aboard north-bound freights and pay coyotes to cross the border don't speak English. What chance do they have at getting a job? They exchange one kind of poverty for another. It's the wealthy immigrants who provide jobs."

"Are they real jobs or a different kind of enslavement?"

Daanish hinged his hand back and forth on the table-top. He wanted to convince Naret. Needed someone fluent in all the Asian languages. "Any job is enslavement. My sister is a teacher. Sure, she makes decent money, but she can't do whatever she wants and show up whenever she feels like. She works hard for her money and deals with lots of district and state bullshit."

"Teaching is a *career*."

"Exactly, and poor immigrants with no skills need to start somewhere."

Naret set down the cup. "Will we be providing any

services for them? English classes? Educational opportunities?"

"We work for the wealthy immigrants—the ones providing jobs—not their future employees."

Naret stared down at her oolong, didn't bother reading the tea leaves. She wanted to talk to the others. They understood her desire to make sure this job provided blessings not curses. Naret did not require their approval, but her friends would suggest flaws and benefits she hadn't considered. Her friends…

Daanish pushed his hair from his eyes. "Are you in?"

Naret's phone buzzed. An ex-goddess group message from Mnem. **Miss everyone! Neiman Marcus. Tomorrow. Eleven a.m.**

Fate handed her the gift of friendship. Moving on with your life doesn't mean breaking ties. It meant moving forward with a new perspective. One only other ex-goddesses understood.

I'm in. Naret tapped SEND with a lightness she hadn't felt since before their argument. Her friends. Her *real* friends.

"Well?" asked Daanish. "Do you want in on this great opportunity?"

Naret lifted her head. "I'll let you know tomorrow afternoon."

"Great." Daanish swiped through his phone. "Since you're worried about its legality, here's the visa program specifics." He pushed his phone across the table. "I'll send it to you. It's all perfectly legal."

Its legality didn't mean it was just. Naret lived through too many unjust edicts deemed lawful in her lifetime.

THIRTY-SIX

M nem was the first to arrive at Neiman Marcus. She wandered around the cosmetic counters, checked the price of a new expensive wrinkle cream and grimaced at the ingredient list. Wrinkle cream. Never in her wildest dreams did Mnem imagine she would need it.

Axie, in white jeans and white silk shirt, came alongside and gave her a quick hug. "Horrible, isn't it?"

Mnem set down the tiny hundred-dollar jar. "The ingredients or the price?"

"The whole aging mortal experience. No wonder mortal women spend all their money to look younger." Axie picked up a tube of anti-aging serum. "Did you get a chance to get a better photo of the funerary stela in the conservation room?"

"I didn't have a chance to sneak down there again." Mnem didn't try either. If the artifacts were fakes, she had a serious problem on her hands. And Mnem didn't need any more problems. "My daughters think I bombed FEM," she whispered.

Axie looked up from reading the label on a two-hundred-dollar eye serum. "Why is that?"

"They know how angry I am. I may talk violence, but I wouldn't dream of doing anything like that."

Naret joined them next. "Thank you for inviting me." She wrapped her arms around Mnem first, then Axie. "I've miss you all so much. Let's not argue anymore. I *need* all of you."

"We need each other," said Mnem.

"Actually," said Axie. "I think we should argue. Mmm… maybe argue is the wrong word. Debate is better and helps us figure out whatever mortality throws at us next."

"Agreed," said Naret. "Friends help you make tough decisions."

Inna, an Eze Gear tie wrapped like a headband, waved from across the cosmetic department. "Sorry I'm late."

"Don't you get tired of wearing Duncan's ties all the time?" asked Axie after all the hugging.

"It's starting to get old." Inna lifted her brown eyes to the ceiling. "But I never know when I'll get an opportunity to take a spontaneous photo." She glanced at the creams and potions on display. "Ugh. There must be thousands of these products on the market."

"It's Greek olive oil for me," said Mnem.

"Coconut oil is my skin care," said Naret.

Inna wagged a playful finger, her tone that of a prissy schoolmarm. "Those oils don't tone or smooth or exfoliate."

Axie laughed. "I'm not going to fight the aging process."

The four ex-goddesses meandered from counter to counter, tried to pronounce the ingredients on the labels.

"Remember when we used natural soaps and makeup?

When did this all become so complicated? Powders, creams, pencils. Tubes, sticks, pots, pallets. Shimmers, frosts, matte. I used to put finely ground rubies on my eyelids." Inna batted her eyes.

"Kohl lined mine." Axie fluttered her fingers around her perfectly applied eyeliner.

"I mixed red iron oxide into bees wax for lipstick." Mnem kissed the air with pursed lips.

"Mashed papaya makes an excellent face and body exfoliator." Naret turned her cheek to show her flawless skin.

They wandered through the shoe, accessories, and designer clothes department next. Sighed over prices they no longer could afford and considered sewing their own clothes again.

"We really did get lazy," said Naret. "All the automation and technology. People almost live like gods and goddesses themselves with all the innovations. Click a button, you get a thousand channels. Push another, you have coffee."

"Tap a few keys and get all the facts, lies, and half-truths you ever wanted," said Axie.

Mnem returned a silk Balenciaga blouse to the rack. "Remember when mortals went to a sage or an oracle?"

"They're called psychiatrists now," said Axie.

They went to the local coffee shop, ordered their favorites, and found a table on the patio.

"I need everyone's opinion about a new business venture," said Naret and launched into her dilemma. "Am I overthinking this? Will both rich and poor find prosperity? Is it just?"

"There will always be the rich and poor," said Mnem. "How many governments and regimes have we lived through? Thousands? It's always the same. The haves and the have-nots."

"The powerful and the powerless," added Inna.

"The ratio of those groups is the only thing that changes," said Axie.

"Should I take the job then?" Naret swirled the straw around her Thai tea. "Even though Daanish doesn't care about helping people and he's in it for the money?"

"Take the job. It might be a steppingstone to something more meaningful." Mnem met each of their eyes. "That's what we all want, isn't it? A job that's meaningful."

Inna bobbed her head. "Our immortality is gone, but our morality remains."

"We can't change who we are," agreed Naret. "Nor should we have to."

Four ex-goddesses were lost in thought. Thousands of years helping humankind don't just wither way. Or maybe it did. Decaying at the same speed as their mortal bodies. Mortal morals corrupted easily enough.

Mnem broke the uncomfortable silence. "That looks interesting." She pointed across the courtyard.

Near the water fountain stood a kiosk with a dozen colorful tops fluttering in the breeze. A woman sat in a high stool beneath a seventy percent off sign. It was music to their broke ears.

After finishing their drinks, they made their way over to the kiosk.

"Not much variety," Mnem whispered to Axie.

There were four sizes and two neckline styles, crew cut and a plunging V.

Mnem touch the tops. "They're silk?"

"Washable silk." The salesclerk responded with pride.

"Is this your booth?" asked Inna.

"Sure is." The owner stood up from the stool and

pulled a top down from the display. "All my tops are made in Uzbekistan and Thailand. I buy direct from families who have been textile artisans for generations." She handed the pink and green top to Naret.

Inna removed a large size. "I could wear this as a short slouchy dress."

"You certainly have the flair and body to pull it off," said the owner.

"Why are they seventy percent off?" Axie held up a swirling white and ivory patterned top.

The owner heaved a going-out-of-business sigh. "They didn't sell at my original price, or even a reduced price. I wanted to start my own business. Pay workers a fair wage."

Mnem, Inna, Naret, and Axie turned their heads in unison. "And?"

"Quality cannot compete with cheap." The owner unfolded a red and purple design from the stack. "Look at this." She pointed to the seams. "You don't see workmanship like this anymore. These are all vegetable dyed, and are a timeless style, and—oh, that looks wonderful on you."

Inna had pulled the top over her head and restyled her mock headband into a belt.

"They're great for traveling." The owner rolled one tight. "You can pack a dozen of these in a carry-on. They're cool and comfortable, easy to wash—hand or machine—and dry fast." She snapped her fingers.

"This is a closeout sale?" asked Mnem.

"Yes. Everything must go." The owner refolded the top. "Renting the kiosk takes all my profits."

"I'll buy two at full price," said Mnem.

"Me too," said Inna.

Naret and Axie bought two each as well.

"Take a picture of me." Inna handed her phone to

Mnem. "In front of the water fountain." She struck a pose, one lean toned leg extended, a hand on her hip, the other behind her head. "See how spontaneous I am?"

"Perfectly spontaneous. Every woman stands that way." Naret mimicked her overly posed stance.

Mnem snapped a few more photos.

"I wish there was a way to find clothes and goods like these silk tops," said Mnem. "I'll pay more knowing it was ethically sourced."

"I pay extra for organic groceries," said Naret. "Never passed up a farmers market yet."

"There should be a website for ethically sourced goods," said Axie.

"With a rating system," added Inna.

"Exactly," said Mnem. "And it would be nice to know if the company gives back to the community."

"I'd definitely choose products like that," Naret agreed.

"Me too," said Inna.

The four ex-goddesses looked from one to another. Behind them the water fountain glistened brighter, each water droplet a speck of light. The sun shone brighter. The sky became a clearer deeper blue.

"Why don't *we* make one?" said Mnem.

THIRTY-SEVEN

Mnem, Axie, Naret, and Inna sat close together—sharing a secret close—on the steps of the water fountain. Behind them, the water spouted high and arced to a happy tempo.

"What are you doing?" asked Axie, her shoulder pressed against Inna.

"I'm making an InstaPic account." Inna tapped her phone. "We need a name for our venture."

"Ethical Buys," suggested Naret.

"Bo-ring," said Inna. "It needs to be fun and catchy."

"What about Feel Good Goods?" asked Mnem.

Inna laughed. "That sounds like a company that sells sex toys."

"Are there ethically made sex toys?" Axie glanced up, noticed the rainbow made by the water fountain. "Ben Wa balls could definitely be made of natural materials."

"Don't mind, Axie, she has sex on the brain right now," said Mnem. "Should she or shouldn't she with Professor Hottie."

"Have sex." Inna looked up from her account creating to look Axie in the eye. "Unless there's an issue."

"A big one." Axie nodded.

"We'll talk about this later." Inna tapped her chin. "We need a name. Come on, we're ex-goddesses, we should be able to come up with a name."

"Does it matter?" asked Naret. "It's just an InstaPic account."

Inna gave her a hard look. "Why did Shee fire us?"

"We were no longer relevant and…" Naret's mouth made a little 'o' of realization. Obscurity was always a megabyte away. Insignificance, a few missed posts a week. "We need a great name."

Mnem looked up at the sky. Was is her imagination that the sky appeared washed clean? That the sun shone like pure gold? "Let's call it Goddesses Inc."

Axie frowned. "We're not goddesses anymore."

"No, but remember what Inna said? Our immortality is gone, but our morality remains. Our desire to do good fills our soul." Mnem set a soft hand on Axie's knee. "Peace, justice, victory." She touched Naret. "Abundance, wealth, and prosperity." She tapped Inna's bare leg. "Protection, promises, justice." She patted her heart. "Creativity, knowledge, and history. We know Good when we see it. We understand the importance of those values. Now we get to celebrate and promote it."

"Goddesses Inc." Naret nodded. "I like it."

"We need a profile photo," said Inna.

They asked the owner of the handcrafted silk tops to take it. She was happy to oblige.

"We need a bio." Inna uploaded the photo.

"Right this minute?" asked Naret.

"Yes, and we need more photos and products and I

should make a website and…" Inna looked up from her phone.

Mnem, Naret, and Axie stared wide-eyed at her.

"Are we doing this or not?" Inna crossed her arms.

"We're doing it," said Mnem.

"But we haven't planned it out." Axie ran her hand through her hair. "We need to think it through."

Naret nodded. "She's right."

"We don't need to talk about it. Let's just do it." Inna punched the air with an excited fist. "We need more doing, less talking about doing. This will be fun."

Axie laughed, shook her head. "I could use some fun in this new mortal life."

"We need a rating system," said Mnem. "Stars?"

"Overdone. What about hearts? Because we *love* the product." Inna's head bobbed with enthusiasm. Her heart thumped harder. Her blood pumped faster. Excitement coursed through her veins.

"Love it." Naret made a heart sign with her hands.

Inna turned to Mnem. "Create a great bio—keep it short—and figure out the specifics of our heart rating system. I'll build a basic website." She turned to Axie and Naret. "Look for ethically-sourced products. I'll post one of Eze Apparel's ties. And the tops we just bought will be our next post."

"I might know a business or two," said Naret.

"Do we start today?" asked Axie.

"No, I need a few more photos. With at least one of us in them. And we need a bio and the rating system." Inna slipped her phone in her purse. "Are we all in then?"

Axie gave the thumbs up. She was already making a mental list of products and businesses to consider.

"I'm in." Naret dragged her teeth over her bottom lip

as she thought about companies that sold ethically sourced goods.

Mnem clapped her hands. "This is going to be so much fun!" *Almost as much fun as watching a mortal drink from her divine spring.*

IT TOOK three days for the others to agree on Mnem's proposed description of Goddesses Inc. Four different personalities don't agree on much.

> **4 goddesses in search of divine & ethically sourced products. Hope. Integrity. Humanity. 5 ♥♥♥♥♥ Contact us for a review.**

THIRTY-EIGHT

"These are perfect." Inna scrolled through the photographs on the phone.

She sat with Naret on the patio of Uba's. The Nigerian restaurant made the traditional foods *almost* as good as she did. It wasn't fair. Goddesses spent years perfecting their culinary skills. Inna's stews were divine. Unbroken oaths were spoken over them. Promises kept. Justice realized. Spirits purified. Her stews were once powerful. Which is why she visited Uba's almost every day since beginning Goddesses Inc. Never underestimate the sacred power of yams.

"What about this one?" Naret pointed to a photo of her stretched out on a bed, a flower and vine carved teak headboard behind her. She lay on her stomach, knees bent, ankles crossed, her chin resting on her hands.

"Love it."

"This is my favorite one." Naret tapped the photo of her straddling a chair, both elbows propped on the chairback.

If there's one thing goddesses mastered, it was how to

make even the mundane appear artistically pleasing. Even a kitchen chair.

"This is all your own furniture, right? All these are from Teak Land?" asked Inna.

"Everything. I found Teak Land by accident a few years ago when I was redecorating. Mr. Yoontong went into great detail about his furniture. He told me all his hand-crafted pieces were made by his family."

"You believed him?"

"I wasn't totally convinced, so I made a few calls. He checked out. It's why I bought from him and not the less expensive furniture at another store."

"Do you know if he donates a portion of his profits?" Inna favorited a few of the photos. "That's the difference between a four and a five-heart rating."

"I don't know. He never mentioned it."

"Four stars it is." Inna tapped away on her phone, then looked up. "Did you take the job?"

"I did." Naret plucked a yam fritter from the little paper food tray. "I also explained my concern that our wealthy clients might exploit their own."

"Harsh." Inna grimaced. "What did he say?"

Naret beamed. "He wants me to create an incentive program that provides continuing education and English classes for their immigrant employees."

"The best of both worlds." Inna sipped on a spoonful of egusi stew.

"How come you're not wearing one of Duncan's ties today?" It was the first thing Naret noticed when she met Inna at the restaurant.

Inna set down the plastic spoon. "Guess I was too busy thinking about Goddesses Inc."

"Can you manage both InstaPic accounts?"

"How hard can it be?"

．　．　．

GODDESSES INC. LAUNCHED with four photos. The first was of the four ex-goddesses by the water fountain at the local mall. The second of Inna in a silk tunic dress she bought at the kiosk. The third, Inna wearing one of Eze Gear's Nigerian print ties. The fourth showed Naret on the four-poster bed from Teak Land.

They got twenty new followers in one day. And a woman from Bakersfield, California messaged about her natural goat milk soaps and lotions.

THIRTY-NINE

"Four hearts? Why only four hearts? I gave you very good service. A good deal. Delivery. All excellent. I want five hearts!" The voice on the other end was angry and loud.

Naret held the phone away from her ear. "Who is this?"

"I am Mr. Yoontong from Teak Land. This is Phra Naret, yes?"

Naret's jaw dropped. Only four days passed since Inna posted the photo. "How did you get my phone number?"

"You gave it to me. You bought a whole houseful of furniture. We needed it for the delivery." Mr. Yoontong sounded like a father scolding his child.

"Oh, I—"

"Why did you only give Teak Land four hearts?"

Naret switched the phone to speaker mode and set the phone on the table. "How do you know about that?"

"The last few days I have had more business than usual. Many people came to my shop." His voice boomed over the phone. "I asked a lady, a nice lady from Westwood, how did you hear about Teak Land. She showed me this....this Insta-picture on her phone with you on one of my teak beds. Then I see you only gave me four hearts. Not five."

Naret stifled a laugh. "Did you sell a lot of furniture since then?"

"Yes, but that's not why I'm calling. I want to know why Teak Land did not get five hearts."

"To get five hearts you must donate a percentage of your profits to a charity."

Mr. Yoontong grunted. "I give to the church."

"That's different."

"I demand to know what the criteria is for these five hearts."

Naret didn't blame Mr. Yoontong. He felt personally attacked. "Goddesses Inc. has a rating system. The product must be ethically sourced, ethically priced, and demonstrate ingenuity or creativity."

"My family makes the best teak furniture in the state."

"I agree. Another criterion is that women are an essential part of the business."

"Eh?"

"I met your wife and sister-in-law when I was at the store. I assumed they work with you."

"Sometimes they think they're the boss." Mr. Yoongtong let loose a phlegm-filled laugh.

It was another reason Naret bought the furniture from Teak Land. Both women mentioned how proud they were to be an integral part of the business.

"The fifth heart is given for a business who gives back to the community, who donates to a worthy cause." The fifth heart was criterion all the ex-goddesses instantly agreed on.

"I want five hearts."

"I understand, but it seems to me you should thank me for increasing your sales. You're most welcome."

Mr. Yoontong snorted. "My wife talks about a charity for children of migrant workers in Myanmar and Cambodia."

"That sounds wonderful." Naret had a soft spot for children of migrant workers.

"I will talk to my accountant. Then we will talk again. I want five hearts." Mr. Yoontong disconnected.

Mr. Yoontong's accountant was his sister-in-law. Naret hoped she would agree to it. Family businesses had their own kinds of problems.

Naret went into the kitchen and scooped oolong leaves out from a tin, took one look at them and poured them back in. Sometimes it's better not to read tea leaves.

FORTY

How are you?
Everything okay?
Feeling better?

M nem scrolled through nine phone messages. Each one from her nine daughters. She answered each one. Not with honesty. She did not do that to her children. Refused to burden them with her daily mortal aggravations and annoyances. They wouldn't understand anyway. Like a mother explaining love for one's children to a person without any. They might nod their head and affirm your feelings, but they would never, ever truly understand.

I got a kink in my neck yesterday. There's a wrinkle at my left eye. My job is boring. I need a purpose. Life without meaning is soul-crushing.

Send those replies? Not a chance. Mnem told her daughters what they wanted to hear, fine and great. Mnem understood her daughters' concerns. Momma was going to die. An event they never anticipated. Sadly, each **how are you** reminded Mnem of her looming death.

Mnem lifted her head, rubbed the back of her still-sore neck—one quick turn was all it took—and breathed in the flowers and foliage of the museum's statuary garden. It was her favorite place to take her lunch break. Reminded her of Greece and Rome. Of garden strolls and the occasional tryst with Priapus. Ovid had the tale all wrong. Well, at least about his impotence during intercourse.

Mnem set the phone on the bench. Why stare at technology when admiring nature and art was much more gratifying? Why clutch a phone when you could inhale fragrant blossoms and bask in the ancient artistry of symmetry and form? Mnem watched visitors stroll about the multi-terraced gardens. The lunch hour was always more crowded, even museum personnel ate their lunch outside in the sunshine.

A woman holding a lunch-sized plastic cooler walked down the path towards Mnem. She glanced at Mnem's lanyard, required identification for any museum employee. "Beautiful day, isn't it? It's good to get out of the basement."

"You must be from the conservation room." Mnem gave her the once over. The woman certainly didn't look like an international black-market art forger. Nothing furtive about her pocketless pants or dangerous about her gray t-shirt. Everything about her was plain, from her hairstyle to her face.

"Sure am." The woman held out her hand. "I'm Vicky Wright."

"Mnemosyne Athanasiou."

"Wow, that's a mouthful." Vicky Wright giggled.

"Are you the only conservator?" asked Mnem assuming a new conservation room meant more employees.

"Today I am. Actually, most days. Robert left a few months ago." Vicky snapped open her mini cooler.

"There's another conservator, but I've never met her because she works the night shift."

"The museum is building a new conservation room for only two employees?"

"They plan to hire more. It's part of their expansion project." Vicky rifled through her cooler, pulled out a container of sugared yogurt. "It will be nice to have someone to talk to again." She settled on the opposite side of the bench. "Although sometimes it's annoying."

"Do you ever run across fakes?"

"Do you mean replicas?" Vicky peeled back the yogurt container's lid. "A copy or replica references the original."

"No, I mean a fake."

"Not at this museum. Did you know forgery, besides prostitution, is one of the oldest professions?" asked Vicky.

"I know," said Mnem. "Did *you* know wealthy Romans paid a small fortune for what they thought were ancient Greek statues to put in their gardens? Happened all the time. Those same fakes are worth a lot of money now."

Vicky gave Mnem an odd look. "Most people don't know that. They think art forgery is a new thing." She rolled her eyes.

"Since the day after the beginning of time." Mnem twisted the cap on her water bottle—the store brand, the French Alps brand was over her budget. "It was nice to meet you." She walked back to the museum, her step a bit too fast and springy. There was no time to waste.

I hope Vicky is a slow eater.

"Where's Phoebe?" asked Mnem as she passed Ashley waiting for the next group tour.

"At a martini lunch with Senator Dreamboat."

Mnem stopped in her tracks. "Who?"

"Senator Flores." Ashley fluttered her hand in front of

her face. "That man is smokin' hot! He can filibuster me any day."

Mnem's breath hitched. *Is Phoebe trying to get more funding for the museum? No, that's not her job.*

Politics. It must be politics. Nothing like living a few thousand years to understand the marriage between art and politics.

"I wish we were allowed to have martini lunches," said Mnem. "Some visitors are a bit…"

"Annoying?" Ashley laughed. "Oh, here comes my 1:30, the Friends of the Canine Club."

"Have fun." Mnem continued through the lobby, down several hallways, and turned into the vestibule. A few minutes later, she stepped out of the elevator and hurried to the deserted conservation room. The door was unlocked this time.

Mnem hurried inside and photographed the possibly fake funerary stela of the cameleer, this time zooming in on the engraved text and details of the carving. Photos taken—in focus this time—Mnem turned to go and accidently kicked a crate sticking out from under a work bench.

A few Styrofoam packing peanuts spilled out.

"Damn," Mnem muttered and crouched down, dragged out the crate, and plucked the packing peanuts from the floor. She closed the top flap. Froze. Checked the label a second time. The recipient was Dr. Azam. Axie's professor. Mnem flipped open the flap and thrust her hand into the box. The object was rough, narrow, and long. Shaped like an obelisk.

A bang echoed through the hallway and Mnem startled. She shoved the crate back and hurried to the door.

Axie transcribes texts, she doesn't authenticate artifacts. Why am I involving her? And blessed goddess, why in Hades am I doing this? Fakes and forgeries are a part of life.

Mnem knew exactly why she was curious. Replicas and copies were fine. It was a way for more people to enjoy great art. But fakes were wrong. Either the museum was being duped or they were duping the public. Whichever the reason, Mnem needed to know. Old habits die hard.

A man with a hard hat and clipboard pushed away the thick plastic sheeting across the corridor as Mnem closed the door behind her.

"Hi." Mnem smiled brightly. It was an age-old rule. Act like you belong there.

"Hi." He barely gave her a glance, his attention on the clipboard. "No, the inspector hasn't been here yet." He spoke into the microphone dangling from his earpiece. "Get him on the phone for me." He continued down the corridor to the service entrance.

Mnem let out a relieved sigh.

Once in the elevator, she tried to make sense of her suspicions. Maybe the board members of Gallery Hall knew about the fakes in their collections. Maybe the originals were on tour at other museums. Maybe the originals were sent to a specialist at a high-tech facility. Maybe law required them to return the original to the country of origin.

That was a lot of maybes. Too many for Mnem.

FORTY-ONE

"What are you doing?" Duncan Eze's height might have dwarfed the average glass sliding door, but not his custom gigantic ones. The west-facing living room wall boasted a multimillion-dollar-contract view. He stood at the threshold, a two-liter water bottle dangling from his hand. "Hey, I said, what are you doing?"

Inna wasn't admiring the view. Or Duncan's perfect physique. She stared at the computer screen. "Working on the Goddesses Inc. website."

Two Duncan-sized strides brought him to her side, where he loomed over her like a father of a disobedient toddler. "Why aren't you working on photos for Eze Gear?" His voice was polished obsidian, dark and smooth.

Inna lifted her eyes. "I'm quite capable of doing both." Her tone matched his. Arrogant superstar basketball players didn't frighten Inna. She knew his type. Even admired and enjoyed it.

He peered down. "Is Eze Gear on there?"

"Yes."

"Did we get the five-star rating?"

"Five hearts and yes, you plan to give back to the community, right?"

"Sure will." Duncan puffed out his already sizable chest. "One scholarship and there's a plan to open libraries in a few of the villages."

Inna tapped the screen. "There it is, five hearts."

Duncan's jaw stiffened. "Why isn't Eze Gear on the home page?"

"That wouldn't make any sense." Inna elbowed his knee. "Goddesses Inc's mission and rating system is on the home page."

"Are you mining my customers?" Duncan's voice turned a shade darker and deeper.

"What customers? You haven't launched Eze Gear yet."

"You're using my followers. I don't like it. You should be building my brand. *My* brand. You don't have time for this bullshit."

"It's not bullshit." Inna met his hard eyes. "I don't care for your tone."

"No? Then how about this one?" Duncan tugged down his basketball shorts.

"It's very nice but I have a bit more work to do. I should be done in ten minutes."

"Now." His voice threatened like thunder before a lightning strike.

Inna closed the laptop. "Excuse me?"

"Now. I want you now. Not in ten minutes. Not in five minutes. Now."

Inna set the laptop on the table with perfect calm, then stood, her head tilted to look up at Duncan's sizable nostrils. "This is important to me. You should respect that."

His eyes narrowed. "I should be more important."

"I'm not one of your star-struck fans. I'm not here to service your needs."

Duncan glared. Inna knew the look. The press dubbed it Evil Eze Eyes. His opponents knew the glowering expression meant he was about to wipe the floor with them.

Inna squared her shoulders. "Do you know who I am?" asked the ex-goddess and protectress of the harvest, justice, and promises. If only she could tell him the truth. Not that he would believe her anyway. But for a split second, Inna felt the surge of divine strength burst through her mortal body.

Duncan's eyes widened. He stepped back. "Damn, babe. That's sexy. You demand respect. For a moment there…"

"What?" Inna's voice was dominatrix sharp.

Duncan's head bobbed with approval "I don't know. You were…"

"I was what?"

"I can't describe it, babe. But it was hot. Very hot." He backed away. "I'll be waiting in the bedroom."

Inna went back to the Goddesses Inc. website. Time slipped by. When she finally went to Duncan he was snoring softly. She smiled, climbed into bed beside him and scrolled through the Goddesses Inc. photos she posted on InstaPic. There were lots of likes and comments and followers. It was gratifying. More gratifying than building Duncan Eze's brand. More gratifying than anything she had done in her life for a very long time.

Inna wanted it all. The full mortal experience. A hot man and a great—well, Goddesses, Inc, wasn't a real job—but it certainly made her heart and mind race with excitement. Maybe a mortal *could* have it all.

FORTY-TWO

I t was wrong. Misspelled. The blessing didn't make any sense.

Axie studied the cameleer's funerary stela photos Mnem sent her. Was that a shadow or a mark? She zoomed in. Difficult to tell. Axie sighed. One particular letter was problematic, it changed the meaning.

Axie rubbed her itchy eyes and set the phone down. Another day. Maybe tomorrow. She needed to study it with fresh eyes. Besides, it was time to leave and she had Goddesses Inc. research to do waiting for her at home.

Goddesses Inc. certainly made Axie see products in a new light. Mnem was right about one thing though, mortals needed a meaningful life. Meaning made everything sweeter. Minor annoyances no longer bothered her as much. Each hour was treasured. Goddesses Inc. filled the void. Researching ethically sourced products gave Axie less time to feel sorry for herself.

"Are you Axtis Khan?" A friendly-looking woman stood in the doorway of Axie's tiny office. Her styled hair, red lipstick, and gray Armani skirt suit was a hundred percent business-chic.

Axie smiled. "Yes, I am. How can I help you?"

The woman's pleasant demeanor vanished. "You bitch!" She stamped into the room.

"What?" Axie's back pressed against the office chair. "I…I…"

"Don't have anything to say, do you?" The woman balled her fists.

"What's this about?"

"Do you know who I am?"

Axie had a pretty good idea.

"I'm Amir's wife!"

"I—"

"How dare you!" The woman slammed her fist onto the desk. "How dare you seduce my husband, you vile bitch!"

"I did *not* seduce your husband."

"Don't deny it!" The woman picked up a stapler and threw it into the corner. "How often are you fucking Amir?"

"Never."

"Liar. I know he's having an affair with you. He said your name—*your* name—while we were in bed last night."

Axie's lips formed a little 'o.' "I swear on my honor, we are not having an affair."

Mrs. Azam thumped the desk again. "I spit on your honor. How long has it been going on? Since you started working for him?"

"I told you, we're not— "

"Amir won't leave me. He will *never* leave me. Do you understand?" Mrs. Azam asked the last question with exaggerated slowness, as though she spoke to a person with bad hearing.

"Perfectly." Axie met Mrs. Azam's kind before. They were in every harem. Jealous women whose anger should have been directed at the husband but never was.

"Don't play the innocent with me. You're not the first slut he's fucked, and you won't be the last."

Axie blinked. She suspected as much.

"You're just another one of his sluts. He'll tire of you in a few months and then kick your ass to the academic curb."

Axie crossed her arms. "I appreciate your courtesy visit."

Mrs. Azam's eyes tapered. "Go to hell."

"You're worried, aren't you? Amir never said another woman's name before, has he?"

Mrs. Azam's finger shook as she pointed to herself. "He won't leave me. He loves money too much." Her face puckered. "Find another job and stay away from my husband."

Axie tilted her head. "Why do you stay with a cheater?"

Mrs. Azam pushed off the desk with both hands. "I love him."

Axie nodded. "You're a very understanding wife."

"And you're a dumb slut who fucks other women's husbands."

That wasn't true. Not for a long time. Several hundred years at least. Axie rose from the chair, met the scorned wife's eye. "You may leave."

Mrs. Azam stepped closer. "I know Amir is taking you to Göbekli Tepe."

"Amir mentioned it a few weeks ago. I never agreed." Pity washed over Axie. "I'm not a slut and you spew your venom at the wrong person. Take your grievances to your husband." Axie lifted her arm, palm side up, like a host telling a guest to partake of the buffet. "Look into your soul, Mrs. Azam. Ask yourself why you stay with such a man. Only you know the reason. If you truly love him as you claim, then ask yourself why you choose to love a cheater."

Dark thoughts shadowed Mrs. Azam's face. She knew why she stayed with Amir. It wasn't about love or honor or duty either. "Bitch!" She turned on her heels and stamped from the room.

Axie stood at the desk until Mrs. Azam's clicking heels faded away. Then she dropped into the chair and stared at the text on the computer screen. Axie wasn't going to let some jealous wife frighten her into quitting. Goddesses, even ex-goddesses, did not accept disrespect from anyone. Nor should a wife.

Axie smiled. Professor Azam needed to be taught a lesson.

But which one would she teach him?

FORTY-THREE

"I have no experience with this," said Axie. "I'm like a virgin."

Inna, Mnem, and Naret burst out laughing.

"Not since for forever," said Mnem.

Axie giggled, her friends knew how to make her laugh. "I don't know anything about website design." She tapped the computer screen. "It looks great to me."

"What about the color scheme?" Inna clicked through the various pages.

"Blues and tans are soothing." said Mnem.

"Uncluttered and calming." Naret nodded.

Inna slid her phone across the table. "Check this out."

Axie eyes bugged. "Goddesses Inc. has three thousand followers?"

Mnem took a pad of paper from the kitchen table. "Here's a list of the companies who want us to review their products."

Naret eyes ran down the page. "For free?"

"Some free. Some at a discount." Mnem passed the list to Axie.

224

"Free is good," said Axie.

"Not necessarily." Mnem crossed the room, her back against the blue sky and the even bluer ocean. "Were our blessings and favors free? Never. Mortals had to *do* something. Make an offering. Repent. Apologize. Pray." She counted them off with her finger. "Give. Build. Create. Forgive. We know free is never free. Mortals should have learned that by now. There's always a cost. Emotionally, spiritually, financially, physically."

"That's a no to free stuff then?" asked Naret.

"Not exactly. We need a policy." Mnem went back to the table. "Or ask them to submit theirs."

"This talk of policies and hidden costs makes me think you've dated the senator for too long," said Axie. "Time to cut him loose."

Old celestial habits clung like nettles to a wool sweater. It was advice immortals gave to each other. Long term relationships with mortals always ended in heartbreak. One of the pitfalls of eternal life. A mortal's promise to love forever teetered on the edge of funny and pathetic.

"You're right." *Except I'm not ready to.* Mnem handed each goddess a list. "Until we have a policy or know theirs, we should purchase the product. I don't want them to expect a good review."

Naret ran her finger down her list. "Ooooh, soy candles with natural scents in shells found on the beach. No waste."

"I love this brand. I'm wearing it now." Axie tugged at her white blouse, which was knotted above her white jeans to show three inches of smooth stomach.

"Mnem and I have been doing a lot of research." Inna already knew what products were on her list. She and Mnem worked together on curating one tailored to each goddesses' specialties. "We have a separate list. Some of the products you may already use, but I'm worried that our niche—ethically sourced products—might be too broad."

"This is already getting too complicated." Naret dragged her teeth across her lower lip.

"It's not," said Inna. "Look into the products on the list. Mnem and I will handle the business side."

"What business side?" asked Axie.

"Getting on the list of social media companies, reaching out to them, putting together a media kit," said Mnem as she headed for the espresso machine.

"Ugh." Axie grimaced. "Doesn't sound fun."

"No? What about this?" Inna tapped the computer screen. "You're a detail person, Axie. Check for typos and read through our policies and disclaimers page to make sure they are ethical."

Axie grinned. "You know me too well."

"Um…" Naret set down her list. "We have a problem." She told them about Mr. Yoontong from Teak Land and his anger at only getting four hearts.

"You did the right thing. Let him earn his five hearts," said Inna. "Maybe those with only four will be inspired to give back in some way."

"I agree." Mnem walked out with a tray of lattes.

"We need to give back too." Axie took a glass cup from the tray. "It would be hypocritical if we didn't."

"We don't make any money on this," said Mnem.

Inna tapped the air with her finger. "Yet."

"We have to do *something*," insisted Axie, her need for integrity sharpened by a celestial whetstone. "A charity or scholarship: something we start now and expand upon as needed."

Mnem grimaced and pressed her hand to her stomach.

"What's wrong?" asked Naret.

"I ate something that didn't agree with me." Mnem set

down the demitasse cup. "I definitely have more respect for mortals now. Their bodies are overly delicate."

"I had my first headache the other day." Axie pinched the space between her eyes. "Spent too much time staring at a computer screen."

"I don't want to talk about our aches and pains." Inna smacked her hands, rubbed them together. "Are we ready for a photo shoot?"

Ten primping minutes later, they stood on the beach in front of Mnem's house. Once the tripod was stuck into the sand, they laughed and giggle and frolicked in front of the camera. They made goofy faces and struck sexy poses. They forgot they were ex-goddesses. They were women. Friends having fun. Feeling the breeze in their hair and the sand between their toes.

"Ow!" Mnem lifted her foot. "I stepped on a broken shell."

Blood oozed out, a crimson reminder of their lost immortality.

FORTY-FOUR

Ribbons of pink and orange clouds sprawled wide in the darkening sky. An ocean liner moved across the horizon. A pelican skimmed the waves. It was another gorgeous sunset at the uber exclusive Beachfront Club restaurant. Wealthy and powerful members only. No fans. No reporters. No media. Just privacy and exquisitely prepared food from local growers, a discreet staff, and a clientele who didn't bat an eye if the President of the United States walked in. Which he had on several occasions.

"Have you thought about my offer?" Miguel looked every inch the sexy stud senator with his rolled-up sleeves, loosened tie, and five o'clock shadow. The man was a dish fit for the gods.

Mnem plucked a green olive from the silver charcuterie plate. "What offer?" She remembered alright—it was on her mind all week—yet couldn't resist teasing him.

Miguel smeared brie on a small slice of bread. "To be my official girlfriend."

"What are the requirements?" Mnem tapped her fingernails against the stem of the martini glass.

"Twenty-four-hour devotion. A hundred percept loyalty and daily kisses." He flashed his campaign smile.

"I must decline. You're much too needy." Mnem sipped her martini, extra dirty.

"Me? Needy?" Miguel pretended confusion.

"You have a staff. Don't you pay them to take care of your needs?"

"Not the need I want from you."

Mnem's cheeks warmed. When was the last time a man made her blush? She didn't remember. Which was a much different problem. Proof that she was losing her ability to remember.

"Seriously, Mnem, I want more of you."

"How much?"

"As much as you'll give."

Mnem selected another olive from the platter. "You're in Washington, DC most of the time."

"Come with me." He opened his mouth, let her feed him.

"I have a life here." *Not a great life, but my friends are here, my support team.*

"What about a weekend visit?"

"I suppose, I haven't been to Washington since…" *The Kennedy assassination.* "I don't remember."

Miguel reached over the table and took Mnem's hand. "You're unlike any woman I've ever met."

"There you go again, Senator Cliché." She withdrew her hand to give his a playful smack.

Miguel reached into his pocket and set a small leather jewelry box on the table.

"What's that?"

"A going steady gift. Go on, open it."

Mnem lifted the lid, sucked in her breath. "It's beautiful." She lifted the gold necklace from its silken nest. The evil eye pendant was mother of pearl; the pupil a sapphire stone. It was a simple and elegant design. Goddesses loved gifts. Extravagant or humble. Especially unexpected gifts. Miguel's gift, however, came with an expectation that made Mnem's heart race like a runner during the Lupercal festival.

"I hear all Greek women have them." Miguel walked around the table to put on the necklace, his fingertips brushing across her neck as he moved her hair aside.

Mnem touched his cheek, guided him to her mouth for a kiss. "You're very sweet." *He tastes so good.*

"Sweet?" Miguel pushed out his lower lip. "I was going for devastatingly sexy."

"That, you already are." She touched the necklace. "Thank you."

"I hope it's the first of many." He sat back down, his expression expectant.

"You're a young ambitious governor. You're going places. I don't know if…" Mnem sighed. There was too much she could never explain.

"Let's play it by ear for now, okay? You're wary, I get that. No rush."

"It's not that, it's politics. It's exhausting and predictable. The scandals, the lies, the back-door meetings. Nobody wins. It's all posturing and demagoguery and bluster." Mnem spoke from her heart and from experience with thousands of years of political rulers and regimes.

Miguel chuckled. "Tell me how you really feel."

I don't know how many years I have left. One, twenty. Fifty. Do I want to be caged in a political glass house? "I don't want to live under a political microscope."

His smile slipped, his mouth a straight line, his brow

furrowed. "I appreciate your honesty. I need more honest people in my life."

The waiter, a fifty-something man with a waxed handlebar mustache, set down a twelve-inch tower of seafood.

Mnem pulled a succulent chunk of octopus from the third tier. "I heard you had a martini lunch with my boss the other day."

"Phoebe?" Miguel rolled his eyes. "Everybody wants something from me. Usually money. Or legislation that makes them money. It wasn't lunch though. Is that what she told you?"

"No, someone else."

"Jealous?"

"Hardly. But I *do* want something from you." Mnem lifted her martini, her voice all husky innuendo.

"I like how you said that," said Miguel. "How is Goddesses Inc. going? Looks like you're getting lots of engagement."

"Are you stalking our InstaPic?"

"More like perusing."

Their dinner arrived and as they supped, Mnem shared the triumphs and concerns of Goddesses Inc. Miguel offered prudent advice about ethical business practices and the harsh cyber world.

"I want a private room." A loud baritone voice from the other side of the dining room drew Mnem's attention.

"Those rooms are booked weeks in advance, sir," said the maître d'. "It would be our great pleasure to accommodate you in this dining room."

Mnem's eyes widened.

"Who is it?" Miguel's back was to the entrance.

"It's Duncan Eze," whispered Mnem. "He's with Verushka Volkov."

The six-foot ice-blonde super model with Barbie-length legs stood in the doorway as though posing on a Paris runway.

Mnem slid her phone from her Chanel clutch.

"No photos allowed." Miguel stayed her hand. "Maybe it's a business meeting."

"In a mini-dress and five-inch heels?" Mnem watched the maître d' seat Duncan and Verushka on the opposite side of the room. "I doubt it."

Miguel, his expression serious, regarded Mnem with sudden curiosity. "Will you tell Inna?"

Duncan leaned over the table to plant a kiss on Verushka's collagen lips.

Mnem's left eye narrowed. "Definitely."

"Maybe you should stay out of your friend's private life."

"This isn't just any friend. It's Inna. She would want to know." Mnem dabbed at the corner of her mouth with the linen napkin. "Wouldn't you want to know if I was seeing another man?"

"Yes." Miguel swallowed, glanced out the window. "How will Inna take it? Is she one of those I'll-give-him-another-chance type of women?"

"I have no idea." Goddesses usually forgave mortals. Mortal mess-ups were the expectation, after all. This, however, was different. And they weren't immortal anymore. "Guess I'll find out."

FORTY-FIVE

"WHAT?! That cheating lousy bastard!" Inna paced the room like a caged tiger. "We had a disagreement. The man had the nerve to say I spent too much time on Goddesses Inc! Who does he think he is?"

"The darling of the NBA. A superstar. You know fame corrupts most mortals."

Inna's eyes flashed with anger and her nostrils flared. She looked downright lethal. "I am not his sex toy! I am a woman! A goddess!"

Mnem put her finger to her lips.

"I thought we had something special. He said…well, it doesn't matter what he said. He never made any promises." Inna glanced over her shoulder, lowered her voice. "I was created to inspire promise-keeping. Mortals felt compelled." Inna balled her fist and set it over her heart. "Duncan never technically promised anything and evidently my promise-keeping power is long gone." Inna sunk into the Italian leather armchair.

Mnem perched beside her. "Sports stars expect to be

adored. Men like that don't make good boyfriend material."

Inna rested her head against the chairback, stared up at the rustic wood beams—shipped in from some castle in Spain—which ran across the twenty-foot ceiling. "He was irritated I didn't hop into bed with him at that precise moment." She snapped her fingers.

"Where is Duncan now?" Mnem delivered the bad news to Inna in Duncan's house, a mansion actually. Inna claimed the view inspired her.

"Practice. He won't be back for a while." Inna sighed. Loud. "It's really gone, isn't it? Our goddess glow, the essence that made men fall at our feet." She turned her head to Mnem. "I *really* miss that."

"Me too. We took everything for granted."

Inna mumbled Nigerian expletives, sat up, slapped both hands on the arm of the chair, and jumped up. "Come with me."

Mnem followed her down the wide marble hall, up a wide bleached oak staircase, and into a gigantic bedroom. Inna grabbed her Louis Vuitton duffle bag and threw open a closet door.

"You keep clothes here?" asked Mnem.

"A few stretch pants and t-shirts." Inna folded them into the duffle bag.

"What about the bathroom?"

"Medicine cabinet on the left."

Mnem gathered Inna's creams and lotions. There wasn't a lot. A face cream—a brand she was reviewing—mascara, a small bottle of perfume, lip balm, eyeliner, and a trial-sized bottle of makeup remover.

"What are you going to tell him?" asked Mnem from the bathroom.

"Nothing." Inna tossed her bra and panties into the duffle.

"Why not?"

"There's nothing to say and whining is beneath me. Anything I say will only sound pathetic. It's over and done." She grabbed a pair of tennis shoes from the floor. "I should have never left all this stuff here. I should have never—"

"Stop it. You did what you did. Don't beat yourself up about it." Mnem dumped the stuff next to the duffle bag.

Inna wrapped her arms around Mnem. "Thank you for telling me."

"What are you going to do about your job as his social media director?"

"I need the job." Inna set the cosmetics in the bag. "I'm angrier at myself than him. I let myself be wowed by a playboy. I should have broken off with him the minute FEM fired me. I want a life partner now, something I never cared about before. Mortality changed more than just my lifespan, it changed what I want in life." She tapped her forehead and her heart. "Here and here. It all changed. I want to find my special someone. Stupid, right?"

"Not at all." Mnem meant it. She felt the same. Actually, she fought the feeling every day.

"You have your daughters to love. I have nobody."

"The world is full of people who don't have a special someone. In fact, throughout history, women and men endured loveless marriages."

Inna scowled. "Why are you telling me this?"

"Because I don't want you to have unrealistic expectations."

"I want the full mortal experience." Inna hefted the bag. "I'm done here." She marched out of the bedroom.

Maria, her hand clutching a kitchen towel, waited at the bottom of the stairs. "Are you taking a trip, Miss Inna?" She looked at the duffle bag in Inna's hand. She knew a pissed off woman when she saw one. "You will be back?"

"No. Maria, thank you for everything, especially all the delicious soups you made me."

"I will miss you, Miss Inna. You are a ray of sunshine. God's light shines from your soul."

Inna set down her duffle bag and hugged Maria. "You're a goddess, Maria. Always remember your worth."

Inna and Mnem walked out the front door and down the wide marble steps to the driveway.

Mnem stopped, blanched, and put her hand to her stomach. "Wait a minute." She heaved breakfast between two agave plants.

"You're sick." Inna pulled a tissue pack from her purse.

"I caught a bug." Mnem wiped her mouth. "My stomach's been upset for the last few days. You would think thousands of years among mortals would have improved our immune system."

Inna rubbed her back. "Are you running a fever?"

"No, it's nothing, it'll pass."

"Are you sure?"

"I'm fine. Mortals are always sick with something." Mnem hurried to her car.

"Mnem…" Inna's voice was barely above a whisper.

Mnem opened the car door, turned around. "I had too much seafood last night. Don't worry. My digestive system hasn't adapted to mortality yet." She smiled, hugged Inna. "Call me anytime."

FORTY-SIX

Inna let the phone ring three times before picking up.

"Babe. Sugar. Why is all your stuff gone?" Duncan's deep smooth voice purred over the phone.

Inna expected Duncan's call. But not so soon. Not five minutes after he returned home from practice.

"You cheated on me with Verushka Volkov." Inna's tone was calm, a major feat of control. She refused to sound angry or hurt. Suspected Duncan made these kinds of calls often. Probably expected certain responses. Undoubtedly had a game plan in his Casanova playbook for each female response. If the woman is angry, then...

"We didn't have sex." Duncan's voice was measured, unworried, not a drop of shame or remorse.

Inna, her fingernails digging into her palms, pretended to sound bored. "You had a date with her."

"That was it. A date. That's all."

Inna knew better. "You took a super model to dinner and didn't have sex with her? Don't play me for a fool."

"I'm telling you the truth."

Inna flattened her fingers. Wanted to go Full Goddess

on him. It was a thousand times more intense than a full court press. Duncan would have been on his knees, head to the ground, shaking in fear. "Your definition of sex is different than mine. Mine is much broader and includes the mouth, tongue, and fingers."

"Babe..." Duncan's voice hitched. "You don't pay attention to me. I was lonely." He sounded like a little boy caught with his hand in the proverbial cookie jar.

"Blow jobs are sex in my book." Inna shifted the phone to the other ear. "I don't have time for this, goodbye—"

"Wait! Don't hang up. It was wrong. I was wrong. But you made me mad. You think you can stay in my house and then tell me no? I'm Duncan Eze. Women don't tell me no."

"I told you to *wait* until I finished something that was important to me." The conversation was too predictable, a messed-up mortal guidebook to pathetic excuses. Inna was ready to tap END. "How would you like it if I came to your practice and demanded sex?"

Duncan laughed. A genuine laugh.

Inna didn't. She felt powerless and undignified. Muttering Nigerian swear words under her breath, she dragged the kitchen chair to the window, and stood on top of it. There it was. A view of the valley over the rooftops. Perspective. It changed everything. A smidgeon of her former glory bolstered her bruised ego.

"Babe? You there?"

Her chin high, Inna spoke to the vista. "You're a man who cheated on his girlfriend. Your superstar status does not bestow you extra privileges or leniency."

"Let me explain—"

"You already did."

"Babe, you're my goddess."

Inna's heart did a little flip flop. "Excuse me?"

"Hear me out before you hang up. No woman ever treated me like you do. It's confusing, babe. It's messing with my mind."

"You mean your ego."

"Fine, my ego, but Verushka, she doesn't mean anything. Her blowjob wasn't even that good. Yours are—damn—mind-blowing."

"A blow job is sex. I'm hanging up now."

"Wait!" Duncan cleared his throat. "She talked about you all night."

"What?"

"You and Goddesses Inc. Verushka has some kind of caviar makeup line from Russia and asked if you would review it. The blowjob kind of happened. Honest. She's showing me the caviar cream one minute, rubbing me the next."

Super model Verushka Volkov followed Goddesses Inc? Why not contact them directly? The answer was obvious. Because Verushka was a superstar too. Famous people didn't go through the normal channels. Inna wavered between irritation and delight. It didn't matter though. Duncan cheated. One thing nagged Inna.

"I have one question, Duncan."

"Okay."

"Am I still your social media director?"

There was a long silence as Inna held her breath.

"Yes." His voice was firm, unwavering. He knew Inna was the best person for the job.

Inna breathed an inaudible sigh of relief and stepped down from off the chair. "Send me the ties. Goodb—"

"I love you."

The world stopped, froze in time. Duncan *loved* her. Not as a goddess but as a mortal woman.

"Inna, babe, did you hear me? I love you. Please forgive me." His voice was deep, husky with emotion.

"I heard you." Loud and clear and damn damn damn, great goddess damn. It's what she wanted, didn't she? A relationship with a special someone. To build a life together.

Inna needed strength, but her bones felt soft. Did she love Duncan? She didn't know what mortal love felt like. If it was mushy and warm and as twisty as a corkscrew then yes, she loved him.

Inna sat on the chair. Forgiveness. Duncan asked for forgiveness. It's what goddesses did. In the past, she forgave far worse. But forgiveness did not mean forget. It also did not mean exoneration. Forgiveness was a heart and soul thing. Benefitted the mortal forgiver the most.

Old habits die hard.

"I forgive you." Inna pressed END.

A DAY later Inna received a box of sample ties. Nestled in the middle was a Harry Winston jewelry box. Inna guessed its contents from the size. She opened the lid and smiled. While securing the ten-carat diamond bracelet around her wrist, she admired the sparkling facets. Not bad. Not bad at all.

Inna had worn better. Rare gems commissioned by kings made this bracelet look like a trinket. Yet it was the simple shell bracelets strung by young children with love, hope, and innocence that surpassed Duncan's generous gift a thousandfold.

Inna removed the bracelet and placed it back in the box. She returned it the next day.

Goddesses cannot be bribed with jewelry.

FORTY-SEVEN

The porcelain goddess. Mnem worshipped her all week. This morning it was with gifts of undigested bagel and spewed coffee. She heaved again and again. Until there was nothing left in her stomach.

It's not possible.

Her nine nights with Zeus had been glorious. He was power. She was memory. Their union perfect, because reason is born of both power and memory.

Reason. It's what set mortals apart from the beasts. Allowed them to predict events and outcomes. Allowed their deeds and feats to be remembered. Without reason there was no civilization. Before mortals learned to write, they shared remembered stories, passed down knowledge and experience, and gave birth to civilization. Long ago, Mnem was one of the most important goddesses ever. But *this* defied reason!

Not. Possible!

Mnem flushed the toilet, swooshed water in her mouth, spit a few times, and sat on the velvet stool by the vanity. She wiped her mouth with the back of her hand.

Miguel is a mortal man. A nobody in the great scheme of the universe.

The box on the counter stood between a vase of pink roses and a collection of Jo Malone perfume bottles. The box didn't belong here. It belonged in the drugstore, in a mortal home, anywhere but in her bathroom.

Mnem snatched the box and read the directions while she fought back another wave of nausea.

It's a mortal flu. Sensitivity to a food additive. Some kind of infection. Easily remedied with a wide range of medicines.

The humbling task accomplished, Mnem returned to the stool and closed her eyes. Time skuttled sideways like a crab, thousands of memories flashing through her mind. Her inception. Father, Cronus. Mother, Gaia. Her time as a Titan. The battles. The fall out. Years spent as a goddess. Roaming the earth. Living and loving.

Then Zeus. Nine wonderful nights with a man who knew how to show a goddess a good time. The nine days of births that followed. Nine beautiful daughters who lit up the mortal world with the songs in their hearts.

Miguel Flores wasn't immortal. Wasn't a god. Wasn't even Greek!

Mnem opened her eyes, dragged them toward the stick. The air whooshed from her lungs.

"Noooooo." Mnem beat the marble counter with her fists and, for the first time since being fired, wept. She howled, wailed at the goddesses, and shuddered with heaving sobs.

Pregnant. I'm am unwed woman cliché.

Mortal mothers-to-be once came to Mnem for encouragement. She stroked their hair and spoke reassuring sentiments. Mnem recalled her words: A babe is a gift from the goddesses. A treasure that both gives and takes. An offering to the world that is uniquely yours. That makes you weaker and stronger, braver and more cowardly, hopeful and hope-less. A child will fill you and empty you. Deplete and restore you. A child is All.

Mnem didn't want All. She wanted to live out the rest of her mortal days selfishly, savor each sunset and sunrise, find a purpose.

This was a new purpose. One she definitely did not choose.

Mnem touched her belly, flat and unmarred by the births of nine daughters, her nine gifts to the world. This child would be a nobody. One of a multitude. Destined to eke out an existence. To toil all day. To die.

Mnem burst into hot tears. And then a ripple of horror exploded through her body. Childbirth. She must give birth as a mortal woman. Labor. Maybe for days. Writhe in pain and deliver in blood. Mnem stared at her stomach, past the firm skin and network of vessels, and into the womb. Imagined the mortal babe clinging to life.

Another new horror seized her. Miguel. She imagined the headlines. **Senator Flores's Love Child! Daddy Duty Disaster for Senator Flores.**

Mnem did not want to do that to him. Did not want to destroy his career and thwart his ambitions with an out-of-wedlock child.

A third horror swept over her. Although she appeared young, healthy, and fit, Mnem was ancient. Too old physically and spiritually.

Mnem pressed her hand to her womb. A baby. After so long. A mortal child. A tiny human growing inside of her. To love and protect.

Protect?

Mnem's stomach constricted, those waves of horror rising as bile in her throat. She vomited again. Who was she kidding? She was unable to protect this child from anything. Not pain or trauma or fear or worry or disease.

Mnem tossed the pregnancy stick in the trash and headed for the bar. She needed a good stiff drink. A Bloody Mary would take the edge off—

She stopped. No alcohol, wasn't that the mortal rule? No coffee, no cold cuts, no smoking, no drugs.

Pregnancy was a stroll through a celestial park for a goddess. For a mortal it was a lumbering hormonal trek up a mountainside.

FORTY-EIGHT

Inna *knew*. Felt someone's eyes at her back. Pretending to look at a shirt on the rack, Inna whipped her head around. There he was again. This was the third time the man lurked in her periphery.

The man tugged down his baseball cap. He was nondescript, average height and build, his gray t-shirt and jeans ordinary. Even his skin tone was difficult to describe, his race unclear. Sunglasses covered his eyes. Inna's stalker was average and forgettable.

Inna noticed Mr. Bland at the farmers' market first. He was the only one without a basket or bag. The coffeeshop was the second. This time he stood behind her.

The third time was at the Bullseye Super store. Inna loved Bullseye. It reminded her of the markets of ancient times. Trinkets and clothing and food and housewares; anything anyone ever needed. Inna had picked up a box of bandages—a first-time purchase—when Mr. Bland walk past the aisle. Inna tossed the bandages in the cart, added a first aid kit—better play it safe—and hurried to the next aisle. Mr. Bland turned the corner.

Coincidence? He obviously lived in the same neighborhood. Still, it unsettled Inna. Goddesses, even ex-goddesses, didn't believe in coincidences. They knew better. The question was, why would anyone follow her? Was he a stalker? A fan?

Today Mr. Bland lurked near the women's shoe department of Bloomingdales. He loitered too far away for her to approach yet was too close for comfort. Inna set down the Louboutin boot and meandered toward the perfume department. Mr. Bland might stay out of the shoe department, but men often purchased perfume as gifts. He might close the gap.

Inna paused, picked up a perfume bottle, set it down, perused the displays. The mirror behind the counter reflected Mr. Bland's position. He didn't take the bait, so Inna moved away. The department was too open. Mr. Bland didn't need to close the distance, he had line of sight. If only he came closer.

Inna strolled to menswear for two reasons. To check out Eze Gear's tie competition and to find a place to disappear between the racks. After strolling past two Armani-clad mannequins, Inna ducked down behind a rack of shirts. Stealthy as a lioness, she prowled to the sweater display and moved behind the trousers.

Inna circled back and came up behind Mr. Bland. "Why are you following me?"

Mr. Bland spun around. "Huh?"

"Don't play stupid." Inna kept an arm's distance away. "You've been following me for days."

Mr. Bland stepped back, palms out. "Lady, I don't know what you're talking about. I've never seen you in my life."

"Don't deny it." Inna studied his features, which was next to impossible since they were hidden behind sunglasses and shaded beneath the baseball cap's brim. "Why are you stalking me?"

Mr. Bland turned his head from side to side. "Security." His voice was a fraction louder than a normal discussion.

Inna, her feet rooted to the floor, lifted her chin. "Good idea, call security. You might want to raise your voice though." She scrutinized him. There was a mole near his jaw and two telltale tiny holes in his ears. Brown hair peeked out from under his no-name baseball cap. "Who are you?"

Mr. Bland shuffled backwards.

Inna advanced. "Where are you going? Don't leave. Here I am. What do you want?"

Mr. Bland held out his soft smooth hands. Not the hands of a laborer. "You have me confused with someone else, lady." He turned and hurried away.

"Two can play at this game," she mumbled as he walked out of the menswear department.

Her heart racing, Inna went from rack to rack, made sure to keep Mr. Bland in sight. He glanced over his shoulder once, but Inna ducked behind the jackets.

Mr. Bland was calm, yet his gait was purposeful, like a shopper who used the store as a short cut from the parking lot to the mall's outdoor pavilion. No meandering or lingering at a display.

Inna fell in behind a giggling group of teen girls flaunting tiny tops and big attitudes.

"Like that designer is so grandma," said one pushing open the door to the mall's pavilion.

"You mean great grandma. *My* nana is always on point."

Mr. Bland checked over his shoulder again before veering to the coffee kiosk. Inna hunched down behind the teens, then dashed behind the sunhat hut nearby.

Mr. Bland ordered his coffee, his attention diverted for a moment, while Inna peeked around a hat rack. After paying, he sauntered to the pick-up counter. Inna was close enough to hear every word.

"This is Seth. She made me, but I still have the information you want… okay, okay …no problem, Mr. Eze."

Inna's heart dropped like a boulder off a cliff. Crashed hard into the pit of her belly. Every muscle stiffened with anger. Duncan Eze did not know who he was dealing with.

FORTY-NINE

A nswer the door. Inna jabbed at the phone's touchscreen.

There was no response.

Inna rang the doorbell. Again. She heard its deep descending notes in the house. Thousands of years of life teach patience. Or rather *impatient* patience. It was a learned goddess skill, an art requiring both an understanding of how the world moves versus how mortals act.

Inna pressed the doorbell again. For the fifth time. She wasn't leaving.

The door opened and Maria poked her head out. "Hello, Miss Inna." She smiled but her eyebrows were pinched. She looked embarrassed. "Mister Duncan wants me to tell you he is very busy right now."

"Is he with another woman?"

Maria shook her head, opened the door wider, retreated, her new Duncan Eze athletic shoes squeaking on the marble floor. "No, Miss Inna." Her voice was louder this time. "You cannot come in!" Maria winked, backed up again, the door wide open.

Inna mouthed thank you and stepped inside. She pointed to Maria's footwear and gave her the thumbs up before heading to the living room.

Duncan sat on the massive sectional Chesterfield leather sofa, his huge bare feet propped atop the over-priced reclaimed wood coffee table. A deep-sea fishing show played on TV. The fisherman explained the proper way to rig a flying fish bait for hooking a blue fin tuna. It was Duncan's next project: learn to fish. He already bought the boat.

Inna stopped, her breath hitching. Duncan appeared like a beautiful god in thoughtful repose. No wonder women threw themselves at him. With his looks, wealth, and charisma he was woman candy. Yet it didn't matter how sweet he was, Inna did not put up with cheating. She looked past him, past the floor to ceiling glass wall that showcased the gorgeous view of the valley. A reminder, Duncan once told her, of his intent to stay at the top of his game. Whatever the game.

"Why did Maria let you in?" Duncan sounded sad, resigned.

"Why are you having me followed?"

"You're talking crazy." Duncan's voice rose an octave. Too high. Too guilty. "I don't follow old girlfriends." He didn't take his eyes from the fisherman attaching the flying fish to a kite.

"I have proof, a photo of the private detective."

Duncan shrugged, his eyes glued to the TV.

"Look at me." Inna tried to summon her goddess voice.

Duncan picked up the TV remote and increased the volume.

Inna stomped into the living room, swiped the remote from his hand, clicked OFF, and stood in front of him.

"Are you a child? Are you too afraid to answer my question?"

Duncan bristled, his jaw tightening. "I'm not afraid of anything, least of all you."

There it was! He *was* afraid.

Inna bit back her grin and flung the TV remote across the room. "Do I have your attention now?"

Duncan flashed his famous Evil Eze Eyes.

"Save that look for the basketball court. The man said your name, Mr. Eze, after I confronted him at Bloomingdales."

"Mother f-er." Duncan crossed his arms. "He came highly recommended."

"Why are you stalking me?"

"Babe—"

"Don't babe me." Inna stiffened her spine, stood tall. It was the oddest thing. She felt taller when she was a goddess. She had not shrunk—she knew that for a fact—but somehow mortality made her feel shorter.

"Inna, I'm not stalking you. You left me and just when I was about to…" Duncan stood and pointed an accusatory finger. "Who are you?"

"What?" Anxiety rippled down Inna's backbone.

"You don't exist, Inna. After you left me—left *me*, Duncan Eze," he pounded his chest, "I decided to look into you."

"You know who I am." The back of Inna's neck grew hot.

Duncan stepped forward. "You don't have a birth certificate."

"Not in this country."

Duncan loomed over her. "You have no medical records. No school records. No photos of when you were a kid. No baby pictures. No yearbook photos. No nothing.

It's like...." His eyes widened. "Are you in witness protection?"

It was an easy out. A way to explain that made sense. But then starting Goddesses Inc. would destroy any chance of anonymity. Not if she wanted to fly under the radar. Duncan was smart enough to know that.

"No, of course not," said Inna.

"Who are your parents?" Duncan circled around her. "Are they alive? Dead? Where in Nigeria are you from?"

FEM was good at a lot of things. Creating new identities for every generation was not one of them. Sloppy of FEM. And really inconsiderate. Unless other goddesses received believable identities. Perhaps, only the top goddesses did.

Inna refused to be intimidated by an intimidation pro. "Why do you care? We're through, over, done."

Duncan faced her again, the anger in his eyes replaced with pain. "Because I...I love you." His face was soft, eyes warm as he looked into hers. "I wanted to know who you are. Your past. I have big plans for my life. I'm going places. Places of power and influence. I'm not playing ball forever."

He loves me. Me, the mortal. Inna's rigid spine wilted, turned plastic and pliable.

"I was going to introduce you to my parents. That's a big thing in my family. For me. My father said not to bother bringing around any women until I found The One." Duncan touched her cheek. "You are The One. I was ready to..." Duncan swallowed, then he spun around, and walked away. He leapt up the two wide steps to the spacious dining area. Duncan liked to eat at the table's far end, claimed it made him feel like a king overlooking his kingdom.

Duncan ran his hand over the massive built-in shelves

arranged with his trophies, medals, awards, and photos of him with famous people. The shelving unit slid back to reveal a steel door.

Inna stifled a smile. Every king has a treasure room.

After Duncan entered the code, the door opened. The vault was a small room with one wall of steel shelves filled with plastic storage containers, memorabilia, and numbered metal boxes. Another wall held his gun collection and equipment for his latest sport, archery. Inna smiled. She never told him that not only did she make her own bows, she had killer spear skills too.

Duncan picked up a small velvet box from off the shelf. "I was this close to proposing, babe." He opened the lid.

The nickel-sized diamond ring glittered and shone. Inna received bigger diamonds before. Not near as well cut and polished but that was lifetimes ago. She stared up at Duncan.

"Sweet Jesus, Inna, how can you look at that engagement ring and be indifferent?"

"You don't know me. Don't know what I've seen in my life. What—"

"Exactly." He snapped the lid shut. "Which is exactly why I hired a private investigator." He put the ring box back on the shelf, walked out, and tapped the keypad. "You want to know one reason why I love you? Because of your reaction to a twenty-carat diamond ring. Things don't impress you. Money doesn't impress you. You're quality, babe. I hoped you and me could make some real changes in this world—local and national. Changes for our people. Real change. Not just political bullshit, but changes that go deep." He thumbed his chest. "Right here."

His words struck Inna like a sharp arrow. Punctured deep. Once the catalyst for change, Inna touched hearts and minds. But time passed. Beliefs transformed like clouds on a windy day. Change wasn't as easy as Duncan thought.

"Then why let a Russian supermodel give you a blow job?" Inna crossed her arms.

Duncan grabbed Inna's left hand. "I didn't put the ring on your finger yet. It doesn't count until the ring is on. When it is, the only person who's going to be blowing me is you."

Inna yanked her hand away. "Not with that attitude."

"That's what the ring means. Commitment."

Inna's nostrils flared. "It's a *promise* of commitment." She knew her promises! "You need to prove your future commitment first before you promise it." Inna turned away and started down the hall. "Call off your PI," she said over her shoulder. "I'm not interested in your offer of marriage."

Duncan laughed.

Inna spun around. "What's so funny?"

"Offer of marriage. Like from the old days." He laughed again, his mouth wide and large, then stopped mid laugh, as though Inna's expression sucked the air from his lungs. "Who are you, Inna?" he whispered.

"Not your girlfriend." Inna strode down the wide hall and out the front door, her heart beating like a bird caught in a cage.

"I'll find out," he called from the doorway as she hurried down the steps to the driveway.

He wouldn't. Divinity was something you had to see with your own eyes and now that Inna was stripped of it there was nothing left to see. No divine powers to witness. This made Inna both relieved and sad.

"You'll still be my social media director, right?" he shouted.

Inna opened her car door and turned around, her

smile wide and beautiful. "Our personal relationship will not impact our business one." She needed the income. Needed to eat and pay utilities.

Before she turned the car into the street, she checked the rearview mirror. Duncan stood like a god in the doorway. Towering and robust and gorgeous. Inna's heart squeezed like a constrictor around its prey. She loved Duncan. Still loved him. But he cheated and showed his true self. She didn't trust him. And if she didn't trust him with his sexual urges, she could never trust him with her deepest secret. Not that he would believe her anyway.

Tears ran down Inna's cheek. She wanted love, a relationship, family. It seemed like such a minor thing. An achievable goal. Now she understood what a gift it truly was.

FIFTY

"I can't tell him." Mnem, her back to the others, gazed out the window to the sea. Oh, how she wished it was the Ionian or the Aegean. She longed for her homeland. Gave serious thought to returning. It seemed to be a realistic plan for her future. Mnem imagined living out the rest of her life in hiding. Playing mommy in a nice stone house with a view of the Aegean some place near her olive orchards.

Inna pressed her hand to her own womb. A baby. Problematic, but very nice. Wonderful even. A gift from the go —she frowned and removed her hand.

"You have to tell the senator." Naret's gentle voice was sprinkled with pity. "He has a right to know."

"You sound like a character from a sappy movie." Mnem studied the horizon, the opposite direction of a flight to Greece. In retrospect, living on the eastern coast would have been better. Her homeland wasn't as far away then.

"You have a moral obligation to tell him," said Axie.

Mnem spun around. "To Hades with honor and ethics

and all that noble crap." Her voice was as shattered and sharp as broken glass. "Those things don't work for our lives anymore."

"Isn't that why we started Goddesses Inc.?" asked Naret. "To give our lives meaning and purpose?"

"That's different." Mnem puffed out her irritation.

"It's not and you know it," said Inna.

"Stop trying to convince yourself otherwise," Axie added.

"It's his baby too," whispered Naret.

"I asked you to come here to give me comfort and all I get is a scolding." Mnem glanced at the bar. She needed a drink. Maybe two.

Naret noticed, understood the look on Mnem's face, and went into the kitchen.

"My womb is ancient." Mnem patted her belly. "All our wombs are ancient. A baby cannot possibly grow in it."

"You delivered nine daughters." Inna watched Naret open the refrigerator.

"Thousands of years ago," Mnem spat.

"Then what's your plan?" Axie's eyes met Inna's. "We all know the old ways."

Every country in the world, every hill and valley and desert, had an herb for the deed. Every medicine woman and healer knew how to prepare the mixture to dispel the new life within.

Naret entered the living room and thrust a drink in Mnem's hand.

Mnem wrapped her fingers around the cold glass, felt comforted by the tinkling of ice cubes. A vodka and cranberry with a slice of lime *would* hit the spot. "I can't drink alcohol."

Inna bit her lip to keep from smiling.

Axie smiled with relief.

Mnem looked down at the glass. It was a trick. A well-played trick to understand her heart. Mnem burst into tears.

Naret patted her shoulder. "It's non-alcoholic."

Mnem collapsed on the sofa, buried her hands in her head and wept.

Inna, Naret, and Axie never saw Mnem weep before and it frightened them.

Naret rushed to Mnem's side. "We will all help you rear the child."

"It will be fun." Axie draped her arm over Mnem's shoulders. "The child will have four mothers."

Mnem lifted her head, her eyes wet, puffy, and red.

"If you tell Miguel it's another man's child, he'll probably leave you." Inna joined the group hug. "Problem solved."

"*Half* the problem." Mnem smeared her tears across her cheek.

"You know," said Axie. "If the senator really loves you, he may not care."

"What do *you* want?" asked Inna. "Do you want to be with Miguel?"

"I don't know." Mnem threw back her head, tears streaming down her cheeks.

Axie stroked Mnem's hair. "You don't have to decide anything today."

"That's right, you have time before you start to show." Naret offered a hopeful smile. "Plenty of time."

"It's more than telling him. It's everything else." Mnem wiped her eyes. "I'm...afraid." There, it was out. "I'm afraid of the unknown. A mortal pregnancy. A mortal birth. Responsibility for a mortal child. I'm afraid that this is all part of FEM's evil plan for making us suffer even more."

The room grew silent as Mnem's fear sunk in. What else did FEM have in store for them? What other mortal complications? There was no way Shee would let them live out their lives without trauma and heartache and suffering.

Naret and Axie shared a look. Knew what the other was thinking. Mortal relationships complicated everything! Sexual dalliances had consequences.

"I wouldn't mind being pregnant." Inna imagined a child in her arms, someone to love, someone to love her. Need her. Part of the fun of being a goddess was that mortals needed you. Which reminded Inna of another problem. "I hate to bring this up now, but since we're all here…" Inna grit her teeth.

"That sounds ominous," said Axie. "What is it?"

"After I broke up with Duncan, he hired a private investigator." Inna told them about her encounter with Mr. Bland, their argument, and the engagement ring.

"It was bound to happen sooner or later." Axie sighed. "No parents, no records, anyone would be suspicious."

Naret dragged her teeth across her bottom lip. "I know a guy."

"What kind of guy?" asked Inna.

Naret rubbed the back of her neck. "He gives people an identity, but it's not cheap."

"How much?" asked Axie.

"Not sure," said Naret. "I'll ask."

Mnem's belly felt bloated with baby and worry. "*If* I tell Miguel I'm pregnant he's going to want to know all about me. If he finds nothing…" She closed her eyes, pressed her forehead. It was all too much.

Axie, her ten fingertips bouncing off each other in thought, crossed the room. Twice. "Here's the plan. Don't make any decisions to tell the senator about your pregnancy until Naret finds out more about creating a new identity."

"This is wrong." Mnem brimmed with tears once again. "We have a history, a beautiful glorious history of power and prestige. We should not have to live a lie."

Inna studied her hands as though the truth might be in the creases. Living a lie went against every fiber of their being. "What other choice do we have?"

FIFTY-ONE

M r. Addison Austin, wearing a custom-tailored suit, Gucci tie, and jade cufflinks, pinched a chunk of raw tuna with his carved ivory chopsticks and regarded the young woman on the other side of the table.

Naret blinked. "I'm sorry, could you please repeat that?"

"You deaf? You heard me. That's the price for a new identity." Mr. Addison Austin popped the tuna into his mouth, watched her with the intensity of a poker player looking for a buff.

Naret dared not show emotion. Not so much as a twitch. She sat in the gilded chair across from Mr. Addison Austin—or was it Austin Addison?—and reined in her astonishment.

Mr. Addison Austin pointed with his chopsticks. "You can afford it." He squinted. "You dressed down to meet with me, but I know quality when I see it. That blouse is designer. The jeans too. But it's the way you carry yourself that tells me you live a life of easy wealth."

Naret tried to remember how she even came to know

of Mr. Addison Austin's services. How *did* she find out about the man whose identity business was done out of the private room of an upscale sushi restaurant? Then she remembered. During her goddess days about a year ago, she overheard the whispered conversation of two elderly women waiting in line behind her at the dim sum shop. Naret stored the nugget of information away. At the time, Naret bristled at the illegality of it all, but here she was, asking Mr. Addison Austin the cost of a new identity. It soured her stomach.

"Do you offer bulk rates?" Naret purred as she gave him her most seductive smile.

Mr. Addison Austin ran his hand through his slicked-back hair. "If I'm the bulk." He picked a piece of tuna up with his fingers, slurped it in between his lips with a nasty grin.

Naret knew his kind well. "Thank you for your time. I'll relay the cost to the intended party, who currently seeks other potential service providers."

"I'm the best in the business. Fast, efficient, discreet, and thorough." Mr. Addison Austin squirted sriracha sauce in his sushi bowl. "You need more than the usual. You want a family history."

"Your name isn't very discreet."

Mr. Addison Austin laughed, an ugly sound like choking on phlegm. "It's forgettable, mix-up-able."

Naret stood. "I'll get back to you."

"You will."

FIFTY-TWO

"Fifteen thousand dollars!" Mnem nibbled on an olive. She craved them lately.

They sat outside on the deck of Mnem's house. Naret wanted to deliver the news in person.

"Not really," said Naret. "It's five thousand dollars a person. Each of us needs three identities. One for us and one for each fake parent. No one—not even the senator—will look past that."

"What do we get for this new identity?" asked Axie.

"A driver's license—"

"We already have that courtesy of FEM," said Inna.

"A social security card, birth certificate, high school diploma, bachelor's degree, and a master's degree if you want. He'll make sure our birth certificates match our homeland as well."

"What about a certification of citizenship?"

"That too." Naret sipped her tea.

"This is wrong," said Mnem.

"Not always." Axie tapped the table. "The government gives endangered witnesses new identities all the time.

People escaping an abusive situation and political refugees do it for survival."

"Goddesses don't lie. They don't deceive. They don't—"

"Die," murmured Inna.

"It's wrong and we all know it." Mnem huffed and crossed her arms.

"It's not wrong," said Inna. "It's about our survival in this mortal world. The truth," she held up her hand, "and do not tell me it will set you free. We all know there is no Truth. At least not the way mortals understand it. There's nothing wrong about making ourselves legitimate."

Mnem bristled. "We're all legitimate."

"Really? What's the birthdate on your driver's license?"

Mnem looked away.

"FEM took care of that for us," said Axie. "Which means if FEM lies, we can too. Anyway, we're not hurting anyone if we get a new identity."

Naret tapped her phone. "I sent you Mr. Austin Addison's—"

"Addison Austin," corrected Axie.

"Right, whatever." Naret giggled. "If you want a fake life, you know where to get it."

"A fake life." Mnem frowned. "That sounds horrible."

Inna pressed her temples. No wonder mortals suffered with headaches all the time. "Don't be Patty Proper. We have to live in the now. An antiquated sense of honor isn't going to work for us anymore."

"Please stop bickering," said Naret.

"We're becoming *them*," whispered Axie.

"We already are!" Inna smacked the table. "We need to do what is best for us."

Silence descended. Four ex-goddesses considered their life, their needs, their too-short futures. Mnem stared at the

GODDESSES INC.

ocean. Naret looked sheepish. Inna folded her arms, and Axie pretended to study her perfect manicure.

Mnem found the answer in the horizon. "Thank you, Naret. We appreciate your visit to Mr. Addison Austin." One never reached the horizon. It wasn't a fixed position. Like their future. There would always be an unknowable Beyond. "Inna is right."

"I am?" Inna's brows lifted. "Damn right I am."

"We must do what is best for us." Mnem patted the table. "Change of subject: Inna has news about Goddesses Inc."

The heavy air lifted like the sun dissipating a fog. Three ex-goddesses perked up.

"I've been mulling over this for a while," said Inna. "We've gained new followers, and our account is getting major traction and good reach, but we need more engagement."

"How do we do that?" asked Axie.

"Ask our followers to tell us how they feel when they used the product."

"Feelings are fleeting," reminded Axie. "Short-lived and changing."

"This is different. It's about purchases that make you smile whenever you use them," said Mnem. "We all own things like that."

"Would we have to change our five-heart rating system?" asked Axie.

"Not if we asked our followers to do it," suggested Naret.

"What do you mean?" Inna tapped on the Goddesses Inc. profile.

"In the bio, we could add something like, use MMS for it 'makes me smile'."

"I love it!" Inna looked at everyone. "Are we in agreement? I'll add it now. It may increase engagement."

They agreed.

Mnem dug into her jean pocket. "This came in the mail today."

Axie rolled her eyes. "*More* lip balm?"

"This one is different. The tube is biodegradable. Decomposes quickly in dirt and water." Mnem passed it to Inna. "The woman wants to start a whole make-up and skin care line but she's still looking for investors."

Inna twisted the tube. "It smells fresh and clean."

Naret leaned over. "Mmmm…lemon and mint."

Inna rolled it on the back of Naret's pale hand. "Goes on smooth. Has a nice rosy tint." She applied the balm, moved her lips over it. "Not sticky either."

"She sent one for each of us. I want a full lip balm report from everyone in a few days." Mnem paled, pressed her hand to her stomach. She leapt from the chair and raced inside.

"Mortal morning sickness strikes all day long," explained Inna.

"Has she told her daughters yet?" asked Naret.

Inna shook her head. "I honestly think she's embarrassed by her pregnancy."

FIFTY-THREE

T he tiny hairs on the back of Axie's neck lifted. Somebody was watching her. Not just watching. Appraising. Lusting for. Axie lifted her eyes from the computer screen.

Professor Amir Azam stood in the doorway, his arms folded, his head tilted. "Which project are you working on?"

"The pottery shard with references to the little-known djinn, qutrub."

"Ah, the corpse-eating ghoul. One of my favorites." He grinned. "Anything interesting?"

"The pronoun here is feminine."

"Well, that *is* interesting and highly unlikely. Are you certain?" He waved a dismissive hand. "Forgive me, your knowledge of ancient languages is unparalleled. I have another project I'd like you to work on. A personal one. If you're interested and have the time. Purely off the record."

"What is it?"

"A special artifact." Amir came into the room and rounded Axie's desk.

Axie smelled him, a mixture of manly desire and cologne. "You're a tease."

Amir's pupils dilated. He crouched down, his body a hair's breadth from hers. He pulled his phone from his pocket, angling it in a way that required Axie to lean forward to see the photograph.

Axie moved closer. Felt his warmth and desire.

"What do you think?"

Think? Axie was too busy wrestling with her conscience. Imagining herself on top of him. Bouncing to the earth's carnal rhythm…

Axie grabbed his phone and yanked it forward. Leaned away from temptation. Her eyes widened. A funeral stela of a cameleer. Mnem sent her a grainy version a few weeks earlier. This photo was high resolution. "Looks similar to murals found in south-west Saudi Arabia."

"Gorgeous isn't it?" Amir gazed into her eyes.

"Yes." Axie's breath came heavy.

"A collector is interested in it."

"Doesn't it belong in a museum?" asked Axie.

Amir's fingers wedged under her hand, took back his phone. Axie's heart quickened. His touch set a shiver through her, the action overly intimate.

"It's a replica of a real one that's in a museum." He licked his lips.

Their mouths were too close. If Axie closed her eyes for a second longer than necessary, Amir would assume she was inviting a kiss. He wasn't the sort of man to ask for permission. It was part of his charm. Bold broody men: Axie's greatest weakness. Did he see that flaw in her? Her hunger for a sweep-me-off-my-feet tryst posed great risk now that she was mortal.

Axie swallowed. "Why does a collector want a fake?"

"Who knows? Impress his friends, maybe? I don't ask."

His attitude set off warning bells in Axie's head. She forgot about kissing him. This was no fake. No replica.

"What exactly do you want me to do?" asked Axie.

"Compare it to the real one. Make sure the markings are absolutely identical."

Axie's brow furrowed.

"You're so adorable when you're befuddled." Amir tapped her chin with his finger.

Adorable?! Axie was not adorable! Adorable was for puppies and kittens and children. Not for ex-goddesses accustomed to declarations of their transcendent magnificence. Axie pushed away. Thank goddess for chairs with wheels.

Amir's brows shot up. "Did I—"

Axie wagged a finger, which encouraged him more, if the devious smile on his face was any indicator.

"Sorry, I crossed a professional line." Amir didn't look or sound sorry. He looked aroused. "That's why I like you, Axie, you're smart and no nonsense, and keep me in my place." He stood. "Will you do it? You'll get five hundred dollars for the replica inspection."

"They must be paying a lot for the fake."

"Like I said, high quality replicas are difficult to come by."

"Okay." Axie had no choice but to say yes. Mnem would want her to. It might be the proof Mnem needed for the museum. A piece of the forgery puzzle.

"Excellent, I'll send you the high-resolution photos." Amir slipped the phone in his trouser front pocket.

Axie looked. Shouldn't have. It was part of his game: Look at my crotch. Amir was obviously aroused.

"You're awesome, Axie." He turned to leave.

"Before you go…."

"Yes?" He pivoted in the doorway.

"Your wife paid me a visit."

"Did she now?" Amir smiled, not a single concerned crease on his face.

"She thinks we're having an affair. I assured her otherwise."

Amir rubbed his chin, trimmed with the perfect amount of stubble. "I like women, Axie. Always have, always will. My wife knew that before we married."

Axie gasped.

"You're surprised." He chuckled. "I'm honest about my adultery. My wife and I have discussed it many times. She's free to leave me or take other lovers. She doesn't. I will never deny who I am." He cocked his head. "Do you hate me now?"

How could she? She lived in the time of harems and sultans. Made love to rulers and kings while their first and lesser wives waited in the seraglio. A few times the first wife watched. Axtis was a goddess, after all. What ambitious wife would deny her husband such an honor? "You're a man who makes no excuses for himself."

"That's right." Amir left the room.

Axie waited until he rounded the corner of the hall, then tapped out Mnem's phone number.

FIFTY-FOUR

M nem embraced Axie at the front entrance of Gallery Hall.

"How are you feeling?" Axie's gaze dropped to Mnem's stomach.

"Some days are better than others." Mnem walked her passed the admission desk. "What's going on? Your message was cryptic."

"I think Professor Azam is part of the art scam. He asked me to inspect a replica funerary stela." Axie put her hand on Mnem's arm. "Remember the photo you sent of a cameleer holding a sword? *That* one."

Mnem's brows lifted. "But the one in the conservation room is supposed to be real. Which means…"

"They're swapping them out."

"Do you think the professor knows this? Or is he an innocent pawn?"

"I have no idea but I'll tell you this, nothing about the man seems innocent," said Axie. "I'd like to compare the photo to the one in the conservation room. Can we get in there?"

"Only one way to find out." Mnem headed toward the vestibule. "It all makes sense now. No wonder I couldn't sense any vibrations from those pieces of art."

"Why do you still have that ability? Inna, Naret, and I lost all of ours."

Mnem stopped, her brow creasing. "I was a Greek titan, and it's not so much a divine ability as it is a learned skill. I'm older than all of you, remember."

"Maybe Shee forgot to remove it."

Mnem stared up at the ceiling, through the plaster and roof, and to the celestial sky above. "Shhh, let's not remind Her."

Axie looked up as well. Shee was there. Everywhere.

Mnem didn't want to consider the Why of that divine ability. It was an exercise in futility after all. What she had today may be taken from her tomorrow. "Anyway… someone is making replicas and swapping them out in the conservation room. I met one of the conservators the other day, Vicki Wright. She didn't seem the type."

Axie quirked an eyebrow. "Since when does greed have a type?"

"It has to be an inside job." Mnem turned right into another hallway. "I thought it odd that your professor was invited to the gala."

Axie scowled. "Amir is not *my* anything. He's an adulterer."

"Did you…" Mnem's question hung in the air.

"No, thank goddess. His wife came into my office to berate me. I feel bad for her. Amir claims they have an open marriage, except she won't participate."

Mnem exhaled her annoyance. "Then it isn't an open marriage."

"It's called polyamory now."

They turned into the freight elevator vestibule. Mnem's

eyes widened and Axie tracked her gaze. A security camera in the corner blended into the white walls.

Mnem grimaced. Since when was a camera mounted there? Was it part of the updated security installed for the new conservation room?

Axie pointed to her ear.

Eavesdropping. The way of the world. From hidden holes in stone walls to acoustically designed rooms to mini microphones. High-tech spying for a low exploit. Mnem shrugged and tapped FABULUS on the keypad.

The elevator door opened.

Mnem looked for another camera as she stepped inside. There was none.

"The world hasn't changed, only the names," Mnem said when the door closed. "Our hearts and souls are too old to live in this mortal world. We're too jaded."

Axie smiled. "Maybe that's why FEM fired us. Goddesses aren't supposed to be cynical."

"Tell me, Axie, are the people worse in this century or does it seem that way because there's billions more people?"

"Both."

"Spoken like the peace-keeping ex-goddess you are." Mnem touched her stomach. She did that a lot. Without thinking, an instinctive reflex. The gesture was not lost on Axie.

"Have you told the senator?"

"No."

"Your daughters?"

"Goddess, no!" Mnem's voice rang hollow in the old elevator.

"What are you waiting for?"

"I don't know. Divine intervention?" Mnem looked at Axie.

The absurdity of it all. They had once been divine intervention.

"Mnem, it's unsettling to see you like this. You are Mnemosyne, a titaness. Nothing ever frightens you. You always have all the answers. You're our rock! If you're unable to make a decision about this—"

"Don't put that on me," snapped Mnem. "I don't want to be everyone's rock."

"It doesn't matter what you want. You *are*. You can't change that. Just like you can't change that little mortal growing inside of you."

The elevator rattled to a stop at the ground floor.

"You don't understand. There is no good way to tell Miguel, a sitting US senator, that I'm pregnant with his love child. The media already hounds him. His opponents will crucify him. I will not be responsible for destroying the man's professional image."

"You're being overly dramatic."

"Trust me, I'm not." Mnem stepped from the elevator.

"Sounds to me like you care more about him and his image than what's best for you."

Mnem stopped walking. "Miguel is a good man. I care about him. I also care about my life. What's left of it."

Axie wrapped Mnem in her arms. "You'll get through this."

Mnem felt Axie's love infuse her skin and soak into her bones. Was it possible to give a transfusion of love and hope? Every goddess knew it to be so.

Love was the answer. It was always the answer.

Except Shee hadn't shown much love or compassion when she fired her less-than-popular goddesses.

"You're making me cry." Mnem pulled away and dabbed at her eyes. "And ruining my eyeliner." She winked. "Let's see if there's anybody in the conservation room."

"Doesn't look like it," said Axie.

The room was dark.

"Good. We got lucky." Mnem hurried forward and turned the doorknob. It was locked.

"This time I came prepared." Axie zipped open her Chanel purse. "You lived thousands of years and never learned how to do this?" She pulled out a pin and worked the lock. "It's a forever skill."

"Looks like yours is a bit rusty."

Half a minute later, Axie switched on the lights and located the cameleer funerary stela on the far worktable. Seating herself in front of it, she took a magnifying glass from her purse. "There's lots of ways to identify a fake. The folds of the clothing, the intricacies of the face, an item from the wrong time period, mixing styles, an off color. All those are clues to authenticity. Thermoluminescence indicates if an artifact was kiln-fired, but most museums can't afford that kind of testing."

"You know a lot for someone who translates ancient texts," said Mnem.

Axie looked through the magnifying glass at Mnem. "Part of the job. Amir traces Middle Eastern myths, which means that fake artifacts lead to fake research results." She returned to examining the funeral stela.

"Does the professor realize how thorough you are?"

"Probably not. Like you said, we've lived too long and have seen too much deception." Axie slipped the magnifying glass back into her purse. "I believe this is an excellent fake made by skilled forger."

"Can you prove—"

A loud *clank* made them both freeze.

"What's that?" whispered Axie.

"Sounds like the elevator." Mnem hurried to the door, switched off the light.

"I wonder how many people are in on this scheme. Do think Amir—"

Mnem put her finger to her lips. "I have a plan. Hurry." She grabbed Axie's hand, left the conservation room, crossed the corridor, and tugged her between the plastic sheeting into the construction area.

"Is there only one way out?" Axie whispered.

Another *clank*. This one followed with a metallic groan.

"Someone's coming down the elevator." Mnem pointed. "There's a delivery exit around the corner but it's locked and alarmed."

"We're trapped."

FIFTY-FIVE

The *clack-clack* of chunky-heeled shoes echoed in the hallway. Mnem and Axie shared a worried glance. This area was off limits to most Gallery Hall personnel. Only a few people knew the elevator code. It might be the construction superintendent or a county inspector. Might even be someone on the board of directors.

The back of Axie's neck bristled. "What are we going to do? Hide down here all day?"

A slow smile curved Mnem's lips. "Nope." She snatched Axie's hand. "Go with it." Mnem rattled the plastic sheeting. "Geeze, they make it difficult to get out of here." With a loud flourish, she pulled back the sheeting. "That's the new conservation room that Miguel wants to get more financing—oh!"

"What are you doing down here?" Phoebe Lawson, in a severe black suit and starched white shirt, glared at Mnem.

Mnem wrapped her arm around Axie's waist. "I'm sorry but I wanted to show my friend around. She's a—"

"You don't have clearance for this floor." Phoebe's chin jutted forward. "How did you get here?"

Mnem widened her eyes. "The elevator. It was open. I just walked right in."

Phoebe's eyes narrowed. "Open, you say?"

"It's a really old elevator. It probably got stuck?" Mnem shrugged, did her best to look innocent.

Phoebe lifted the small two-way radio from her jacket pocket. "This is Lawson. Call the elevator company and the alarm company immediately." She clicked off. "You're not permitted down here, and you should have reported the broken elevator."

"I didn't see the harm. I've been down here already, remember? With the senator?"

"With. The. Senator. That's entirely different."

"I didn't realize. I won't do it again. Promise," said Mnem.

"That's right, you won't." Phoebe put out her hand. "Give it to me."

"Give what? Do you think I took something?"

"I want your Gallery Hall employee identification." Phoebe pointed at the ID hanging from a silk cord around Mnem's neck. "You're fired."

Mnem's eyes widened further, this time for real. "For showing my friend the new room under construction?"

"For going into a prohibited area." Phoebe gestured to the old conservation room. "This area has priceless artwork and artifacts. Insubordination and a flagrant disregard for our rules will not be tolerated." She wiggled her fingers. "Now."

Mnem handed over the badge.

Phoebe clicked on the two-way radio again. "This is Lawson. I need security to meet me at the basement elevator. They need to see an ex-employee out." She clicked off.

"Follow me, ladies." She marched down the hall with loud, fast Ferragamo clacks. "Your friend is also banned— forever banned—from Gallery Hall." She pressed the UP button, then turned around to snap a photograph of Axie.

The door rattled open. "You may have an unparalleled knowledge of ancient art, Mnem, but neither I nor the board will tolerate insubordination. Even if you *are* currently fucking the senator." She stepped into the elevator.

Axie's lips made a little 'o'.

Mnem tilted her head. "Do they tolerate fakes in their museum?"

Phoebe turned her head whiplash fast. "Excuse me?"

"There are fakes in the museum." Mnem met her eyes.

"That's absurd. The board does not display forgeries or replicas."

"I beg to differ."

Phoebe lifted her chin, her nose in the air. "You don't have an art degree, do you? You only know some ancient artifacts and tell a few enchanting stories about the times. Stories mixed with a few facts. Entertaining for our visitors to be sure. But you're not qualified to determine what is authentic or fake, are you? Or did you leave that bit of schooling out?"

"I'm not technically trained." *Maybe I do need Mr. Addison Austin's services. I'll pay extra for a master's degree in art history.*

"Every item in Gallery Hall has been authenticated by experts." Phoebe looked down her nose at Mnem. "You're a hack, a nobody."

Mnem's finger hooked around a tendril of her dark hair. "A nobody with a senator boyfriend."

Phoebe's face turned glacial. "For the senator's sake— because he is a supporter of Gallery Hall—I will do my best to make sure that your dismissal for endangering museum property is not made public."

Mnem's mouth dropped open. "I didn't endanger anything."

"No? You claim we have fakes in our museum. That's slander." Phoebe glared, looked like she was ready to pounce. "I see the headlines now: Senator's Lover Slanders Museum After Attempt to Destroys Priceless Artifacts."

"What?! You can't do that, you can't—"

"Keep talking and it will get worse."

The elevator doors slid open. Two security guards stood in the vestibule.

"Miss Mnem?" Carlos, the security guard, blinked, then looked at Phoebe. "Not Miss Mnem. I love her stories."

Phoebe scowled. "Escort Mnem and her friend off Gallery Hall premises."

"My purse is in the employees' room," mumbled Mnem.

"Fine," Phoebe snapped and turned to Axie. "Have we met before?"

"No." Axie masked both her annoyance and relief at not being recognized as Amir's date for the gala. Not surprising. People like Phoebe only remembered important people. "It's the first time I've been to Gallery Hall. Looks like it will be my last."

Phoebe lifted her haughty chin and strode away.

After Mnem retrieved her purse, the security guards escorted them out.

"I'm sad to see you go, Miss Mnem. Your stories helped me understand art a whole lot better. They were funny too," said Carlos.

"Thank you. I'll miss this place."

Axie sidled close to Mnem as they headed for the parking lot. "Your boss over-reacted, don't you think?"

"That's just her, rude and full of imagined self-importance," said Mnem. "Were you able to tell if she lied about there being no fakes in the museum?"

"That power is gone. If there was even a grain of sand left of it, I would have figured out Amir's game in a flash." Axie glanced over her shoulder. "She's watching us."

Mnem looked back.

Phoebe Lawson stood there with her hands on her hips, an inscrutable look on her face.

FIFTY-SIX

She had to do it. Now. Best to get it over with. She hated confrontation. Wasn't very good at it. It wasn't her fault. The ex-Thai goddess of good fortune, wealth, and beauty spent a thousand lifetimes helping others make their own good fortune. Not herself.

Naret put her hands together. Five mind-clearing breaths later, she knocked on the door and poked her head into Daanish Das's office. It was furnished with an unsuccessful attempt to impress with oversized leather club chairs, a glossy desk, and an American flag in the corner. A large pot of lucky bamboo stood in the other. His office would not fool his wealthy immigrant clients who were familiar with authentic luxury, not cheap leather and a shiny particle board desk.

"Did you have a chance to look into those programs we discussed earlier?" asked Naret.

Daanish looked up from his computer. "It's in the works."

"You said that two weeks ago."

It seemed simple enough. Establish a program whereby

wealthy immigrants subsidized their less fortunate employees' vocational training and English classes. The lucky
helping the less fortunate.

"These things take time. You can't get them started like
that." He snapped his fingers.

"I understand, but establishing the program was a
condition of my working for you. Of being the Asian arm
of your business."

"More like tongue." Daanish guffawed at his joke.

Naret didn't smile. "My linguist tongue makes you
money."

"And my business savvy cuts your paycheck."

"I want to help the less fortunate."

"That's what I love about you," said Daanish. "You
keep me honest."

"That's not my job." Naret managed a fake smile. She
wanted this discussion to be productive, not accusatory.
"What can I do to untangle the red tape?"

Daanish leaned back in his chair. "That's a kind offer,
but I *am* working on it."

Naret's lips pushed into an irritated pout, then she softened her expression and tried a different tact. "You're very
busy. The program will make no money; however, it will
earn good will, which is invaluable. Let me do the foot
work, I'll get it up and running for you."

Daanish shifted in the chair. "There's protocol to
follow. Toes I don't want to step on."

"Are you saying I don't have the skills or
know-how to—"

"Don't misunderstand." Daanish lifted both hands,
palms forward. "I want it to happen. Rich immigrants help
their less fortunate compadres. It's a great idea, but there's
a lot of bureaucracy to wade through, laws I have to make
sure we don't break, you know?"

No, she didn't know. But she knew an excuse when she heard it. "Creating a non-profit organization isn't that difficult to set up."

Daanish flipped back his long bangs. "I'll get on it the moment I have time." He slid a six-inch-tall stack of folders across the shiny mahogany desk. "These are the new requests for expedited citizenship. Review the files and make contact."

Naret saw through his little power play. Didn't give him the satisfaction of reacting. "When did all these come in?"

Daanish's eyes lit up. "Word's getting out. It's happening like I told you. We're going to make some serious money."

Naret picked up the stack, returned to her desk, and set down the folders as gently as her anger allowed. She imagined throwing them across the room. Watching the papers flutter through the air. These cases were *her* case. Like her hopes for the future, scattered and reliant on someone else. With a heavy sigh, Naret opened the first file and made the overseas call to China.

The hopeful immigrant was wealthy and charming but ignored Naret's attempts to discover anything but the vaguest information about his business. Import/export. Trinkets. People love trinkets. He had a family. A large one. All eager to invest in America. Ready to employ people. Ready to live the American Dream. Lots of relatives in the import/export business.

Mr. Big Import/Export said it without saying it. I'm willing to pay big dollars to get to the head of the immigration line.

Naret explained the process. Assured him their service was a hundred percent legitimate and legal. Mr. Big Import/Export asked where she came from. Naret glanced at his address, noted the province, and stated another.

Alliances and family were important to her people. She didn't want Mr. Big Import/Export to claim ties. Although it didn't matter. Money—more specifically the opportunity to invest in America—fast-tracked a wealthy immigrant.

Discussion concluded, worries allayed, Naret hung up. She was the goddess of wishes, abundance, wealth, prosperity, luck, and beauty. Her dealings with Mr. Big Import/Export guaranteed his wish for wealth. His luck was in finding a service that expedited his continued prosperity. It was a beautiful thing for him and his family. But it turned rancid in Naret's stomach. Like rotten fruit. With worms.

Naret checked her bank account. Too many withdrawals. Her balance dropped faster than sand through an hourglass. The rancid feeling in her stomach congealed into a putrid sludge. A few months ago, Mr. Big Import/Export and she had not been all that different. She never worried about money. Never worried about anything. Never considered, really considered, what it was like to stare at a dwindling bank balance. If she wanted something, she bought it. When she tired of it, she discarded it.

Naret considered all the beneficent things she could have done. *Should* have done while a goddess. Found trade schools. Provide small business opportunities. Write inspirational articles or books.

Naret glanced at the stack. Hours' worth of work were ahead. All the same. Wealthy people paying to go to the head of the line. Wealth buying more wealth. Although, there was nothing wrong with that *per se*—the world would never be fair, could never be fair—these people did not require an ex-goddess's help.

The phone buzzed. It was a group message from Inna.
Ten thousand followers!

Inna pushed the stack away, as if putting another few

inches of distance between her and the case files might soothe her sour stomach. She walked back to Daanish's office.

"Remember when I said I would try this job out?" she asked.

Daanish tossed his head, his long bangs messy. "Uh-uh."

"I tried. It's not working out."

Daanish's jaw slid from side to side. "You want a raise."

"No."

"Ah, very clever." He bobbed his head. "You want a percent of the profits?"

"No. Thank you for allowing me to try out this job, but it's not a good fit."

Daanish's bushy brows knitted close. "Are you joking? You're the perfect fit. Clients love you. You're fast, accurate, and upbeat. How can this job not fit you?"

"It's too small for my soul." Naret went to her desk, grabbed her Gucci purse from the bottom drawer and, head held high, strode out the door.

Naret's sour stomach settled. She had real work to do. Goddess worthy work. Naret just didn't know what it was.

FIFTY-SEVEN

Professor Amir Azam looked yummy with his three-day-old stubble, tailored gray suit, and Bally wingtips. No wonder women swooned. He oozed sexual prowess. He stood with his wife and four notables with PhD after their names and clinked champagne flutes in celebration. The university and other distinguished academics celebrated the completion of Dr. Amir Azam's new book. All the academic Somebody's were present. They gobbled down cold shrimp, bacon-wrapped dates, and mini goat cheese pizzas.

They hailed it as the definitive book on Middle Eastern mythology. A superlative codex of ancient myths, explanations, and lexicon. Axie heard all their fawning compliments. A champagne flute in her hand, she stood at the bar and surveyed the room. Amir had invited only a few PhD candidates. Women only. They were eager, fawning co-eds with an over fondness for the ancient world. A world of tyrants and slaves and hardship. A world of breathtaking beauty, magnificent craftsmanship, and unparalleled wisdom.

Axie sipped the champagne. She knew one thing they did not. The modern world was a diluted version of everything. Of sky and sea and terra. Of morals and laws and purity and wisdom. Yet these mortals, instead of becoming more temperate and tolerant, became less so.

Despite Axie's joining Amir's research team late in the process, she provided a nuanced understanding of the oldest texts. Subtleties long covered by the shamal winds. Her knowledge alone gave Amir's book the scholarly edge.

Axie plucked a lamb morsel from a passing server. It was sweet and tender. The opposite of her feelings when Amir had set the final copy of the manuscript on her desk a week ago. "All done. Not a comma error in sight." He leaned close, his lips hovering over her ear. "I need you, Axie. You're my muse. Please consider going to Göbekli Tepe with me."

Axie read the acknowledgements page first. All ten gratitude-coated pages. Her name was missing. She flipped to the reference section at the back of the book. No name there either. Axie, her anger rising like a river after a storm, pushed away the manuscript. Disgust clogged her throat. Disgust for Amir. Disgust at herself for not navigating the shark-infested waters of humanity.

Ancient memories rushed back as Axie watched the academic elite toast their cerebral superiority. They knew nothing. Understood nothing. No, that wasn't true. They understood greed and arrogance. Academic elitists took the place of kings and royals. Same authority, different name.

Axie emptied the champagne flute. Was Professor Amir Azam part of the forgery scam at Gallery Hall? Or was he an unwitting participant? There was no way to know.

Axie sauntered toward the tight knit group of academics while Amir's wife threw dagger looks at her approach.

"Ah, Axie, come here." Amir waved her forward. "This is one of my research assistants, Axie Khan. This woman was a godsend, her gift for translating ancient texts has no equal. I have no doubt she will go far."

Amir's wife narrowed her eyes in warning despite the polite smile frozen on her lips.

"Will you be working on Amir's next project?" asked a middle-aged man with a scraggly beard.

Axie tugged at her French cuffs. "Perhaps. A trip to Göbekli Tepe sounds exciting."

Amir tossed Axie a quick look, his mouth politely curved, his eyes alight with naughty pleasures.

"Will you be going, Yasmine?" An old man in a tweed suit turned to Amir's wife.

"Not this time," said Yasmine. "I have two commissions to finish."

Tweed Suit glanced at Axie. "Not only does Yasmine have a doctorate in art history, she's a world-renowned artist."

"Oh, Robert, you do exaggerate." Yasmine pretended humility. "I only have a few pieces at two art galleries in Qatar at the moment."

"What's your preferred medium?" asked Axie.

"Sculptures," said Tweed Suit. "Incredible sculptures. Breathtaking in their detail." He turned to Axie. "Well out of this professor's price range."

"Yasmine," said Scraggly Beard, "Will you carve a soap bar for me?"

Everyone laughed. Axie too. But she hoped her champagne flute was not shaking.

It all made sense. Amir and his wife's invitation to the museum gala. His wife's insistence that he would never leave. Who better than an artist to make fakes? It wasn't culture obligations that kept them together. They were both thieves in an art fraud scheme.

A hundred questions danced on Axie's tongue. She asked none of them, instead she studied Amir and Yasmine. They didn't *look* dangerous or corrupt at all.

Yasmine steered the discussion back to her husband and his agent's pitching the book to film producers. "The real money is a documentary deal."

Did Yasmine have access to the museum's conservation room? Axie wanted to ask. Caution stopped her.

During a lull in the conversation, Axie excused herself. A strategically bad move for a nobody rubbing elbows with the academic elite. Axie needed fresh air, air free of arrogance and superiority. The bench overlooking the campus green was the perfect place to collect her thoughts.

To message Mnem or not. That was the question. Axie had no proof of Amir's guilt. It was sheer speculation, a deduction on her part.

"There you are." Amir walked outside and sat next to her. "Is everything okay? You hurried off. Dr. Thornbeck wanted to ask you a few questions."

Axie shifted. Amir sat too close. This time it wasn't flirtatious, it felt intimidating.

"Why would I be angry?" Axie pouted her lips, pretended confusion.

"Yasmine and I filed for a separation." Amir spoke quietly. "We haven't made it public yet."

Axie bit back the urge to laugh in his face. "Why are you telling me this?"

"We have feelings for one another." He scooted close, his voice low and husky. "Feelings you and I must no longer deny. Axie, you're my goddess. I can't stop thinking about you."

Axie moved away.

"You're angry because your name isn't listed in the acknowledgements page. I couldn't." Amir ran his hands through his curls. "My wife, my colleagues—it's just not done. The next book for sure. I promise." He glanced back at the doors to the reception room. "I love you, Axie. I've never met anyone like you. I crave your body. Dream of you."

Axie rose from the bench with the regal elegance of a goddess. "Goodbye, Professor Azam."

His brow furrowed. "You're not leaving the party now, are you?"

"I'm leaving, period. I quit."

Amir's brow smoothed into a relieved but sad smile. "You don't have to do that for me. Once my divorce is final our relationship won't need to be a secret."

"We don't have a relationship. We will never have one." Axie reached down to get her purse from the bench.

Amir grabbed her wrist. "You want me. Don't deny it. I can offer you the world."

Axie twisted away. "No thanks."

"You're a nobody, a research sparrow in a cage of academic hawks."

Axie stepped back and considered the pompous mortal with newfound pity. "I ride the Roc and am mightier than you imagine."

The mythological bird with the wingspan and strength to carry an elephant was a prophetic and feared omen in her land.

Axie refused to be involved in art fraud or give her love to a womanizer. The ex-goddess of peace, justice, and victory refused to settle for anything less than respect and honesty.

FIFTY-EIGHT

Secrets were more fun when I was a goddess.

Mnem's secret weighed on her. Luckily, it didn't bother her too much during Miguel's weekday phone calls from Washington DC. The weekends he visited were more problematic, a double-edged sword of sorrow and happiness. The touch of his lips, his scent, his skin's warmth, his adoring eyes… Mnem's conscience pressed on her heart. Shame and guilt were heavy twins.

"Water, no ice, with a lime wedge, please." Mnem set down the menu.

"What's wrong?" Miguel's square jaw slid to the side, his lips compressed tight.

"Why do you ask?"

"You always order a drink, a stiff one at that."

"What are you insinuating?"

"Nothing." Miguel was calm. "I pay attention to you. That's typically a good thing, a caring thing." He unfolded the cloth napkin. "You've been different the last few weeks."

Mnem aligned the silverware. "Really?"

"You're fidgeting. You never fidget. Unless you're worried about something. Is it work?"

Mnem looked up, her face beaming. "Goddesses Inc. exploded, especially after we hit ten thousand followers. Businesses are sending us their products to review, and Inna is learning about all the ways we can monetize."

"That's not the work I was referring to."

Mnem's stiffened. "Goddesses Inc. is work!"

"Whoa," said Miguel, "I didn't say it wasn't. I mean Gallery Hall."

"Oh…that." Mnem dropped her hands in her lap. "Phoebe fired me last week."

Miguel's brows shot up. "What? You know everything about ancient art. Why didn't you tell me?" He looked genuinely hurt.

"I don't want to bother you. You're dealing with lobby-ists and congress and who knows what else. My being fired from a dead-end job isn't important." Her hand toyed with the edge of the linen tablecloth. Mortal pregnancy *did* make her fidgety. And always a breath away from crying. Mortal hormones were horrible.

"Your life is important to me," said Miguel. "What happened?"

"I was in an unauthorized area, the new conservation room."

"Phoebe fired you for that?" Miguel pulled the phone from his pocket. "That doesn't make any sense. I'll take care of this for you."

"Don't." Mnem set her hand over his phone. "I don't want to go back."

"O-kay." Miguel sipped his whiskey. "Why does it feel like you're leaving something important out?"

"Axie was with me. That's all." *We were looking for evidence of art fraud. No big deal. Just two ex-goddesses with an ethical itch in an immoral world.*

"That's all?"

Oh, and Axie suspected the cameleer's funerary stela was fake because of an obscure detail known only to someone who lived during that time.

"That's it." For a split second, Mnem imagined confessing the entire truth. Miguel would be polite and diplomatic, hide his pity, and then he would cease all contact with his crazy ex-girlfriend.

Which was one way to end the relationship.

There was another reason. The art forgeries business was huge, their net wide. Mnem didn't want Miguel embroiled in a scandal he could be connected to.

Miguel tapped his phone. "One phone call, Mnem, and I get your job back."

Mnem shook her head, sipped the water. "I appreciate the offer but no."

"What are you going to do? Apply at another museum? You're the perfect fit for that."

Mnem's brow furrowed, indignant. "Is that so!" She forgot how Miguel saw her. He didn't see a thousands-year-old woman. He saw youth and inexperience.

Miguel narrowed his eyes, the cleft in his square jaw deepening. "You're knowledgeable. Your stories about art are riveting. It was meant as a compliment." Familiar with the grandstanding, tantrums, and melodramas in Washington, he figured Mnem was having a bad day. God knew, he had plenty of them. "I have an idea, maybe you should write a book."

Mnem's irritation melted. "A book…" She looked away, her mind sweeping through the centuries. "Why haven't I thought of that?" *Because it doesn't pay the utility or grocery bill. Because goddesses are not permitted to publish.* Mnem's lips curled into a genuine smile as she thought of the possibilities now open to her as a mere mortal.

"When you're ready, I'll give you the name of a few agents," said Miguel.

Mnem studied the man across the table like a detective in search of a clue. Senator Miguel Flores. Tall. Robust. Handsome. Calm. With enough charisma to fill Mount Olympus. Charming and unflappable. Perfect. Too perfect. Everyone had faults. Mortals and immortals alike. What was Miguel's?

"Do you ever get riled?" Mnem dipped the bread into the olive tapenade.

"Never in public."

"I've never seen you upset in private either."

"Why would I be upset if I'm alone with you?" He grinned. "You're the highlight of my week."

Mnem's body warmed under his gaze.

Miguel basked in her glow, then cleared his throat. "If you need professional connections, I'm your man. Just ask."

It was tempting. Except then Mnem would feel beholden to Miguel. Another complication she didn't need.

"I'll let you know," said Mnem. "Thanks for the offer."

"Have you considered my *other* offer?"

Mnem shifted in her seat, scratched at her palms. Every topic of tonight's discussion made her nervous. "About making our dating official?"

"That's the one."

The server set down dinner, roasted lamb for Mnem and pan-seared shark for Miguel.

"Sweeten the deal with a rider." Mnem purred, her old goddess spunk emerging despite her worries.

Miguel's brows lifted. "Somebody's been studying legislative verbiage. A rider…mmm." He rubbed his palms together. "You also get my heart, amazing sex, fabulous parties, scandalous gossip, and to be part of the VIP crowd."

"It's the VIP crowd that's concerning."

Miguel sliced into the shark. "It's nothing you can't handle."

"I need more time." *More time to figure you out. More time to adjust to mortal pregnancy.*

"I understand." Miguel set down his fork, his eyes warm. "Don't break my heart."

Mnem's heart tightened. That was her plan. Even though she was falling hard for him. Secrecy and relationships don't mix. Besides, their relationship would never be healthy when Mnem's soul was sick. When her pregnancy interfered with his ambitions. When her ancient past had to remain hidden.

"Break your heart? Never. But I may bruise it," said Mnem, her tone falsely playful.

HOURS LATER, after a vigorous sexual romp, Mnem left the bed to sit on the deck overlooking the ocean. Miguel loved her, but she no longer loved herself.

Mnem loved the child in her womb yet suspected mortal motherhood tested all women in a million different ways. She wrapped her arms around her knees and let the tears flow.

Miguel watched Mnem from the bedroom. Saw her shaking shoulders and suspected she hid secrets. Big secrets. Secrets he must uncover before the press did.

FIFTY-NINE

"It's what mortals do. Celebrate. That's why they invented champagne."

Mnem begged to differ but kept silent.

"Twenty thousand followers are a big deal." Inna was as proud as a mother watching her child graduate from college. "It's an accomplishment."

Inna insisted on the celebration. The guest list was short: Four ex-goddesses and nine muses. Inna ordered lunch from the local organic restaurant, bought a pink cake with sprinkles from the bakery, and purchased five helium balloons.

Mnem tied the shiny mylar puffs to a chair. "Why five?"

"Because we're aiming for fifty thousand followers by the end of the month." Naret pulled five wish boats from a paper bag. "Inna wants us to be influencers."

Calliope hugged each ex-goddess. "We're so proud. And I have to admit, we were worried about you all."

Eight muses nodded in unison.

"Looks like you became each other's muse." Calliope winked.

"Muse and annoyer." Axie held a wish boat of white camellias, daisies, and heliotrope.

"In a good way," said Inna.

Melpomene made herself a drink at the bar. "Have you heard the latest about FEM?"

"We're out of the birdie loop, remember?" said Inna. "We don't hear a peep."

"FEM dismissed more goddesses than initially thought," said Polymnia.

"How many?" asked Inna. "Fifty? A thousand?"

"No one knows." Calliope gave her sisters a warning look. "But everyone is talking about it."

"Not in the FEM building." Clio fiddled with the gold charms on her bracelet, her fingers brushing against the finely crafted book, scroll, quill, and ink pot.

Mnem knew all her daughters' mannerisms. Knew when they were bothered or hiding something.

Clio rubbed the gold quill charm between her fingers. "The layoff and the bomb are causing a lot of speculation."

"Do you know something?" asked Mnem, knowing perfectly well she did.

Clio glanced at Calliope, who gave an affirming nod.

"Not about that, but about the uptick in unusual bird sightings." Clio let go of the charm bracelet.

"Shee's spying on everyone, is that it?" asked Naret.

"Every goddess and ex-goddess," nodded Terpsichore. "We're all walking on eggshells."

"Tell them about the email," said Melpomene.

Calliope poured herself a small glass of ouzo. "We're not a hundred percent certain, but we think everyone received the same one. It said, the world is experiencing an unprecedented amount of change and FEM must change with it."

"And the merger with MAS is still being negotiated. Merger? Ha!" Thalia laughed. "Our past mergers only mucked up thinks for mortals. Except for us." She twirled around. "Best merger, ever."

Melpomene rolled her eyes. "Everyone anticipates more downsizing."

Mnem crossed her arms. "The world never stops changing but mortals don't change at all. Not at their core. We know this. FEM and MAS know this."

"Momma, I'm sorry to disagree, but you're wrong." Erato twirled her finger around a tendril of hair. "The struggles for food, education, and shelter are greatly reduced. Mortal adults desire play more than ever. They want to be taken to a magical and fantastical world. They crave twenty-four-hour amusement. Entertainment is their opiate and they have it at their fingertips." She jiggled her phone.

"Someone still has to create that entertainment," said Axie.

Calliope dropped ice cubes into the glass. "Sometimes, but often it's as easy as videoing an event on your phone."

"The more mortals consume entertainment, the less deeply they think," said Melpomene. "It's a tragedy."

"There are many impoverished countries where mortals struggle for basic necessities." Inna frowned. "That's the true tragedy."

"Yes, but only because of evil regimes. Man-made reasons." Thalia joined her sister at the bar.

No one disagreed. Mortals were their own worst enemies.

Inna and Mnem set the fresh spring rolls, Greek wrap, chimichurri bowl, and Persian pomegranate stew on the table. The conversation turned to lighter topics. The growth of Goddesses Inc, the assortment of products they tested, and their techno mishaps.

"Where do you find the time for Goddesses Inc?" asked Euterpe as she plucked a fish taco from the platter.

Inna, Mnem, Naret, and Axie wore identical grimaces.

"Well…." said Axie. "Mnem, Naret, and I all quit our jobs."

"Why?" asked Calliope. "You were happy when you got them."

"A variety of reasons." Mnem waved her hand dismissively. "We'll find better ones."

The nine muses were not fooled.

Mnem, her heart overflowing with pride, watched her daughters as they chatted and moved around the feast-filled table. Each daughter was a delight. A gift to humankind. More important to the world than mortals were capable of comprehending.

My children.

The proud smile slid from Mnem's face. *The child growing inside will toil and struggle. Will experience mistakes, mishaps, and misery. I will be powerless to protect the blood of my blood.* Fear clung to Mnem like nettles on a wool shawl.

"Oh, Momma, why such a wistful look on this happy day?" asked Thalia.

"She doesn't have a drink, that's why," said Calliope.

"I'll get it." Terpsichore headed for the bar. "What do you want? More champagne? An iced ouzo? How about a nice dirty martini?"

"A sparkling water with a lime wedge sounds delicious," said Mnem.

Terpsichore stopped in her tracks, her head whipped around. "What?"

"You heard me."

Ourania scanned the room. "Momma, where's your champagne glass?"

Mnem waved her hand in the general direction.

Melpomene picked it up. "It's full."

Nine muses shared a troubled glance.

"Why are you not drinking, Momma?" asked Calliope.

Mnem shrugged, waved off their concern. "I have a mortal body now, remember?"

"Inna," Calliope's eyes narrowed. "Why isn't Momma drinking?"

SIXTY

Nine muses felt the air shift. Untold secrets were storm clouds, dense and dark and threatening.

Inna didn't dare look at Mnem. This wasn't her secret to tell. "Maybe she's not thirsty."

Calliope frowned. Knew a lie when she heard it. "Axie?"

"Maybe Mnem is hung over." Axie crossed her arms.

Calliope next aimed her stare at Naret.

Naret plucked a spring roll from the platter. "These look delicious. Mmm, I smell lemongrass."

"Are you on medication, Momma?" asked Melpomene. "Did you catch a mortal disease?"

"No." Mnem ladled Persian pomegranate walnut stew into a bowl. "You're making a big deal over nothing."

"Are you on a mortal diet that forbids alcohol?" asked Clio.

"Mortal diets are a form of torture." Erato bit into a wrap stuffed with feta, lamb, olives, and cucumbers.

Mnem felt Calliope's studied stare from across the table. Her daughter was going down a mental list of reasons why Momma wasn't drinking. Calliope was methodical and logical. It wouldn't take too long until she concluded that—

"Modern mortal women do not drink alcohol when they're pregnant," said Calliope.

Eight muses burst out laughing. Thalia snorted champagne from her nose, sending them into another fit of laughter. Except for Calliope. She watched her mother's reaction. Watched her blush a deep rosy pink. Saw her eyes drop to her belly.

"Momma…" Calliope's voice was soft, hesitant.

Mnem swept her gaze over each daughter. "I'm pregnant with Senator Miguel Flores's progeny."

Melpomene paled, her face slack with horror. "Momma, you're too old!"

Euterpe's hands flew to her cheeks. "You can't possibly be pregnant! Your womb is ancient."

Inna sucked in her lips to keep from laughing.

"I hope it's a girl," said Polymnia. "It has to be a girl."

"Oh dear." Clio rubbed the back of her neck. "A mortal baby."

"How horrible," whispered Melpomene.

Clio shoved her sister. "I think it's wonderful."

"I'm going to be an auntie!" Terpsichore wiggled in her seat. "I'll teach her to dance and sing and—"

"I will teach her the power of words and stories." Calliope rounded the table to give Mnem a hug. "This child will be the most creative, educated, and amazing mortal child ever!"

Ourania wrapped her arms around Mnem. "I'll show this child the world."

They all gave Mnem a hug. Some more joyful than others. Their respect and love for Mnemosyne was not reduced. Quite the opposite. They were in awe of Mnem's emotional strength and courage.

"I hate to burst your bubble, but it may be a boy who wants to play football," said Axie.

"Then he will play football and still be the most educated and creative child in the world," said Calliope.

Inna, Naret, and Axie watched the muses' comments fly across the table like a tennis ball during a match. The forehands. Easy volleys. Lobs. Backhands.

"What did Miguel say when you told him?" asked Melpomene.

There it was. The Smash.

Mnem set her spoon down and stood up from the table. "I haven't told him." She folded her arms.

"What!" The chorus of nine rose from the table.

"He has a right to know." Calliope was indignant.

"This isn't *The Iliad* or *The Odyssey*," said Mnem. "This is real life."

"You're going to tell him, aren't you, Momma?" Erato's lower lip pushed into an offended pout. "You love him, don't you?"

Mnem burst into tears. "Damn these mortal hormones. I don't know what to do. It will ruin his career."

Clio waggled her arms, her charm bracelet clinking. "It may temporarily put a dent in his career—"

"Dents can be fixed." Euterpe added. "A flat note in a political melody, that's all."

"It won't crash his career," said Terpsichore. "It's a stumble, a misstep, no big deal."

"He's the savior of the party." Calliope, repeating the press's oft-spoken words, lifted both hands to the sky as though beseeching the goddesses.

"Muses!" Inna's sharp voice jolted the muses silent. "This is about your mother not the senator."

The muses looked from one to the other. Their eyes speaking louder than their collective voices.

"Inna's right," said Calliope. "Any of us are able to help the senator whenever we like. But, Momma, there must be a reason *why* you haven't told him."

"We'd like to know too." Inna plucked a Greek wrap from the platter.

Mnem stared down at her plate, her body still, her mind spinning with the ferocity of Charybdis.

"Are you afraid?" Erato's voice was a whisper.

Mnem lifted her head. "I'm petrified." She touched her belly. "I'm petrified of this tiny mortal growing inside me. It will be defenseless in this world. It will bleed. Get hurt. And die. This child will die."

"Goddess willing, not for a very long time," said Calliope. "Eighty years is the average mortal lifespan these days."

"You'll be dead when that happens." Melpomene cringed the moment she uttered the last word.

Everyone else winced.

Mnem dropped into her chair and closed her eyes.

Calliope's hand rested on Mnem's shoulder. "You must tell him, Momma."

"I'm not ready." Mnem lifted her head again. She hated that her daughters saw her this way. Weak, defeated, afraid.

"Mortals are never ready for any of the big changes in their life," said Clio. "It's what makes them uniquely irrational."

"When *will* you be ready to tell the senator that you carry his child?" asked Inna.

When indeed.

SIXTY-ONE

Inna tapped SHARE on InstaPics. Another product review posted. Five hearts for the lip balm in a compostable tube. She clicked on their website— Goddesses Inc. was three-hours short of a fulltime job now —when the doorbell rang. Again and again. Probably an obnoxiously persistent delivery person.

Inna added **get post office box** to her to-do list.

The doorbell ran three more times.

"I'm coming," shouted Inna as she hurried down the hall. She flung open the door.

"I don't care about your past. I miss you." Duncan stood on the front porch. A baseball hat was pulled down low over his forehead, his muscular body concealed in an off-brand t-shirt and baggy sweatpants. A superstar incognito.

Neither his Maserati, Mercedes, nor Range Rover were in the driveway. Maria's Honda was.

"We need to talk." Duncan pressed his large hands together, his long thick fingers perfectly aligned. "I had an epiphany." His eyes were soft with hope, his mouth curved into a shy smile.

Inna's heart thumped fast and hard. Denial was futile. Duncan was special, made her feel as giddy as a teenager and as excited as a bride.

In spite of her better judgement, Inna let him in.

"Thank you, babe—Inna." Duncan's lips spread into a relieved smile.

Inna strode into her living room and crossed her arms. "I'm waiting."

"Huh?" Duncan's eyes darted around the room, took in the desk, large computer monitor, small stacked boxes, and large parcels piled on the floor.

"Explain your epiphany." Inna tapped her foot.

"Is this all for Goddesses Inc.?"

"Yes. Epiphany, please. I'm busy."

"I found God, Inna. I found him." Duncan patted his chest. "I lost him a long time ago. Money and contracts and fame had become my god."

"Did you forget to pay homage to him?" Inna asked, knowing quite a few gods who required weekly, if not daily, rituals of worship.

"Huh?" Duncan cocked his head. "Oh, I get it. It's true, I paid way too much homage to myself and not enough to God. But when you left me, I started to think about my life, my goals and successes, and I discovered something." His fist pressed to his heart. "Success is nothing without someone to share it with." He moved toward Inna, took her hands in his. "I want a family and children. Lots of children. I want to give back to my community. I want to share my success."

The warmth of Duncan's love traveled through Inna's hand, up her arm, and nestled in her heart. She looked up into his loving eyes.

"I don't care if you have some horrible past you want to hide. I look at you and I see love. I look at you and I see hope. I see honesty and—this is going to sound weird —bounty."

"Bounty?" Inna whispered. It was a familiar word. One describing the ex-goddess of the harvest, justice, and protection. Her eyes grew hot, tears welling. One slipped past her armor of composure to slide down her cheek.

Duncan's face glowed with adoration. "I promise never to cheat on you. Ever. I'll sign a prenup that gives you fifty percent of what I'm worth." Duncan knelt down. "My soul needs you. My heart needs you."

Inna's lower lip quivered. "I don't like needy men."

Duncan grinned. "I know you don't. That's why I'm going to be the man *you* need. The man who fills your days with joy. The man you can rely on for anything." He glanced at the desk in the corner. "The man who will never hold you down from your dreams and goals." His lips pressed onto her palm. "You're my goddess, Inna. I live to serve you."

Inna pushed his baseball cap off his head. "I'm your goddess?"

"I will worship you the rest of my days."

Ripples of happiness coursed through Inna's body. Men and women had said this before. But never that way. Their devotion had been abstract and pious. This was real. "Then I suggest you visit my altar."

Hours later, glowing and tingling with love's afterglow, Inna traced the ridges of Duncan's god-like abdominal muscles. For thousands of years, Inna's power inspired promise keeping. Oaths taken in her name were binding. Did a vestigial trace of the divine power remain? Was it enough to keep his marriage vows? Or was Shee playing a lesson-in-mortals joke on Inna? Was Shee's intent to make the protectress of justice and promises a lovestruck dupe?

"Mmm." Duncan opened his brown eyes, hazy with love and satisfaction. "Will you marry me?"

"Yes." The affirmation came despite Inna's better judgement.

"Will you have all my babies?"

"All?" Inna's fingers walked up his chest. "How many do you want?"

"As many as you will have."

"Let's take it one at a time." Was pregnancy a possibility? Why not? Mnem conceived.

"I have a request." Duncan rested his head on his hand. "Even though I'm a Christian man I want to name our children after the Nigerian gods and goddesses."

"Why?"

"As a testament to the spark of the divine in all of us."

Inna's full heart burst and joyful tears flowed down her face.

SIXTY-TWO

It felt like a bee sting in her belly. A pricked pain followed by an outward spreading. Mnem knew the feeling. It was a premonition. Whether it was divine residue or mortal intuition didn't matter. The feeling began the second she opened her eyes in the morning and increased with each passing hour.

Mnem glanced at her Rolex. Noon. The uneasiness now permeated every part of her being.

The doorbell rang. The premonition spiked, set Mnem's heart racing. She opened the door.

"There she is, the woman who makes my heart and loins ache." Senator Miguel Flores flicked his thumb over his shoulder. "Your chariot awaits."

The chariot was an old orange Jeep with the top off.

Mnem stayed in the doorway. "Aren't you supposed to be in Washington this week?"

"Change of plans. Came home early. Thought I'd surprise you with a quick trip." Miguel grinned, his brows high. He looked like a little boy on Christmas morning.

"Now?"

"Yes, that's why it's a surprise."

"Where to?" Mnem put her hands on her hips.

"A little place I know. It's very private."

"Am I dressed appropriately?" Mnem tugged on the frayed hem of her denim shorts.

Miguel's gaze roved up and down her body, from her messy top bun to the Converse All Stars on her feet. "Perfect."

Mnem blushed, pretended to fuss with the sleeves of her rolled-up white shirt. "I'll get my purse."

The purse was a Louis Vuitton backpack, one she stuffed with a package of saltines. It helped stave off the nausea that struck without warning. Five minutes later, Mnem strapped on the seatbelt. "A trip sounds divine." *I need something to divert my attention from joblessness and pregnancy.*

Miguel smiled but Mnem could have sworn his brow creased for a fraction of a second.

"Where are we going? Someplace rugged, I'm guessing."

"Don't let the designer suits fool you, Mnem. I'm a country guy not a city boy. I prefer wide open spaces and the grass beneath my feet."

"Your Brooks Brothers suit fooled me." Mnem tugged on his tie.

"My clothes are in the duffle in the back seat." Miguel gripped the stick shift. "How is Goddesses Inc. going? Looks like you have a lot more followers."

Mnem shared their latest successes. Their conversation flowed easier than the drive—Los Angeles rush hour was twenty-four-hours long. They laughed, commiserated, and poked fun at one another. Mnem's premonition vanished. Miguel always put her at ease. Mnem was herself. Well, almost.

"Homes as far as you can see," said Mnem as their

eastbound drive took them past countless cities, towns, close-packed homes, and strip malls. *Millions of mortals.*

"Everyone wants to live here." Miguel merged onto a northbound freeway.

"The mountains?" Mnem missed the jagged peaks of the Greek mountains. Missed the fragrance of her homeland, the scent of the air.

"I bought a small place a few years ago. Used my sister's name."

"You have a sister?" *I don't know this man at all.*

"Her name is Gloria," he said. "I'd like you to meet my family one day."

"Tell me about this secret place you're taking me to."

"It's secluded and has a wonderful view of the lake."

"This is a long drive for an evening out."

"Oh? Didn't I tell you? I'm kidnapping you until tomorrow." Miguel dragged his fingers through his already wind-tousled hair. "May I tie you up?"

Mnem pantomimed tying a fisherman's knot. "I'd rather tie *you* up."

"Even better." Miguel took the off-ramp onto a two-lane highway.

The terrain was spectacular as it snaked up the mountain pass. Mnem leaned against the headrest, inhaled the fresh pine air, and watched the valley pass. Her soul longed for home. The idea of returning to give birth in Greece, to live out the rest of her days looked better and better each day.

Fifteen minutes later, Mnem set her hand on her belly and groaned.

"Car sick? The windy roads will do that. Keep your eyes straight ahead, we're almost there."

That only worked for motion sickness.

Miguel slowed down and turned onto another road. "Not far now."

"Do you take all your kidnapped girlfriends here?"

Miguel braked at the stop sign. "You're the first and only."

Mnem's heart lurched in time with the Jeep. The premonition returned, found its way in Mnem's belly again. It didn't mix well with the nausea. "Do you expect me to skinny dip?" She leaned over and kissed his cheek.

"House rules." Miguel kissed her quick and deep, one eye on the road.

Two more turns later, Miguel steered the Jeep into a twisty long flagstone driveway. Mnem waited for the house to appear after every curve but it was hidden in the thick woods.

The next curve opened into a clearing.

Mnem sucked in her breath. "I expected a cabin."

The house was mansion-sized, a custom log home with multiple steep roofs and a bright red rocking chair on the front porch. A cardboard box blocked the door.

Miguel pulled under the portico. "I like space. Helps me think. Do you like it?"

"It's certainly a big house for one man."

After grabbing his duffle bag from the back, Miguel opened Mnem's door. "Maybe one day it will be full of children." He took her hand. "Only my immediate family knows about this place. If you tell anyone…" he winked and slid his eyes toward the pine forest.

"I'll rise from the dead to haunt you forever." Mnem slung her backpack over her shoulder.

Mnem fell in love with the house the moment she stepped inside. The home was huge but warm and inviting with colorful handwoven textiles, aged wood, and inter- esting art. She wandered around the living room, ran her hands over the wool blankets, and large stone fireplace. "South American art?"

"Yes, most of it is Mayan." Miguel set the box on the marble counter that separated the kitchen from the living area.

"You're from Mexico?"

"My ancestors come from central America. There might be a Mexican or two in there." He pulled containers from the box. "I ordered lamb for you and steak for me."

"Is this a real jade mask?" Mnem touched the primitive piece. She felt the artist's fear of making a mistake while carving it. Felt his pride at a job well done. Felt the power of the ceremonies it was worn for.

"One of my favorites." Miguel put the containers in the oversized refrigerator.

"You have an impressive collection."

There were textiles, masks, figures, panels, and what looked like a carved throne in the living room.

Mnem touched another mask, this one with its tongue sticking out. "These are museum quality."

Miguel shut the refrigerator door and strode to the bar. "Not really." He pulled a few bottles from the shelf. "My grandfather collected them. Their old, but not ancient."

"Old fakes?" asked Mnem. *Something's not right. I feel the art.*

"I really don't know much about their origins." Miguel gave Mnem an odd look. "My grandfather was a ship captain, traveled up and down the central and south American coasts. Rumor has it, he kept a wife and kids in every port. Who knows where he came upon this stuff?" He gestured to the lake view. "Go outside and enjoy the fresh air."

Mnem opened the oversized sliding door and sat on one of the six sturdy rocking chairs that lined the back deck. The lake view was beautiful, the air fresh with pine, the sky a smog-free azure. It should have been calming. It wasn't.

Was Miguel part of the art forgery scam? His lunch meeting with Phoebe makes sense now. And my being fired.

Miguel came outside and set a glass of iced ouzo on the little table next to Mnem. "Your favorite."

"Thank you, but I'd prefer some water."

"With vodka?"

"Just water."

"Still woozy from the drive?" Miguel kissed the top of her head and went back inside.

The lake was blue and inviting, surrounded with towering pines and distant mountains. Birds twittered. A soft breeze caressed her skin. Memories rushed at her.

Mnem was back in ancient Greece. A time of small villages and large temples. When one heard a snake slither across a path and a bee's diligent hum. When watching clouds drift across the sky was considered thoughtful not lazy. When technology's noises did not intrude upon a perfect day, your hopes, your dreams.

When there was time to ponder life, the divine, and the world.

Other memories bubbled up into Mnem's conscious-ness, real enough to snatch out of the air. Pinpoints in time. Mortal faces of lovers and friends. Cities, old and new; conquered and reconquered; destroyed and rebuilt.

Immortals were able to handle the maelstrom of count-less memories. Mortals could not.

Goddess no, I'm having a mortal anxiety attack!

"What's wrong?" Miguel set down her water and kneeled in front of her. He brushed back her hair and wiped the tears from her cheek.

Mnem's body shook with convulsive sobs. "I'm s-s-sorry."

Miguel lifted her chin. "What's wrong? What happened?"

"I was sitting here enjoying the view and then all these memories came from out of nowhere."

"Nature is magic, isn't it? It makes you think. Now you understand why I bought this place. I can't hide from myself here. The silence demands authenticity from me." Miguel sat on the rocker next to hers. "Are your tears happy or sad?"

"They're nostalgic for a time long, long ago."

Miguel's brow furrowed, one eye narrowing with amusement. "You sound like an old woman."

What a stupid mistake. "It feels like a long time since I was a young girl in Greece."

"You were born there?" He popped the tab on his beer.

"Yes."

"When did you leave Greece?"

"When I was five."

"Really? That's impressive. I don't remember much of anything at that age."

"I have a good memory." Mnem tapped her head and forced a smile. Pregnancy hormones were much too inconvenient. She simply must get a handle on them. "It's beautiful here." She sipped the water. "I'm fine now, I promise."

"Are you sure?"

"Kiss me." She wrapped her arms around his neck.

Mnem melted into his warmth, taste, and tongue. Let it dissolve all the memories. Let it dispel her ridiculous suspicions about his being an art thief.

She craved physical pleasure. Needed to lose herself in it. That was the only thing that remained the same since being made mortal. The anticipation, teasing, build-up, sensations, and blissful release kept her sane. Let her touch the delight of divinity for a moment or two. Three if she had any say about it.

Miguel's breath came heavy and urgent. "Mnem…"

Mnem nipped at his lip, pulled away, rose from the chair, and unbuttoned her shirt. She kicked off her shoes and shimmied out of her denim shorts.

Miguel watched with rapt attention. "I love nature."

Mnem flung her bra and panties at him. "Come and get it." She skipped down the steps and ran down the path.

By the time she reached the dock's edge, Miguel was naked and running towards her, his tie, shirt, trousers, and shoes discarded along the way.

Mnem dove in, the chilly water awakening her senses. She wanted to swim across the entire lake, feel her limbs burn with exertion, absorb the water into the skin. Instead she went under and kicked until her lungs came close to bursting. Mnem emerged refreshed and happy.

"Show off!" Miguel dove in, surfaced and shook his head like a wet dog. "Were you on the swim team?"

I swam across countless Aegean and Ionian coves. Dove from high rocky cliffs. Rode upon Neptune's shoulders, scolded sirens, and partied with nymphs. "I like water." She treaded water as he swam towards her. "Took you long enough." She wrapped her legs around his hips and sunk down. "Ahhh…perfect."

Miguel moaned and nuzzled her neck. "This is another reason why I love you."

Afterwards, she wrapped her arms around his shoulders as he made his way slowly towards the dock.

"Hungry?" asked Miguel as they sat on the edge, their legs swinging over the side.

"Starving."

"Good, I also have stuffed grape leaves, potatoes with lemon and oregano, and a *real* Greek salad."

Mnem patted her belly. "Can't wait." Greek food and more Greek food: Her pregnancy cravings. "Is there a Greek restaurant nearby?"

"First generation Greek owner. From..." Miguel tapped his chin. "Gero—something."

"Gerolimenas. It's a tiny village on the Peloponnese coast." Mnem sighed. "It's a beautiful place. We should visit sometime."

"I'd like that." Miguel smiled, but the sudden depth in his gaze made Mnem shiver. "I'd like to ask you something." His voice was light, belied the intensity of his stare. "I need you to be a hundred percent honest."

Mnem's premonition, the one that lurked all morning, came back a thousand-fold strong. "Okay."

"Who are you?"

SIXTY-THREE

The hairs on Mnem's arm lifted. "You know who I am." *Did Miguel bring me all the way up here for this?* She was naked. Physically and emotionally. The breeze chilled her skin. It was a well-played and chilling move on his part.

"I know your name, a few details, but nothing else." Miguel walked to the edge of the dock, opened a large plastic chest, and tossed Mnem a towel.

Mnem wrapped it around herself yet still felt exposed. She shivered and suddenly stopped. Stood stock still. Already? Mnem did the math, then bit her lip to keep from smiling. There was no mistaking the fluttering in her womb.

Miguel wrapped a towel around his waist. "Tell me who you really are." His voice bore a superior tone, one Mnem never heard before. She didn't like it.

"Don't talk to me like that." Nose in the air, Mnem strode past him and up the path.

"Like what?"

"Like I'm an inferior. Don't look at me like that either. I'm not a con artist or liar." Mnem ran up the deck steps where she pulled on her denim shorts and tugged on her shirt. The fluttering happened again. The baby's first kicks!

"I dug into your past." Miguel's voice was powerful, like a king's issuing a decree.

"What?" Mnem reeled back. *I should have expected it. Duncan did the same thing to Inna. Hades, I should have bought a history from that guy with two last names.*

"I did it for political reasons."

"Take me home." Mnem buttoned up her shirt.

"I must be prepared. Better that I find a skeleton in your closet than the press." He grabbed Mnem's sneaker away from her.

I have thousands of years' worth of skeletons!

"Give me my shoes and take me home." Mnem stomped into the house.

Miguel, the towel wrapped around his torso, followed. "Don't you want to know what they found?"

"No." Mnem slung her backpack over her shoulder.

Can I drive a stick shift with no shoes? It's been awhile.

"Nothing. *Nada.*" He stepped in front of her. "You claim you came here when you were five years old. There's no record of that."

"I said I left Greece at five. I didn't say I came here." Europe was ever so much more wonderful than the wilds of the northern continent. "We moved around a lot. My parents were diplomats. I attended small private schools and had tutors. We were never in one place for long. I speak many languages—Spanish, French, Romanian, Polish, Russian, German, Turkish, Italian, Ukrainian, Dutch, and Estonian."

Miguel's eyes bugged. "That's impressive but—"

"But what?" Mnem held out her hand.

Miguel gave her shoes back. "Tell me about your parents."

Uranus, Father Sky, Titan, lived in Mother's shadow. Gaia, Life Mother, Mother of Titans, Life Strategist par excellence.

Mnem sat in a wide armchair and tied on her Converse All Stars. "They were both very ambitious. Mother is a down-to-earth type while father was always aiming for the sky. They make an excellent couple despite their differences."

Miguel's eyes tapered. "Are they still alive?"

Always. "Yes."

"I'd like to meet them."

Mnem opened her mouth, about to make an excuse. "I'm sure they'd like that." She stood, glanced at the door.

"Don't go. Please." The dominant look and tone were gone. Miguel appeared intrigued. "Where did you go to high school?"

"Is this an interrogation?" Mnem crossed her arms.

"Like I said, I don't want a politically sensitive issue cropping up when I least expect it. My team needs to prepare." Miguel removed her backpack. "Please, Mnem. I need honesty not mock indignation."

His comment sliced like the precise blade of a surgeon.

"I'm not hiding anything." *Just everything.* "I already told you, I didn't go to high school. I had tutors."

"What have you been doing for the past ten years?"

Traveling the world. Indulging. Fornicating. Shopping. Nothing. Nothing that mattered to mortals. "I don't need all this bullshit. And I don't need you."

Miguel's stare was intense. His charm was legendary, his smile plastered across social media and multiple magazine covers, but this particular expression sent a shiver down Mnem's spine.

Senator Miguel Flores looked downright wicked. "You're not going anywhere."

"Excuse me?" Mnem stiffened her spine. How dare a mere mortal issue a command.

"I love you, Mnemosyne. I want you by my side. I also know you're hiding something. What is it? A stint in drug rehab? An arrest? Are you the high priestess of a wiccan cult? Were you in juvie? Are you married? Did your ex-boyfriend commit crimes against humanity? *What?*"

Mnem blanched.

"Ah." Miguel stepped back. "Which one is it?"

Mnem looked down. All she wanted to do was lie on that big comfy sofa, close her eyes, and feel the little mortal life move in her womb.

"I don't care, Mnem. I just need to know. I love you, warts and all."

Mnem glowered at him.

"That is if you had any warts." Miguel smiled, his eyes softening. "Let me get you a drink. Maybe I can pry out your deep dark secret after you have a few stiff ones."

"I don't want a stiff anything."

"You're turning down a drink again? I brought your favorite brand of ouzo."

"No, thank you." Mnem moved away from him.

Miguel laughed. "What, are you pregnant?"

Mnem lifted her eyes to his. His mouth opened and he stood expressionless. Each second felt like an hour to Mnem.

"Oh my god." Miguel stared, shock and amazement and alarm vying for dominance on his face. "You're pregnant. That explains why you haven't been drinking. Why you've been different."

Mnem's lips pushed into an indignant pout.

Miguel came forward, set his hand on her belly. "My baby."

"That's right, I carry your progeny."

"My progeny? I like the sound of that." Miguel gazed at her stomach as though a miracle happened. "This is wonderful. A baby. My baby. Our baby!" Miguel kissed her long and deep. "How far along are you?"

"Eighteen weeks." *Or thereabouts. My belly is more rounded than usual. Who am I kidding? There is no usual for me!*

"Why didn't you tell me immediately?"

"I didn't know what to do." Mnem watched as Miguel's fingers splayed wide over her belly.

Miguel looked up, his head cocked, hurt dimming his eyes. "With me or the child?"

"With you."

Miguel exhaled, relieved, and knelt down.

It had been a long time since someone was on their knees before Mnem. She never expected such gallantry from Miguel. Disappointment and resignation, yes. But joy? She heard it in his voice, saw it in his eyes, and felt it in his touch. Senator Miguel Flores had big political aspirations. He was dubbed the golden boy of the political party, their hope for a better tomorrow and the architect of the nation's future. Long ago, they would have built statues in his honor and wrote poems praising his wisdom and bravery.

Miguel pressed his lips to Mnem's belly. "You will make me the happiest of men if you agree to be my wife, Mnemosyne. Will you marry me?" He rested his chin on her belly and looked up with the most beautiful eyes Mnem had ever seen.

SIXTY-FOUR

"You did what?" The cup of double espresso Calliope set down clattered in the saucer.

"You heard me." Mnemosyne sipped from a mug steaming with mint tea.

"You can't be married!" Calliope slammed her hands on the table. "You are Mnemosyne, goddess of creativity, knowledge, history, art, and memory. You don't get married."

"*Was* a goddess. Mortal women get married." Mnem blew steam across the mug. "This mortal child needs a father and a future."

"What about us?" Calliope patted her heart, her tone like a child just told no.

"What about you? You're still my daughters. Nothing's changed. I don't understand. It was you and your sisters who insisted—right here at this table—that I tell Miguel immediately. You told me it was morally wrong if I didn't. What did you expect to happen?"

"Not marriage."

Mnem's six-carat diamond ring caught the morning

sun and sparkled with memories of the past weekend. Miguel had called a judge, a good friend who lived in the area. They were married the next afternoon, Inna and Duncan, their witnesses. Monday morning, Miguel did two things. He bought the huge diamond and posted two words on his social media accounts, Got Married!

Calliope reached into the pink box of donuts. "How are you going to explain nine women coming to your home and calling you momma? Are you disowning us?"

Mnem set down the mug, "Don't be silly, Calliope. This is unlike you. You can visit all you like. I'll tell Miguel you're my cousins and calling me momma is a family joke."

"Sounds like you've thought all of this through. The lies, the half-truths, the obfuscations—you and I both know that never works. Truth prevails in the end."

"This isn't the same as you helping mortal kings do the ethical and right thing. Our truth does not exist for them." Mnem reached into the pink box, selected a glazed donut. Another craving. "I have more news."

"I don't think I can handle any more."

"I went to the obstetrician. I'm having twins, a boy and a girl."

Calliope lifted her hands to the sky. "Thank goddess, it's not nine babies."

Mnem was relieved too. It had been one of her mortal pregnancy worries. One she didn't dare mention to anyone.

"Are you selling this house?" Calliope looked around. Not one box was packed.

"No, it will be the headquarters for Goddesses Inc. We've grown over the past few weeks. Now we have two hundred thousand followers. It's become a fulltime job for all of us."

"That's wonderful, Momma. Are you really making that much money?"

"Not yet. If need be, Naret and Axie offered to sell their homes and move in here."

"What about Inna?"

"Inna is engaged to Duncan." Mnem recalled Inna rushing into her arms with the news. It was a happy-sad moment before they all went into the judge's chambers. Goddesses didn't marry, didn't need to. Yet here they were, in-love with mortal men. Their transformation to mortality complete.

Calliope put her hands atop her head. "I thought they broke up. He cheated on her. I don't understand what's gotten into you both. Marriage to mortals!" She lifted her face to the ceiling.

"Such theatrics." Mnem pushed away the donut box. "Are you channeling Melpomene? Everything changed once Shee removed our immortality. Everything. We don't know if there's a tomorrow for us. How long our future will be. Please understand, *nothing* is the same." Mnem clasped her daughter's hand. "We're like milk with an expiration date. It's petrifying. We've been everywhere, done everything—yet all that means nothing anymore."

"That's not true." Calliope squeezed her mother's hand, felt the bones beneath her flesh. Mortal flesh.

"Inna wants children. We want a mortal life—the whole baker's dozen. It would be ridiculous to want anything else."

"But marriage? Children?"

"It's not a curse," said Mnem, her voice soft. *It felt like a curse at first, a punishment worse than Hades. But each day brought new emotions and experiences and once-in-a-lifetime opportunities that made mortality bearable and even enjoyable.*

There were no once-in-a-lifetime experiences when you

live a thousand lifetimes. Mnem did not want to tell her daughter that the capacity for joy was a suitable replacement for immortality.

"Sounds like a curse to me."

Mnem lifted Calliope's hand and kissed it. "Because you're a goddess and divinity is fused into every microcosm of your being."

"I won't pretend to understand what you did, but I do accept it." Calliope wrapped her arms around her mother, the truth as hard-hitting as a Poseidon-sent tidal wave. Each hug was precious.

SIXTY-FIVE

"I'm stunned." Naret sliced open a package, one of many stacked on the table. "You haven't been mortal for that long. Why rush into marriage?" She pulled a pretty pink box from the tissue paper. "Especially you, Inna."

"Do you think I made the wrong decision?" Inna sat at the computer, a product spreadsheet on the screen.

"Maybe. I'm worried about both of you. I want you to be happy." Naret read the label. "This is a face cream called Amari De." Naret squinted. "The name sounds familiar."

"She's a Romanian goddess," said Mnem. "What are the product specifications?"

"It's a toning and brightening cream." Naret tapped the ingredient list. "All natural. Says healthy skin is beautiful skin. The package is compostable." She passed the cream to Axie. "Do you think this is actually Amari De's cream?"

"I wouldn't be surprised." Mnem sniffed at it. "Fresh."

"Let's email her," said Inna as she typed the information into the spreadsheet.

"And say what?" Mnem rubbed a dollop on the back of her hand. "Are you mortal now or is that the name of your business?"

They laughed until Axie killed the mood. "Do you think Amari De bombed FEM?"

"Any goddess enraged about being fired is suspect," said Mnem. "Remember how angry we were at the time?"

"Whoever the ex-goddess is, she did a very bad thing. She could have hurt someone." Axie twisted close the lid on the face cream. "What if there was a semi-divine and quasi-divine being in the lobby at the time? They're tough but they do bleed."

"There's no way a real goddess would have let a bleeding-out quasi-divine goddess in the lobby long enough to be rescued by a mortal." Inna plucked the container from Axie's hand. "I don't want to play Who Bombed FEM anymore. Are we testing this or not? My heart tells me we might be helping out another failed goddess."

Their decision was a unanimous yes.

"Have you started planning your wedding?" Axie opened another package.

Inna shook her head. "I wish we could elope like Mnem and Miguel. The guest list is already five hundred people. I guess that's what you get when you mix a traditional Nigerian wedding with fame."

"Have you chosen a venue?" asked Naret.

"Not yet," said Inna. "Did you design the new logo?"

Naret showed them the design on her phone. It was her fourth attempt. "How's this?" She waited for the criticism. Wrong font. Wrong color. Too this or too that. Four ex-goddesses don't tend to agree on much. Thousands of years of getting your own way and calling the shots doesn't translate into teamwork.

"It has my vote," said Mnem.

"Mine too." Axie nodded.

Inna smiled. "This one is perfect."

"Will we use it for our video channel too?" asked Axie.

A video channel was Inna's idea. Assigning each of them responsibilities, Mnem's.

Mnem was the idea person. Axie, the scriptwriter. Naret styled the video, from clothing, to location, to how the product was displayed. Inna was the main speaker.

"I think we should include baby products," said Mnem.

"We're adding a lot of categories." Inna tapped the computer screen.

"If we're going to add baby stuff then why not weddings?" Naret sliced open the next parcel.

Inna swiveled around in the chair. "That's genius! Why didn't I think of that? A green wedding. We need to announce our wedding category." She grabbed her phone. "Ready?"

"We need a script," said Axie.

"Not for this, it will be more fun if it's impromptu." Inna beckoned them forward. "Let's all do it together. Live."

They huddled together in front of the phone.

"Hi everyone," said Inna. "Goddesses Inc. is hard at work reviewing products that are earth-positive and women-affirming. We have the best job in world and want to thank all of you for your support."

"Keep those divine comments and heavenly suggestions coming," added Naret.

"Today, we decided to add another category," said Mnem.

"Weddings!" Axie waved both hands.

"Some of you may know I'm planning my wedding; you may even have heard of my fiancé. Right now, we're looking at venues." Inna sighed theatrically. "I need help. Does anyone know of a green wedding venue?"

"One that serves local organic food," said Mnem.

Axie spoke next. "We'd love your suggestions for eco-friendly wedding gifts."

"Cool compostable party favors," added Naret.

"What about bridesmaid dresses?" asked Inna.

"Inna, please tell me," said Axie, "you won't make us wear some horrid bridesmaid dress."

Inna tapped her chin. "Mmmm, I think woven grass or seaweed dresses is a smashing idea." She mugged for the camera, a close-up of a mischievous grin.

Mnem, a horrified look on her face, tugged Inna away. "Tell us your suggestions. Thank you, everyone, and keep your innovative goddess-worthy products coming. We're adding another new category soon." She pressed her finger to her lips.

"We also have five more product reviews that you are going to love," said Naret.

"See you soon," said Axie. "And—"

Inna, cheek to cheek with Naret, interrupted. "Help me find a green wedding venue!"

They blew kisses, their signature close.

Inna clicked OFF. "That was perfect. We make a great team."

Axie burst into tears.

"What's wrong?" asked Mnem. "I'm supposed to be the hormonal one."

"I'm so happy." Axie accepted a tissue from Naret. "We *are* a team. We made a life. A life that matters. I haven't been this proud since I can't remember when."

Their impromptu video received one hundred likes in fourteen minutes.

Inna's phone buzzed. "Duncan messaged. He said I'm a marketing genius."

"Guess that's why you decided to marry the man," said Axie.

Two hours and ten product rejections later they decided to take a break.

"Let me just check our private InstaPic messages," said Inna as they stood up from the table. "Look at this! Two five-star hotels messaged to say they would be honored and delighted to launch their new Green Wedding Option with Inna's and Duncan's wedding."

Mnem's heart warmed. Everything was going well. Goddesses Inc. was taking off. The work filled their souls. Life—mortal life—was working out. Mnem set her hand over her belly. A boy and a girl. She couldn't wait to meet them.

SIXTY-SIX

"This is intimidating." Axie put on the headphones and adjusted the large professional microphone.

The studio was cluttered with stools, microphones, and music stands. Cords snaked across the floor.

"Nervous?" Mnem smoothed her blouse over her blossoming belly.

"Oh, don't be, you women are divine. Seriously, I mean you even look like goddesses." Deena Diva flipped through a stack of papers. "Just act like you usually do in your videos. Don't let all this," she waved her hand about, "bother you. Any fub or gaff I edit out." She pointed to the large monitor on the wall. "If you say something you want me to cut, point to the monitor. My production engineer will mark the time."

A month earlier, Deena Diva—her real name was Deena Rosenberg—ran across one of their product reviews on InstaPic. Intrigued by their motto, goddess-worthy products and divine reviews, Deena Diva, always on the hunt for content for her Women First podcast, contacted them.

Inna sat up straight on her stool. "This is going to be so much fun."

Axie swallowed, her mouth dry.

Naret passed her a water bottle.

Mnem was nervous. Deena Diva only gave them a brief outline of the interview, claimed she liked to keep things spontaneous.

"Ready?" asked Deena Diva. "Be your fabulous selves." She held up one finger…two… three, and then pointed to the production assistant on the other side of the glass. "Welcome, darlings, it's your host, Deena Diva and this is Women First, a podcast where I dish about the fabulous and the scandalous. Today, I have four amazing guests for you. If you're on InstaPics—and, darlings, if you're not you should be—you might already follow these four gorgeous, and I mean stunningly beautiful, women of Goddesses Inc. They have a review site where the ethically, sustainably, and organically inclined crowd can check out the very latest products. Mnem—did I pronounce that right? —Tell me more about Goddesses Inc."

"Thank you so much for having us on your wonderful podcast. It's such an honor to be here."

"It's my pleasure, darling. I am *in-love* with your company's purpose."

"Thank you. Well, Deena, we at Goddesses Inc. want to showcase products that meet five divine criteria. It must be ethically and sustainably sourced, ethically priced, demonstrate ingenuity, make women feel good about themselves, and give a portion back to the community."

"That certainly makes it goddess-worthy," said Deena Diva. "Inna, tell me how you all know each other and how you got started."

Inna laughed. "How long is this podcast?"

"Only an hour, darling. Can you give us the short version?"

Inna explained that they were friends who loved to shop and were very particular about quality. Naret provided a few examples and Axie shared the moment they decided to start Goddesses Inc.

A half hour into the podcast, Deena looked straight at Mnem. "You ladies are fabulous. You are an inspiration, and I know I'm certainly going to pay more attention to who gets my money. Now let's move on to the scandalous."

Mnem braced herself.

"Mnem, I heard you were fired from Gallery Hall. Do tell! We also want to know what it's like to be married to the fabulous political hottie, Senator Miguel Flores. An elopement is always such a delicious scandal."

"I loved working at Gallery Hall. Everyone there was wonderful and friendly. And the artwork! Who wouldn't want to be surrounded by such artistry all day? Unfortunately, I broke a major rule with my friend, Axie."

The moment Mnem said Axie's name, she regretted it. Something nagged at her and she wasn't sure exactly why. Nonetheless, Mnem lived long enough to know that giving away too much information was never a good thing.

Hades, mortality makes me careless.

"Oh my," said Deena Diva.

"What can I say? I'm a rulebreaker," said Mnem, her voice deceptively worry-free.

"What rule did you break, darling?"

"If I told you, I'd have to kill you, Deena."

"Oh my, that does sound intriguing. I bet I know what it was. I heard that your stories about the artwork were quite colorful. Even scandalous. Not a problem with me and my listeners to be sure. Did others take offense?"

Deena Diva did her homework!

Mnem shrugged, then remembered a listener couldn't hear a shrug. "Most art involves elements of the scandalous."

Deena Diva chuckled. "Tell us about the senator. His marriage shocked everyone. And I'm sure broke a few hearts as well. Is he really as fabulous as he seems on TV?"

"Even more." Mnem shared a few harmless stories about him, things listeners might relate to, like his love for restoring old cars, the outdoors, and Mexican food.

"A certain political someone told me the senator has presidential aspirations."

"Doesn't everyone in politics?"

"Good point, well I for one think you will make a fabulous first lady," said Deena Diva.

"Oh Deena, I think our country is full of women who will make fabulous *presidents*."

"Right you are!" Deena Diva turned to Inna. "Inna darling, don't think you're not without scandal. You're engaged to basketball superstar Duncan Eze. We want to know *everything*."

Inna followed Mnem's lead with a few amusing stories about watching her first basketball game and the perils and perks of dating during basketball season.

"That's a wrap," said Deena Diva after her close. "You're all naturals. That was a lot of fun."

Deena Diva aired the podcast episode three weeks later.

Goddesses Inc. doubled their followers overnight.

Mnem forgot the nagging feeling about mentioning Axie's name.

SIXTY-SEVEN

"Fresh chocolate croissants and coffee from Brew Me?" Axie selected a flaky chocolate-filled one. "What's the occasion?"

They gathered around Mnem's kitchen table, the early morning light reflecting off the surf.

Inna, looking especially regal in a tall updo and a white dress tied with a colorful sash, sauntered to the computer. "Goddesses, we are moving up."

Axie, Mnem, and Naret looked up at the heavens. It was a reflex. They regretted it the moment their chins lifted.

"Not that." Inna flapped her diamond-bracelet—courtesy of Duncan—adorned hand. "Look at this. SoCal Sunrise wants to interview us. Also the radio show, Female Creation. Even better, we are starting to make some money. I've already decided to take my share and add it to the Goddesses Inc. scholarship fund."

"I'll do the same," said Mnem.

"Naret and I still need a paycheck," said Axie.

It was a touchy subject. Mnem and Inna didn't need

the money and put their share back into the business. In fact, Miguel and Duncan had both suggested it.

"Don't be offended," said Mnem. "We all want Goddesses Inc. to grow. This is our way of helping."

"It doesn't feel equal anymore," said Naret.

"Then come up with a better plan," said Inna.

Axie rubbed the bridge of her nose and heaved a heavy sigh. "This would never have bothered me when I was a goddess."

Naret nodded. "It's true. Mortality is under my skin." She scratched her arm. "It's like a constant itch, I'm taking offence to the stupidest things."

"We all are," said Inna. "Let's change the subject. Have we reached a decision about hiring more people?"

"Mortals or ex-goddesses?" Naret poured tea from the pot.

"Mortals. Less ego to deal with," said Axie.

"I disagree. We need ex-goddesses. They understand at their core what we're trying to accomplish." Mnem sat on the sofa, croissant in one hand, a decaf coffee in the other. She set the croissant on her blossoming belly.

"We owe it to our goddess sisters. Remember how lost we felt?" asked Inna. "This is a chance for us to do more good."

"Mortals need jobs," said Axie.

Naret spoke over the teacup's rim. "I'm afraid Shee will smite us."

"Turn us into dust? Set us aflame? That kind of smiting?" Inna nibbled on her croissant.

"No...yes. I don't know." Naret set down the tea with a clatter. "Remember, Shee's out there." She pointed into the blue horizon. "Don't you ever wonder what Shee's thinking?"

"No, and I don't care. Shee washed her hands of us."

Inna slapped her hands together. "I'm not concerned with her anymore."

"Let's not argue," said Mnem.

"Good idea," said Naret. "I'd rather talk about Mnem's pregnancy anyway. How are you feeling?"

"Mostly good. The female mortal body is nothing short of incredible. I'm excited to meet my two babies. But Miguel…" Mnem wagged her head.

"What's wrong?" asked Inna.

"Sometimes I catch him staring at my belly in the oddest way. Like he's not sure of something, you know? It's worrisome. I mean, he's the one who wanted to get married right away." Mnem rubbed her belly. "He's still kind and thoughtful and loving, yet sometimes his actions don't square with that look in his eyes."

"Did you ask him about it?" asked Axie.

"A few times. His answer is always the same: Twins are high risk, I'm worried about you, that's all."

"Maybe you're getting a glimpse into him as a father," said Inna. "It's probably nothing. Your hormones working overtime."

"There's another thing. He's always telling me to stay hydrated, as though water is the cure all for every pregnancy ache and pain."

Inna exhaled with a loud *pfft*. "You'd think after all these millennia, men would understand a little bit more about pregnancy."

"What about you, Inna?" asked Naret. "Do you want children?"

Inna looked away from the email-filled computer screen. Hundreds of startups, people, and companies requested product placement, endorsements, and reviews. Followers mostly commented or asked questions. A few trolls spewed hateful venom.

"Duncan and I both want a family." Inna smiled bravely then returned to the computer screen. "What's this?" She leaned close, tapped the keyboard with renewed enthusiasm. "Mary Star from Women Entrepreneurs wants us to speak at their next event."

"When?" Time was split into two for Mnem. Before and after her due date.

"Next month." Inna fist pumped the air.

"What are we, the backup plan?" asked Axie.

"Yes, but who cares. Mary Star said one of their speakers cancelled and after listening to Deena Diva's podcast—I told you that gig would be our springboard—they knew we would be the perfect fit for a twenty-minute speech on the power of female teamwork." Inna bared her teeth as her brows shot up.

Mnem spewed her decaf coffee. Naret snorted tea through her nose, which sent everyone into another fit of laughter.

"Axie, I'm glad you're going to write that speech," said Mnem. "Because we mostly argue."

"Ah," grinned Axie shaking her finger, "but I'm going to say we debate, which inspires us to see past our personal limitations."

Inna clapped. "Perfect." She wiggled her shoulders and head. "This is exciting."

Mnem hauled herself off the sofa and went to the kitchen for a glass of water. The feeling came back. The same one she had during the Deena Diva interview.

I can't remember what spooked me. Ugh, I've gone full mortal.

The rest of the morning they worked, each to their specialty. Inna handled the tech stuff and emails. Axie composed the reviews and all things written. Naret planned and designed photos. Mnem was the idea and businessperson.

Ping.

"Too many emails." Inna slumped in her chair. "The more I delete, the more show up in the inbox." She rubbed her eyes, blinked, then returned to the screen. Her mouth dropped open, her heart racing like never before. "Wh—wh…" She rolled the chair back, pointed to the screen.

Naret noticed first. "What's wrong? What is it?"

Inna stared straight ahead, through them, past them, to an unknown point Beyond.

Beyond. They knew the place.

"Inna," said Mnem. "You're scaring us."

Inna drew a ragged breath. "Oh. My. Goddess. I can't. I just can't."

SIXTY-EIGHT

M nem, Naret, and Axie gathered around the computer.

There it was. FEM.

"Oh no." Axie swallowed, her mouth suddenly as dry as the Sahara.

"This can't be good," said Naret.

"Open the email," said Mnem.

"Delete it." Axie's hand covered the keyboard. "It's junk mail."

"I won't." Inna dropped her hands in her lap.

Mnem pushed away Axie's hand to hover protectively over the keyboard. "We're not cowards. We'll deal with whatever it is. Shee made us mortal. How bad can it be?"

Axie flicked Mnem's hand away. "Delete—"

Mnem tapped the key.

They sucked in a collective breath.

Dear Goddesses Inc,

This is an official summons on behalf of Shee, CEO of FEM. Shee expects your presence this Friday at three p.m. A prompt response to this email is required.

. . .

Have a nice day,
    Omega,
    Executive Secretary

"Have a nice day." Axie lifted her hands to the sky. "How can we have a nice day after this?"

"Who the hell does Shee think she is?" Inna stomped across the room. "Shee can't order us around. We're not goddesses anymore."

Mnem protected her belly with both hands. Shee might strike at any time. Shee wielded unlimited power.

Naret dragged her teeth across her lower lip. "Shee's going to smite us."

"Stop with the smiting already," said Axie.

Inna folded her arms. "Shee fired us. Dumped us out into the mortal world like garbage."

Mnem murmured in Greek to her twins.

Ping. Ping. Ping. Ping.

Everyone's phone sounded.

"Shee's secretary messaged me." Inna threw the phone on the sofa.

"Me too." Naret tossed hers next.

"Same." Axie lowered her head. "I'm going to be sick."

"Shee's going to kill us."

"Why schedule a meeting to do that?"

"We're as good as dead anyway."

"Yes, but none of us was planning on dying this Friday."

Inna returned to the computer, jabbed at the keyboard with the flourish of a conductor. "There. I deleted the email. I feel better already."

"You don't look better," said Axie. "Your face is all—"

"It's gone. Bye-bye." Inna slapped her hands together.

"It's still in your Trash folder," said Mnem.

"I know that. I'm making a point. Shee threw us in the trash. So that's where Her email went."

Mnem frowned. "I don't need this kind of anxiety in my third trimester."

Naret held up her phone. "I deleted the message."

"Shee abandoned us," said Inna as though anyone needed reminding.

Each of them deleted the message.

"There, it's like nothing ever happened," said Inna.

They all knew better.

Mnem grew still, looked past them and at the deck outside. The cloudless sky, the blue Pacific, the white-capped waves breaking on the beach—the scenic view was a blur. Something else captured her attention. *The Bird* perched on her railing. "No no no."

"What?" Inna spun around.

"Holy goddess," mumbled Axie.

"Maybe it escaped from the zoo?" whispered Naret.

"No, it's a hoopoe." Mnem sighed. "Twice the size of a regular one."

A hoopoe bird. The bird of messages. Emissary of great kings. Bearer of bad news. Giver of glad tidings. Diviner of water. A magical and mystical bird. The hoopoe ruffled its head, a crown of black-tipped feathers adding to its unusual size. The bird hop-walked along the railing, its pinkish tan chest puffed out.

Mnem pulled the glass sliding door wide open. "You have our attention."

The hoopoe opened its majestic black and white striped wings, opened its long, sharp beak and *hoo-hoo'ed.*

And kept *hoo-hoo-ing*. Twice, the bird lifted off the railing as though for emphasis.

"Anyone understand this?" asked Inna.

"I got nothing." Axie shrugged.

Only goddesses understood.

"We don't have to understand the words. The message needs no translation." Mnem closed the sliding glass door and drew the drapes.

"The bird is going to tell Shee you did that," said Axie.

Naret peeked between the drapes. "The hoopoe flew away."

"Now what do we do?" asked Axie.

"We carry on. Business as usual." Inna strolled back to the computer.

Naret sat down, drew her legs up and close to her body. "I wonder what Shee wants."

"It doesn't matter," said Mnem.

SIXTY-NINE

Monday passed. Tuesday and Wednesday too. No one mentioned Shee's email or messages or the hoopoe's appearance. They had products to test. Reviews to write. Photos to take. Ideas to turn into realities. They worked side-by-side, but Shee's summons was like a storm on the horizon. They saw it coming. Felt the change in the air pressure. Sometimes, the hair on the back of their neck lifted for no apparent reason.

"I'm telling people it will be at least three months until we're able to schedule a time to review their product," said Inna. "We need to hire another person."

"Not this argument again." Axie looked up from writing a review.

"More products, more followers, more revenue stream." Inna pushed away from the computer desk. "My opinion hasn't changed. We hire ex-goddesses."

"How do you plan to do that? Put an ad in the paper?" Axie stood and stretched. "I'm hungry. Let's try that new place down the street."

A half hour later they sat on the rooftop restaurant with an ocean view.

"Business lunch: that's a write off." Mnem tapped her phone. "Are we all set for the Women Entrepreneur's speech?"

"I want to go over it one more time," said Axie.

"We really got lucky with that one." Naret set down her menu.

"Was it *really* luck?" Mnem shifted in her seat. Her belly grew bigger and heavier each day. Today it was especially weighty. "You'd think that with our thousands of years of collective divinity we would have figured out how Life works. It feels incredibly random at times."

"I know what you mean." Inna laid the paper napkin on her lap. "I used to be absolutely convinced that life was directed by the Hand of Shee."

"It's obviously Shee's hand," said a fifth voice.

A woman dressed in white chiffon stood at the table. Her long tunic fluttered in the sea breeze, gave the impression of an angel about to take flight.

"Who are you?" Mnem set down the menu with a heavy sigh.

"I'm Omega. Mind if I join you?" The woman snatched a chair from a nearby table and scooted between Inna and Mnem. "None of you responded to Shee's email, message, or hoopoe summons."

"What happened to Shee's other executive secretary? The bald one." Axie looked Omega up and down. This one wasn't near as beautiful and lacked sex appeal.

"Tao?" Omega picked up the menu, ran her black-lacquered fingernail down the offerings. "You didn't hear?"

Four ex-goddesses exchanged puzzled glances.

"We're not privy to FEM gossip." Mnem picked up a glass.

Omega closed the menu. "Shee eviscerated her."

Mnem coughed, choked on the water. That *never* happened. Not once! Shackled for an eon, forced to wander the desert, thrown into a pit, changed into a hideous form, yes. Eviscerated? Never.

Four ex-goddesses lost their appetites.

"Can I take your orders?" A perky waitress chirped, a pen and pad in her hand.

Omega ordered for them. Ordered the exact items they would have. Which was a good thing because Naret, Axie, Inna, and Mnem were speechless. And petrified.

"Tao did a very bad thing," said Omega when the waitress left.

Four ex-goddesses remained silent; their eyes glued to Omega.

"Tao was upset because of her eons-long wait to become a full goddess. Went a bit crazy. It was a brilliant plan really, executed to perfection. Shee might never have found out because there were many possible suspects." Omega uncurled a finger at Mnem first. "Like you...and you...and you...and you." Omega wiggled her four fingers. "There are many enraged ex-goddesses. Hopeless and helpless." She leaned back in the seat and crossed her arms. "But Shee found out, Shee always does, and eviscerated her."

Mnem leaned forward. "The bombing of FEM was semi-divine?"

"Did mortality make you stupid?"

"No, but your attitude makes you rude," snapped Mnem.

"Tao was quasi-divine." Omega shuddered. "Shee created her that way."

"The wrong way," muttered Inna.

Omega lifted her chin. "I'm Shee's final creation. I won't let Shee down. Not like you four."

Axie rolled her eyes. "Why are you here?"

"Shee summoned you. Shee expects you tomorrow at three pm. Do not disappoint Her."

Omega's subtext was clear. Evisceration. Shee did it once, Shee will do it again.

Four ex-goddesses looked from one to the other. Mnem's eyes tightened with sadness. Naret bit her lip. Axie wore the same expression as the day she almost committed suicide. Inna's lips pushed into a frustrated sulk.

The waitress set down their plates.

"We'll be there," said Mnem.

The others did not disagree.

Omega smoothed out her napkin. "Glad to hear it. Is there anything I can help you with?"

Mnem dug her fingernails into her palms. Imagined slapping the smug smile off Omega's face.

Inna poked at her vegetable flat bread. "How is the merger with MAS?"

Omega looked at Mnem. "Don't your daughters tell you anything?"

"No, because none of that matters to us anymore," said Mnem.

The nine muses tried to keep their mother updated on FEM, but one day—Mnem couldn't remember when, which was a problem in itself—told them to stop, that all it did was remind her of an existence no longer available.

"Still in progress. It's a delicate situation. You know how the male ego is." Omega spooned lobster bisque into her mouth.

"We know the male ego and the female ego better than you," snapped Naret. "You're an upstart. How long have you been around?"

Axie, Mnem, and Inna stared. Naret never lost her temper.

"If you're measuring divinity and wisdom by millennia then it's one reason why you are all mortal and I'm not." Omega smirked as she slurped on her soup.

"Your arrogance is why *you* are not divine yet." Inna smirked back.

"Ladies." Omega set down her spoon. "Don't shoot the messenger. And don't be stupid with your attitudes when you meet with Shee."

"What does Shee want?" asked Inna. "None us want to walk into the lion's den."

"I did that once," said Axie. "It wasn't fun...for the lion."

Inna, Naret, and Mnem laughed. The first time since Omega's arrival. Then they looked at Omega with a collective amused glare. You're not a goddess for thousands of years without learning a few intimidation techniques.

Omega reached for a sourdough roll. "I don't understand why you aren't jumping at the chance for this meeting. Why aren't you thrilled to be in the presence of the divine?"

"Look around. Open your semi-divine eyes," said Naret. "We *are already* in the presence of the divine. Every. Day. The sky and the ocean."

"The mountains and deserts."

"The flowers and trees."

"The bird and bees and all the creatures who share this sphere."

"Mortals can't hold a grudge for thousands of years."

"They must live in the moment."

"Yet consider the past and future."

"Mortals live at a hundred percent."

"Get smart fast."

"Deal with their mistakes."

"Live life in four dimensions."

"Three physical and one temporal."

"Mortals live a limited and confined life."

"Yet their mind is limitless."

"Their spirits, free."

"They must take chances. *Real* chances."

"They create meaning and purpose from thin air."

Inna snapped her fingers. "Like a job. Like Goddesses Inc."

Omega pressed her back to the seat, her eyes darting from one to the other as they spoke. She picked up her spoon, unused since the ex-goddess barrage and dragged it through the lobster bisque.

"You ought to get out more," said Mnem.

"See the world." Inna, suddenly ravenous, tore off a bite of her vegetable flatbread.

"Shee shouldn't keep you cooped up in that sky-high office," added Naret.

Axie tapped the side of her right eye. "Perspective is all."

Omega bared her signature smug smile. The curve was the same, but her eyes were wary. Omega lifted her hands as though in prayer and then clapped. Softly and slowly. "Well done. I hope your performance is as equally excellent for Shee."

SEVENTY

They met at Mnem's beach house. They needed each other's comfort and energy. Individually they were strong, together they were stronger. One thing they did not say—that did not need to be spoken—was that this might be their last time together.

"I was sick to my stomach all night." Axie patted her belly.

"Duncan said I acted like a caged tiger with all my pacing," said Inna.

"I made a bunch of wish boats. My best designs ever." Naret smiled. "I set them in the ocean early this morning for all of us."

"What did you wish for?" asked Mnem.

"Grace."

Inna gave Naret a hug. "Thank you. It's the perfect all-purpose wish."

Mnem took a deep breath. "Ready?"

Axie nodded. "I hope the weather isn't a sign of what's to come."

The gentle rain started at sunrise. Each hour the sky grew darker and the rain beat harder.

MNEM, Inna, Naret, and Axie, the rain pelting their umbrellas, lifted their heads to stare at the top floor of the FEM building.

"Does it look taller because we're mortal?" asked Inna.

Axie's brows drew together. "I don't recall it being this ominous."

A thunder crack startled them.

"Shee's putting on a good show." Mnem walked around a puddle to reach the intercom by the door. "Good afternoon. Axie, Inna, Naret, and Mnem have an appointment with Shee."

"One moment," came a cheerful voice.

They waited, heard another sharp thunderclap.

"Thank you. Please look into the camera on the right-hand side…. Thank you. Enter the building and go directly to the first elevator. Do not attempt to go anywhere else."

"We wouldn't dream of it," Inna said into the intercom, her voice soaked with sarcasm.

The door opened and four ex-goddesses went inside, their umbrella's dripping rainwater, their anxiety trickling down their spines.

"Welcome to FEM, the originator of divine, semi-divine, and quasi-divine female empowerment and resources." The familiar voice floated above them.

"Was the lobby always this gorgeous?" asked Naret.

"Well, they did rebuild after the bombing," said Mnem. "This is a definite upgrade. The pink marble glows like it's lit from within."

"Love and fertility are on the tenth, eleventh, and twelfth. Grievances are on the thirteenth…"

The celestial announcement was white noise. It didn't apply to them anymore. It didn't matter if the departments moved floors, grew or shrank in importance.

Inna looked back. "We're leaving a dirty trail."

"Isn't that symbolic," said Mnem. "Where once we rode on the clouds, we now walk through the puddles."

Two goddesses striding across the lobby did a double take. Both lifted their hand in greeting but hurried away.

"Consult the Information Desk for all other departments…"

Inna inhaled. "I miss the café. Their coffee was heavenly."

"I miss the library," said Axie. "I could have translated those texts for Amir in half the time."

"Whatever happened to him?" asked Naret.

"Have a nice day," purred the ethereal voice.

"I don't know. My guess is he's hitting on another researcher."

Inna stepped up to the gold panel next to the elevator. "I didn't floss this morning."

Naret giggled. "You're bad."

"Shee probably smells your mortal breath from here," said Mnem.

"Like I care." Inna blew onto the panel, fogged the shiny gold plate.

The elevator door opened without a sound, they stepped inside, and the door closed.

Axie looked from side to side, up and down. "Feels like a tomb in here."

"An expensive sepulcher," whispered Naret.

Mnem turned around to face them, her back to the door. "I think Shee's going to try to pit us against one other. Divide and conquer. Shee will say my marrying Miguel was a big mistake. That Inna must not marry Duncan. That Naret should have kept working to help immigrants. That Axie's translating artifacts to connect ancient myths was wrong. Shee will find ways for us to blame each other and try to prove that our choices were horrible. No matter what Shee says or does, we stick together. Agreed?"

"Agreed," they said in unison.

The elevator door glided open right on cue. As if it knew. As if Shee knew. Which Shee did.

Four brave ex-goddesses stepped out onto the plexiglass, the city many stories beneath their feet.

Mnem considered the view before, above, and beneath her. Contemplated the bruise-colored layers of thick ominous clouds hovering over the sea of humanity. *Nice touch, Shee.*

"This isn't *really* a floor, is it?" asked Naret. "Not a mortal floor. That's why I'm feeling—"

"Don't say it," said Axie.

"Is the whole building real?" Axie stared out the window.

"The lobby was real enough to be bombed." Inna smudged the glass. "Mortals would laugh if they knew about all the floors devoted to divine bureaucracy."

"Shee once told me bureaucracy was the tenth level of hell." Mnem looked down the glass hall to the door at the end. "We can't stand here all day. Let's get it over with."

The other goddesses gave her a look, a This May Be Our Last Minute On Earth look.

"Remember, we're all in this together." Mnem started down the hall.

The door at the end opened.

Omega lifted her head and smiled. "It's good to see

you again. Shee is waiting for you. Go on in. Leave your umbrellas."

The large gold door to Shee's office slid into the wall.

Mnem walked with purpose. Inna, with a defiant bounce in her step. Axie's feet felt heavy and Naret wondered if all the wish boats in the world were enough.

"Had a nice day," said Omega.

Had?

SEVENTY-ONE

Shee's office was as they remembered. Five walls of glass and a ceiling of sky. But this time, dark gray clouds concealed the vista. Shee, her back to them, stood at the window, her multi-hued kaftan glimmering gold, silver, and bronze.

The ex-goddesses looked from one to another. Should they or shouldn't they?

Mnem nodded, lowered herself to the ground—no easy task with a twin-big belly—and did her best to assume the posture of obeisance.

Naret lowered next, followed by Axie. Inna, last.

"A bit of nasty weather today." Shee turned around. "Please, take a seat."

They did, Inna helping Mnem up.

Shee's face looked different, more distorted, like an unfocused camera lens, and yet with milliseconds of sublime clarity. Glimpses of her transcendent faces of All Women.

Shee rounded the enormous ebony desk, perched on the edge, her ankles crossed. "Mnemosyne, Inna, Phra

357

Naret, Axtis. Darlings, you look amazing. Mortality did not diminish your beauty. And Mnem, twins growing in your mortal womb." Shee interlaced her fingers and set them over her heart. "Delightful."

Mnem shifted in the chair, set a protective hand over her belly.

"Inna, engaged to a basketball superstar," said Shee. "Why am I not surprised. The man has the body of a god and the wealth of a king." Her head turned. "Naret, my beautiful Naret. You did the right thing. What was it you said? That's right, 'This job is too small for my soul.' It *really* was. Good call." Shee turned to Axie and wagged her finger. "You had an unfair advantage when you translated and traced those myths. I am very glad you chose not to unearth all the mysteries buried beneath the sands."

Inna tried to look Shee in the eye, but Her glorious radiance made it impossible. "Why are we here?"

"Is that a philosophical question?" Shee leaned forward.

"Why did you summon us?" asked Mnem. "We're mortal nobodies. I'm surprised you didn't wipe our memories clean."

"Mortal nobodies? Heavens, no. You all went out and made a life. A real life with a purpose." Shee picked up a remote and aimed it at the large TV mounted on the wall. Their InstaPic and website appeared on the split screen. "You found a niche. Created something from nothing. You provide a service to the world that is valuable, timely, and relevant. I'm quite impressed." Shee folded her arms, the kaftan sleeves draping like a liquid metallic sheen over her body. "What inspired you?"

The four ex-goddesses were silent.

Mnem found her voice first. "We all lived lives of

luxury. We understand, value, and appreciate that now. We also understand struggles and hardship and righteousness."

Shee cocked her head. "Go on."

"It's something we knew we would be good at, and, to be honest, testing products, writing reviews, and helping people make good choices make us feel good."

"You worked hard for no money because it made *you* feel good." Shee scooted off the desk and stood before them like a mother over disobedient children.

Mnem lifted her chin. "It satisfies our soul."

"Some of your five-heart products are too expensive for people of modest means."

"And some are less expensive than the bargain brands that pollute the earth," said Naret.

"We provide a service." Axie swallowed, her mouth dry. "We're not selling anything."

Shee walked past them to the other side of the room. "You landed a speaking gig on Women Entrepreneurs. Your business will take off. You'll need to hire more people."

Four ex-goddesses swiveled in their seats to look at Shee.

"Will you hire other ex-goddesses or mortals?"

"We're leaning towards ex-goddesses," said Inna. "They have the expertise we need."

Shee returned to her desk. But not by walking past them. Shee just appeared in her ivory chair, her arms on the armrest, her fingers draped over the side. "I have an offer. One I think you will be most pleased to accept. Goddesses Inc. is an admirable service with excellent criteria. You're reaching more women then I thought possible." Shee smiled an All Women smile. "You help women make choices. Life is all about choices, and Goddesses Inc. offers excellent options. The scholarship fund is a great idea, as is the criteria for a business to give back to the community. It's most goddess-like." Shee set her elbows on the armrest, her hands together in prayer. "I want in. I will provide funds for more scholarships and capital to grow your business."

Mnem looked at the others, their stunned expressions offering Mnem no clue how to respond. "Why would we do that? We're doing fine without your divine help."

"Oh, I forgot to mention one little thing." Shee held up a finger. "I will make you all immortal goddesses again."

SEVENTY-TWO

S hee would make them immortal goddesses again. The offer of a lifetime, of a thousand more lifetimes, shook them to their mortal core. Four ex-goddesses sucked in the rarified air, felt the divine possibilities permeate their skin, muscles, and bones. Right down to their Prada-clad toes.

Shee's face was expressionless, but Her senses missed nothing. Their changed breathing patterns, increased heart rates, and dilated pupils told Shee much. A lip quiver, finger twitch, and stiffened jaw told Shee even more.

"You will re-instate us?" Mnem asked.

"Yes." Shee nodded. "Exactly as you were before."

Axie's eyes narrowed. "Will we have full access to all of FEM's resources?"

"Everything as before."

Inna, her brow furrowed, glanced at the others in warning. "But you would be the boss of Goddesses Inc."

"Naturally." Shee rested her arms on the desk, her fingers interlaced. "By virtue of all my vast resources, money, information, and ex-goddesses."

"I assume you will not be a silent partner." Mnem set

her hand on her side, one of the babies was doing an excellent imitation of a bucking bronco.

"We will be obligated to you," said Naret.

Shee's brows lifted. "Phra Naret, my child, the whole world is beholden to me. Forever and always."

Mnem pressed down on the tiny hand or foot that bulged from her belly. Baby gymnastics was evidently scheduled for this hour. "I'd like to see a contract first and read all the deific fine print."

"A contract." Shee smiled, her many faces brightening, glowing with divinity. "How very mortal of you. FEM has no celestial attorneys on staff. I'd have to outsource to Hell."

"I'm serious." Mnem did not appreciate Shee's humor. "We need to know exactly what we're getting into."

Inna folded her arms. "What's to stop you from firing us from our own company?"

"And throwing us out on the street again?" asked Axie.

"Or making us mortal for a second time?" Naret added.

Shee gave each one a prolonged look of pure love and compassion. "You all have done more good in a few short months than many of the goddesses roaming this building. Why would I jeopardize that?"

"Does this pertain to your merger with MAS?" asked Inna.

"The merger?" Shee rose from the chair. "Imagine the universe. Every planet, comet, moon, sun, star, and every particle of creation not yet discovered. Those are the details necessary for any merger between FEM and MAS." Shee sashayed across the room, set a small translucent demitasse cup under the espresso machine. "I will draw up a heaven-clad contract." Shee turned on the machine and the fragrance of ground beans permeated the air.

"I miss the coffee here," whispered Axie.

Her back to them, Shee went through the latte-making ritual with the skilled efficiency of a celestial barista. Latte in hand, Shee turned to face them. "Be advised, my offer is time sensitive. Twenty-four hours after the contract's delivery it will become null and void." Shee inhaled the latte's aroma. "What you have already done, I will do a million times better."

Mnem's jaw dropped.

"Let me get this right, we agree to your terms or you become our competition?" asked Inna. "That's pretty ballsy."

Shee laughed. "My beautiful Inna, Shee power trumps man balls any day." Shee took a sip of the latte, shimmered, and disappeared.

Mnem glanced around the room. "You know Shee's still here."

"Time to go." Inna stood.

"I wonder when we'll get the contract?" Naret headed for the open office door.

Omega handed them a folder. "Here you go, four identical contracts. Have a nice day."

SEVENTY-THREE

Four ex-goddesses sat on the beach in front of Mnem's house. They stared at the horizon and into their potential futures. Sifted grains of sand through their fingers and understood the infinite possibilities. Listened to the surf's roar and heard the unceasing sound of life eternal.

"We should make a pros and cons list," said Axie.

"A list?" snapped Inna. "A stupid list? Logic is not part of this decision."

"Why not?" Mnem dug her toes into the sand. "You know human emotions change on a breeze."

"I'm not talking about emotions. I'm talking about heart." Inna tapped her own.

"We can do a lot more as immortals," said Naret. "More time on earth means more heart."

Mnem tossed a handful of sand aside. "I don't want to be at Shee's beck and call."

"We already are," said Axie.

Inna knocked shoulders with Mnem. "You don't trust Shee."

"The contract is full of loopholes," said Mnem. "Loopholes we don't see and don't understand. It'll end up a hostile takeover."

"Why do you think that?" Axie gathered her long dark hair and twisted it into a knot on top of her head.

"We're nobodies—defrocked goddesses—who got lucky and started a business Shee hadn't thought of to help the feminine collective."

"Maybe Shee put the idea in our heads," said Naret.

"Who knows?" Mnem tossed more sand aside from the hole. "We're just a means to Her end."

"You believe Shee will boot us out with the excuse that it's for the greater good?" asked Inna.

"Absolutely, then we will be right back where we started." Mnem kept digging into the sand. "Immortal goddesses without a platform or a calling. Has-been goddesses with no place in this world."

"I lived for thousands of years in a beautiful delusion," said Axie. "Now I know the truth. We were expendable immortals. But I can make a difference as a mortal. I'd rather a mortal life of purpose and passion than know my immortality can be taken from me at any time."

"So can your mortal life," said Naret.

"Do you hear yourselves?" Inna's voice intoned with disbelief. "You're turning down divinity? Mnem's wrong, we won't make the same mistakes we made before. We know in our heart that service is our calling, what fills our soul. Axie, you're wrong too. We *can* live immortal lives of passionate purpose. This is our second chance. Naret's right." Inna snapped her fingers. "An accident, a disease—there's a million ways to die tomorrow. I was created to be a goddess. This…" Inna pinched a bit of skin on her arm. "This will wrinkle and rot and become food for worms." Inna pointed to Axie. "I see a gray hair."

Axie's hand flew to her head. "Where? You do not."

"Not now." Inna grinned. "I see your gray hair in the next few decades. I see your stamina and the daily struggle of living a mortal life, of aging and the effects of tainted air and water and food on your body. Mortal life wears everyone down."

"That goes for immortality as well," said Mnem as her fingers pressed against the damp sand walls of the hole she dug. "We got lazy. Mortals and their never-ending antics wore us down."

Inna stood, loomed over the others. "We each have a contract. That means it doesn't have to be a joint decision. I suggest we all think real hard tonight. By ourselves." She pointed to the hole beside Mnem. "You dug yourself into a hole, Mnem. Don't drag the others down with you because of your belief in a predetermined and unescapable destiny."

SEVENTY-FOUR

Naret held the *krathong* in her hand. It was the most beautiful floating basket she ever made. Adorned with multi-layered colorful blooms collected from her garden. The flower petals curled at the sides, the leaves imperfect, a few pricked with holes from hungry insects. Which was the point. The flowery floating basket was perfect in its imperfections. An authentic portrayal of Naret's heart.

Naret wedged a long white tapered candle into the middle of the arrangement. Not straight. Nothing in life was straight. Not immortal life either. Everything was at a slant. Even the tilt of the earth.

Naret stripped naked and stepped down into the pool, the *krathong* in her hands. Lifting it over her head, she submerged until she felt the *krathong's* buoyancy. She let go. Stared up at its banana leaf bottom.

Naret had never viewed a krathong from this angle before. Never thought to. Tonight she needed a different perspective. And in the pool's light, the floating imperfect wish basket glowed ethereal under the night sky.

Good fortune, beauty, and blessings. She could be the goddess of those things again. Her power to make mortals realize their way to wealth and recognize their unique beauty would be restored.

Still holding her breath, Naret followed the *krathong's* path across the pool. A single petal dropped off, floated beside it.

Her lungs bursting, Naret emerged from the water with a smile.

SEVENTY-FIVE

"Hey, babe, come look at this." Duncan waved Inna over.

Inna sat down and snuggled beside him on the sofa.

Duncan draped his arm over her shoulder. "My mom dropped this off. It's my old baby book." He flipped back to the beginning of the photo album. "Admit it. I'm the cutest baby you ever saw. Look at those chubby cheeks."

"Hard to believe all those rolls turned into this." Inna poked his bicep.

"Those aren't rolls, babe, that's pure baby muscle." Duncan flipped the page. "Guess how old I am here."

"Five. You look pretty tall."

"Nope. I'm three years old." Duncan grinned. "Mom says I was born tall. Too big for all those newborn clothes." He turned more pages. "This is Dad and Mom getting their certificate of citizenship. I remember that day. I was nine years old." He turned another page and an old photo slid out.

"Who are those people?" Inna asked as Duncan flipped

to the backside of the cracked and faded black and white photograph.

Duncan snugged Inna closer. "That's my grandpa and grandma on Dad' s side. They died about ten years ago. Grandpa went first, then Grandma a year after from a broken heart." Duncan slid the photo back under the clear sticky film that kept the photos in place. "That's the kind of marriage I want, Inna. They were best friends. Each other's rock and foundation. If we can get old together like they did, with a twinkle in their eye and an unshakeable love, then I will have considered my life a success."

Inna swallowed. "Not good works? Not reaching your ambitions?"

"Those are important, sure, but what my grandparents had was powerful. I know they're together in heaven looking down right now. They see you beside me and I feel their love for us."

"Since when did you become so sappy?" Inna pinched his stomach.

A polite cough made them both look up.

"Mister Duncan, Miss Inna, sorry to interrupt," said Maria, her hands clutched in front of her.

"No problem, what is it?" asked Duncan.

"The viewing for my niece is later this evening."

Death, the cost of mortality. Could Inna be any more certain of her decision?

"I'm so sorry, Maria." Duncan touched his forehead. "You told me the other day, didn't you? What happened?"

"A car accident. Life is precious, no? One day you're alive and the next..." She sighed. "Alma leaves behind three children and a husband. It's such a horrible tragedy. I wonder what god was thinking." Maria crossed herself. "Alma was a wonderful mother and wife. A good woman. A good Catholic. She always volunteered at the soup kitchen and battered women's shelter and…" Maria dug into her sleeve for a tissue.

"Let me know if there is anything I can do for the family," said Duncan.

Maria nodded. "God may have taken her to His bosom early, but she will live in the hearts of her family and community forever."

"Take whatever time you need, Maria," said Duncan. "I'll send flowers on your behalf."

"Alma's favorite color was pink." Maria dabbed at her eyes. "Thank you."

Inna watched Maria until she turned the corner.

Maybe death was a gift and immortality the curse. No goddess ever had what Alma had. Or what Duncan's grandparents had. They were adored and loved without divine talents. Without celestial expectations.

Any mortal who loved a goddess expected something. Miracles or luck or good fortune. No one expected miracles from a mortal. Their love was enough.

Duncan turned the page, tapped a photo. "I played center on the community basketball team."

Was it foolish to give up immortality to grow old with someone? How would Inna explain her perpetual youth? At some point she must leave him and their children. Abandon people who loved her with all their hearts. How useful was the divine power of promise keeping if Inna broke her own vows?

SEVENTY-SIX

A xie drove up to the hills. Parked her car at a vacant lookout point with an impressive view of the city and rolled down the windows. It was her favorite place to ponder Deep Thoughts. Tonight, the moon was full and bright, the lights below even brighter. The stars paled in the sky.

Mortal lights consumed energy. Divine light created it.

Axie left her pro and con list at her house. Realized by the time she reached the bottom line of the paper that the reasons for and against were endless. As the ex-goddess of peace, justice, and victory she knew there were countless ways to win or lose an argument. Her decision would come down, as Inna said, to heart.

Axie missed not knowing when a person lied. Conversations with mortals left her uncertain. Truth, be it personal truth or a cultural, political, religious, or ethical truth was still a Truth. One she had worked with, understood, and empathized with. Not recognizing professor Amir's philandering ways left her vulnerable. Not knowing if he was involved with the art scam—thank goddess, she didn't need to deal with that anymore—made her feel powerless.

Powerlessness. It was the reason Axie wanted to run a blade through her heart after Shee fired her. Ironic, really, since Axie did nothing with her power for hundreds of years.

Was an unused power as much a crime as making fake artifacts? One was a moral crime, the other, legal. Restitution paid for the second, but never the first.

The crunch of gravel interrupted Axie's thoughts.

A white BMW convertible pulled beside her. A bearded man leaned over from the driver's side. "I can leave if you want." He left the car running.

"Leave?"

"I don't want to make you uncomfortable."

"Are you a serial killer?"

"No, but I played a lovable one in a film once." He grinned.

"Oh." Axie didn't recognize him. Didn't know what movie he referred to. "You're an actor."

"Yup. I've been coming to this lookout point for a long time—since my bartending days. This place helps me think. Sometimes a man just needs to count the stars—the real ones, not those on the Hollywood Walk of Fame."

"Do you have a star there?"

"A star in the sky is brighter than one incased in concrete. The thing is, they both burn out eventually, right?" The man smiled. "Sorry to interrupt you. I'll shut up now." He leaned back against the headrest; his famous profile obscured by the darkness.

Axie stared at him. Hard.

He turned his head. "You're drilling a hole into the side of my skull with that stare of yours."

Axie giggled. "Thank you. You solved my problem."

SEVENTY-SEVEN

Senator Miguel Flores ran his fingers through his dark waves. "Everything okay?"

"Why do you ask?" Mnem ran the brush over her hair.

"You were quiet last night, and this morning you're distracted." Miguel buttoned his white shirt.

"Pregnancy is tiring." *Deciding whether to be immortal is exhausting!*

"You will tell me if there's something wrong, right?" Miguel lifted up two different ties.

Mnem selected the blue and burgundy stripe. "You'll be the first to know."

"It's the speech for Women Entrepreneurs, isn't it? Want me to have one of my people look at it?" His chin lifted as Mnem put on his tie.

"I'm confident in Axie's speech writing skills." *Axie has more experience than a thousand speech writers.*

Miguel kissed Mnem's cheek. "Can't seem to get close enough to you anymore." He bent down, set his hand on her belly. "How are you, my children? Oh, there's a kick."

He checked his watch. "I've time for a quick breakfast this morning."

They went downstairs, Mnem plodding behind him.

"I forgot to tell you last night, Phoebe Lawson from the museum called." Miguel dropped a bagel into the toaster.

Mnem's stomach lurched. "What about?"

"Mostly museum stuff. She gave me an update about the new conservation room and asked about you."

"That's odd."

"Not really. I'm a senator after all. People want to stay on my good side." He set the cream cheese on the table.

"She fired me."

"I think she feels bad about that." Miguel poured his coffee and smeared his bagel with cream cheese. "Phoebe asked about Axie too."

Mnem's heart thumped in her throat. "Why would she ask about Axie? She doesn't even know who she is."

The interview with Deena Diva. Mnem recalled her mistake... *I loved working at Gallery Hall. Everyone there was wonderful and friendly. And the artwork! Who wouldn't want to be surrounded by such artistry all day? Unfortunately, I broke a major rule with my friend, Axie.*

Phoebe heard the podcast.

"Axie was with me when Phoebe fired me for checking out the new conservation room." Mnem lowered herself onto the kitchen chair.

"Phoebe is a person who likes to wield whatever power she has over others. I see it all the time." Miguel popped the last bite into his mouth.

Mnem drummed her fingers on the table. Inna, Naret, and Axie were scheduled to meet at nine this morning to discuss their decision.

"Are you working today?"

"I work every day."

"You don't have to." Miguel balled the napkin in his hand.

"Not this again. I want to work." Mnem touched his arm. "I need to work."

Miguel patted her hand. "My offer still stands. Work from here. There's plenty of space."

"I like my house. I like looking outside and seeing the ocean."

"You're a stubborn woman." Miguel set the coffee cup in the sink.

"That's why you love me."

"More than you will ever know." He read the new message on his phone. "Good news, they rescheduled an appointment, which means I have time to attend the Goddesses Inc. speech."

Mnem pushed herself up, rubbed her belly. "Really? Do they let men in?"

"Only the handsome ones." Miguel stood behind Mnem, his arms wrapped around her. "I'm the luckiest man in the world. Besides convincing you to marry me, this may be my greatest achievement." His hands rested on her belly.

"Wait until they're teenagers. You may think differently."

"Children are a gift. Through them we live forever." Miguel nuzzled her neck. "I have a light day. Are you up for dinner at our favorite restaurant?"

"Sounds wonderful."

"Excuse me." An aide walked into the kitchen.

Miguel kissed Mnem's cheek before releasing her.

"Senator, the meeting begins in half an hour." The aide handed Miguel a folder.

Mnem grabbed Miguel by the tie and yanked him close. "That's another reason why I want to keep my own place. Twenty-four-hour privacy. No aides walking in on us." She kissed him full on the lips.

After the front door closed, Mnem stared at her belly. "What should I do? If I become immortal, I will watch you both age and die. I don't think I could bear it."

One of the babies kicked.

"Yes, I have nine more, but you are both special."

Two more kicks. One on either side.

"If I chose immortality, I will see your children and your children's children forever more." Mnem waited for another kick. "What? No kicks? If it's a sign, I don't know what it is."

SEVENTY-EIGHT

Mnem sat on the deck overlooking the ocean, a cup of tea in her hand, when Naret, Axie, and Inna arrived. "Well? Did everyone decide?"

Inna sat beside her. "I choose to be mortal."

"What! Why? I thought you were Team Divinity."

"I was, until I saw an old photo of Duncan's grandparents." Inna wrapped her arms around herself. "Naret? What about you?"

"Mortality. I want to be the banana leaf, not the flower and not the candle."

"I don't know what that means," said Mnem, "but it sounds like it has something to do with a *krathong*."

They turned their eyes to Axie.

"I had sex with Lance Hardwood last night."

"What?!" Inna's, Mnem's, and Naret's voice squawked in unison.

"It was wonderful. We did it in the front seat of his car."

"Axie, that's...that's not like you," said Inna. "What happened?"

"We met each other last night at the lookout point where I do my best thinking. It was late. Past midnight. We connected."

"You think?" Inna snickered.

"We connected spiritually before that. The sex was just an extension of our soul connection." Axie settled back in the chair and grinned that Good Sex grin.

"Soul connection?" Mnem blinked, looked at her friend like she was crazy. "He's not your type at all. You like them broody and dangerous. Lance Hardwood is America's sweetheart."

"I changed. People can change." Axie rubbed sleep thick eyes. "Stop staring at me like that. For once in my life I did something outrageous and it was wonderfully freeing."

Naret cleared her throat. "Soooo, immortality or no?"

"Mortality. The experience—our connection—was amazing. I've never felt anything like it." Axie yawned. "I'll need a few espressos to get through the day." She pointed to Mnem. "What about you?"

"I choose to be mortal." Mnem looked down at her belly. "For my mortal children."

Inna burst out laughing. "Mortality addled our brains."

"No, it gave us more heart," said Mnem.

"Good." Axie slipped a folded paper from her purse. "Our speech is a week away. Tell me if it has the right amount of heart."

SEVENTY-NINE

A xie hurried down the bright hallway of the hotel and opened the door at the end. "It's packed. Every seat is taken."

"Did you see Miguel?" asked Mnem as she added bronzer to her cheeks.

"He was talking to Mary Star, the president of Women Entrepreneur's."

"Why am I not surprised. The man never stops campaigning."

"Duncan was there too," said Axie. "You can't miss him. I feel sorry for the woman sitting behind him."

"Who's nervous?" asked Mnem.

"Are you kidding?" Inna smoothed her blouse into her skirt waistband. "We've all spoken to a whole lot more people during our goddess days."

"So…that's a yes." Mnem quirked an eyebrow.

"Yes." Inna, Naret, and Axie laughed.

"Does everyone have their speech?" asked Mnem.

Inna waved a piece of paper. "Right here."

The door opened. A woman wearing jeans, t-shirt, and

a headset entered. "Hi ladies, I hope you're ready. You all look fabulous. Follow me."

Inna, Naret, and Axie took their speeches with them. Mnem did not. The ex-goddess of memory knew how to memorize a speech.

They followed the assistant event coordinator down the hall to the grand ballroom.

"I love your InstaPic," said the assistant event coordinator. "I'm all about sustainability now." She led them through a door and into a room adjacent the stage. "Walk out when Mary Star introduces you. Make sure to speak into the microphone. When you're done, Mary will come back out and announce the lunch break. All good?"

"We're good," they answered in unison.

Axie sidled next to Mnem. "I'm not a hundred percent certain, but I'm pretty sure I saw Phoebe Lawson in the audience."

Mnem stiffened. "Who is she with?"

"I didn't see."

Weird. Or is it? The Women Entrepreneurs' event draws all the female movers and shakers. Still, I don't like it. I have a bad feeling. Does she intend to embarrass me in front of everyone? Make a scene?

"Many of you may know our next four speakers," said Mary Star.

That was their cue.

"If you don't, I suggest you take out your phones right now and follow Goddesses Inc. on InstaPic. These gorgeous young women have taken the retail world by ethically sourced storm. They graciously agreed to take time from their day of product reviewing and photo-taking to talk about how and why they began Goddesses Inc." Mary Star turned her head and clapped.

Naret, Axie, Inna, and Mnem approached the podium, their hearts fuller and their energy higher than ever before.

EIGHTY

The speech was flawless. Perfect in its delivery. Each goddess's part of the speech flowed into the next. It was verbal choreography meant to show teamwork. It came off without a hitch. The applause was earthly music to their mortal ears. After Mary Star announced lunch, she waved them over.

"That was fabulous," said Mary Star. "Incredibly inspirational. Are you interested in being our keynote speakers next year?"

"We would be honored," said Inna.

A woman whispered in Mary Star's ear.

"Ladies, I almost forgot, we like to post signed copies of the speeches on our Memory Board. If you would be good enough to sign them."

"I left my part in the room. I'll get it now." Mnem waved to Miguel who, with Duncan, worked their way slowly through the crowd toward them—not easy considering their fame—and started back to the room.

Mnem climbed the steps to the stage and went out the side door.

Walking. Mnem would never take it for granted again. Each day she lumbered and swayed more.

The door to their room was unlocked and Mnem went inside. A sweatshirt, a wrinkled blouse, and several bobby pins were discarded on the bed. All their purses were on the table. Mnem gathered them up—knew Inna would want to check her phone every minute for new followers—and grabbed the copy with her part of the speech. She signed it Mnemosyne Athanasiou Flores.

What a mouthful.

Mnem turned around and started.

"Hello, Mnem." Phoebe Lawson stood in the doorway. "It's nice to see you."

The hair on Mnem's neck lifted. "Hello. What brings you here?"

"Where's your friend, Axie?"

"Why do you ask?" But Mnem already knew. Realized the consequences of saying Axie's name during the podcast.

Phoebe opened her Fendi purse. "We didn't put it together until I heard Deena Diva's podcast."

Mnem swallowed. "We?"

"Amir, his wife and I." Phoebe pulled out a shiny black pistol. "You snuck Axie into the old conservation room to confirm the fake."

Mnem stepped back.

"Amir was stupid to ask her to authenticate one of the pieces. That man has no common sense. All he and his wife see are dollar signs."

"I don't know what you're talking about."

"You knew. Somehow you *knew*." Phoebe wagged the gun. "Why didn't you tell anyone?"

"Tell them what?"

"Don't play stupid. Why didn't you tell anyone what you and Axie suspected?"

"We didn't have any real proof." Mnem's eyes darted around the room. There was nowhere to go. Nothing to throw at her.

Phoebe smiled. "Well, we won't take any chances that you may find some." Phoebe pulled the trigger.

EIGHTY-ONE

Thousands of years rushed past Mnem. All her many lives. Her divine cronies, mortal friends, lovers, the faces of each of her beloved muse daughters, her mother, father, nine days spent with Zeus, every philosopher, the imagined faces of the twins in her womb, Miguel's voice, Miguel's touch…

"Mnem… Mnem… can you hear me? Mnem, hold on."

Mnem's eyes fluttered. She felt the wall against her back. The room came back into focus after a few blinks. *Why am I on the floor? How long have I been here?* "What happened?"

Miguel jolted back. "You were shot. Phoebe shot you. Where's the wound? Where does it hurt?"

Mnem shook her head. "Nothing hurts."

Miguel moved the folds of her silk tunic. "I saw the shot, Mnem. It went into your chest. You're in shock. Don't move."

"Shot?" Mnem looked down. "I don't feel anything." She scooted sideways.

"I said don't move—" Miguel gasped, his attention focused on the space behind her.

"What is it?" Mnem followed his stare.

The bullet was lodged deep in the wall.

Miguel sat back, his mouth agape. He blinked, swallowed. Stared hard. "Mnemosyne. My god, you're *the* Mnemosyne, the goddess of remembrance." He laughed, a deep throaty laughter Mnem never heard before. "I should have known." He shook his head in disbelief. "Hello, goddess Mnemosyne, allow me to introduce myself. I'm Yumil Kaxob, the Mayan god of flora."

"You're a god?" Mnem poked his arm.

"Afraid so." He grinned. "Well, that explains the amazing sex."

"I'm not immortal anymore. FEM fired me."

"That bullet went through you. I saw it."

"Did you do that?" Mnem pointed across the room.

Phoebe Lawson was unconscious on the floor, her hands and feet bound with electrical cord.

"Couldn't let her get away." Miguel helped Mnem up from the floor. "Do you want to tell me why Phoebe tried to kill you?"

"She's part of an art forgery scam. I figured it out when a few of the artifacts didn't speak to me and Axie confirmed one of them was probably a fake. Phoebe fired me because she suspected I was snooping around."

"Which you were."

"I had to know." Mnem's hand slid over the bullet hole in the wall. "I should be dead. Why am I immortal again?"

"I think I know why." Axie stood in the doorway. "We proved ourselves worthy of our divinity."

Inna walked in. "The choices we made were a hundred percent goddess."

"We chose love," said Naret. "We chose selflessness."

"Anybody have a knife?" asked Axie.

"This should do the trick." Naret pulled a pearl-tipped pin from her updo. "Allow me the honors." She poked Axie's finger first. Inna was next, followed by Miguel's and, just to be certain, Mnem's. Naret pricked herself last.

No one bled, but Phoebe groaned.

"What are we going to do with her?" asked Inna.

"What happened?" Phoebe moaned. "Why am I tied up?"

"Don't even start that amnesia stuff with me." Mnem touched Phoebe's forehead. The ability to restore someone's memory came in handy.

Phoebe's eyes widened. "H-h-how are you alive?"

Inna touched Phoebe's arm. "Promise to tell the truth when the police arrive. Promise to confess."

"Sure, whatever." Phoebe looked at Inna like she was crazy, but Inna just grinned.

Naret, her hands folded in front of her, stood over Phoebe. "Do you have something to say to Mnemosyne?"

Phoebe turned her head, tears streaming down her cheeks. "I had no choice. They said it would be easy money, that no one would ever find out. They threatened to expose me."

"Who's they?" asked Miguel.

"Amir Azam and his wife," said Phoebe. "They're part of an international art ring."

Axie crossed his arms. "What exactly are they threatening to expose?"

Phoebe closed her eyes. "My father is an illegal arms dealer."

"Didn't see that coming," said Inna.

Mnem looked at Axie. "Is she telling the truth?"

Axie nodded. "Afraid so."

Duncan Eze strode into the room, took one look at everything, and rocked back on his signature rubber-soled heels. "What the hell happened?"

EIGHTY-TWO

After the police arrived and they made their statements, Miguel and Inna returned to Mnem's beach house.

With Miguel's help, Mnem sat down on the sand.

"I fell in love with a god," Mnem giggled. "Tell me exactly who you are again?"

Miguel settled beside her. "My Mayan name, Yumil Kaxon, means Owner of the Crop."

"Like maize, corn?"

"You know your ancient history." He nestled closer. As the god of flora—"

"Flores, your last name!"

"Right again, my people gave thanks for their harvests." Miguel took Mnem's hand. "I'm like the phoenix, Mnem, I grow old, die, and rise again. In this life, I have been tasked with bringing this great country together." He nudged her knee. "MAS expects miracles, no doubt."

"You age and die?"

"Yes, but when I'm reborn I know who I am and what I have to do."

"How will I find you again?"

"I'll find *you*. Always and forever." Miguel put his hand on her belly and shook his head. "Are they…"

Immortal?

"I honestly don't know. I was mortal when you knocked me up." Mnem set her hand over his.

Miguel laughed. "The gods don't play fair."

"Neither do goddesses. Or, for that matter, the Highest Powers. Then again, what isn't fair to us, may be Fair to them." Mnem clutched Miguel's hand. "Do you think FEM planned all this? Knew Inna, Naret, Axie, and I would start Goddesses Inc? Planned our falling in love and this pregnancy? Is it all part of some grand scheme?"

Miguel lifted their intertwined fingers to his lips. "We'll never know, will we?" He kissed the back of her hand.

They watched the sun set, enjoyed the lavender sky and pink clouds as the golden sun lowered behind the blue horizon. The wet sand reflected the sky, painting a spectrum of hues on the beach.

Mnem turned to Miguel. "When you go into the FEM building, Shee lists the departments on every floor."

"Really? Same with Hee. His announcement always ends with, thank you for your contributions to humanity. H—"

"Have a nice day," they said in perfect unison.

The End

OTHER TITLES BY AUTUMN BARDOT

Historical

The Emperor's Assassin

The Impaler's Wife

Dragon Lady

Historical Erotica

Confessions of a Sheba Queen

Legends of Lust, Erotic Myths From Around The World

Amazon

Urban Fantasy Titles by LZ Marie

The Merkabah Recruit

The Merkabah Deception

The Merkabah Temptation

The Merkabah Obsession

Amazon

ABOUT THE AUTHOR

Autumn Bardot is a multi-genre author who writes stories about fearless women and dangerous passions. In addition to writing novels, she has been teaching advanced literary analysis and writing for almost twenty years. Autumn was the featured author on Stoya's Book Club and has an article on writing erotica in BooksbyWomen.org. She has been a guest on several podcasts and speaks at writing clubs and reader groups. Autumn is currently writing her next novel and making videos for new writers on her YouTube channel.

Autumn has a passion for history and a special affinity for the unsung courageous females that history neglects or misunderstands. Autumn lives in Southern California with her husband and ever-growing family. She wishes she was one-tenth as brave as the women she writes about.

To connect with Autumn, visit her at: www.autumnbardotbooks.com and on Facebook, Twitter, Instagram, and BookBub.

Made in the USA
Las Vegas, NV
12 March 2021